THE SOUND OF YOU

DAVID TELFORD

Kindred Voices
Press

The Sound of You

Cover design by **Seve**

ISBN (eBook): 979-8-9939736-1-6

First Edition

Published by **Kindred Voices Press,** an imprint of Kindred Voices Media, LLC.

Charlotte, North Carolina

KET IN ACTION™

This book is part of *KET In Action*, a commitment by Kindred Voices Media to practice Kindness, Empathy, and Trust not only in what we publish, but in how we publish it.

KET In Action reflects the choices made throughout the creative process: how stories are shaped, how people are represented, how collaborators are treated, and how readers are respected. It is not a label of approval or a claim of perfection, but a visible promise of intention.

If you're curious what that looks like in practice, you can learn more at

kindredvoicesmedia.com/philosophy/ket-in-action

Every life is a song. This is his.

PART I

OVERTURE

"Without music, life would be a mistake."

– Friedrich **Nietzsche**

LISTEN.

HER FINGERS TREMBLED UNDER HIS, barely noticeable. He tightened his grip, grounding himself in the softness of her skin and the shape of her hand. He didn't dare look at her. Not yet. Not until he heard it.

The hand he held was small and delicate. It fit nicely into his own as he covered it on the bench, his right over her left, fingers haphazardly entwined. Beneath her hand, the faded carving in the green-painted wood reminded the world that "Tomas" had once been there, whoever he was. He moved to lace their fingers together, palms facing each other, covering the past with their presence.

He felt her warmth next to him, warm despite the cool air dancing around them that mid-spring morning. A biting wind gusted off the lake, reminding them it wasn't too late for snow in that part of the world. He studied her manicured nails, the freckles on her knuckles, and the fine hairs on her wrist. He smelled her perfume. He couldn't recall what it was, but he promised himself she would always have it on her vanity. He could taste the lingering sweetness of the ice cream they had shared before they came to the park—before the playful sway of the swings, before they sat together on the weathered bench, and before the words were spoken.

He breathed, listening, his other senses satisfied. The world around him seemed muffled. The voices of children playing in the park, dogs barking, the wind blowing through the new young leaves, and traffic flowing on Route 13 all sounded untuned, like wet cotton stuffed in his ears. He wasn't listening to the sound of cars or the wind in the trees. He wasn't listening to the children on the swing set she had been on only minutes earlier. He wasn't listening to the idle chit-chat of passersby or to dogs barking. He wasn't listening *to* anything. He was listening *for* something—for a specific sound.

His free hand shaped the chord in his palm as if he were squeezing invisible guitar strings beneath them. His ring finger pressed more firmly than the others.

Third fret—Second string, he thought. He knew that if he heard that note, that clear tone, his life would change. He had memorized her sounds before memorizing the shape of her smile, and this—this was her note.

If he heard *Third fret—Third string*, he would be devastated. It was a minor shift on the fretboard but a significant change in her song. He heard that tone just minutes earlier when she expressed frustration with his behavior. She made that sound in his presence whenever he did or said something that annoyed her. Was this one of those times? What if this was too much for her?

But it wasn't just the note. That was the frequency that would carry the word. The word was the source of his anxiety, the answer to a question he had never dared to ask before.

The tension in her hand reflected her frustration leading up to this moment. He braced himself for the worst and listened intently. His thumb brushed her knuckle, trying to soften the rigidity.

Her finger encircled his revealing the ring—a small diamond glinting in the sunshine. She lifted her hand while his followed, turning it to let her see the ring.

From the shadows, Tomas peeked up from the wood at their intertwined fingers.

Then he heard it.

Third fret—Second string.

The root of the D chord. The sound she made when she was happy. A lifetime's decision unfolded in the vibration of a single breath. Years later, he would still remember how the air moved as the sound reached his ears.

Third fret—Second string.

"Yes," was all she said.

But that single syllable contained everything—a song that began the day they met, filled with laughter and music, stolen kisses and late-night whispers, along with all the moments in between. His heart, which had been holding its breath in fear, finally exhaled. He let out a quiet, stunned laugh, his grip tightening around her fingers as if to anchor himself to this new reality. She had said it.

"Yes!"

The sound escaped involuntarily from her lips, traveling against her inhale. This new sound conveyed arousal and passion, something he had never heard from her before that night.

The motel room was small, but the universe fit inside it. Their hands, fingers knotted together, gripped each other tightly, anchor points in an ocean of storming desire. Their bodies struggled against one another, each trying to find a rhythm. They were two stones thrown into a pond, creating interference patterns, concentric disturbances, colliding and then moving together before spastically colliding again, occasionally finding harmony within the discord. This wasn't a new song for either of them, but it was the first time they had sung it together.

Their coupling was a fusion of emotions and nerve endings. He felt the rhythm within the dissonance as she moved alternately with him and against him. He tasted the salty kiss of sweat on her cheeks. He smelled the stale air of this cheap room, the candles, and the carpet. He heard the syncopation of her breathing as she rose and fell on the waves of their passion. He could see the tacky neon sign of the diner across the street reflected in her eyes, and in that dim, artificial light, he saw a lifetime of love beneath lustful hunger and the unspoken demand for more and more and more.

"Oh!"

Her manicured nails dug reflexively into the back of his hand, seeking purchase, balance, and stability. The chaos vanished, and they moved together, their cadence harmonious and amplified, spiraling toward the summit. He made a sound he did not expect, and she joined his song.

"Oh!" she cried again, the ache of it bringing tears to her eyes, her mouth slightly falling open, her breath halting as she crested the wave. He felt himself being pulled into the slipstream of her ecstasy, joining her as the universe split open before them.

She moaned loudly, another note he had never heard from her before, but he wanted to hear it every day for the rest of his life. Her tears spilled over, and his slid down his nose to join them on her cheek.

They collapsed, hands released, finding each other in the dark, lips and fingers, kisses and touches, until the raging seas within them settled again. They lay wrapped in each other's warmth, breathing the same air and sharing the same space.

The vows were spoken, the rings exchanged, the toasts delivered, and the contract consummated. Now, they looked at one another and saw themselves in each other's eyes. They were united in a new life. They were One.

BUT NOW THERE was this one. Her hand was so tiny, resting on his own.

She did this, he thought, stroking the delicate pink palm with the tips of his calloused fingers. *She did this alone.*

She had gone to the hospital alone, fought through the pain alone, and after six hours, she had triumphed alone.

His band had been playing at a festival across the river. When he called home to tell her they were finished and heading back, a neighbor answered the phone and told him where she was. He broke almost every traffic law to get to the hospital in Suffern.

When he entered the room, with panic on his face and shame in his heart for not being there sooner, he found her exhausted but alert. Yet, with a smile upon seeing him, she showed she shared her victory. It was *their* reward for *her* strength.

She never ceased to amaze him. Despite her stature, she was stronger than he was in all the ways that mattered, carrying their dreams, struggles, and love. He had always believed strength meant endurance, found in the tension of muscle and bone. But watching her cradle their newborn daughter, exhaustion visible on her face and yet her smile steady, he understood. Strength was not resistance. It was the willingness to bend, to lift others, and to love despite the burden.

And she was more intelligent, patient, kind, and compassionate. She was willing to let him follow his dream as a musician while she paid the bills with her steady job as a high school teacher. She would tell her friends that he wasn't lazy but aspirational. He didn't understand what she meant, but each night his band had a show, she would kiss him goodnight as he left and again when he returned. Some nights, the stench of beer, sweat, and cigarette smoke clung to him like a shroud, but she wouldn't flinch, and her lips would find him every time. She was a goddess if such things existed anymore. And to him, they did, and she was.

"Ally," he heard her say. *Third fret—Second string.* Happiness.

He looked up from the perfect being before him, his eyes filled with rivers of joy.

"Ally?"

She nodded. "Allison, officially, but always and forever, Ally."

He looked down at the tiny creature in front of him, and the creature looked back. *Her* eyes. *Her* mouth.

"Ally," he said to his daughter, the first word she would hear from him. *Third fret—Fifth string.* The root of C in his cracking voice. His sound of happiness.

The baby cooed, and he smiled. *Third fret—First string.* There would be harmony in their songs.

Their love and her strength brought this child into the world.

Now, he had to be strong, but he didn't know how. She had always been the strong one, the wise one. He held her hand, much older and more fragile than the one he remembered from another time in another place. As warm as he recalled her touch that long-ago day, it felt icy cold now. He cupped it in both hands and pulled it to his lips, using his breath to warm it.

Where are her rings?

Her nails were cracked and rough from her battles against the pain, tugging on sheets until they split, weakened by the chemo and radiation treatments. Her skin was loose from abrupt weight loss, as fragile as parchment, and peppered with faded patches of brown yet still soft. He kissed her fingers and felt them move slightly against his lips, the faintest trace of perfume now barely clinging to her skin.

There was movement in the room, but he didn't look up. Voices he recognized, some he didn't. He wasn't religious but prayed silently to whichever deity would listen. He didn't know what he wanted other than to hear her again.

Third Fret—Second String.

Just one word.

The machines, their cords snaking into her, hissed and pinged, establishing a mechanical rhythm that kept time against the looming threat of silence. It was a hospital symphony— steady, measured, and merciless—illuminated by cold white, fluorescent bulbs and transmitted through air that tasted of disinfectant and despair.

Nineteenth fret—First string. A high B note bent out of tune. The heart monitor beeped a tone that had meant nothing to him before, but now he would hate forever. His fingers tightened around hers, desperate to keep the warmth from slipping away.

"Sarah," he whispered into her hand. "Not yet, baby."

The sounds in the room were muffled and dull, with the higher notes drowned out by the pounding of his heartbeat in his ears—except for that hateful ping that seemed to pierce right through him.

"Not yet," he whispered again, holding her hand to his lips.

"Paxton?"

He looked up, startled to see her eyes open and looking around, the brown beads of glass haloed red by broken blood vessels. He couldn't fight the tears or find the words to respond, but he kissed her fingers to let her know he heard her.

"Pax?" A whisper, toneless and confused.

He heard someone behind him say something. *Mom*, maybe? She turned her eyes toward him and smiled.

"There you are," she said, her voice a discordant rasp. "I heard you."

He nodded, holding her hand but not too tightly.

"Hi," he said, blinking through tears.

"Pax?"

And then that tone, that bent fucking B, fucking nineteenth fret on the fucking first string, chirped and didn't stop. It stretched out too long, like the final chord of a fading song. The room filled with commotion as he felt her hand relax in his. He heard himself saying "no" repeatedly. Then, a hand on his shoulder—who was that? A muffled voice, also full of tears, familiar yet distant.

"Dad."

He closed his eyes and tried to summon her back. He wasn't ready to be alone.

"Dad, let them work."

He turned and looked into *Her* eyes, but it wasn't *Her* face. *Her* mouth moved, but it wasn't *Her* voice.

"Dad, let them work. Please."

Someone finally turned off the machine, and his awareness of the room faded. He saw Rob talking to one of the doctors. Rob was nodding. That was good, right? Nodding is good! But when his son looked at him—*Her* eyes, not *Her* face—he shook his head.

"I'm sorry, Dad."

And then silence, as the room went black.

PART II

THE LOSS OF YOU

"Grief is just love with no place to go."

– Jamie **Anderson**

CHAPTER 1

THE PHONE BUZZED on the arm of the chair.

The caller ID on his flip phone showed "Kiddo," his nickname for his daughter, his firstborn, his reminder of *Her*. Kiddo for Ally, Kiddon't for Rob. He thought it was funny, but Rob didn't.

"Hi Kiddo, what's new and unusual?"

She had been crying, and he could hear the notes of it in her voice.

"Hi, Dad."

"What's wrong, Ally?"

There was a pause, then "Nothing, Dad."

"That's a dollar for the lie, Kiddo. What's going on?"

She laughed a little at the reference to the dollar. As a child, she instituted a Swear Jar to curb his tendency to curse. She taped a sign on an empty mayonnaise jar that read "$1 for most swears. $5 for the F word." Pax had filled that jar many times in the subsequent years, calling it their College Fund.

Then, when Ally and Rob were in middle and high school, he grew tired of the constant dishonesty that comes with puberty and created a new jar called the Lie Jar. The sign read, "$1 for most lies. $5 if you lie to your mother."

He could hear the sour notes in her laugh and knew something was wrong.

"It's okay, Dad," Ally insisted. "It was a tough day, and I just wanted to hear your voice."

"Russell?"

Silence meant, *Yeah, Russell.*

He had never liked Russell, so much so that he tried to avoid attending their wedding. He knew that the volatile mix of his anger issues, free liquor, and the likelihood that the idiot would insult his wife or daughter during the reception meant that either he or Russell, or both, would end up in the emergency room. But Ally begged him. She loved Russell. He was a changed man. So, he went. No blood had been spilled, but the hostility between Russell and Pax didn't fade.

"Leave him, Ally," he said plainly. "Take the kids and leave him. Go stay with Rob."

She sniffed but didn't respond.

"He's nearby?"

"Mm-hmm," she replied quietly.

He searched for the next thing he could say to calm her, but his rage was building. He heard Russell in the background say something, the sound getting closer. Ally tried to quiet her husband's side conversation, but he heard it.

"Who you talking to?" Russell asked, his mouthful of tobacco making him sound dumber than usual.

"Dad," she replied quietly.

"Hey, Pax!" Russell shouted. "Bye, Pax!"

"Go fuck yourself, Russell!" he shouted back, but Ally translated it.

"Dad says 'Hi.'"

He heard a door close, and Ally returned to the call.

"Did he hit you?" He needed to calm down.

"No, it's not that, Dad."

"It's what then?"

She started crying.

"He's cheating on you?" he probed for the thorn he could help pull to ease her distress.

"I don't think so," she replied, but she was uncertain, and he could hear tears and snot in her voice. "It's just that—"

He took a deep breath to cool his blood and waited.

"It's just that... I'm not Mom."

He let that sink in. That meant what? He's a shithead like me, and she doesn't have her mother's skill to deal with this kind of shithead?

"She was one of a kind, Kiddo."

She sobbed louder.

"I miss her so much, Dad."

He felt something turn over in his chest. It wasn't butterflies. He had always thought that was a silly metaphor. This wasn't cute. This wasn't pleasurable. This was painful. This was empti-ness. This was a black hole inside him, sucking away all the joy of the world. Sarah had been gone a little over a year, and every thought of her still felt like ripping the bandage off a wound that wouldn't heal, pouring gasoline on it, and setting it on fire.

"Dad?"

He gathered himself and managed a weak, "Yeah, Kiddo?"

"Why don't you come down for a nice long visit?"

He closed his eyes and fought the urge to tell her in no uncertain terms why that was a bad idea. The words in his head would have contributed at least $50 to the Swear Jar. He preferred hearing her voice. He wasn't ready to see those eyes. *Her* eyes. Both Ally and Rob had them.

"I don't know, Kiddo," he started, not sure what he would say next.

"I know, Dad. Just think about it." And then, as if it might help. "Rob has a girlfriend."

He chuckled at her effort to lighten the mood.

"Good for Rob," he said, genuinely smiling and happy for that news.

"Just think about it?"

"I will, Kiddo. Tell Rob I said hey," he said as he moved to close the flip phone and heard Ally.

"I love you, Dad."

He closed the phone. He was never good at goodbyes or showing affection to anyone except Sarah, and with her gone…

The phone rang almost immediately. It was Zim.

"Yo," he answered before the phone got to his ear.

"I'm outside."

ZIM WAS LASHARON ZIMMERMAN, his friend for over twenty-five years. His bandmate for nearly as long, and the Best Man at his wedding. The only person on the planet who knew more about him than he knew himself.

Zim was there when he officially started dating Sarah. He loaned Pax the money to buy the ring. He showed up for the birth of Ally and Rob, and Sarah's funeral. He was always there. Pax couldn't remember a significant moment when Zim was not by his side or just behind him, playing the keyboards.

Pax glanced at Zim as he climbed into the step-van, trying to hide his disgust at the cramped space. As soon as he inhaled the trapped air inside, he knew Zim had been sleeping in there again and probably not alone. The stench of stale sweat and sex, old Chinese food containers, unwashed clothes, and beer assaulted his senses.

The van, gloriously named Gloria after his favorite aunt, was

Zim's only possession despite his family's wealth. It served as his transportation, office, studio, shaggin' wagon, and more nights than not, his bedroom.

Zim had access to an apartment nearby, but there was a problem, and her name was Erin. He rarely discussed his relationship with Erin, often replying to questions about his living arrangements with, "Yeah, there's a problem." Though he didn't know her well, Pax had always assumed that the van served as Zim's bunker against the potential wrath of Hurricane Erin.

Pax slid the case with his battle-scarred acoustic guitar into the space behind the seat and climbed in. Sarah had written "Tomas" with a Sharpie on the bare wood beneath the broken pickguard. It was her tribute to the park bench from all those years ago when she had said "yes."

Third Fret—Second String.

These days, the band Butler Service consisted of Zim and himself, but they often brought in other gig musicians depending on the event and the type of music being played.

"Bringing Tomas tonight, Pax?"

"Yeah, feeling off," he responded. "Who's playing with us?"

"Reggie and that kid, Steve? Sam? Smoothy?"

"Seth," he corrected, glancing at his hands and noticing how much deeper the lines had become over the past year. They trembled slightly after the call with Ally, his pent-up rage toward his son-in-law still not fully defused.

Zim eyed him with concern.

"We don't have to keep doing this, man. Maybe you need more time to grieve."

He shot a look at Zim that, if it hadn't been Zim, would have sent chills through the person receiving it. Zim laughed and shifted the van into gear.

"Ok, brother. Tonight, we play unplugged."

During their prime, Butler Service traveled the East Coast

circuit between New York and Miami. There were four of them then, and they had a small but dedicated following along the coast. During the summers, when school was out, Sarah and the kids would join them, often spending time on the beaches of the oceanfront cities where they had bookings. Everything changed when Sarah received her first diagnosis.

Now, for the past five months, what was left of Butler Service played a weekly gig at the only place in Middletown that would have them. The Club—so named because the author of this part of the creation story was lazy, bored, or just uninspired—was located between a hardware store and the park. On nights when The Club was busy, the party would spill into the park, and shenanigans would follow. Many future residents of Middletown were ejaculated into existence in that park after closing time.

As he helped Zim unpack the gig equipment, he looked at the pavilion where Ally was conceived and smiled. There wasn't any significant place in this town where he and Sarah hadn't made a memory. He felt a twinge, but he needed that pain. He needed that longing, the ache for something that couldn't be fulfilled. It reminded him he was still alive and that Sarah was still somewhere, waiting. Despite what his grief counseling group sermonized, "closure" was not his friend. Not yet, anyway.

"You sure we're gonna do this acoustic, man?" Zim asked again.

"We'll see," he replied. "Bring the Strat in, just in case."

"That's more like it! We've got holiday shoppers tonight, man. Labor Day on Monday and days of labor in nine months."

The club paid the band a percentage of the liquor sales, so the more jumping, dancing, sweating, thirsty patrons they could draw in, the thicker the envelope at the end of the night. Pax took a moment to talk to Louis, The Club's owner, as the band set up inside. He had known Louis nearly as long as Zim, but although they were friendly, they were never close. He suspected Louis might have given them this regular gig out of sympathy. Louis had been sweet on Sarah.

Louis put a hand on his shoulder. "How is it tonight, Pax?"

He looked at Louis and forced a smile. "Hard, like every other night she's not here."

"I bet," Louis replied, the pleasantries out of the way. "You should have a good crowd tonight. What's the line-up?"

Pax looked at the patrons' faces to decide what kind of music would keep the bottles pouring.

"A little '70s. Blues. Southern Rock. We'll make them dance, and you make them drink."

Louis nodded and gave him another pat on the shoulder. "Tear it up, Pax. You're the man."

He walked to the stage and saw that the boys had finished setting up. Zim was playing soundlessly on the electric piano. Reggie Murphy was still tuning his bass. He was a regular at most of their gigs, though not an official band member. Seth, a kid fresh out of college, sat at the drums, grinning widely as he watched the attractive college girls in the growing crowd. Pax had heard Seth playing in That Music Store and asked if he'd like to gig occasionally. The kid had chops.

Pax placed his hand on Zim's shoulder, as close to an act of affection as he had ever shown to anyone except Sarah. Zim read his mind and said, "Strat's ready." He nodded, picked up the road-worn Fender, and plugged it in. Zim had it tuned, cranked up, and ready to be bled.

He closed his eyes, uncertain of what he would do next. He gazed out at the crowd. Something about it reminded him of those early days. The same faces, different hairstyles. The same booths, but no clouds of cigarette smoke drifting over the crowd.

He remembered a girl in a SUNY New Paltz T-shirt. Those eyes. That smile. He had sung Joni Mitchell's version of *Wood-*

stock and never looked away from those eyes. She sang along from the floor in front of the stage.

He needed to experience something visceral, like Joni's gut-wrenching version of that song.

Pax looked down and gently pulled at the strings, skillfully bending each note to perfection. The crowd paused, watching and listening as he brought the Strat to life, the opening guitar solo of Pink Floyd's *Shine on You Crazy Diamond* bleeding onto the stage. Tears welled in his eyes as the notes flowed from his fingers.

When he reached the final crest of the opening movement, ready to dive into the main riff, he paused and looked up. Blinking away tears, he glanced back at Zim, who was also fighting with his emotions. Pax smiled, then turned back to the microphone.

"That was my wife's favorite song," he shared with the crowd. "She was my crazy diamond. Shine on, baby."

The crowd cheered and whistled, and the band applauded.

"I'm Pax," he said, returning to the present. "And this is Butler Service."

He turned and counted out the first song, and the night began.

IN THE STERILE fluorescent light of the exam room, Pax looked down at his hand and moaned. The mottled mix of greens, browns, yellows, and reds looked like chaotic camouflage. The ER doctor slowly turned his hand, inspecting the damage. She glanced at him and offered a grim smile.

"I hope you don't need this hand for a while," she said with a rare tone of compassion for an ER doctor, who usually sees injuries like a banker sees a bounced check. "We're going to do some minor surgery on this tonight, but it will take several weeks to heal and go through physical therapy."

"I make my living with my hands," he replied.

She nodded, then shifted her focus to his elbow.

"Your CT scan shows a minor concussion from that lump on your forehead. The X-ray reveals two broken fingers, two other fractures in your metacarpals, and a hairline fracture of the olecranon process. That one isn't so bad. Just painful."

"Fractured what?" he asked, feeling the throb of his pulse in the injured hand.

"The pointy part of your elbow."

"Fuck," he muttered under his breath. "Sorry. I'm a musician. This sidelines me for a long time."

Zim entered the curtained section of the ER. His jaw dropped at the sight of the injuries.

"Pax, wow. This is bad."

"Ya think?"

That was all he could manage. His sense of humor hadn't made the trip in the ambulance.

"Pax," Zim stuttered. "There's more."

Zim seemed to be on the verge of despair.

"Pax, Tomas."

He straightened up, alert. *What about Tomas?*

"He didn't make it," Zim choked on the words.

The doctor stood up and began to offer her condolences.

"My guitar," he said to her, pain in his heart outweighing the pain in his hand.

"Oh, I see." She paused for a moment, unsure of what to say, then walked away.

Zim sat beside him and grasped his uninjured hand. "Fuck, man."

"What happened, Zim?" he asked, sniffing. "I turned to give you the nod, and the next thing I know, I'm on the floor."

Zim wrapped his arm around Pax and replayed the scene.

"Oh man, you pulled out Tomas and told everyone we'd take a break after one more song. Then you started playing Sarah's song, and man, it was gold! The crowd was digging it. You got to the bridge and gave me the high sign to do my solo, and then your foot hit the edge of the stage, and you went down —hard!"

Pax took it all in. The brief moment of gravity from the stage to the floor was a blur, but he remembered hearing something snap and then feeling another thing crack. The pain in his hand and chest was immediate, each vying for his attention as his forehead hit the floor.

"The band was tight," Zim said, almost nostalgically. "Our best show in a long time."

Pax remembered smelling beer as he lay on the floor at the foot of a young woman wearing a SUNY Purchase T-shirt. He looked up at her, holding his hand to his chest. In his mind, he heard Joni Mitchell's plaintive refrain as consciousness faded.

He leaned into his friend's shoulder, waiting for the anesthesiologist to arrive and relieve his pain, even if just briefly, while the doctors did what they could to fix the rest.

It was Ally.

He pushed the buzzing phone away and took another sip of tequila. He knew he shouldn't be drinking while on painkillers, but in his defense, he had been left unsupervised. The phone stopped buzzing, only to start again—Rob.

He took another sip and fiddled with the pins poking out of his hand through the cast, keeping the fragile bones aligned as they healed. The itchy cast stretched from his fingernails to his bicep, wrapping his hand and elbow in a smooth curve of fiberglass. Even though Pax threatened to club him, Zim had signed it, adding a big smiley face with hearts for eyes.

The loss of Tomas, so soon after Sarah, was devastating. It felt as if someone were taking the pieces of his soul and systematically erasing them. The painkillers eased the physical pain of the injury, and the tequila helped him handle the emotional pain, but neither was enough.

The phone buzzed. He resigned himself to endure the conversation and flipped it open.

"Hi, Kiddo."

"Dad! You have to answer the phone when we call. For God's sake, you're—"

"Old," he finished for her when she stopped mid-sentence.

"Dad. What happened?"

Zim, he thought. *Zim called her.*

"Tomas is gone, Ally." He wept as he succumbed to his physical and emotional pain, with the agave and opioids amplifying his sorrow rather than numbing it. The dam of his heartache broke, unleashing a flood of tears mixed with snot, saliva, and tequila. The core of grief inside him had borne fetid fruit, and he could no longer hold it in.

He unloaded everything onto Ally, and she poured out all her grief in return. Their shared sorrow created a pungent, bitter cocktail of anguish. They talked for over an hour, trying to find answers to questions they knew couldn't be answered, all of which started with the word *Why*.

Eventually, the shouting, swearing, and raging against the storm of despair quieted until all that remained was a chorus of sniffles.

"Come down, Dad," Ally begged. "Come down, and let's get through this together."

He sat in silence. The painkillers were wearing off, and he felt unmotivated to take any more.

Just let the pain come. Make me feel something real.

"Dad, I'm not asking."

He smiled at her tough-guy attitude. She carried a lot of fearlessness in that small frame.

"What will your husband say?" he asked, trying not to sound snarky, but... well... tequila.

"He'll have to deal with it. You'll need to be nice to each other, or I'll have to smack you."

"Nice?" he replied. "Perhaps you've forgotten, kiddo. I'm a fucking delight."

He snorted as he laughed. She heard him and started laughing too.

"Ok, Kiddo," he said.

THE TRIP SOUTH WAS DULL, just endless miles of highway, gas stations, fast food joints, and traffic. Pax looked out the window at the trees rushing past the van. He figured there was a tree for every dog that had ever existed to pee on.

Zim chattered away, filling the van's silence with a rant about how love is a form of quantum entanglement, claiming that when you think of someone you love, it's like resolving the superposition of entangled particles.

"Yeah!" Zim chirped. "I mean, what is consciousness, if not some kind of quantum-level packet of energy bouncing between dimensions?"

"I don't know, Zim."

"ESP, ghosts, and spectral phenomena—all of it is energy moving between quantum dimensions. Right?"

"You may be onto something," Pax said absently.

"Yeah!" Zim punctuated his stream of consciousness with confirmation of his theory, then fell silent.

They rolled steadily down Interstate 81 through Virginia. Zim sang along with songs on the radio in a key that Pax thought didn't exist. He played keyboards without a microphone for a reason. During commercials, he pontificated on fate and how Pax's current situation might be a cosmic setup for something important. Clapton's *Wonderful Tonight* came on the radio, and Zim sat quietly, knowing Pax was thinking about Sarah.

Pax absentmindedly spun his wedding ring with his thumb, an old habit he defaulted to when lost in thought. Zim noticed.

"Maybe it's time you put that away. To help yourself heal, brother."

He turned sharply toward Zim. The tone was unmistakable.

"Maybe it's time you shut the fuck up. Brother."

Zim smiled and nodded, his eyes moving back to the highway.

"Shutting the fuck up, sir."

Russell opened the door when they arrived. Pax forced a smile at Russell's smirking face.

"Russell," he said, trying to keep his promise to Ally that he would at least attempt to be civil with his punk of a son-in-law.

"Holy shit, Pax!" Russell pointed at the cast with his beer hand. "You totally fucked yourself up!"

It wasn't calling out the obvious that bothered him, but rather the idiotic laughter that followed, as if other people's pain and misery were Russell's preferred form of entertainment. He opened his mouth to retaliate verbally, but then just smiled.

"Yeah, I did."

Zim came up behind him carrying his bags.

"Russell," Zim said, grinning from ear to ear.

Russell's smile faded as he moved away from the door, leaving it ajar.

"Too friendly?" Zim asked.

"Too Jewish," Pax responded, then stepped through the door.

Ally held him tightly for a long time, sniffling through her tears. Pax hugged her back, trying to hide his discomfort, both from the awkward position of his wounded arm and his general dislike of public displays of affection. Ally looked up, cupped his cheeks, and kissed his forehead.

"Thank you, Dad."

He nodded. Ally turned to Zim and hugged him, thanking him sincerely for bringing her father to her. Zim blushed, smiled, and eagerly returned her hug with enthusiasm.

"How long can you stay?"

Zim scowled. "I have to head back tomorrow, sweetie."

"Erin?"

Zim nodded. "Yeah. That's the problem."

She laughed and handed Zim a beer, then went back to her father and led him down the hall toward the room she had prepared for him.

Zim looked at Russell, who was quietly watching a football game on TV.

"Who's playing?" he asked, attempting to engage Russell for no other reason than to make Russell uncomfortable.

"Gamecocks," Russell replied, still not looking up.

Zim plopped onto the couch next to Russell and took a long sip from his beer. He stared at Russell until Russell felt compelled to return the gaze.

"So, Russell, what do you know about quantum physics?"

The room Ally prepared for him had previously been used by his namesake grandson, Paxton, known as Puck to his friends, even though he didn't have any yet. The single bed, large enough for a five-year-old who was "a big boy now," was low to the floor, and Pax knew his knees and back would be complaining soon enough.

He smiled as he took in the Americana-themed wallpaper and deep blue carpeting, with Russell's self-styled patriotism influencing the bedroom's decor for a child too young to understand what it all meant. Pax was surprised there wasn't a red "Make America Great Again" hat tacked to the wall. Still, he was sure there was one somewhere in the house.

"I have a doctor lined up for you, Dad," Ally said while unpacking his suitcase.

"I can do that, Kiddo," he said as he moved toward her, reaching for the clothes. But when she looked at his arm, pinned and frozen in a cast, he conceded.

"You can share the bathroom in the hall with Puck. He's a big boy now and uses the potty by himself, though I think he inherited his father's habit of taking his time with Number Two. Lainey and Puck can share a room for a little while until you get your arm back."

Pax laughed and thanked her for everything.

"Dad," she said, turning to him and holding his good hand in hers. "Thank you for being kind to Russell when you got here. I could tell by your eyes you were fighting back the words."

He smiled and quickly shifted the subject.

"What's the deal with the doctor?"

THE CAST CAME OFF FAIRLY QUICKLY, but the pins proved to be a whole different story. The doctor warned that it might hurt a little, and by a little, he meant a shitload. They doped him up nicely for the removal, but once the anesthesia wore off, the pain took over.

The doctor prescribed more painkillers, but they made him nauseous, so he fought the pain with tequila and willpower. Eventually, the pain eased enough for him to cut back on the agave.

His arm, weakened from the lack of fiberglass and steel and

slightly atrophied after eight weeks of restriction, wouldn't respond to his brain's commands. During his last visit to the orthopedist, the doctor assessed his range of motion—lift, bend, thumb-to-pinky, pick up a ball. The professional diagnosis for what he was experiencing was *immobilization syndrome*. Pax's pain-fogged brain translated the medical speech into a simple message: You're a fucking mess.

No medications were available to help him with this part of his recovery. The prescription he required was called Audra.

Audra Boyd was "not one of those Boyds," whatever that meant. She was, however, a highly recommended physical therapist, skilled at turning his "fucking mess" into a functioning limb. She was also attractive, which didn't help the fact that she was a total pain in the ass about him doing his therapy outside of her office.

"Pax, honey," she would say, "Professionally speaking, I don't care if you ever play guitar again. However, if *you* care, do the work, and I will help you get there. Or don't do it and be a miserable cuss for the rest of your life. I get paid either way."

Sometimes, he didn't like Audra, especially when she made him squeeze a stress ball a hundred times or when she slowly closed his fist, forcing him to fight to keep it closed after she let go, only to painfully open it again. But at the same time, he liked her a lot. She never said "Pax" without following it with "honey," and he enjoyed the feel of her warm hand on his wounded one. She was gentle and patient, yet firm and determined. So, he did the work slowly at first, but he improved each day.

After eight weeks, the day finally came when she said, "You're done with me."

He felt strangely confused by that statement.

"I'm not done with you," he stammered, shaking his head.

"Well, Pax honey," she laughed. "I'm done with you."

That hurt, almost worse than his injury. He hadn't realized

he had developed feelings for Audra during the time she tortured him back into shape. Although their relationship had only been professional so far, this felt personal. It was like the sting of a breakup.

"Ok," he managed, feeling strangely disoriented. "What?"

"Your range of motion has significantly improved. Your fingers are moving as they should. I understand you're still feeling some discomfort, but that will pass. You're whole again, sir."

She smiled, and the impact of her words hit him.

"I'm fixed?"

"Yes, sir."

Without asking, he hugged her, feeling for the first time since the accident that he might be okay. If only Audra could repair the hole in his soul, he would never let go of her.

"Pax, honey," Audra whispered, patting his back.

"Pax, honey," she said, a little louder.

"Mr. Butler."

Pax released her and stepped back, smiling foolishly as he looked at her face, finally seeing her as a person and not a medieval torture device. He was torn. Audra was the first woman he had felt anything for since Sarah. It wasn't the same, but it was something. He thanked her and then walked to the door of her office.

He turned and asked, "Would you like to get a drink someday?"

Audra smiled like a woman who had heard this question before. He expected the awkward rejection that other men had experienced countless times in the bars and clubs where he performed.

"Someday," she said.

Pax nodded and smiled back. "Someday," he repeated.

GETTING BACK to playing guitar was tough. His fingers didn't move like they used to. On the electric guitar, he played with a pick. On the acoustic, he was a fingerpicker. In this new world, he relied on his thumb, awkwardly rolling through the basics of plucking patterns. His index and middle finger patterns were sloppy, and the ring finger patterns were a hard no.

He disliked using a pick on the acoustic, so he practiced his rolls daily, trying to apply the discipline he learned in PT to regain the stretch and agility he once had. It was slow progress, and improvement was barely noticeable. His frustration grew as the weeks passed.

He knew that Russell was sometimes outside the door while he practiced. He could hear him breathing and the occasional sniff. One day, he decided to find out why.

"Need something, Russell?"

Russell rolled around the door frame to look into the room.

"No, just listening," he said without his signature sarcasm. "Sounds like you lost something."

Pax looked up, uncertain whether Russell was being kind or... well... Russell-ish.

"Yeah."

"Think you can get it back?" Russell asked with genuine interest.

"Maybe some, but not all of it," Pax said reluctantly, not only because it gave Russell fodder to be a dick but also because he didn't want to believe it himself.

Russell nodded and turned away, walking down the hallway. Pax wasn't sure what had just happened, but it almost seemed like Russell was showing empathy.

He returned to practice, guiding his fingers through the patterns and trying to carve out a verse or two of Dylan's *Don't*

Think Twice, It's All Right. He didn't like how it sounded, so he thumbed a few blues riffs and set the guitar on the bed. Maybe performing was behind him, he thought. What's next? Teach?

He heard his phone ring and realized he had left it in the kitchen. Russell answered it.

"Pax!"

He walked into the kitchen, where Russell was stuffing a sandwich into his mouth.

"It's a girl, ooooh." The more familiar version of his son-in-law had returned.

He grabbed his phone off the counter.

"Pax here."

It was Audra.

"So, Pax, I guess maybe today is someday."

He grinned broadly, knowing Russell was watching.

"Is it now?"

"Well, if you're busy—"

"No, no, no," he interrupted. "I could really use some professional advice."

"So, this will be a business meeting?" Audra laughed.

"Depends," he said coyly. "What are we doing?"

AUDRA BECAME a fixture in his life and his children's lives. She was the shoulder Ally cried on while navigating her difficult divorce from Russell—yes, he had been cheating on her. At their request, she read to Puck and Lainey whenever she was there around bedtime. Audra and Rob shared a love for the same movies, video games, and cheesy jokes. She introduced Rob to her friend Naomi, and they connected in a meaningful way, leading to baby Jasmine. Any major event in the Butlers' lives included Audra.

For Pax, Audra was the best medicine he could ask for, both physically and emotionally. She was quick to laugh, even when he wasn't being funny. She accepted his social awkwardness as something endearing, not as something to endure. She enjoyed watching his strange alchemy in the presence of women and how he would shyly flirt back with many of them. She understood that, to him, it was about kindness, not about sex. She accepted that he was not ready to say or even hear the words "I love you," so she would say, "You make me smile, Pax honey."

Audra convinced Pax to ride the big rollercoaster at Carowinds. She got him to float in the greenish murk of Lake Wylie, even though she knew he disliked being surrounded by water. She urged him to ease off the tequila but introduced him to apple pie moonshine.

In return, Pax introduced Audra to various types of music. He took her to small venues in Charlotte, Columbia, and Charleston, where they experienced everything from alternative rock to bluegrass. He also introduced her to ice hockey and lacrosse, and he thought she looked terrific in her Charlotte Checkers jersey. They often stopped for ice cream, never each getting a cone, just one to share, with him usually eating more. They hiked many trails and greenways in the area, spent time touring the mountains in Asheville, Blowing Rock, and Boone, and walked the beaches of both Carolinas when the weather was nice.

They argued, often about generational differences and what was good or seemingly awful about growing up in different decades. He started calling her "Kid" to make her feel younger and to remind himself of their age gap. Being proudly Black and liberal in a red state, Audra tried to get Pax to take a stand on the issues flooding the news, but he refused, saying that the only thing that matters is if people are good to each other.

"It doesn't matter what they look like or who they pray to or who they love," he would say. "If they can't be kind, then I have no use for them." She found it difficult to argue with that logic.

The relationship wasn't physical at first—just two people enjoying each other's company. He would never assume she wanted him in that way. He wasn't even sure how to pursue a sexual encounter, as his experience was limited before Sarah, and even on their honeymoon, Sarah was the one who initiated contact. Audra made the first move after a night of dancing in Uptown Charlotte. It was a slow and subtle gesture, but he understood the intent, and when the song started, he was ready to sing.

At first, it bothered him that he didn't feel guilty about sleeping with Audra. He wondered why it was so easy to be with her. The struggle with the lack of guilt lessened over the weeks, and eventually, he spent more nights at her house than at Ally's.

And that was good.

Ally had met someone.

Travis was as much like Russell as an apple is like a walrus. Silently strong, kind, and patient, Pax knew Travis was good for Ally and the kids, but he could never fully trust anyone after witnessing the disaster Russell caused during the divorce. He wanted Ally to be happy, and Travis seemed to have the skills to make that happen. So, Pax stayed out of the way. He was glad to feel something good after the long deluge of misery following Sarah's illness and passing. Zim had been right. Something significant had truly been on the horizon.

ONE MORNING, Pax leaned back on the bed, his head supported by his arms crossed beneath it. The early summer sun, low in the morning sky, shone through the trees, casting shadows on the wall, while the moving branches created the effect of an old-time movie. Audra snored softly beside him, smiling in her dream state. He wondered if he was part of that dream.

He was reminded of a time when he had watched Sarah sleeping like this. *Dream of Me, Please*, the song he was playing at The Club on the night he destroyed his arm and killed Tomas, was written while he watched Sarah sleep. As he thought of her, he felt calm in his mind, not overwhelmed by grief. It felt strange. He remembered a different time.

"Don't be alone, Pax."

Sarah watched him write as he sat up in bed. He glanced at her. Earlier that week, they had received the worst possible news. Incurable. Inoperable. It was a slow descent with only one outcome. He struggled with the thought that she would soon be leaving him.

"Shut up," he replied, looking away, and immediately regretted his words.

She laughed, which turned into a cough. One cough sparked another, and soon she was choking. Pax pulled her into his arms and held her tightly, singing softly into her ear to soothe her and help her breathe steadily.

She nodded thankfully and pulled back, looking into his eyes, her voice soft and husky.

"I mean it, Pax. Don't be alone. Find someone to love. You can be so closed off sometimes. It would help if you let it out. You need to let that beautiful music in your heart sing."

"I'm not talking about this," he said matter-of-factly. She laughed again, though quietly.

"I'm not saying you should go out and start dating at your age, baby. Still, it would be fun to watch that from the afterlife. You have a lot of living to do and plenty of love to share. Find someone to share it with."

He remembered feeling angry at her for that conversation. He also recalled her pulling him close and kissing him until the anger faded.

They made love. It was slow, awkward, and imperfect. Her condition added an unspoken caution in Pax, which dulled the passion of their intimacy, preventing it from reaching its usual heights. They laughed about it and apologized to each other for their lackluster performance.

She tried once more to get him to promise that he wouldn't be alone, that he would love again. He declined to respond.

He felt Audra stir beside him, pulling him back to the moment. He watched her hand wrap around his waist—her beautiful ebony skin contrasting with his, her Carolina blue-tinted braids spread across the pillow around her head. Had he found someone like Sarah had told him he should? Did she know he would? Did she make sure he stayed open to it? Something in his chest stirred, and he chuckled.

"Stupid butterflies," he said softly, but not softly enough.

"Butterflies?" Audra asked, looking at him.

"Forget about it," he said, as he took her hand.

"Pax, honey," Audra smiled as she spoke. "Have I ever told you that I love your accent?"

He smirked. "I don't have an accent, Kid. You do."

"Down here, honey, you're the one with the accent."

He turned onto his side and supported his head with his hand.

"Has anyone ever told you that they didn't understand anything you just said? I bet they have."

She looked at him, her golden-brown eyes sparkling with delight at his Yankee sarcasm.

"Because," he continued, "nobody has ever said that to me."

She laughed and stuck out her tongue. He pulled her head toward his and kissed her. They made love quietly, yet with no lack of passion.

The sun was fully up when they collapsed in exhaustion, sweaty and flushed, their minds hazy with dopamine. Pax settled back into his position, his head resting on his hand, supported by his elbow.

He looked at Audra, her eyes closed and a blissful grin spread across her face. She was the "someone" that Sarah told him to find. He felt certain of it. The year and a half they had spent together felt much longer. The meals they shared, the laughter, the thrills, the sex—oh yes, the sex—and the music, always the music. All of it seemed perfect. Something he never thought he would experience again in his lifetime.

"Hey, Audra?"

She opened her eyes when she heard her real name slip from his lips.

"What's wrong?"

He smiled while shaking his head. "Nothing. No. Nothing is wrong."

Audra turned toward him, her eyes wide with disbelief. He took her hand, and she squeezed it, still uneasy about his sudden switch from calling her "Kid."

"I was wondering," he began, choosing his words carefully. "I was wondering if maybe we should—"

His pause increased her anxiety.

"We should *what*, Pax?"

No, *honey*. He heard the difference, just like she did. He decided to speak his mind quickly and be damned if the words didn't come out right.

"I was wondering if you would... maybe... like to get married?"

Her face shifted. It was subtle, but he noticed it. She relaxed slightly, then tensed again, but in a different way—more around her mouth, less around her eyes. Her hand that had been gripping his loosened. He waited.

"Oh, Pax, honey."

He heard the shift in her tone—sharps and flats fighting for dominance. She caressed his cheek and kissed him softly. He waited.

Her smile was genuine, and her copper eyes sparkled. Then, she shook her head slowly.

"Honey, you are a most amazing man. I love what we have and know you would be an equally amazing husband, but—"

But.

She gently held his face in her hands, her eyes fixed on his.

"Pax, honey, I can't compete with a ghost."

He felt the motion in his chest again, but it wasn't pleasant. These weren't butterflies; this was a knotting sensation, like swallowing a live snake.

He felt anger building inside him and took slow breaths to control it.

"What?"

Audra noticed the impact of her comment and let his face go. She sat up and wrapped her arms around her bent legs.

"Pax, honey," she tried to stay calm amid his growing disappointment. "You must know that you talk about Sarah quite often. I know all about what she liked and disliked. What she would do and what she would never do. How she liked to dress, what she enjoyed drinking, how she liked to dance."

He sat on the edge of the bed, looking away as Audra's voice bounced off his bare back.

"There's almost nothing we do together—except maybe in bed—that you don't bring up how Sarah would act in similar situations."

"Stop saying her name," he said through clenched teeth.

"Pax, honey," she continued, "I love you. There, I said it. And I love being with you, but I can't replace something you never let go of. I can never be her. I love this—what we have—but it will have to be all there is for us because I will never be enough to replace her."

A void of silence filled the room. She waited. He exhaled.

Audra reached out to touch his back, and his sudden recoil revealed everything she needed to know. Tears streamed down her face.

"Oh, Pax." No *honey*.

He stood, dressed, grabbed his wallet and keys, and began to leave. Audra bounded from the bed and positioned herself, naked and defiant, between Pax and the door, arms wide open, chest lifting and falling with her breath.

"No!" she said. "You don't get to unleash that Paxton Butler rage on me. Not on me. You stay here and talk to me about this."

Pax stopped mid-step, his face shifting with every breath— anger, disappointment, fear, and his old enemy, despair, all vying to take control.

"I can't do this," he said through clenched teeth.

"You can't or you won't?" she asked, trying to hold his attention.

Pax said nothing. He looked at her, this beautiful woman who had captured his heart and now squeezed it.

"You will do it," Audra replied. "We have too much between us to just walk away like this."

"I can't," he repeated. "Not now."

"Then when?" Her tone softened, and she lowered her arms.

"I don't know," he said, stepping around her and walking out the door.

He didn't hear her call after him. He didn't hear her sob. He didn't hear the door close behind him or the roar of his engine when he started the car. He heard nothing. For the first time in his memory, he heard nothing.

He drove aimlessly. The argument looped endlessly in his thoughts. He reflected on the places he and Audra had visited and the experiences they had shared. His auditory memory replayed conversations that validated Audra's remark about his frequent comparisons with Sarah. He realized she might be right, and worse, he possibly wasn't ready for a relationship of this magnitude.

As he drove, his rage turned to guilt, and he almost talked himself into turning around and heading back. He decided to visit Ally's house to relax before trying to reconcile with Audra.

His phone chirped as he drove. The caller ID read, "Zim." Pax flipped the phone open and said, "Yo, good timing. I need to talk to you, man."

Sobs came through the earpiece—sharps and flats like those he had just left, but in a different tone. He listened.

"Pax?" The voice was a gentle soprano, thick with tears.

"Erin?"

"SHE'S THE ONE," Zim said, arranging his mixing board in the off-stage area at The Chance Theater.

Pax smiled, having heard his keyboardist say the same thing many times before, but the "She" part always referred to someone different. He had known Zim for nearly eighteen years, and during that time, Zim had fallen in and out of love so many times that Pax had lost count. Zim probably had too.

"I think I've heard you say that before."

Zim looked at him as if he were remembering something important that he had forgotten, then laughed.

"Yeah, you have. But this time, man, it's different."

"Where did you meet her?" Pax asked.

The "this time" Zim referred to was named Erin. She was a student at Vassar and considerably younger than Zim.

They met at Darkside Records, where Zim was browsing sheet music and saw her with some friends across the aisle. She asked Zim if he played an instrument, and he proudly told her he was in a band that was "going places," a stretch at that time unless "places" meant various clubs in the Hudson Valley.

They talked about music until her friends, worried about Erin's virtue around this much older, long-haired, rough-looking man, gathered her to go back to campus.

Zim watched them leave, waiting for the pretty girl to look back. She did.

"What's your name?" she called across the store.

"Zim."

"I'm Erin," she replied. "See you later, Zim."

He returned to the store every day for a week until he saw her again. After that, they shared lunch, then dinner, followed by movies, and finally drinks and dancing. On the night she kissed him, he was completely lost.

"Pax," he said. "It was magical. Cosmic. I haven't felt anything like it before."

"Good for you, brother," Pax replied, expecting to hear about the next "she's the one" within a month.

"Hey, is Sarah coming tonight? Erin and some friends are coming, and maybe they could sit together."

"No," Pax replied. "The kids are being a pain. Teenagers, right? We don't feel comfortable leaving them alone in the house right now."

"Drag," Zim replied. "I want her to meet Sarah."

"You like this one, huh?"

"Yeah," Zim said, smiling. "This one's gonna be a problem."

ERIN PICKED Pax up from LaGuardia and quietly drove to his house in Middletown. Pax had let Zim stay in the house while he was in South Carolina, and knowing that Zim was somewhat of a slob, he expected to find the house layered with fast food containers and used condoms. He was pleasantly surprised to find it relatively clean.

He arrived in New York just in time to wash up and change into a black suit before they had to leave for the synagogue. The funeral was already scheduled a day later than Zim's sister Rachel wanted. She had flown in from Miami, and although she had always liked Pax, she wouldn't wait for him to arrive, and certainly not for Erin.

Erin was ready to go when Pax came downstairs.

"I've never seen you in a suit," she said. "You should wear them more often."

"Not a chance," he replied with a faint smile.

Pax sat beside Erin in the back row of the synagogue. Zim had not been an active practitioner, but Rachel wanted him to have a proper funeral. He was relieved it was a closed-casket event. Erin told him that the car accident had been brutal, and he wanted to remember Zim's face as he had seen it last—bearded and grinning.

He glanced down at Erin's hand, clutching his own tightly. He knew she was close to tears, wanting to shout at the universe for this theft. They would grieve together after the burial. For now, Rachel was in charge, and they accepted their roles as friends of the departed.

After the service at the synagogue, Erin drove them to the cemetery. During the short drive, she tried to discuss Zim with Pax several times. Each time, he raised his hand to stop her and eventually asked her to wait.

"I'm not ready yet, Erin. We can talk after all of this is over, okay? All night if you want."

Erin agreed, and they continued in silence.

Once the prayers were said and the family's duties were complete, Zim was laid to rest. Pax took Erin's hand, and they walked toward the car.

"Pax," Rachel called to him. He turned toward Zim's sister. "Are you coming to sit shiva with us?"

Pax turned to Erin, who was staring down at her shoes. He knew Erin wouldn't be welcome, and honestly, he thought that was pretty shitty.

"No, Rachel," he smiled as he delivered his disappointing response. "Erin and I are going to get drunk and tell stories about your brother."

Rachel tensed and shot a contemptuous look at Erin.

"He would have preferred that over all of this," Pax finished, gesturing toward the cemetery and the people dressed in black. It was his way of emphasizing that he and Erin knew Zim much better than Rachel did. He turned, and the two headed to the car.

They talked about Zim. They got drunk. They laughed. They cried. They voiced their regrets and frustrations with a man who couldn't get his shit together even into middle age.

"You know," Erin said, her drunken voice a few notes higher than her usual soprano. "I know he always told you that I was a problem."

"No—" Pax started, trying to lie to blunt Erin's grief.

"Hush. I know he did. Shut up."

Pax laughed, poured another tequila for Erin, and then poured one for himself.

"He did," she continued. "But the truth is... here's the truth, Pax. The truth is, I would have dropped everything to spend the rest of my life with that idiot."

Pax squinted, both from the alcohol and the words Erin shared. Except for their early days, Zim had never discussed his feelings for Erin or hers for him. He spent nights with Erin and sometimes days, but Pax always saw their relationship as friends with benefits.

"The problem," she said, waving her tequila glass around

and splashing the table as she pontificated. "The problem was that big idiot didn't think he deserved me."

She downed her tequila in one gulp.

"He would never commit to me because of you, Pax—you and Sarah."

Pax sat up and set his drink on the table.

"What are you talking about?"

The alcohol haze suddenly lifted, and he wanted to understand what she was saying before the agave curtain fell again.

"Yup," Erin hiccupped. "He was in love with how you and Sarah loved each other. He talked about it all the time. But he felt like he could never give me that. So, he didn't try. That was the problem."

Erin tried to slam her tequila again but found her glass was already empty. She waved it at Pax to fill it, but he was lost in thought. The gaping hole he felt where Zim had occupied his soul suddenly widened. He thought of times when Zim would drop in unannounced and stay longer than he should. He wondered if that was to bathe in Pax and Sarah's love. He couldn't wrap his mind around Zim being afraid to even try to love Erin because he felt inadequate.

Erin sighed deeply and poured herself another glass. "You were his hero, Pax. The way you and Sarah loved each other was—"

"He said that each of you was a force multiplier for the other," Erin slurred, the word "force" coming out more like *fortz*. "He said that together, you had more love than either of you had on your own."

Pax reflected on the old saying that people should never meet their heroes unless they want to risk disappointment. He believed a better truism is to avoid meeting those who see you as a hero, out of fear of causing that disappointment.

"He was my soulmate, Pax," Erin sniffed. "And he didn't fucking know it."

Grief came to Pax not as a wave, washing slowly over him, but like a truck at full speed, as big and as fast as the one that had taken Zim. He fought it, but between the tequila and the breaking news Erin had dropped on him, that struggle was short, and he lay his head on the table and wept.

Erin's grief, dry kindling waiting for a spark, ignited into flame, and she collapsed to the floor, kneeling beside Pax with her head on his lap as their sorrow sang out in the kitchen—more sharps and flats competing for dominance.

In the morning, Pax sat on the front steps of his Middletown house, watching the dew glisten in the sunlight that slanted through the neighborhood. His head throbbed slightly with the beginnings of a hangover, but he knew from experience that deep breaths of fresh air were an excellent way to ward off the worst of it. Erin had passed out on the couch after their wake for Zim. He thought she might be in worse shape than he was.

He learned many new things about his oldest friend from Erin, whose rage at the universe and grief for what would never be were worsened by the truth serum from Jalisco. Knowing the hidden message behind "the problem" Zim always mentioned when talking about Erin, Pax felt furious with his lost brother. He also wrestled with the guilt of not having gotten to know Erin better before last night. He could have guided Zim onto a better path if he had. Maybe.

"What now, Pax?" a croaking soprano voice came from the door.

He looked up to see Erin holding a cup of coffee. He reached out to take her hand, but she gave him the mug and produced another from behind the door frame. He thanked her and sipped the bitter, hot brew, feeling it enter his system almost immediately.

"I don't know how you take it, so it's just black," she said, almost apologetically.

"If it's not black, it's not coffee. It's just coffee flavored."

She laughed, and a tear welled up in her eye.

"Zim used to say that," she sniffed.

"Yeah, I know. Sorry." Pax hadn't intended to reopen the fresh wound of Zim's loss.

He reached out his hand once more, and this time, she accepted it. They sat silently, gazing at each other, not as potential lovers but as long-lost friends who had only recently met.

"I wish I had gotten to know you better before all this, Erin," he said. He wanted some absolution for his negligence. "I assumed what he said meant one thing when it meant something completely different. I can't tell you how sorry I am."

Erin squeezed his hand and nodded, holding back tears. The silence settled again as they sipped their coffee, watching the sun's rays seep into the neighborhood and light up the morning.

"Did Zim ever talk to you about quantum physics?" she asked.

Pax gave Erin a crooked grin and nodded.

"I didn't quite understand it, but he made it sound interesting."

"He did!" she emphasized. "He thought about it a lot, how these bodies are just transport mechanisms and that our consciousness is some subatomic particle. He was pretty convinced he was onto something important."

"Who knows," Pax responded. "Maybe he was."

"He said that you and Sarah were," she paused to find the right word, "tangled?"

"Entangled, I think."

"Yes, entangled, and your atomic particles were forever connected in some multi-dimensional way. He was very sure about that."

"He mentioned something like that on the drive south."

"I think that means the two of you are always linked and still connected, even though she's not here in person."

Pax thought about it, and it felt right. Even though Sarah had left the world, he could still feel her presence. He truly believed she was out there somewhere. He longed to find a way to locate her.

"Do you think Zim and I were entangled, Pax?" Erin was seeking comfort from the emptiness she felt. "Do you think we're still connected?"

"Do you feel him out there?" Pax chose not to comment on Zim's metaphysics, quantum physics, or whatever. He simply wanted to help Erin cope.

She sat silently, contemplating, listening, and feeling, then looked at Pax and nodded.

"Well, there you are."

Pax squeezed her hand and looked back at the neighborhood, now glowing in the dawn light. He spun the wedding band on his finger as he thought about Sarah. He desperately wanted to find her. He needed to hear that root of D: *Third Fret —Second String*. It was the sound of her joy and the cause of his own. He would go out into the world and listen for it. He had no idea where to start, so it would take time and a lot of driving.

He turned and looked at the door of the old house.

"Erin, do you know a good realtor?"

CHAPTER 2

HE STARED AT HER. *Through her. Into the ether beyond her.*

"What do you mean you're pregnant?"

Sarah laughed, took his hand, and placed it on her belly. He sat up in bed and stared at his hand, covering the spot that would soon nourish a tiny human.

"You put a baby in here, you big dummy. That's what I mean."

They had only been married for ten months and planned to wait at least two years before starting their family.

"But I thought you had that diaphragm thing?" Pax croaked, panic seeping into his voice.

"Well, I guess this little one was a strong swimmer and somehow found a way around it."

He blinked a few times. His ears were buzzing. His mouth felt dry.

"A baby?"

"A baby."

"Do you know if it's—"

"No, silly, I don't think even the baby knows what it is yet. But we can find out eventually if you want to spoil the surprise."

"No. No."

"But," she said with a gleam in her eye, "I feel like it's a girl."

The weight of the moment overwhelmed him, and he found himself weeping as the hand touching her skin trembled. She watched him for a moment and then understood she had to save him from himself.

"We have time to plan, Pax. It won't be here tomorrow."

He nodded and slowly began to regain his senses.

"I'll get a job, Sarah. I'll shut the band down and get a job. I'll take care of you."

"Oh no, you will not, Pax Butler. You will not shut down the band. You and the band will keep playing and bringing in what you can. You're too good not to be noticed. It's going to happen. We'll start cutting back on some of our more frivolous expenses. No more eating out or drinking in bars. Home-cooked meals and discount beer from now on. We'll live on my income, and whatever money you bring home, we'll put it in savings for the future. But you keep playing and recording, making Butler Service a household name."

He looked at his wife, his soulmate, the woman who brought music to his soul and breath to his voice. She was incredibly strong and unafraid of any of this. He felt that everything would be okay if she handled the practical aspects of their lives. She would let him be who he believed he was meant to be while she took care of everything else.

"You're going to be a great father, Pax."

ALLY WAS PISSED.

She was furious that Pax had stayed so long in New York without calling. She was angry that Pax had sold the house in Middletown. *Our house! Our family home!* And now she was even more upset because sixty feet of truck and trailer were parked on the street outside her house, nearly blocking access to the cul-de-sac. She and Travis had been in the house a little over a month, and now Pax was causing a scene that the neighbors would definitely talk about.

"What the fuck, Dad?" Ally pointed at the fifth wheel as Pax climbed out of the shiny new truck pulling the extended trailer. Ally rarely cursed, but when she did, she called it "getting her Pax on." She would never have thrown the f-bomb at her father, but—

"Slow your roll, Kiddo," Pax interrupted her follow-up tirade. "It's only for a day."

Ally stared at the spotless, new mobile apartment, her mouth hanging open as she unconsciously shook her head. It took several long seconds for his words to sink in.

"What do you mean 'for a day'?"

"I'm hitting the road tomorrow. Not sure when I'll return."

Pax draped his arm around Ally's shoulder and guided her back to the house. She was in shock, and he had a lot to tell her.

Puck and Lainey ran up to him, shouting "Papa!" as he entered the house. He lifted each of them one at a time and hugged them tightly, giving big, messy smooches on their cheeks, which made them giggle. Travis was making Sunday breakfast for Ally and the kids. He acknowledged Pax's presence with a calm, unflappable nod and asked if Pax wanted something to eat.

"Yeah," Pax replied, leading Ally to the kitchen table. "Whatever you're making is fine, Russ... sorry, Travis."

Travis glanced at Pax over his glasses as he stirred scrambled eggs in the pan. Pax gave him an apologetic smile. This wasn't the first time he had made that mistake. Ally smacked the side of his head to get his attention.

"Speak!"

Pax took a deep breath and began speaking. He talked continuously for twenty minutes without hesitation, about Audra and how he let his anger take over. He shared details about Zim and Erin, including the harsh truth Erin had delivered to him in New York. He described his accident, the damage to his hand, and how he felt as if he had lost so much so quickly.

He talked about Sarah. He fumbled as he tried to describe Zim's idea of entanglement, sharing how he felt his late wife's presence in the universe and that he needed to find her. He told her what Audra had said about competing with a ghost, admitting that she was right. He hadn't made peace with Sarah's passing because he still felt her presence.

"I'm lost without her, Ally. Your mother was always the decision maker."

"That was good because you're terrible at it," Ally interrupted, pointing toward the fifth wheel parked in front of the house.

Pax placed his hand on hers to *take back the mic*, as he used to say.

"She was the strong one. She gave birth to you while I was at a gig. She worked hard to give me a shot at my dream and made sure that the little money I brought helped keep that dream alive. She was too much of a presence in the world to be snatched away like that. Even though her body is gone, I know she's out there. I know it as truly as I know anything, Kiddo."

Ally held his hand, her voice adopting the professional tone of the counselor she had become, as if she were speaking to a patient facing a serious medical situation.

"Dad, you're over sixty. I know you're in good health—great health, in fact—but you're talking about driving several tons of vehicle across the country in search of a feeling."

Pax nodded, smiling. *She gets it*, he thought, *even if she disagrees with it.*

Ally looked up at Travis as he was putting strips of bacon into the pan.

"A little help here, Travis?"

Travis was overly rational, but he would share his view only when asked. He looked up from the stove, first at Ally and then at Pax.

"What do you need for your trip, Dad?"

Rob was torn. He felt excited about the odyssey Pax was undertaking, and if he were still a childless bachelor, he might have joined him. But he also understood Ally's anxiety and questioned Pax about the timing and the decision to go solo on such a journey. Pax responded by hugging Rob tightly—something he had never done before—and thanking him for understanding, and for the collection of CDs, which, combined with the pile Travis gave him, provided a week's worth of driving music without hearing the same song twice.

In the morning, Ally went missing for a few hours. She returned carrying a box and handed it to Travis, who opened it and began working on its contents.

"You need to call," she told him. "You need to make sure we know where you are regularly. Not daily. Well, maybe daily at first."

"It's time you had a smartphone, Dad." Ally showed Pax her own, which she used for work at the medical center. "It's a phone, but you can also use it for email, texting, the internet, and navigation. Even listening to music or watching videos. But in your case, it's a phone. Use it. Regularly."

Travis spent some time helping Pax learn how to use the mobile device. As a musician, he found technical details easy to grasp. Travis then transferred contacts and important information from Pax's flip phone to the new one.

"All of our phone numbers and email addresses are there, Dad," Travis told him. "Mine is listed as Tech Support."

Pax laughed and thanked Travis for the guide.

"Try it out when you reach your first stop. Let us know where you are. Send me an email. Call Ally and Rob. And always remember to plug it in at night. That battery should last a couple of days, but keep it charged, okay?"

Pax promised he would.

"And if you don't call us," Ally added, "we'll call you. Always answer the phone when one of us calls, Dad. Always."

At midday, he played with the grandkids while lunch was being prepared. He wrestled with Puck and Lainey on the floor, hoping they would remember him when he returned. Jasmine was too young to know who Papa was, but he hugged her, kissed her cheeks, and made her laugh. *Her* eyes, again. All of them had *Her* eyes.

He wanted to reach Nashville on the first leg, and the longer he stayed, the more likely he was to end up driving into unfamiliar territory at night. To Ally's relief, he decided to stay another night and leave early the next morning. She still held out hope that she might be able to talk him out of it.

However, in the morning, after coffee and pancakes with the kids, after hugs and kisses and promises to call, after tears and laughter, he climbed into the truck. Ally stood on the curb next to the passenger's window to lean in and remind him once more to call. She noticed a small white box on the passenger seat.

"What's in that box?"

He clenched his jaw, searching for the right words.

"Your mother," he said. "Her rings."

Ally began to weep.

"I promised her a long time ago that I would take her across the country. I put it off for too long, and then it was too late. So..."

Ally dabbed at her eyes.

"Kiddo," he said quietly so only Ally would hear. "If you see Audra, tell her—"

"Tell her yourself, Dad. Travis put her number in your phone."

PAX LOOKED at his reflection in the Tennessee Welcome Center restroom mirror as he washed his hands. He had only been on the road for a few hours but needed to stop and gather himself before moving on. Driving the fifth wheel through the mountains between North Carolina and Tennessee was one of the most nerve-wracking things he could remember doing. He drove cautiously, probably too slowly for many others on the road. He nearly had a heart attack when he encountered a lane closure that forced him to steer those tons of metal through a narrow, winding section of road without sliding off the shoulder. After what felt like a lifetime of stress, he made it through the mountains, and relief washed over him as he entered the open lanes of Eastern Tennessee.

He left the rest area cautiously, smoothing his way back onto the highway. Still uncomfortable maneuvering the hulking house on wheels, he stayed in the right lane and kept his speed around fifty miles per hour, much to the annoyance of those who periodically got stuck behind him for a mile or two.

He waved and smiled at the middle fingers from passing cars and other RV drivers, who were more confident in this task than he was. He let the music from the stack of CDs keep his mind out of the panic zone as he headed to Nashville.

The RV dealer who sold him the fifth wheel let him practice backing it into a parking space until he felt comfortable. He knew the real test of that skill was coming outside Nashville when he rolled into his first KOA. He hoped he wouldn't look too silly in front of the regulars at these nomad stops. He didn't regret buying the fifth wheel, but a nagging voice in his head said, "You could have stayed in hotels, Pax."

Periodically, he glanced at the small white box in the

passenger seat and smiled. This wasn't the trip they had planned, but as the philosophers say, "Man Plans. God Laughs."

He slid *Dark Side of the Moon* into the CD player, Rob's favorite album, popped some cashews into his mouth, and sipped his coffee. Then he nudged the beast up to fifty-five as the sun moved across the clear blue Tennessee sky.

HE MET her at the age of six.

His mother took him to the neighbor's house because Mrs. Bing had brought home her new baby girl. As an only child, Pax had never seen a baby up close, and he felt both excited and scared. He knew he had once been one of these little creatures, but his childlike mind couldn't understand how that was possible. His memories began when he was already walking, running, and playing. How could he have ever been so tiny?

Mrs. Bing and his mother were good friends, part of the same neighborhood committees, members of several charities, and respected women in the community. Mr. Bing worked in science at the College on the Hill, while Pax's dad worked for the city of Ithaca. They were two good American families, descendants of survivors of the Great Depression and the War to End All Wars, as well as the wars that followed. Americans living in houses they owned, at the dawn of a new era of prosperity. These were the days they would someday refer to as The Good Old Days.

And there she was.

"Pax, this is Sarah."

Mrs. Bing sat in a chair, cradling the tiny person in her lap. The baby was asleep, her bottom lip protruding slightly, her mouth gently moving as she sucked on something invisible in her dreams.

Pax knelt beside the chair and gazed at her, feeling speechless. Thin strands of brown hair framed her otherwise bald head. Her tiny nose, just a bump between her chubby cheeks, twitched as she suckled. He examined her fingers, so small and delicate, and slowly reached for that little hand but paused. Looking up at Mrs. Bing for permission, he saw her smile and nod.

"Go ahead," she said softly.

Pax touched the open palm of the little hand, and it closed around his finger. His eyes widened. His heart raced. He heard his mother make the sound she makes when she sees something she likes. He looked up into the baby's face and saw two brown circles, like glass beads, looking at him. He was lost.

"What do you think, Pax?" his mother asked softly.

He paused to find the words. His mind was lost in those eyes.

"I love her," he whispered.

Mrs. Bing and his mother both made that happy sound. He didn't care. He didn't have time to care. His life was laid out before him in that little face. He would be her protector, her best friend, and the person she needed when no one else could help. He didn't know any of this yet, or even the words for what he was feeling, but someday he would. Someday, he would realize that what he felt that day was destiny.

And it appeared that destiny was mutual.

The tiny fingers clenched tighter around his own as if testing him, claiming him. He barely breathed, afraid that any movement would shatter the strange, sacred moment between them.

A breeze fluttered the sheer curtains of Bing's sitting room, rustling the leaves of the ivy plant by the window. The house smelled of lavender and bread rising in the kitchen, with a timer ticking away, counting down to when it was time to put the dough in the oven. Somewhere outside, a motorcycle rumbled past. Pax heard none of it. His focus was on the soft suckling sound of Sarah's lips and the murmur of their mothers talking above him.

"She likes you," Mrs. Bing said with a laugh.

Sarah yawned, a small squeak escaping from her mouth. Her grip on his finger loosened, but Pax adjusted, curling his hand slightly to keep his hold. Mrs. Bing smiled.

"Looks like you've made a new friend, Pax."

He nodded solemnly, as if accepting a responsibility he hadn't known was his until that moment.

"Yeah," he said, glancing at the adults before looking back at Sarah.

His mother chuckled, but Mrs. Bing gave him a thoughtful look. Sarah made a soft noise that was part sigh and part hum, and for a moment, Pax thought she had fallen asleep again. But no. Her eyes—those brown eyes—remained fixed on him, her expression unreadable. He tightened his grip, and she responded by grasping him back, firm for such a tiny hand.

He didn't know it yet, but someday he would hold that same hand on a park bench by the lake. Someday, those fingers would stroke his cheek when he was tired, grip his shoulder when she was angry, and interlace with his own in the dark when words weren't needed. Someday, he would hold that hand in a hospital room, feeling it grow cold, wishing it would stay warm.

But for now, she was just a baby, and he was just a boy. And without realizing it, they had chosen each other.

PART III

THE SCENT OF YOU

"Smell is a potent wizard that transports you across thousands of miles and all the years you have lived."

– Helen **Keller**

CHAPTER 3

HIS HEART RACED, and a bead of sweat rolled down his temple as Pax felt the cold beer bottle strike his palm while a meaty hand shook the other.

"First time?"

"Hard to tell, huh?" he replied.

"Ah," the man laughed. "We were all rookies at one time or another. I'm Leo Murphy."

"Pax," he said, shaking the offered hand and then sipping the beer, "Thanks for this."

"Just Pax?" The woman walking up to the two men asked, a beer bottle hanging from her fingers and a cigarette in her other hand. "Is that like Cher? Just the one name?"

"Pax Butler. Paxton in full. But, yeah, just Pax."

She clinked her bottle against his and said, "Claire."

"Nice to meet you, Claire."

"This one belongs to me," she said, leaning into Leo. "First time backing into a tight space?"

Pax looked at the fifth wheel. It was parked—if that meant not moving—and mostly within the designated space, if one was generous. It was inches from a tree on one side, crooked as it extended out of the slip, and the front of the truck was just over the line into the lane between sites, which meant it was technically covering most of the space.

"Yeah," he said, grimacing at the awful park job. "I'll get better."

"I don't doubt that," she said. Pax thought her tone might have implied something different.

"We're that one," Leo said, pointing at a soft-blue RV a few spaces down. "We call her Robin. Does yours have a name?"

"Uh, no," Pax replied, wondering why people give vehicles names. "Not yet."

"I counted eleven," came a voice from the other side. Pax and Leo turned to see a compact, middle-aged woman walking toward them, her hands shoved into the pockets of her jeans and her cotton shirt open to her breastbone.

"Eleven is right," Leo said.

"Eleven?" Pax asked.

"Eleven times forward and back until you had your baby in the cradle."

The woman's accent was thick with New England flavor. She extended her hand, and Pax took it, feeling her firm grip, like that of a salesperson.

"Sally Cornish," she said. "Sal, if ya like."

"Pax."

Sal smiled.

"Well, Pax, it wasn't any kind of record, but it was a lot of fun to watch. Got one of those for me, Leo?"

Leo reached into his back pocket, pulled out another bottle of beer, and handed it to her. Sal used the post at the end of the parking space to pop off the cap.

"Here's to first-timers," she said, raising her bottle in toast. "Cheers to beers and legs behind your ears!" Pax heard *cheeahs t' beeahs 'n legs ba-hind ye' eeahs.*

The small group talked as evening fell. Pax mostly listened but shared a few parts of his story whenever asked. He wanted to be more open about his life and situation during this trip, but for now, he would only answer questions and not offer unsolicited details. He wasn't searching for a therapist. He wasn't exactly sure what he was seeking other than *Her*.

Leo and Claire were both retired. Unmarried and widowed, they met through Craigslist—one was selling a car, and the other was buying. They traveled seasonally, usually moving north and south, but always east of the Mississippi River. They had a home outside Columbus, Ohio, to stay grounded. He had been a research chemist at Ohio State University, working on new types of polymers, while she had owned a moderately successful insurance agency with her late husband. They were an unlikely pair, as mismatched as Pax had ever seen, yet they seemed to enjoy each other's company.

Sal was a software consultant. She had no home base, but because she was afraid of flying, she navigated her nomadic life by driving to projects across the country wherever her skills were needed, including her current gig at Nashville International Airport. She was quite the talker, so much so that she not only shared details about herself with Pax but also filled in gaps in some of Leo and Claire's stories. Eventually, Claire had to interrupt her.

"Sally, give the man a minute to digest. He just got here."

Pax saw Leo point to the bottle in Sal's hand, and she nodded in response. Then he and Claire said goodnight before going back to Robin to eat and relax for the evening.

Sal gave Pax a tour of the campsite. She waved to people she knew and introduced him to those she wanted him to meet. She talked nonstop, not giving him a moment to interject, even when she posed questions. He found it strange but charming. It saved him the trouble of coming up with things to talk about.

She told him it was her fourth time at that RV park, that she had been there for a month, and that her current assignment would keep her there for another month. She liked the park and the people.

"Some of these places," she said, "the people are just snooty. They pull up in their luxury rolling hotel suites, with their pop-out sides and fancy cars in tow. They don't talk to real people like us."

"I see."

"The folks here, though," she continued, unaware that Pax had made a sound. "Real people. Good people. Lend-a-hand and share-a-beer types. Sure, they come and go, but while they're here, you can count on them."

Pax nodded and tossed his empty bottle into a trash can. Sal quickly reached in, grabbed the bottle, and slid it into her back pocket. That's when he noticed her other back pocket held her own empty bottle. Pax smiled at the oddness of this woman.

"Leo makes the beer. He has me and others collect the empties so he can clean them and reuse them for his brew."

"Leo made that beer?" Pax asked, surprised.

Sal smiled broadly and nodded. "Good shit, huh?"

Pax agreed and promised to save his bottles for Leo.

"What do you do, Pax?"

"I'm—"

"Or I guess, what did you do? Retired, probably, huh?"

"No," he responded, hoping he didn't look that old. "I guess, maybe? I don't know. I'm a musician."

Sal paused and looked at him as if he had claimed to be the second coming of Christ.

"Shut up," she said, a smile crossing her face. "Me too!"

"Really, what do you play?" he asked, genuinely interested.

"Mandolin," she said. "Got it from my dad. Piece of crap won't stay in tune, but I can't let it go."

"Mandolin? I didn't realize that was a popular instrument in, what, Massachusetts?"

"Screw you," Sal retorted, laughing. "New Hampshire. Close enough, I guess. The way I said beer gave me away, huh?"

Pax laughed. "I have an ear for things."

Sal continued, "Yeah. Dad was from West Virginia. Moved to Hampton after Vietnam. What's your instrument?"

"Guitar.

"Nice. Let's jam some night."

He agreed as they stopped in front of a small trailer, which was a little worn but still tidy.

"This is me," Sal said. "You want to come in for a beer?"

Pax looked up and saw the first stars peeking through the fabric of the night sky.

"Another time? I need to get my rig set straight."

"Set straight," she replied. "That's funny. Might need another eleven tries to straighten that sucker out."

He laughed, thanked Sal for the tour, and then headed back to his own space.

"Hey, Pax," she called after him. "Bonfire on Friday. Be there. Bring your guitaaaah."

He waved without looking back, listening to her laugh at her self-deprecating joke.

Pax connected his utilities at the fifth wheel, turned off the battery, and plugged into the park's grid. He climbed inside and tested the lights. Pleased with himself for successfully completing this part of his first overnight, he took a microwave dinner out of the cooler. While he ate, he listened to some Crosby, Stills, and Nash, then cleaned up and lay down in bed. The first day of this adventure was over and had been a whirlwind of strangeness.

He took out the shiny new phone and called Ally. Her phone

went straight to voicemail, much to his relief. He was too exhausted for a long chat.

"Hey Kiddo. Made it to Nashville. I'm at a KOA on the...I guess the east side, I don't know. Met some nice people. I'm tired, so I'm going to hit the rack. Talk soon."

He set the phone on the bedside table next to his traveling companion, the small white box holding Sarah's rings. He gently touched the box, turned off the light, and quickly drifted off to sleep.

PAX WOKE BEFORE DAWN. He was not usually an early riser, but the unfamiliarity of his current situation made him open his eyes. He knew that if he went back to sleep, he would feel terrible when he finally woke up for good, so he rolled out of bed and made some coffee.

My favorite fruit, he heard Zim say in his head.

A gentle knock on his door startled him, causing him to spill some coffee on the floor. It was Sal, dressed and ready to drive to her work site.

"I noticed your light was on, so I thought—"

"Coffee?" Pax asked, as he sipped his own.

"Oh, uh, no, thanks. Gives me the shakes."

"Are you heading to work?" Pax asked, leaning on the door frame. He thought he should invite Sal in but considered that it might be too early in their relationship for that sort of thing.

"Yeah, yeah, but I want to show you something. It doesn't happen often, but today is your lucky day. Put your shoes on. The grass is wet."

Pax slipped his sockless feet into his sneakers and joined Sal outside. She led him to the playground near the center of the RV park and pointed. Pax followed her finger and was awed by the vista of stars before him.

"Usually, there are clouds, or it's overcast, or the moon is too bright, but today... Damn, huh?"

"Damn, huh, is right." Pax echoed.

Sal pointed out several planets and constellations. Pax recognized most of them, but his new friend wanted to share her knowledge, and he was happy to let her. He inhaled the morning air, sipped his coffee, and smiled at the sky.

"How long are you staying, Pax?"

He shrugged. "I don't have any specific plans, so I guess I'll be here for a little while. I want to go into town and listen to some live music."

"Yeah? Cool. I'll go with you if you want some company. I don't usually go clubbing in most of the places I stay. I'm not... comfortable in crowds."

Pax laughed and looked at Sal. "Really? I feel like you would be in your element with an audience."

Sal chuckled. "I'm not sure if that's a compliment or an insult, but yeah, I can see how you might think that."

"You said bonfire Friday?"

"Yeah, you going to be there?"

Pax nodded. "Yeah. Then we'll hit Broadway on Saturday night?"

Sal agreed, patted Pax on the shoulder, and went back to her truck. Pax stayed in the playground, watching the stars until he finished his coffee, then went back to his site to decide what to do next.

He spent the day reviewing the owner's manual for the fifth wheel and testing all the features and connections to make sure he understood where everything was and what each component did. As a traveling musician, he was used to figuring out how to connect things and where to hang cords. Understanding the fifth wheel wasn't as straightforward as that, but it wasn't overly difficult either. It was just work, as he would say.

Pax learned more about the other campers in the park. Most were on vacation with their kids, but older nomads like him occupied a handful of sites. He wasn't eager to share too much about his current situation, except to mention that he felt the need to see the country and wanted to experience as much live music as possible. All the residents asked if he would attend the bonfire on Friday night. It seemed to him that it would be quite an event, and he planned to bring his guitar in case anyone wanted to sing. Sal was right. These were good people—friendly, open, and pleasant.

Leo would visit occasionally, sometimes with Claire and sometimes alone. He discussed his years as a polymer chemist and his love for brewing beer. Pax shared his experiences as a musician and some of the gigs he played over the decades. Occasionally, one of them would reminisce about their late wives, although Pax wouldn't initiate such conversations unless the discussion naturally drifted in that direction. He preferred not to mention Sarah unless it was relevant to the ongoing topic, and more often than not, he tried to steer the discussion away from his personal life—an old habit that conflicted with his new approach to living, but he was making an effort.

Every night before bed, he would email Ally and Rob. He called once or twice but only reached voicemail. Occasionally, he saw missed calls from either of them. Their busy lives and his disinterest in constantly being connected made live conversations unpredictable. When he finally figured out how to include both kids in a single email instead of sending separate messages, he felt like he had found the Holy Grail.

Every night, he saw Audra's name listed in his contacts, but bypassed it. It became easier with each passing day.

THE BONFIRE WAS MORE like a campfire—maybe a little bigger—but nothing like what he remembered from his high school camping trips. Claire and Leo hosted it as a bring-your-own-everything event. Pax had wisely packed a foldable chair, planning to spend time outside the fifth wheel. He brought his guitar and a flask of tequila and settled into a spot across from Claire, who watched him as she smoked. Meanwhile, Leo kept the fire well-fed.

Other campers wandered in slowly, and the area around the fire began to fill in. Being the new guy, not many people sat too close to him, but that didn't bother him.

A younger couple and their two small children arrived. Darnell, Kenya, and their twin ten-year-olds, Eden and Michaela, were on vacation from Charlottesville. Eden was especially interested in Pax's guitar and asked if he would play it.

"Would you like that?" he smiled, thinking of Lainey.

Eden nodded, and Michaela, eager to join, shouted, "Me too!"

Pax grabbed the guitar from the travel bag and motioned for the girls to come over.

"This is how I tune it to make sure it sounds good."

The girls watched as Pax adjusted the tuning pegs. He let each of them pluck the strings while he tuned them. He made faces when the notes didn't sound right and smiled and nodded when they did. The girls loved being part of the process.

"What song should I play?"

The girls talked for a moment, then said together, "Let it Go."

Pax looked at Darnell and Kenya and shook his head.

"It's from Frozen," Kenya said. "Mr. Butler probably doesn't know that one, girls."

Pax laughed. "I don't know that one, but here's one that maybe you have heard."

Pax stretched the fingers of his strumming hand and began to play and sing *Blackbird*. He played slower than the usual tempo to ensure his hands didn't betray their diminished skill. Eden and Michaela sat on the ground with their legs crossed, chins resting on their hands as Pax performed. When he strummed the final G chord, both girls stood up and clapped before running back to their chairs.

Kenya thanked Pax for his kindness to the girls.

"Oh man, if I knew you were that good, I wouldn't have brought this crappy thing with me."

Sal stepped into the firelight, clutching a worn mandolin.

"Hey, Sal," Pax said as she pulled her folding chair next to his. "Looks like your friend there has been through it."

"Yeah," Sal replied. "She's a little beat-up, but I think she mostly sounds good."

"Play something!" Eden shouted.

"What do you know, Sal?" Pax asked, not wanting to start anything she wouldn't be comfortable playing.

"Do you know Copperhead Road?" Sal asked hesitantly.

Pax smiled, thinking it was a solid mandolin song.

"I know it, but I've never played it. But you start, and I'll catch up."

Sal spent the next five minutes tuning the old instrument, then slowly and softly began strumming the opening riffs. She sounded a bit stiff, but Pax found the key and smoothly transitioned into the song as background, helping to mask Sal's choppy chord changes.

When she began to sing, Pax smiled widely. She had Steve Earle's growl just right, and her tone was spot-on. That Nor'easter accent blended with a touch of the mountaineer twang she picked up from her father. They played together as she belted out the lyrics, and by the end, the group around the fire gave them both a rousing ovation.

Pax played again, and Sal sat quietly listening with the others. Then, they performed another duet before helping the growing crowd of children make s'mores. Pax felt light. He felt good. He felt welcome in this strange community. He thought of his family and how he would like to experience the same with them. He remembered feeling like this before, but that was when *She* was there.

After the fire was put out and the families returned to their sites, Pax walked Sal back to her trailer.

"We still on for going into town tomorrow?"

"Yeah, I want to check out some of the clubs."

He felt comfortable with Sal, quirks and all. She had a bit of Zim in her, but the rest was all Sal. It felt great to sing and play for people again, and despite her fumbles with the mandolin chords, she proved to be a good partner.

In front of her trailer, Sal suddenly stopped and grabbed his hand. She turned him toward her and moved close in an intimate way. She looked at him, waiting for him to lean down, but he didn't. Instead, he took her hand, holding it between his own.

"Sal," he said softly, trying to find the right words to let her down without hurting her feelings. "I need a friend. But right now, I don't need more than a friend. I hope that's okay."

Sal's disappointment was visible in the tightness of her face. He felt he should speak, but kept his mouth shut and waited. Her recovery showed she was used to rejection. A faint smile appeared on her lips as she nodded.

"Sure, Pax," she said, patting him on the chest. "Sure."

They said goodnight, and Pax went back to his trailer.

"A friend with benefits?" Sal shouted after him, laughing.

Pax raised his hand to wave without turning around and kept walking toward his trailer.

Lounging on his bed, he called Ally. The call went straight to voicemail, and he was unsure what to say, so he kept it short.

"All's well, Kiddo. Have a good night."

He scrolled through his phone, looking for messages when Audra's contact appeared. He touched it and starting writing a text, but then stopped. He didn't have the words.

Not yet, he thought.

SAL FOLLOWED him as he wandered toward Southern Blues Junction. The club was tucked away off the main street in downtown Nashville. Pax knew that the larger venues on Broadway catered to tourists, so the style and variety of music wouldn't be what you'd find just a few side streets over.

He stopped to read the sign in the window listing the bands performing that month and saw that the night's entertainment was a trio called Three Little Birds. He thought of the song by Bob Marley and wondered if they were a reggae band.

"What do you think?" Sal asked. "Check it out?"

"Yup," he said. "If they suck, we'll find another place."

They entered and found a table just off the small dance floor, close to the stage, already set with microphones and a small drum kit. Sal said she would handle the first round, and Pax happily ordered tequila on ice. Sal preferred vodka and tonic.

He estimated the club could seat about three hundred people, but only around sixty were scattered across the tables. The band stepped out and didn't seem surprised by the small audience. They took their positions—the lead singer with a hollow-body Gretsch guitar, the bass player on a stand-up, and the drummer at the snare and cymbal kit.

"Rockabilly," Pax said, mostly to himself, but Sal heard him and smiled.

The band started, and Rockabilly was on point. They were outstanding, truly outstanding.

Sal tried to keep rhythm with the drummer, slapping her legs in awkward syncopation. When she attempted to sing along with some of the songs, Pax touched her arm to quiet her. He wanted to hear the band, not Sal.

Like many other musicians, Pax watched the frontman's fingers as he tore off riffs up and down the neck of his guitar. He had never had the skills to play this kind of music and deeply respected anyone who could do it well.

The frontman saw Pax looking at him and gave him a nod, recognizing another player in the audience. Pax nodded back.

When the band finally took a break, Pax and Sal applauded loudly and looked around to make sure the other patrons were also clapping, encouraging them with whoops and calls of "Come on!"

The frontman thanked them and left the stage to get a drink. Pax called their server over and told her not to let the band pay for their drinks. He would take care of it. She went back to the bar to update those involved.

"So, what do you think, Pax?" Sal asked. "Stay here or find another joint?"

Just as he was about to respond, the band's guitarist approached their table.

"Thanks for the drinks, sir."

"Sir? Ha." Sal chuckled. "It's because you're old."

"Pax," he said, shaking the man's hand. "You can call my friend Sir if you like."

Sal backhanded Pax on the shoulder.

"I'm Bobby Bird," the man said, then pointed back to the bar. "Those are my brothers, Deke and Rick."

Pax waved to the other band members, who lifted their drinks in recognition.

"Ah," Pax said. "Three Little Birds. Got it."

"You play, don't you?" Bobby asked.

"I do," Pax replied. "But not like that."

Bobby laughed. "I saw you looking at my hands. I do that too when I'm watching a band."

"It's how we learn, man," Pax said. "You're terrific. Crisp. Fluid. I'm a fan."

"You want to play?" Bobby asked. "Maybe something slower, not so much flash?"

"Do it, Pax!" Sal shouted, her third vodka tonic rushing through her small frame.

Pax laughed, contemplating his depleted skill. "Not a fucking chance."

Sal felt disappointed and slapped his shoulder.

"Get up there, Pax! You're really good!" she slurred.

"How about singing something?" Bobby asked, seeking a compromise. "You sing?"

Pax nodded, feeling a desire to step back onto the stage.

"You guys know 'Come On Everybody'?"

"Know it?" Bobby laughed. "In another life, I was Eddy Cochran."

The break ended, and Bobby talked to his brothers, who agreed to let the old man who bought them drinks get up and embarrass himself. Pax followed the group to the stage and stood next to Bobby.

"This is Pax," Bobby said to the crowd. "I think he might have been around when this song was written."

Pax shook his head and looked at Sal, who was cheering like a maniac. Bobby stepped back and started the opening riff. Taking his cue, Pax grabbed the mic and unleashed his inner Cochran.

At the end of the song, both the band and the other patrons of the club applauded.

"Let's hear it for Pax." Bobby encouraged the crowd as Pax took a deep bow and blew kisses to them. His third glass of tequila had erased what little humility he still had.

He returned to the table where Sal had already ordered another round of drinks. He quickly drank half of his as the band started their second set. Sal took Pax's hand on the table and mouthed the word "wow," her smile as wide as her eyes.

They stayed for the entire second set and then decided it would be smart to soak up some of the alcohol with something starchy and greasy. Waving to the band and leaving a generous tip for their server, they shuffled out onto the street and headed back toward Broadway in search of food.

They found the Waffle Iron diner a few blocks away, which was convenient because Pax wasn't sure how long his bladder could hold out. He let Sal order for him while he used the restroom. When he returned, he saw coffee on the table and loaded hash browns that were just being delivered. He sank into the seat across from Sal, his balance now affected by too much Jalisco Happy Juice.

"Seriously," Sal said through a mouthful of french fries, "you should be performing somewhere. Your voice is sexy as hell."

"That was fun," he said in response. "Not sure I can do the stage scene much. I used to play better before this."

Pax rested his right hand on the table so Sal could see the scars from his surgery.

"Yeah," she said. "That looks like it might have been bad."

"It was. I killed one of my best friends that night."

Sal stopped chewing and stared at him wide-eyed.

"A guitar," he laughed. "I destroyed my favorite guitar the same night I destroyed my hand."

"Scared the shit out of me," Sal replied, relieved. "I'm thinking, oh man, do I want to be this guy's friend?"

Pax laughed and scooped some hash browns into his mouth.

"But no joke," Sal said, not letting the silence between them go unfilled. "Maybe you should treat this trip like a pilgrimage. You're already heading to all the big music cities. Why not make it your mission to get on stage wherever you go? Get your game face back? Be Pax Butler—Rock Star."

He chuckled and pushed hash browns and sausage around on his plate. He thought about what she said. He had no plans except for visiting places he had always wanted to take Sarah. Maybe Sal's idea was a good way to feel like himself again.

His head eventually cleared somewhat from the tequila fog, but he knew they should take a taxi back to the campsite instead of driving. He paid the check, and the two left the diner, trying to figure out where to hail a cab. They agreed that walking back to the main street was their best option. As they turned the corner onto Broadway, Sal saw Leo and Claire walking on the other side of the street.

"Hey, Leo!" Sal shouted.

Leo saw them and crossed, Claire in tow. It was clear to both that Sal and Pax were still a little too pickled to drive home, and Claire agreed to drive Pax's truck back to the site. He thanked her and handed her his keys.

Once back at the KOA, Sal mumbled her "goodnights" and staggered to her trailer. Claire used Pax's key to unlock his door and helped him inside, where he collapsed onto the bed and passed out.

MIDWEEK OF WEEK three in Nashville, as the evening settled on the KOA, Pax lounged in his folding chair outside the fifth wheel, scrolling through emails from the kids on his phone. Ally had attached some pictures of the young ones, which he enjoyed. He missed them. Although he enjoyed his time on the road, he increasingly realized that having Ally and Rob nearby served as a kind of anchor for him. He wasn't ready to return but longed for that feeling of stability.

Sal had been an excellent companion and a suitable replacement for Zim, even though Zim had never once tried to seduce him. In contrast, Sal was persistent but respectful whenever he declined.

They spent weekends exploring smaller clubs. After their first drunken night in town, they decided to limit themselves to two drinks so they could enjoy the music while staying sober enough to drive back to the site without issues. However, a few nights they had a little too much to drink at the KOA, even waking up one morning in the folding chairs outside Sal's trailer as a light drizzle washed away the memories of the night before.

During weekdays, while Sal worked, Pax would walk around the RV park, chat with residents, and tidy up his site and trailer. Occasionally, he would play his guitar and sing to the children and their parents at the playground. Claire would join some of these impromptu sessions and sit nearby, though not too close. Her hand was never without a cigarette as she listened.

And he had started writing again.

At first, it felt forced—pushing ideas into words and words into scribbled lines. Rhyming schemes that made no sense. Rough-hewn poems that didn't lend themselves to music.

Then, one day, sitting on top of the fifth wheel and watching the clouds roll overhead, a voice spoke in his head and gave him something he could work with. Something meaningful. Something good. He nearly fell to the ground, trying to get down and inside where his pen and notebook sat impotently on the table.

Third fret, second string,
Meant happiness and all it brings.
You smile, your laugh, an endless Spring,

A beauty that is true.
That perfect little root of D,
Plays in my mind repeatedly.
You conquered me so easily,
By the simple sound of you.

Now, sitting outside his trailer, he put down his phone and picked up his notebook. Pax read the words that had flowed from his pen that day. He heard the music. He knew this had potential, but it was all he had.

"Penny for your thoughts." A sultry voice snapped Pax back to the present.

He put down the notebook and looked up at Claire, who was leaning against the tree next to the trailer, her ever-present cigarette smoldering in her hand.

"Not sure they're worth a whole penny," he laughed. "Do people even say that anymore?"

She laughed in response, but it seemed forced.

Pax pointed to the other chair, inviting her to sit. She accepted, sitting down and crossing her legs slowly as she watched him watch her.

"How long have you been a smoker, Claire?"

"Too long," she replied.

"Ever think of quitting?" He wondered if his boldness might lead to a better conversation or cause Claire to leave. Either outcome was okay with him.

"There have been times. Leo doesn't seem to mind."

"I bet he does. I don't know any non-smoker who blindly accepts it. It's generally not an attractive trait in a partner or friend. He might see it as an acceptable trade-off to have a beautiful woman want to be with him. More of an insecurity than anything else."

Claire was unfazed. His boldness hadn't even dented her

façade.

"Does it bother you?"

"Always has. But as a musician, you get used to the smell. Clubs are full of it. Or at least they used to be."

She chuckled softly. "The good old days, huh?"

"No," Pax replied. "There's no such thing as the good old days. That's a lie we tell ourselves when we don't like how our life is going now."

"Profound. A musician and a philosopher?"

"No, that was my buddy, Zim. He had some interesting ideas about the universe."

"Had?" she asked, letting her cigarette burn in her hand instead of smoking it.

Pax nodded but said nothing more.

"Oh," Claire said, sitting up a little. "He's... I'm sorry. We've both lost people. It's still... hard."

Her posture shifted from that of a jungle cat to a frightened kitten. She flicked her cigarette onto the road and gripped the arms of the folding chair, caught somewhere between leaving and screaming. Pax empathized with her. Like himself with Audra, there hadn't been enough time to fully absorb the loss of her husband before she found herself with Leo. The distraction of the warm body beside her each night helped her ignore, but not forget, that it had once been someone else there.

"Hey," Pax said, reaching out his hand toward her. "I'm here if you want to talk. Vent. Shout. Curse the universe. Whatever. I'm going through the same thing."

She gently took his hand and squeezed it modestly, thanking him. Then, she rose, softly touching his shoulder before heading back to the path between their sites.

She turned around, and he looked up at her.

"Why are there so few men like you in the world?"

Pax smiled in response, recognizing it as an invitation to extend an invitation.

"Good night, Claire."

"Good night, Pax."

"I GOT CANNED TODAY," Sal said, sipping one of Leo's beers by the Friday firelight.

Pax sat up. "Fired? What the fu—"

"No," she laughed. "Not fired. My gig is ending early. I'm just too damn good at what I do. But I've got stuff in the hopper. I had a couple of phone interviews this week, and I have a partner in Atlanta who gets me work. They have a big project in Florida starting in a couple of weeks. Bus company or something like that. I'll probably take it."

"Do you have enough money to get by?"

"Yeah, Pax. Don't worry about me. I could live comfortably off six months of work at the rate I charge. I keep working because I enjoy staying busy."

Pax relaxed. He had grown close to Sal and didn't want to see her struggling. However, the unspoken part of her message was that she would leave soon.

"So, Florida, huh?" he said, knowing that if she pursued that path, it would be a long time before he saw her again. When he decided to leave, he would be heading west.

"Yeah," she replied, uncharacteristically brief.

Pax looked around at the shrinking crowd at the Friday night bonfire. Many of the people he had met over the past few weeks had moved on or gone home, which made him a little sad. He had always been the one to move on, and he didn't know how to feel about people leaving—Sarah, then Zim, now new friends.

These were unwelcome feelings. He thought maybe it was time for him to do the same and find the next chapter in this strange story he was writing for himself.

His eyes met Claire's gaze. He smiled. She replied. He noticed there was no cigarette burning between her fingers. He wondered if their conversation had registered with her. Leo added a few more logs to the fire and opened beers for himself and Claire. *I bet she tastes better when he kisses her*, Pax thought.

He reached around and pulled his guitar out of his travel bag. The small group gathered around the fire noticed and turned their attention to him. In his brief time at the park, he had become a popular troubadour.

"I have something new I'm working on," he said as he tuned up. "It's nowhere near complete, but I'm interested in your thoughts."

He started fingerpicking slowly, not because of his injury but because that's how he heard the song in his head. He moved through the chords, humming where the lyrics would go. He only knew some of the words but wasn't ready to share them yet. When he finished, he looked up.

"What's it called, Pax?" Claire asked from across the fire.

"The working title is 'Her Song.'"

"Beautiful tune and beautiful title," she replied.

"Thanks."

The group's consensus was the same. What were they going to say? *It sounds a little rushed in the bridge, Pax. Are you sure that chord change should be there?*

He accepted their compliments gracefully, thanked them, then packed the guitar back in its case and stood up.

"We're still on for tomorrow, Sal?"

Sal nodded but said nothing. He wondered if she felt the same sense of finality he did.

He sat in the trailer, trying to write a few more lyrics, but nothing came to him. He took out his phone and scrolled through the messages—nothing new. Audra's contact stood out. His thumb hovered over the call button but then scrolled past it. He wasn't sure when, or even if, he would be ready to call her or what he would say if he did.

ALTHOUGH THEY DIDN'T SAY it out loud, Sal and Pax knew it was their last night in Nashville together. They both sensed that, somehow, one or both would be on the road by the following weekend. They visited several clubs they had been to before but couldn't find the vibe they needed.

As they walked down 5th Avenue past the famous Ryman Auditorium, Pax paused to look up at the historic façade, soaking in the sense of history around him.

"So many incredible performers walked that stage," he told Sal. "Elvis, Dolly, tons of country stars. Louis Armstrong. The Byrds. Any musician worth their salt would want to look out into those pews and see the faces of their fans."

"Can we get in?" Sal asked. "Is there a show tonight?"

"No idea."

Sal walked a short distance down the avenue before turning onto the street that intersected in front of the famous building.

"Hey!" Pax called, running after her.

Halfway down the street, they saw a semi buzzing with activity as men moved equipment boxes out of the truck and into the theater through a side entrance.

Sal approached one of the men who seemed to be coordinating the effort and, in a tone of authority, asked if they had everything they needed to get the load in that night. Pax peeked into the truck and saw a modest stack of equipment, indicating that the show moving in was not a major production, yet he still felt envious of whoever it was.

"Who are you?" the man asked, glancing at a clipboard.

"I'm Sal, man. Sally Cornish?"

She pointed to the building next to her as if it would explain more than just her name. Pax was in awe of her confidence.

"Whatever," the man said. "We got here late. If we don't run into any issues, we'll have everything set up by midnight. The distro is going in now. Dummy check in a few hours."

Sal nodded as if it all made sense.

"You handle merch, or is that a different crew?"

"Different crew," he said. "Look, if you want to do a quick look, knock yourself out. I'm trying to get caught up, Sal."

"We'll get out of your way," Sal said, then pointed to Pax. "That's Pax. If you need anything, come find either of us, okay?"

"Derrick," the man said.

"Either one of us, Derrick," Sal repeated.

The man nodded and then shouted something at another roadie in the truck. As they entered the venue, Pax couldn't stop smiling.

"Holy shit, I think I just fell in love with you," he said as they passed other roadies, with Sal nodding to them.

"Finally," she laughed. "Maybe you'll visit my trailer later."

They wandered through some hallways, falling behind the roadies and their hand trucks guiding them to the stage. Pax stopped just before the entrance, gazing at the stage—an unexpected view from his current angle. Sal waited while he gathered himself. Then, holding his breath and Sal's hand, they stepped through the entrance onto the world-famous Ryman stage.

The handful of roadies were like a hybrid of highly specialized robots and an ant colony. Boxes were moved in, unpacked, and taken off the stage with a level of efficiency rarely seen in other industries. Electricians carried power cables while instrument techs unpacked, cleaned, and prepared guitars, basses, drums, and microphones. Stage setters taped the floor and noted the names of the different marks for the performers.

Pax wandered toward the edge of the stage in a daze, with Sal following closely behind. He stood there, gazing out at the auditorium and feeling a mix of awe, nostalgia, and fear. Sal squeezed his hand to share the moment and to feel safer near the long drop off the stage in case she lost her balance.

"Hey!" Derrick had figured out the ruse. "You're not supposed to be in here, are you, Sal?"

Sal looked back at the supervisor, smiling.

"Nah," she laughed. "But we won't be long. Thanks for being cool about it, Derrick."

The chief roadie looked at Pax, who was still lost in his trance, and understood what he saw—a musician experiencing a moment he never thought he would have. Many roadies, musicians themselves, shared the same dreams. He glanced back at Sal.

"Two more minutes, then you need to fuck off. We clear, Sal?"

"Clear. You're one of the good ones, Derrick."

Derrick talked to another roadie near the side stage before leaving the area, presumably to motivate others to catch up with the load-in.

Pax looked at Sal and smiled.

"Thank you, Sal," he said, squeezing her hand. "I don't know how you did it, but thank you."

"Come on, Pax. Let's grab a drink."

They left the building and walked past Derrick, who was

talking with another roadie. He glanced at them and nodded. Sal tapped his shoulder in gratitude as they went by.

They journeyed back to Southern Blues Junction. The night's featured band was a blues outfit with the unlikely name of The Blues Outfit. They sat at the bar, listening as the solo guitarist and singer poured his heart into his performance.

Pax was beaming. He leaned over to Sal, kissed her cheek, and then leaned in close to her ear.

"I can't say I'll visit your trailer, Sal, but I care about you. A lot. You've been a great friend, and tonight—"

Pax shook his head, feeling overwhelmed by his emotions. Sal patted his arm and sipped her vodka tonic. The two sat quietly, drinking, listening, and growing closer through the shared experience.

Back at the KOA, they decided to visit the playground one more time to stargaze and work through Pax's liquor supply. Sal waited outside as Pax unlocked the trailer and went inside.

As soon as he stepped into the dimly lit trailer, the faint smell of cigarettes hit him. He paused by the door, listening carefully. A soft rustle from the bedroom revealed the intruder and confirmed who had entered his space.

"Claire?"

Silence. Stillness. He listened.

"Claire!"

The light in the bedroom switched on, and Pax saw more of Claire than he had ever expected. She sat up in his bed, bare from the waist up and likely the same beneath the sheets.

"I thought maybe we could resolve this tension between us, Pax," Claire said, her voice reminiscent of an old-time movie, dripping with innuendo.

Sal opened the door and stepped inside just as he was about to reply.

"What's going on? I heard voices."

Sal saw Pax staring into the bedroom, while Claire looked back at him.

"Oh fuck."

"Sal," Pax said calmly. "Go get Leo."

Claire looked at Pax, her expression shifting from seduction to defeat. Sal remained frozen.

"Sal," Pax repeated more firmly. "Go get Leo."

Sal stepped out of the trailer and ran toward the robin's egg-blue RV a hundred yards away.

Claire, feeling defeated by her failed seduction, started to get out of bed.

"No!" Pax shouted, glancing around for something to cover her nakedness. When he couldn't find anything, he bolted from the trailer.

Sal and Leo emerged from the darkness just as Claire, now fully dressed, stepped onto the grass. Leo stopped in his tracks at the sight of her. Sal approached and stood beside Pax.

Claire looked at Pax, reached into her pocket, and handed him a copy of his trailer key. Then, she walked toward Leo. Instead of stopping to say anything, she kept going past him toward their shared trailer. Leo, clearly embodying the role of a cuckold, watched her walk away before turning to Pax, who braced for an attack, whether verbal or physical.

"Leo," Sal jumped in. "We just got back from town. She was there when we got here. Pax didn't do anything."

Pax held up the key for Leo to see.

"She must have made a copy after she drove us home that night when we were drunk," he said. "I didn't give this to her."

Leo glanced from Pax to Sal and then back again, nodding slightly. Pax thought the nod came from a man familiar with this scenario.

"I know," Leo said. "It's not the first time. I need to get her some help."

Leo turned and followed Claire to their trailer as Pax and Sal watched him disappear into the darkness.

"You okay?" Sal asked quietly.

"Yup."

"Still want to get drunk?"

"Nah."

"Yeah, me neither."

"I think I need to pack, Sal."

She looked at him, understanding the implication of his statement.

"Don't leave without saying goodbye," she said.

"Not a chance."

She went back to her trailer while Pax looked over his site and began packing up what he intended to take.

In the morning, they met for breakfast. Pax had already visited the KOA office and paid his final invoice, explaining that it was time to move on. Sal took Pax's phone and entered all her contact information. She also added his information to her own.

They embraced for a long time.

"Call me," she said.

"I will."

"Let me know where you're headed next," he said.

"I will."

"Get up on those stages and sing," she said.

"I will."

"Get that damn mandolin fixed," he said.

"I will."

"I'll miss you, Pax," she said.

"I'll miss you too, Sal," he said.

He cupped her cheeks and kissed her. She blushed, smiled, wiped away her tears, and then headed toward her trailer.

"I'll see you again, Sally Cornish," he called after her.

She lifted her hand and waved without turning as she walked away.

HE LEFT Nashville around noon after enjoying a lunch of local hot chicken. Within an hour, he realized that his culinary choice had been a mistake and pulled over at a rest stop to deal with the biological urges raging in his digestive system.

The parking lot was peppered with Harleys, Indians, and custom choppers—at least twenty, he estimated. Pax had no issues with motorcycle clubs. Butler Service used to perform at biker rallies in their prime. Still, he chose to lock the box with Sarah's rings in the fifth wheel while attending to his business at the facility. He placed the box on a shelf in the pantry behind a roll of paper towels and locked the door as he left.

Walking toward the building, he ran into a couple of men who were members of the "club." They must have seen him come out of the trailer, as one man commented on how nice it was.

"Thanks," Pax replied curtly.

"Watch out in there," the man said, nodding toward the building. "Restrooms are wrecked. Don't you have a pisser in your trailer?"

"Not for what I have to do," he replied, never slowing as he entered the building and headed to the restroom.

Wrecked was an understatement. After struggling to hold his breath in the fetid air of the restroom while tending to his own needs, Pax couldn't believe how much better the air outside the facility tasted as he inhaled deeply to clear out the vapors trapped inside his lungs. Even the diesel exhaust from passing trucks tasted better.

The bikers had left, and his vehicle and trailer appeared untouched. He climbed into the truck and headed back onto the road.

After another hour, he decided to fill the tank before heading into Memphis. He wanted to find an RV park outside of town and get settled before exploring.

He and Zim visited Memphis many years earlier, trying to make Butler Service a household name. Insufficient planning, too few gigs, and an excessive number of liquor bottles made that trip a failure. He'd liked Memphis back then, but, like everything else, he expected it had changed, and he was approaching it now as a tourist. He needed time to get his bearings.

Pax pulled into Loves Travel Stop outside Jackson for fuel and light provisions. As he cautiously maneuvered up to the pump, he heard the roar of a motorcycle and saw the same club from the rest stop clustered at the end of the parking lot. Most of the members sat idly, waiting for something, while others lounged in the grass, soaking up the afternoon sun.

He fueled the truck and parked it away from the pumps, then went inside to buy some beer and snacks for when he arrived in Memphis. As he entered, he overheard a conversation between a biker and the man behind the counter about another group that had passed through on their way to New Orleans.

"Those are my cousin's people," the big biker said, asking how long ago they passed through.

"Couple hours," the cashier said.

Beer was in the back. Pax grabbed a twelve-pack before turning to see the smiling face of the biker from the rest stop.

"Hey, RV man."

"Hey," he said as he grabbed some potato chips.

"Everything come out all right back there?" the smiling biker asked, laughing as if he knew.

His cackle reminded Pax of his idiot former son-in-law, triggering the same urge to unleash his verbal kung fu on the man. However, his better judgment intervened, and he kept his responses to single syllables.

"Yup," he replied.

The tall biker at the cashier turned to look at him, then glanced at the laughing biker before turning back.

"That's my brother," the cackler said, with no shortage of sarcasm. "He's in charge. I have to behave." Then, holding out his hand, he added, "I'm Joe."

Pax accepted the hand offered and shook it. "Pax."

"Pax? Cool name. That means "peace" in Latin."

Zim had said the same thing whenever Pax's anger flared up.

"So, I've heard," he stated.

"Hey, that's a nice RV you got, Pax. Is it new? It's so clean."

Pax replied while grabbing some jerky, "Yup, new."

"Think I could take a look inside?" Joe continued. "I see them all over the place, but I've never seen the inside of one."

"Why?" a voice behind Pax said. He turned to see the large biker Joe referred to as his brother.

Joe seemed annoyed.

"Come on, Mike. Why do you always ask why? I just want to see it."

"I always ask why because you're an unreliable pain in the ass, and I always end up settling your messes for you."

Pax watched the interaction, making sure it didn't involve him by moving to the next aisle and heading to the cashier. The brothers argued more, and the bigger one, Mike, walked out of the store and lit a cigarette.

Joe sidled up next to Pax at the cashier.

"Sooooooo?"

Pax settled his bill with the cashier, thanked him, and left the store without responding. Joe followed.

"Come on, Pax."

Pax glanced at Mike as he left the store, and Mike stepped in.

"If you say yes," Mike pointed his cigarette at Pax as Joe exited the store, "I'll make sure he doesn't mess anything up."

"If I say no?"

"Your prerogative. It will probably mean I have to punch him in the mouth to shut him up, though," Mike glanced at Joe, who scowled back.

Pax shook his head and rolled his eyes.

"Fine," he said, ending the discussion.

Pax unlocked the trailer and stepped back to let Joe inside. He stayed outside with Mike, not wanting to share the cramped space with someone clearly on the edge of instability. The previous night's trespass by Claire put him on edge about anyone else being in his "home," so he decided one minute was all he would allow.

"Heading to Memphis?" Mike asked, making conversation.

"Yeah," Pax responded, not taking his eyes off the trailer. "Kind of a pilgrimage of sorts."

Mike nodded. "Heading to New Orleans to meet up with my cousin's outfit. There's a music festival happening, and the southeast branch of our club is using it as an excuse to hang out."

"Yeah, I heard about that festival. I'm thinking about heading down there after Memphis."

Pax could hear Joe moving inside the trailer, which made him feel uneasy. Mike noticed his growing agitation.

"Joe, now!" Mike bellowed, tossing the cigarette into the grass. "You got a brother, Pax?"

Pax thought of Zim, the closest thing to a brother he would ever know, "Had, sort of."

"Is he a childish jackass like this one?"

Pax smiled. "Yeah, he could be."

Joe stepped out of the trailer. "Man, that is a sweet setup, Pax. I'm going to get me one of these someday."

"Doubtful," Mike said as he moved to the trailer door and looked inside. Seeming to approve of the condition Joe left behind, he closed the door and headed toward the rest of the club, which was still idling at the edge of the parking lot.

"Safe travels, Pax," he said as he passed. "Joe, now!"

"Thanks, Pax, safe travels." Joe hurried off to catch up with his brother.

Pax looked inside the trailer, expecting to see cupboards open and drawers pulled out, but everything seemed to be in order. He put away the beer and snacks and stepped back into the parking lot as the motorcycles rumbled back toward the highway.

Having left the Nashville KOA in a hurry, he hadn't made a reservation for his next stop. He called Sal for advice.

"Pax Butler's office," Sal said as she answered the call.

Pax laughed and told her she was a goofball.

"What's up, brother? Miss me already?" Sal asked, sounding too much like Zim for a moment.

"I need a place to stay outside Memphis. Have you ever parked your rig there?"

"Ah, no," Sal replied. "I always planned on it, Graceland and all, but I never had a gig nearby. Where are you?"

"Sitting in the parking lot of a Loves gas station on the other side of Nashville."

"Try asking the clerk. They usually have flyers, cards, or brochures for parks and such."

"Thanks, Sal, I'll do that. Have you seen... you know?"

"Not yet," she replied. "Not even Leo. But hey, I got a call from that project in Florida. I'm in. Gonna be there for nine months. Not the worst place to spend the winter."

"Good for you, Sal. Try to be a little more mediocre so you can stay on the job longer."

Sal laughed. "I'll try. It's hard, goddamn work, being this good, though."

"Thanks again, Sal. I'll get back on the road as soon as I can make a reservation. Let me know when you get to Florida."

"Be good, Pax." Sal disconnected before he could, outplaying him at his own game.

He returned to the convenience store to ask about RV parks in the Memphis area. As Sal predicted, the cashier gave him business cards for three locations. He thanked the man and went back to the truck to make a call.

The first number rang endlessly, but there was no answer or voicemail. He tried the second number and was placed on hold. He hung up and dialed the third.

As he waited for someone to answer, he glanced at the passenger seat just as his call was picked up. Yes, they had two sites that could fit his trailer. Yes, there was parking for his truck next to the pad. Yes, there was electricity and water. They could hold one if he arrived within the next four hours.

With the reservation booked, Pax hopped out of the truck and headed toward the trailer. A faint smell lingered in the air of the fifth wheel, irritating him. He couldn't tell if it was from Joe's body odor, Claire's lingering cigarette funk, or both.

He opened the pantry and pulled out the paper towels, but the ring box was not there. He took everything out of the pantry piece by piece, yet the box was nowhere to be found. Panic began to set in.

I put it in there and locked the trailer. Nobody could have gotten in to take it.

Then it hit him, and panic morphed into rage.

"Fuck!"

He threw all the paper products back into the pantry, closed the trailer, got into the truck, and pulled out of the parking lot as quickly as he could. He slowed down but didn't stop as he ran the stop sign and merged onto the westbound ramp to Memphis.

The bikers were a mile ahead when Pax spotted them. He sped up to close the gap, burning through the fuel he just bought to move almost 60 feet of metal at better than the speed limit. As he neared the pack, he flashed his lights and blew his horn to get the attention of the bikers in the back. Two of them slowed down and pulled alongside the truck. With the sixty-five-mile-per-hour wind whooshing past his open window, Pax shouted as loudly as he could, exaggerating his pronunciation to make his message clear. "GET MIKE!"

The two bikers sped down the road and passed the tail of the convoy. Pax stayed safely behind the rest of the pack, uncertain about what would happen next. As his patience wore thin, he noticed the pack moving past two bikers in the left lane. The two riders were traveling slowly enough for him to catch up and pull alongside, just as the other riders had, pacing his rolling condo. Mike looked up.

Pax pointed to the ring on his hand, then used his finger to spell J-O-E on his window. He knew his message had been received as Mike's face changed, and he accelerated his custom chopper to the front of the group.

The entire flock of bikes slowed to a manageable pace, and as they approached the next rest stop, he saw turn signals indicating their departure from the highway. Pax followed.

He didn't bother finding a trailer berth. Instead, he pulled up along the grass line and covered several parking spots meant for cars. Climbing out, he walked around to the trailer door, reached inside, and grabbed an aluminum softball bat he brought on the trip in case he ran into a pick-up game, or to chase off wild animals, or if an idiot biker had stolen his wife's wedding ring.

He moved purposefully toward the crowd of bikers, scanning their faces for the one idiot he would recognize.

"Pax," Mike bellowed. "What's the malfunction?"

Pax slowed as he approached Mike, gripping the bat tightly. He thought he could reason with Mike, but he didn't really know him. He just wanted a piece of Joe.

"Your asshole brother took something of mine, and I want it back!" he shouted loudly enough for the whole group to hear.

"Hey!" Mike countered. "I'm the only person who gets to call my brother an asshole. Joe, now!"

Joe stepped away from the group, his hands in his pockets. Pax lunged at him, the bat ready to strike.

"Give it back, you fuck!" He pointed the bat at Joe's crotch. "Give it back, or I'm taking those."

Mike grabbed Pax's collar to hold him back. Pax shook free and turned around, ready to swing at Mike if needed.

"He stole a box with my wife's rings, Mike." He turned to Joe, his face crimson with fury. "Give it back!"

"Oh, come on, Pax," Joe pleaded, his hands open wide and smiling like the cat that caught the canary and planned to pawn it the first chance he got. "I didn't take nothing."

Pax lunged and yelled, "Fucking liar," but was again held back by Mike.

The absurdity of the situation washed over him. Nearly thirty of them, all younger and many bigger than Pax, including some women. He knew he couldn't win a fight, but he wasn't going to let this cackling idiot get away with his wife's rings.

He shook Mike off again, glanced at the group, and then looked back at Joe.

He quietly and intentionally addressed his adversary.

"Let me explain something to you, Joe." He grit his teeth on the last syllable. "I'm going to get that box back, even if I have to beat you senseless to do it. You're bigger than me, sure. Younger. Probably stronger. In the end, you might win. You might even kill me. But you won't walk away from here with both eyes and both balls. I'm taking one of each with me if that's the way it goes. So, it's the rings, or—"

Pax moved in closer, aiming the bat at Joe's groin again. Mike didn't try to stop him. Joe chuckled as if the thought of fighting this old man was just too funny to take seriously.

"My wife is gone. Those rings are all I have left that she touched. But if you keep pushing this, you'll be forever known as the man who was blinded and neutered by an old man because you were too much of a fucking coward to admit your stupidity and make things right."

A large hand rested on his shoulder.

"Joe," Mike growled. "You get one shot to fix this. Right now. Where's the box?"

Joe opened his hands again and pleaded with his brother.

"I don't have it, Mike."

Pax seethed.

"I have it," a female voice said from behind Joe. "I have it. He gave it to me."

A tall, blonde, heavily tattooed woman emerged from behind Joe and approached Pax. She took the white box from her jacket pocket and handed it to him. He quickly looked inside and felt relieved to see both rings still there.

"Thank you," he said quietly.

"He told me he found them at the rest stop," she said, then turned and walked back toward Joe.

"Come on, baby," Joe started, just as she drove her knee into his groin, dropping him to the pavement.

Bending over Joe as he writhed on the blacktop, she spat at him, "You ride alone, you fucking liar!"

Pax turned to face Mike.

"We got this, Pax. Safe travels."

Mike turned Pax toward his truck and gently nudged him. Pax kept walking without looking back. He placed the box on the passenger seat, slid the bat to the floor behind him, and started the truck heading toward the on-ramp.

He looked at the box in the seat and felt a wave of calm wash over him.

"Sorry for all that drama, baby. I won't let you out of my sight again."

CHAPTER 4

T.O. Fuller State Park, located southwest of Memphis, was a beautiful spot to spend a few days before heading to New Orleans. Pax was fortunate to secure a site that allowed him to pull in directly, instead of trying to beat his record by backing the fifth wheel into another tight spot. The site featured a picnic table, grill, electric and water hookups, and a small fire pit, which he didn't expect to use.

He connected the trailer to electricity and water, then consulted the park map to find a dumping station for his waste tank. There were several walking trails on the map, and he thought that climbing to one of the overlooks might help him clear his mind of Claire, Joe, and everything else.

After getting his mobile condo in livable condition, he laced up his sneakers, the best and only footwear he had for trail walking, pocketed the box of Sarah's rings, and set off toward the lookout marked on the park map.

The walk was nice, but the overlook itself didn't offer much of an experience. He had thought it might be similar to many of the trails he explored with Audra in the Carolinas, but it didn't live up to those memories. So, he retraced his steps down the trail toward what he believed was the campsite. However, after an unexpected turn while lost in thought, he realized he was passing sights he hadn't seen on the way up. He checked the map and found he was as far from the campsite as possible on the Discovery Trail.

With nothing better to do, he kept going, eventually completing the loop and returning to his trailer, sweaty, dehydrated, and with blisters on both feet. He then spent the next few hours cleaning up, doing laundry, and driving to the nearest pharmacy for blister remedies.

With his blisters treated back at the trailer, he sat down and tried to conjure more lyrics for his new song. The pen wouldn't move. He wished Zim were there. Zim was incredibly creative and could look at the page and, based on Pax's random beginnings, suggest a direction for the lyrics, including rhyming schemes to improve the theme. But Zim was gone, and his creative block continued until he finally set the pen aside. He conceded defeat, for now, put on a decent shirt, and drove into town to listen to music.

Pax missed having Sal with him as he wandered down Beale Street, soaking in the sights and sounds of one of the most famous music avenues on earth. As in Nashville, he knew the off-the-beaten-path clubs would offer something unique compared to those aimed at tourists. Though he was technically a tourist, he was a different kind. He wasn't looking for a story to share with his buddies at the office. He was searching for a sound, or maybe he was seeking a way to create that sound.

The Blues & Roots Revival Lounge was located in a partially renovated building near Main and Gayoso Avenue. Pax paid his cover charge and headed to the bar, choosing a seat with a good view of the stage and the room. The house music played *Me and Bobby McGee*—the Kristofferson version.

He ordered a beer and sat, listening to the lyrics and

thinking of Sarah with a smile. She loved that song. She preferred the Joplin version, imagining Pax as her Bobby, but the gritty lyrics still conveyed the various and awkward shapes of love. Sarah had a knack for deciphering lyrics that eluded Pax, despite his skill with musical poetry.

"It's about twin souls, Pax," she would say. "It's about people like us. I love it so much, even though the ending is sad. But God, what a ballad to finding that one person and then losing them, yet remembering so clearly how you felt together that you would sacrifice the future to have another day in the past."

The entertainment for the night took the stage. They were a country trio with a hint of blues. It wasn't great by any stretch, but Pax didn't mind. He listened, applauded, and felt light again. Live music always made him feel that way, especially when he was the one performing it.

He ordered another drink and asked the bartender if they hosted an open mic night.

"Not here," the man replied. "Try the Delta Harmony Lounge on Union, near South Front. They don't do it every night, but they have a schedule in the window, or you can find it online."

Pax thanked the bartender, left a tip, and wandered into the night. He tried to use his phone's navigation to find his way to The Delta. However, he wasn't familiar with the app, so he acknowledged his limitations and made his way back to where he parked to get his bearings.

On his way, he came across an Irish pub and spent the next two hours enjoying barbecue, beer, and the blues performed by a sextet called Soulful Six Strings. He missed having Sal by his side, but it was still a very good night.

Back at the trailer, Pax called the Delta Harmony Lounge to ask about their open mic schedule. The booking manager told him they hosted it every Friday and asked if he wanted to add his name to the list of performers. He told her he did and that he was a solo act. She shared some rules about respectful behavior and performing songs with explicit lyrics. Pax chuckled and told her he thought he could behave himself for one night.

After booking his gig, he called Ally.

"Dad? Wow, we get to talk live on the phone?"

By her tone and choice of words, Ally was implying he should have made more effort over the past few weeks, despite his nightly texts and emails. Sarcasm was one of her love languages.

"Yeah, you sound older," he laughed.

"You should talk," she replied. "But it's good to hear you laugh, Dad. How are you doing, alright? Where are you? How are you handling the RV driving?"

"Whoa, Kiddo, slow your roll. Let me answer one question before you ask the next." He laughed again. "I'm good, honey. I am. I'm in Memphis at a state park. Getting better with the RV. You should have seen me try to park it the first time."

Pax settled back into bed and told Ally all about his time in Nashville—the music, the food, and the drinking with Sal. He spent a lot of time talking about Sal.

"She sounds like a pisser," Ally chimed in.

"She is," he replied. "She reminds me a lot of Zim."

He told her about Claire and the whole mess surrounding her attempt to seduce him and how that was what drove him out of Nashville. He didn't mention the bikers, the rings, or the near-death experience involved in trying to retrieve them. She needed good news. She needed positive sounds from him.

They talked for an hour before he brought up needing help from Travis. Ally handed the phone to Travis, who spent almost as much time helping Pax figure out how to use the navigation on his smartphone. Once Pax felt confident he had it, he asked to talk to Ally again to say good night. Travis then handed the phone back to her.

"Dad, I totally forgot to ask you this. Is Erin Watson, 'the Erin' Zim always talked about?"

Pax frowned. Why was Ally asking about Erin?

"Yeah, that's her. Why?"

"Good," she replied. "Honestly, I never knew she had a last name, just that she *was a problem* as Zim always put it. Anyway, she somehow found Rob's address and sent him a box full of CDs. None of them have labels, just blank CDs in cases with a note that says, 'I found this in Zim's things. It might be music. I wonder if Pax might want them.'"

"Huh," Pax responded, dumbfounded. "Can you find out what's on them? Maybe it's some of the demos that Zim and I put together in the studio."

"Yeah, I'll have Travis check and see what's on them. It was, you know, creepy to get that out of the blue, all things considered. I mean, she's kind of a stranger to us, right? We don't really know her."

Pax smiled, thinking of Erin. "She's not a stranger. Not anymore, anyway."

Ally was silent for a moment. "Dad, you didn't... Did you... Dad?"

"No, no, no," he laughed again. "Erin and I spent time together after Zim's funeral, but not like that. She's a friend. She should have been a friend a long time ago, but I'll explain later."

"Ok," she said tentatively, then suddenly, "Did you like the pictures of the kids? Aren't they cute as hell?"

"I loved them, Kiddo. Keep sending them."

Pax's phone beeped, and the screen showed it needed charging.

"Hey, Kiddo, I have to go now before my phone dies. Love to the kids. Thanks to Travis. Give Rob an update. I love you guys."

Ally paused briefly before replying, sniffing, "I love you too, Dad."

He disconnected the phone and plugged it into the charger. The notebook on the table caught his attention, and he opened it, rereading the few lines he had written for his new song, hoping for rhythmic inspiration. Maybe one of the songs he heard that night would match the lyrics, and he would find his flow. He picked up the pen, took a deep breath, and placed it on the paper. After a long silence, he dropped the pen, turned off the lights, and went to bed.

As sleep drifted over him, he thought of his conversation with Ally, feeling like they had connected in a way they hadn't in a long time, and it made him smile.

〜

"Hɪ, Kɪᴅᴅᴏ."

"Dad, what's wrong?" She could tell he'd been crying.

"Everything is wrong, honey. Every-fucking-thing."

Ally began to sob slightly, as she had never heard her father in such distress.

"Please, Dad."

"Mom has cancer, Ally."

The silence was palpable.

"What?" Ally exclaimed in shock.

"She's been having some problems lately, I don't know the details, you know your mother. 'I'm fine.' So, they did some tests, and they found cancer in her breast. I meant to tell you a while ago, but she wanted to wait until we knew more, and then today—"

"Wait, what?" Ally was caught between shock and anger. "How long—"

"It doesn't matter. Today, we went to get test results from the oncologist and..."

"Dad, what? What?" Ally began to cry, fearing the worst. Pax joined in, sobbing inharmoniously across the phone lines.

"It's everywhere, Ally. Fucking everywhere. They say it has even moved to her brain," Pax could barely get the words out.

"Oh God, Dad! Oh God, no!"

"I'm scared, Ally. I don't remember ever being without her. How can I be without her? How can I fucking be without her?"

Ally's sobs were too spasmodic to respond.

"Ally?"

"Dad," she said, regaining control and trying to make sense of what was happening. "I know some people from my new job who might be able to help. I don't know how, but I'll talk to them."

"Okay," his voice was thick with tears and snot. He didn't say the other words. Inoperable. Incurable. Ally needed hope, even when he had none.

"Dad, we're going to get through this." She tried to be the strong one, and the role reversal was not lost on either of them.

"Okay, Kiddo."

"Is she there, Dad?"

"She's sleeping. It was a fucking shitty day."

"Okay, I'll talk to her tomorrow. Dad, call Rob."

Pax sniffed, dreading another call like this.

"Dad?"

"Can you call him Ally? I don't think I can go through this again."

"I'll tell him," she said. "But we all need to get on a call tomorrow to discuss options."

"Okay, Kiddo."

"Dad, go be with her. Lie with her. Hold her. Remind her how strong she is."

"I will."

"Dad, I love you."

Pax hung up and melted into his chair.

HE SPENT the days leading up to his performance at the Delta Harmony Lounge exploring some of Memphis's tourist spots. He walked the trails in the park that served as his home base, visited Graceland, and went to the zoo. But since his primary interest in Memphis was music, he did most of his exploring at night, moving between small and medium-sized venues and listening to a wide variety of music, including a strange mix of industrial and country swing.

When Friday arrived, Pax spent the day deciding which song he would perform. It didn't really matter to him. This was a bucket list item, not an audition. But, as a former professional musician, he wanted to make sure his performance was his best, and he still needed to address some challenges with his injured hand. He settled on his personalized version of *I'm So Lonesome I Could Cry*, the famous Hank Williams song, but with a bluesy spin. He thought the mix of blues and old-school country music would fit nicely into the Memphis scene.

The open mic sessions started at 8:00 p.m., but Pax arrived half an hour early to find a seat strategically placed so he could watch the other acts and still see the audience. The stage was big enough for a four-piece band, as long as little to no movement was needed. It was perfect for one man and a guitar.

He set his guitar case by his chair and ordered a beer. Tequila wasn't kind to his aging vocal cords, but beer always seemed to relax them and give them more depth.

The crowd filtered in slowly, a larger turnout than he expected. He figured that many might be friends or family of the night's performers, which was fine with him. They were all strangers, and he thought they would enjoy his act. Even if they didn't, he was performing for himself more than anyone else.

As the room gradually filled up in anticipation of the first act, Pax noticed a group of three women enter and sit at the table next to him. He was struck by how stylishly they were dressed, as if they were heading to a gala, yet here they were at an open mic night in a small club off the main drag.

Then it struck him. At first, it was subtle, but it grew more obvious with each passing second.

Her perfume, he realized, and he was immediately disoriented.

The club manager stepped onto the stage, welcomed every-one, and invited the first performer. Pax heard none of it. He gripped the edge of his table as the scent from his past flooded his mind, bringing up memories from the his decades with Sarah. It was the scent from the night he took her to her senior prom—the first time she kissed him. It was the scent she wore in the park when he asked her to marry him. It was her constant fragrance from every meaningful moment they had experienced together. It was—

His mind went blank. He couldn't remember the name. Of all the memories that scent conjured, the most obvious—the name—was gone.

He looked up as the second performer stepped off the stage. The time lost during his trip into the past only heightened his agitation. He glanced at the women sitting a few feet away and realized that one of them was the source of the perfume. As the next act got ready to perform, he walked over.

"Excuse me," he said quietly.

The three women looked up at him. From the change in perspective, he spotted her—the trail of perfume leading the way. She was the elegant brunette on the left, in her mid-forties, with a faint smile on her lips that radiated natural confidence. Pax looked up and noticed the performer beginning.

"I'm sorry," he whispered. "Can I just sit here while she performs? I don't want to be rude."

The women agreed, and he sat, listening, his fingers clenching the fabric of his pants as he waited for three minutes and forty-two seconds until the song finished. He clapped along with the rest of the crowd before sliding his chair forward to look at the brunette, who smelled so much like *Her*.

"Hi," he said, a little unsteady and missing his usual charm and confidence. "Uh, hi."

The woman replied, smiling, "You said that."

He chuckled softly and nodded, trying to find his center.

"My name is Pax," he said, extending his hand to introduce himself to Jessica, Camryn, and... Lara. He gazed at Lara.

"This is going to sound weird," he said. "But can you tell me the name of the perfume you're wearing?"

Lara smiled, revealing some teeth, clearly intrigued by this awkward man with a northern accent.

"It's called Must de Cartier," she replied. "My mother used to wear it, and now I do."

He recognized it immediately when she said it and let out a sigh of relief that his memory was still intact. It had just skipped a groove.

"Thank you," he said, the quiver of emotion not lost on the woman.

He shifted to stand up and return to his seat, but Lara touched his arm.

"Why did you want to know?" she asked.

Pax hesitated to share the reason for his emotional response to a perfume with a stranger. The club manager resolved the issue for him.

"Next up is Pax Butler. Did I get that right? Pax?"

Pax stood up, picked up his guitar, and headed on stage.

"You got it right," he said, hoping his voice wouldn't shake from the flood of cortisol streaming through him.

"Okay, great. Pax Butler, everyone." The audience applauded.

Pax slung his guitar, checked the tuning, adjusted the mic, and stepped back. He tried to recall the song he wanted to perform, but, like Elvis, it had left the building. The perfume had sent his plans packing, leaving him frozen for a long, awkward moment.

Then, just as the memories of *Her* were triggered by the faint scent of Must de Cartier, so too was his recollection of another time. A beautiful, yet tragic time.

He dabbed a little perfume on his finger and then applied it to her neck and behind her ears. She smiled.

"Thank you, baby. It makes me feel more like me."

Pax gently kissed her. She felt weak from the radiation, and her hair was gone from the chemo. She was a shadow of her former self, but he could still see that angel in her eyes. Now, with her favorite scent lingering in the air, she returned.

"Sing something, Pax."

He reached past the bedside table and grabbed his travel guitar, a stoic sentinel for those moments when inspiration struck him in the middle of the night.

"What would you like me to sing, my love?"

She squinted, trying to remember the song she wanted to hear. A tear of frustration formed in her eye and rolled down her cheek. He knew the name had slipped her mind.

"The one about the flowers," she said at last.

He nodded and smiled before he started to strum.

Pax stepped up to the microphone.

"I was planning to put a little twist on a classic, but my memories have been a bit jumbled."

He looked at Lara and smiled.

"I sang this song to my wife when she was sick. She's not sick anymore. This is for you, baby."

He closed his eyes and began to strum. He poured his heart out on stage, filling the room with the plaintive refrains of *Red Roses*, the heart-wrenching ballad by the BoDeans. He sang from pain, without clever riffs on the guitar, just chords behind the voice behind the words behind the grief.

When he strummed the final chord, three full seconds of silence passed before the roar of applause erupted. Pax nodded to the audience, thanked them, packed his guitar, and returned to his table. To his surprise, the three women stood and approached his table, with Lara now sitting on his right.

"That was so beautiful," Camryn said, wiping her eyes with a napkin.

Jessica agreed and asked him if she could get him a drink.

"I never say no to tequila," he laughed, blinking back tears.

Lara rested her chin on her hand, gazing at him intently.

"She wore this perfume," she said.

Pax nodded and offered a thin smile.

"She passed, didn't she?"

He looked down and nodded. Camryn started crying again. Lara just looked at him, studying.

"Pax, is it?" she asked. "Well, Pax, they say that scent is the strongest trigger for memory. You might be walking down a city street and smell a cigarette that takes you back to high school. Or you might smell something in a restaurant that reminds you of that first date with the one who got away. Perfume is so personal that—"

He felt overwhelmed, the need to scream building inside him. He needed to step away.

"If you'll excuse me," he said quietly, "I'm going to use the restroom."

He stood to leave, but Lara suddenly stepped in front of him. Without asking, she cupped her hands on his cheeks and kissed him softly on the lips. The contact, the warmth of her lips, and her perfume overwhelmed him, and when she pulled away and stepped back, he knew he was losing the battle. Without saying another word, he quickly headed toward the restroom.

Pax stared in the mirror, fighting the urge to shout. He was having trouble catching his breath and thought he might be having a heart attack. He splashed water on his face and practiced some controlled breathing to regain the remnants of his shredded calm.

When he thought he had sufficiently recovered, he returned to his table. As he approached and the perfume flooded his sinuses, again, he suddenly felt lightheaded. He stumbled forward, grabbed the back of a chair, and sank to the floor. His ears were ringing. He felt flushed. He feared he was dying.

The women came to his aid. Lara took the lead, checked his pulse, and instructed the others to make calls and find the manager. His awareness faded in and out. When he finally felt his balance returning, Camryn was sitting on the floor with him, her fingers on his wrist, monitoring his pulse. Lara was talking to the club manager. Jessica appeared from the front of the club, accompanied by two EMTs.

"I'm ok," he attempted to say, his words slurring worse than a drunk with a mouthful of Novocain.

Camryn chuckled.

"Those aren't words, Pax. Just sit quietly and breathe. You had a panic attack. EMTs were called. Just breathe."

The EMTs carried out their duties and spent quite a bit of time talking with Lara. As she spoke with them, she occasionally looked over at Pax, and then, as they were leaving, she approached.

Camryn said, "His pulse has been pretty steady."

"When was your last check-up, Pax?" Lara's voice grew more assertive.

"A couple of years ago, I saw a doctor after I broke my hand."

"How about a general practitioner? A family doctor?"

Pax shook his head. He could still smell her perfume, but the psychotropic effects on him were milder after his meltdown.

"Well, you've caused quite a scene here at open-mic night," she laughed. "Do you need a ride home?"

"I have my truck," he said.

"Do you think it's a good idea for you to drive after such a severe panic attack?"

"Probably not," he said. "But my daughter would tell you I've made worse decisions."

Lara reached into her small handbag and handed him a card.

She helped Pax stand, and although he was shaky, he felt better being off the floor.

"Please call me tomorrow," Lara said.

Pax agreed to do so, and after thanking the women for their help and apologizing to the manager, he left the club.

Pulling into his campsite, he turned off the engine and looked at the business card, a faint trace of perfume drifting toward him. His mind flooded once again with memories of Sarah.

He thought about how he would stash money from his gigs to ensure she always had a bottle of Must de Cartier on her vanity. His first memory of the scent was the night of her prom —the night of their first kiss. When their lips touched, he heard, saw, felt, smelled, and tasted everything in that moment. The thought of that first kiss immediately took him back to the kiss Lara gave him at the club. He fought to keep his emotions in check, but the dam had broken, and there was no escape.

Pax covered his face and let the flood of tears take over. It was the hardest he had cried since the funeral. His chest ached and heaved. His sinuses, flooded with tears, drained into his hands. He found it hard to breathe, to think, and to move. He might die in this car, and that was fine. Right now, that was more than fine.

He reached into his pocket and pulled out the small white box he now carried everywhere. He took out the wedding ring and held it to his lips.

"I'm so sorry, Sarah."

The kiss Lara gave him was too much like the first kiss Sarah had given him. Guilt compounded his misery, and tears started flowing again.

As he sat, trying to drift above the flood of grief, a late summer rain began, mirroring his tears as drops ran down the windshield. At the same time, a gust of wind moved through the trees, and a sound passed through the campsites, reaching him in his truck. It was a single clear note, produced when air pushed a small piece of wood attached to a disk, causing it to strike a single metal tube of a wind chime. It was a D—*Her* note of happiness. She was telling him that she was with him and that everything would be okay.

He sat for a few more minutes in the truck, listening to the occasional ring of the wind chimes. His calm returned, and the tears dried on his cheeks. His narrow smile widened with each D note carried on the breeze. The scent of the business card mingled with the memories from the chimes, and the words came.

He hurried from the truck to the trailer, sat down at the table, and opened the notebook to the page where the song had begun.

In darkened rooms alive with sound,
The stink of beer and sweat abound.
I catch your scent and turn around,
In hopes of finding you.
But disappointment falls again,

Like bitter tears in summer rain.
The passing memories in vain.
It's someone else I view.

Then, without hesitation, more words flowed.

Second string, third fret,
The note of joy I can't forget.
In my mind, I hear it, yet
My ears can't find the tune.
That single tone remains unblurred.
But missing in the voices heard.
I long to hear a single word
In the perfect sound of you.

He looked at the words, hearing how they would fit into the chords he felt. He would try them out tomorrow. Maybe more words would come, maybe not, but the words that had come so far were perfect for what he was feeling.

Before putting the notebook away, he wrote four words at the top of the page: *The Sound of You.* It was the perfect title for what he was trying to say, for what he was attempting to find—the sound of Sarah.

Third fret—Second string.

He glanced at the messages waiting on his phone, one from Ally, one from Rob. But the evening had worn him out, and those messages, like the words he had just written, would still be there tomorrow.

Pax lay on the bed, holding the box against his chest, Sarah's wedding ring safely reunited with her engagement ring. He watched the light from the streetlamp dance through the rain as it ran down the trailer's windows and drifted off to sleep.

*S*HE ASKED *him to take her to the prom.*

He looked at himself in the mirror, trying on a frilled shirt to match the charcoal gray tux he was renting for the occasion, still stupefied by the prospect. He was twenty-four, and she was eighteen. Why wouldn't she go with any of the classmates who asked her? What was she up to? Teasing them, then bringing her older best friend to keep them away? He felt like more of a bodyguard than a date.

The frills were too out of character for him, something a teenager might find fancy, but he thought it looked foppish. He chose a standard white shirt and bow tie. He had saved enough money to rent the tux for the event, though he had hoped to use that same cash to pay off the black Les Paul he had on layaway. He'd have to wait another month to bend those strings.

"Corsage?"

The salesman waited as Pax counted out the rental money and looked up.

"What?"

"Do you want a corsage for your date?"

Fuck, Pax thought. What have I gotten myself into?

"I'll throw in the carnation boutonniere for you if you buy a corsage."

Pax conceded, wanting Sarah to have a memorable prom. He counted out some extra cash on the table.

"What color is your date wearing?" the man asked.

Pax zoned out. She had told him to get a dark-colored tux but hadn't said anything about what she was wearing.

"No idea," he said, slightly panicked that he might choose poorly. Color wasn't his strong suit. He was a sound guy.

"Cornell or Ithaca College?" the man continued, trying to simplify Pax's decision by narrowing down his options.

Pax stared at him.

"Which school is this for?"

"Ithaca High," Pax said.

"Ithaca High?" the man asked, surprised that someone Pax's age would be going to a high school prom rather than a college formal.

"Yeah," Pax said, his irritation clear. "Ithaca High."

"Ok," the man said. He placed two flowers on the counter: a red carnation and a gold silk rose corsage. "Ithaca High colors. Can't go wrong."

Pax paid the money, grabbed the suit and flowers, and headed out onto the Commons just as the drizzle started to fall.

Aside from being with the most beautiful girl he had ever seen, the prom felt like torture. Knowing that all the other girls in her group would be wearing pastels and creams, Sarah chose a black, full-length gown that flattered her figure and made her look more mature and sophisticated. They seemed more like they were attending a Holly-wood gala than a high school dance.

Pax hated the attention he was getting from Sarah's friends. He hated the stink-eye he was getting from their respective dates. He hated seeing his former teachers look at him like some he was some kind of pervert. He hated the band. He hated the music. He hated the whole fucking thing. But when he looked at Sarah, it was all worth it.

He was feeling something for her that had never surfaced before. He saw her as more than the kid next door who always followed him around. She was more than the girl who entered his parents' house and his bedroom without knocking. She was no longer the girl he protected from the creeps in the neighborhood when she got braces or started wearing training bras. This girl, this woman before him, was none of those things. She was confident. She was poised. She was exceptional.

Near the end of the evening, after dancing, too many photos, and sneaking sips of liquor behind the bleachers in the gym, the two of them stood under the overhang of one of the side entrances to the school, waiting for a break in the rain so they could dash to his car.

Sarah lit up a Virginia Slims she'd bummed from one of her friends. Pax said nothing as he watched her try to look sophisticated while holding and drawing on the cigarette. She coughed, and he flinched at the smell of smoke in his face.

"I wish you wouldn't do that," he said simply.

"Sorry. I didn't mean to cough in your face."

"I mean smoke. At all. Ever." He corrected her in the tone of an older brother.

His expression showed her he was serious, and she flicked the coffin nail into the wet grass.

"Sorry," she said nervously. "I don't like it anyway."

Pax looked up and out, hoping the rain would slow down.

"That whiskey Mikey had was gross, too," she continued.

"I wouldn't know," he said with a smirk. "I was standing guard while you kids were having your fun."

She swatted him on the arm and stood with her arms spread out, as if posing for a movie photo.

"Does this look like a kid to you, Paxton Butler?"

He smiled, then frowned, and forced another smile.

"It does not," he said quietly.

She looked up at him and moved closer.

"Thank you for coming with me, Pax."

"Sure."

"I didn't want to be here with anyone else."

"Why not?" he replied, still a little stung by the cost of the night.

She moved slightly closer.

"Because I didn't want to do this with anyone else."

Her hands gently cupped his cheeks. She rose on her toes and drew his head nearer, closing the gap between them. Her eyes fluttered shut.

He felt her touch on his face. His head moved under her guidance, and his hands instinctively found their way to her hips. The rain drummed its syncopation on the overhang. Her perfume overpowered the scent of wet ozone in the air. Their lips met, and he tasted her lip *gloss. The softness yet insistence of that first intimate touch enveloped his senses, and he was lost.*

She pulled back slightly, her eyes closed, and her lips just barely touching his. They shared a breath for a moment, the cigarette and the lip gloss competing for attention, and she finally spoke.

"I love you, Pax."

HE TOOK a sip of his coffee and looked over the business card.

Dr. Lara Allen. Pediatric Cardiologist. St. Jude's Hospital.

He lifted the card to his nose and fought to contain the flood of memories it brought up. Satisfied that his emotions were in check, Pax called the number on the card. He was directed straight to voicemail. He hated voicemail with his kids and even more with someone he didn't know.

"Uh, hi Lara. This is Pax from last night at the club—the guy with the perfume question. Panic attack. Uh... whatever. Um, I don't know why I called, but I guess if you feel like calling me back, we can talk about... something... I guess. Shit. Which button is delete? Dammit."

He looked at his phone and saw that he had disconnected the call instead of deleting the voicemail, which he meant to do but didn't know how.

"Shit," he said to the empty room. Nobody responded.

He decided to pull himself together and check the maps for an RV park near New Orleans. While he was in the shower, his phone rang. He scrambled to get out, dripping water on the floor, and wrapped a towel around his waist as if the caller could see him in his current state. The phone stopped ringing before he reached it.

"Shit." The room still offered no response.

Then a ping signaled a voicemail. Pax picked up the phone and played the message.

"Dad!" Ally shouted. "Call me right away. It's urgent."

Pax overheard her say something to someone else and laugh as she hung up. If she was laughing, it couldn't be that urgent.

He finished his shower, got dressed, made breakfast, and then sat down with another cup of coffee to call Ally back.

"Dad? Do you know what urgent means?" He could hear the notes of happiness in her voice, which made him smile.

"Yes, it means something happened, and I will call when I feel like I have time to deal with it." He laughed.

"Dad," Ally said, unable to hide her excitement. "Did you read Rob's email or mine?"

He remembered receiving messages from the night before.

"Not yet," he laughed. "Are they urgent?"

"Shut up and listen, Dad," she laughed. "You're on YouTube."

He didn't know how to respond because he didn't understand what that meant. Travis had explained YouTube to him, but it seemed like something he didn't care about, so he filed it away under *Don't Give a Shit* in his memory.

"Is that a good thing, Kiddo?"

Ally laughed. He heard her say something to Travis, who was also laughing in the background.

"Ally, just put me on speakerphone or whatever so I can hear both of you."

The sound in his ear changed, and he heard Travis more clearly.

"Hi, Dad."

"Dad," Ally asked, "did you sing in a club last night?"

Her tone suggested she already knew the answer.

"Yeah," he replied, feeling a bit disoriented.

"It was that BoDeans song that Mom liked, right? Red Roses?"

Pax felt a bit spooked that something he had done just twelve hours earlier was already known by people hundreds of miles away.

"Yeah, but—"

"Rob found it first. He's a YouTube freak. Watches everything. I think it might eventually get him to join a cult. But, anyway, maybe the algorithm matched names because there was a video in his feed shot by someone in the audience at that club. They filmed you performing."

Pax didn't know what to say. Why would someone record his performance? Why would it end up online? What the hell was wrong with people, anyway?

"Can we get it deleted?" he asked, genuinely irritated at the thought of someone sharing his grief with the entire Internet.

"Dad, you don't understand," she continued. "It has—"

"Twenty-two thousand," Travis said.

"Twenty-two thousand views and four thousand likes."

"And that means what?" he asked, unsure if he cared.

"Dad, it means you're a hit!" Ally screamed away from the phone.

"Dad," Travis jumped in. "The comments are the most amazing part. You'll have to go online and read them. You remember how, right?"

"Um, yeah, sure," he said, not remembering but also not wanting to admit it.

"There's an app on your phone, Dad," Travis continued, knowing that repetition was the mother of learning. "Launch the app, then click on the search box and type your name and Memphis into it."

"Dad," Ally interrupted. "Rob's calling. Check it out then call us back."

"Ok, Kiddo. Tell Rob I'll call him later."

The call ended, and Pax looked around the empty room,

feeling confused. What just happened? He finished his coffee and poured another cup before finding the YouTube app on his phone and searching for his name, just as Travis instructed.

Then there he was. From the angle of the video, he thought the person filming might have been sitting near his table. He looked at himself on stage and wondered when he had gotten so fat.

"I still sound pretty good," he said, finding something positive in this invasion of his privacy. This time, he accepted the silence of the room as confirmation.

He scrolled down to read the comments. The name of the person who posted the video caught his attention, and he wasn't sure whether to smile or punch something.

@memphiskidsdoclallen

Lara had filmed him as he poured his heart out on stage, then posted the video for the world to critique. He scrolled down further and saw her opening comment.

This is Pax Butler. I saw this beautiful man perform a tribute to his wife last night at a club in Memphis. When he finished, the whole place was a blubbering mess.

The comment was accompanied by small images, including hearts and other symbols that might have conveyed a positive meaning if he could decipher them.

He continued reading other comments. Many people left similar messages, saying how heartbreaking his performance was, how beautiful his soul must be, and "Why can't my husband be like him?" Not all comments were flattering, but he knew that for every good person, there were probably a dozen shitty ones. He went through the comments until his coffee cup was empty, then called Rob.

"Hey, superstar," Rob said when he answered the phone.

"Hey, Rob," he laughed. "All those years with Zim, and all I had to do to get noticed was have someone post on YouTube."

They talked for an hour, discussing not only the video but also Rob, his work, Naomi, her work, and, of course, baby Jazz. Pax shared details about Sal and Claire. He even mentioned the bikers and made Rob promise not to tell Ally.

He didn't mention the panic attack, the EMTs, or the doctor who smelled like *Her*. He needed to work through all of that before sharing it with anyone.

"Send me some pictures of Jazz, will you, Rob?"

"Sure, Dad. This was fun. Call more often. You sound good."

"I think I'm getting there. I have some hard periods, but I'm getting there." He felt that was as genuine as he could be after the previous night's multiple meltdowns.

They ended the call with banalities, and afterward, Pax felt guilty for not telling Rob that he loved him.

Next time, he thought.

When he returned from his morning walk, his phone displayed a waiting voicemail. Lara's message was just as brief as his had been.

Hi Pax, it's Lara. Funny message. Would you like to meet me at my office? I have something I'd like to discuss with you. There's no need to call if you don't want to. Just show up if you do.

Pax looked at the business card and assumed she meant to meet her at St. Jude's. He cleaned up, struggled to find an appropriate shirt, and then headed to the hospital.

As he neared, he felt a tightening in his gut. His last few hospital visits had been painful: Sarah, then his broken hand, which dredged up memories of Tomas.

He parked in the lot across from the hospital, entered through the main entrance, and the attendant at the front desk called someone—presumably Lara's office. She gave him a visitor's pass, directed him to the elevators, and provided him with the room number.

Pax hated the smell of the hospital. It reminded him too much of the one in Westchester, which made him eager to leave.

Upon entering the outer office, he was greeted by a smiling receptionist who told him that Dr. Allen would be with him shortly. Pax sat in the corner and noticed that the room was filled with toys and children's books.

The receptionist said, "I saw your video."

Pax looked up and scowled, initially confused, but then he remembered.

"Oh, yeah," he responded awkwardly.

"It was incredibly moving," she said. "Just beautiful."

"Thank you," he managed, just as Lara entered the waiting area, saving him from more humiliation disguised as flattery.

She noticed the receptionist beaming while Pax cringed in discomfort, and she smiled.

"Good to see you again, Mr. Butler."

"Same," Pax said, nodding.

In her scrubs and ponytail, she no longer resembled the glamorous brunette from the club. Even from several feet away, Pax could tell she wasn't wearing the perfume from the night before, which he appreciated. She waved for him to follow and headed into her small office.

"First, I apologize for posting that video without your consent. I regretted it this morning and went to remove it, but then I saw all the comments and positive feedback. I couldn't take it down, but I will if you want me to."

"It's fine," Pax said with a chuckle. "My kids seemed to enjoy it."

"How many kids do you have?"

"Two, they're older. Kids of their own." He felt the sting of his mortality in that statement.

"Huh," Lara replied. "I didn't peg you for anything more than the late forties."

Pax nodded, feeling somewhat better. The man in the video looked older than she had estimated. Lara was either poor at judging ages or a skilled liar.

"Sixty-one."

"Wow," she replied. "You are a surprising character, Mr. Butler."

"If you call me that, we can't be friends. Just Pax."

She laughed, and it sounded sincere. He liked her so far.

He spent some time with Lara, Dr. Allen to the many children who were her patients. She talked to him about the night before and diplomatically encouraged him to see a doctor for a physical because a man of his age... blah... blah... blah. He nodded and replied, "Sure," and "Maybe," and "I guess so."

"I want to show you something," she said, then led him out of her office.

"We adults often take our health for granted, especially when we can't tell if anything's wrong beneath the surface. We tend to ignore minor pains, headaches, and similar issues, but these can be signs of something more serious."

Pax thought of Sarah and understood exactly what Lara was describing. Sarah had either ignored or endured her pain until it was too late to do anything about it.

Lara took Pax to a viewing window for the ward's playroom near her office.

"Kids don't ignore things," she continued. "If it hurts, they say something. Sometimes, it's just a headache or a sore muscle. Sometimes it's something more serious. And sometimes the cause of the pain brings them here."

Unable to enter the ward directly, Pax watched the children in the play area through the window as Lara tried to explain some of the conditions the children faced. The technical terms became a blur in his mind, and all he could focus on were the faces of these little ones who had spent most of their young lives in hospitals. He couldn't help but think of Puck, Lainey, and Jazz and how fortunate he and his kids were to have healthy children to raise.

One little blonde girl caught his eye. She was draped in a paper gown with a mask over her mouth and nose, but she laughed and played as if these obstacles didn't exist. She read *Where the Wild Things Are* to other children in the play area, appearing more like a teacher in front of a class than a child fighting for her life. Pax was fascinated by the resilience of these children and wondered at what point their perspective of the world morphed into the cynical view of adulthood.

"Sara kind of runs the playroom," Lara said.

Pax suddenly felt that same clenching sensation from the night before, dropping him to one knee. He felt caught between suffocation and hyperventilation. His heart pounded.

"Pax!" she shouted, but his ears rang. She called someone down the hall while supporting him, one hand on his back and the other on his arm.

He slowly stood up and looked at her, breathing in through his nose and out through his mouth, a pre-show ritual he used before each performance.

An orderly arrived with a wheelchair, but Lara waved it away, helping him into a chair in the hallway and sitting beside him, her fingers instinctively finding his pulse. When his calm returned, he blinked away tears and, to her surprise, smiled.

"Pax?"

"Her name was Sarah," he said, feeling strangely calm as he talked about his missing soulmate. "She was a teacher. That little girl..."

He looked back through the observation window.

"She died three years ago from cancer."

"I'm sorry," Lara said. "I understand why you reacted that way."

"You know what? It's okay. I feel... okay?"

"Is that a question?" Lara asked.

Pax chuckled.

"I feel okay. I was startled, but lately many things have been triggering good memories. I spent most of the past few years dwelling on the bad ones."

"My perfume?"

"That was a good one. I just wasn't ready for it."

She grinned.

"After last night, I wasn't sure what to think," she said. "It may have been a grief-induced panic attack triggered by my perfume, but when I asked you about your medical history, I knew you were one of those tough guys who only sees a doctor when something is bleeding or broken. I wanted to emphasize the importance of seeing someone so you could know for sure. That was a serious episode, and you shouldn't assume anything about its cause."

"I know."

They sat in silence for several minutes, her fingers resting on his wrist, monitoring his pulse as he eased back into himself.

"Why did you kiss me?"

Lara smiled and shook her head.

"I have no idea, Pax. It was... instinct?"

He took Lara's hand as he had taken Sal's when he declined her advances. He confided in her about the prom, the first kiss with Sarah, and why the kiss from the previous night had been so upsetting. Just as he had told Sal, he explained to Lara that he wasn't looking for a romantic relationship. Instead, he was searching for the parts of Sarah that still existed in the world.

Lara chuckled softly and gently patted his hand.

"Don't worry, Pax," she said with a grin. "I'm not interested in a romantic relationship either. My wife would never allow it."

AT HER SUGGESTION, Pax visited Dr. Engel, one of Lara's colleagues, to have a calcium scan performed around his heart. He sat with Lara and Dr. Engel, reviewing the results, which, in medical terms, were "concerning." Pax heard technical terms that his brain immediately discarded, but he also heard "potential widow maker," which made him sit up and take notice. Dr. Engel recommended a stress test to track the blood flow around his heart to ensure there was no blockage. It would take a few weeks to get on the schedule, and Pax knew the New Orleans music festival was off his dance card.

During the wait, Pax spent time with Lara and her wife Maliyah, who was also a doctor at the hospital. Maliyah was a fantastic cook, so Pax never turned down an invitation to dinner. However, he always picked up the check when they ate out to show his appreciation for their generosity.

The doctors shared stories about children they had known, though not all had happy endings. Pax recounted tales about Sarah and Zim, Rob and Ally, and growing up around Ithaca. It was enjoyable, stress-free, and made him feel like himself again.

When he wasn't with Mrs. and Mrs. Allen, Pax would chat with Ally or Rob in the evenings. He told them about his new doctor friends but never about why he stayed longer in Memphis than he initially planned. Ally asked him more than once if he had contacted Audra. His response was always the same.

"No, Kiddo, but I will."

Ally and Rob sent pictures of the little ones. On one occasion, Travis sent a video of Puck playing air guitar to an AC/DC song while Lainey danced. Pax replied, saying they needed to "get the boy some music lessons."

The brief local fame he gained from the YouTube video was

soon overshadowed by the toxic mix of chronic attention deficit disorder and a craving for instant gratification that plagued American society, always on the hunt for the next trending thing. He didn't mind. It wasn't the kind of fame he would ever have sought.

He hadn't been back to open-mic night at the Delta Harmony Lounge since that first evening. Still, he enjoyed live music at various clubs, with or without the Allens. On the rare occasions when someone recognized him from the video, he would smile, nod, and say, "Thank you."

He talked with Sal. Her consulting gig in Florida looked like it could potentially become permanent. She wasn't sure she wanted to settle down, but the offer might be too good to pass up. Pax assured her that she would make the right decision when the time came. They exchanged photos of where they were staying and what they saw. He wanted to share his medical dilemma with Sal, but he decided to wait until he had more information.

On a Monday, as the weather cooled with fall creeping steadily over the city, he walked into Lara's office to find her head resting on her desk. At first, he thought she was asleep on her arms, knowing that sometimes they endured long, overnight battles with chronic illness that drained both the patient and the doctor. When she heard him knock, she looked up, and it became clear to him that she had been crying.

"Lara?"

She managed to smile, but her chin trembled.

"It never gets easier," she said. "Never."

He concluded that one of the children had died.

"What happened?"

"It was just too much for her. She was too frail. The disease was too strong."

"Who?" he asked, uncertain that he wanted to know.

"I almost don't want to tell you, Pax," she said, wiping her eyes.

He sat in the guest chair and reached across the desk to take her hands.

"Sara?"

Lara nodded and started crying again. Pax moved around the desk and knelt beside her, just as Erin had done during his own descent into grief. He let her quite literally cry on his shoulder until, eventually, the sorrow had to be set aside. Even as Lara mourned, Dr. Allen had children who needed her care.

They stood, and Pax held her in his arms—just friends comforting each other—as he thought about the little girl who reminded him so much of the woman from his past who shared her name.

HE PUSHED THE SWING, and she soared into the air, leaning back on the ascent to look at him upside down. It had been years since he had pushed her on swings, and years since they had ridden the carousel at Stewart Park.

She was studying to be a teacher at SUNY New Paltz. He tried to return to school to earn a degree in music but eventually dropped out to pursue his dream of becoming a musician. They wrote to each other, and he sent her cassettes of the songs he was writing. They talked on the phone whenever someone had enough money for the long-distance charges. It was spring break of her senior year, and here she was again, swinging with the other kids.

He was excited to have her near again, but he felt restless, and she could tell. His responses were short and emotionless. When she asked what he wanted to do, he replied, "Whatever you want to do." When she suggested something, he answered, "Sure." She was getting annoyed, and he noticed.

In his mind, he kept hearing Sara by Fleetwood Mac. He loved the sound of that song and wanted to sing it to her—either that or Sara Smile. by Hall and Oates. He thought that would be the most romantic way to—

She jumped off the swing and stumbled in the loose mulch. He rushed over to help her up.

"Take me home, Pax."

He was stunned. They had only been together for a couple of hours, and he still hadn't—

"Say something or take me home. I'm tired of whatever is making you so... boring."

It felt like a slap in the face. He thought he had been giving her a perfect day by following her wishes, but he clearly misunderstood the situation. It was time to act. It was now or never.

"Sarah," he said, his voice trembling slightly.

He looked around. This felt wrong. Not here. He grabbed her hand and pulled her away from the playground onto a trail heading toward the lake. She shook his hand off.

"Pax!"

Third fret—Third string.

Disappointment. Frustration. Annoyance.

He paused and extended his hand for her to take willingly.

"Please," he said, and she complied.

They walked silently for several minutes until they reached a bench overlooking the dark waters of Cayuga Lake. They sat on the bench, its green paint chipped and repainted multiple times over the years.

He held her hand, their fingers intertwined. He had never felt so nervous. She had that effect on him. She was the only person he knew who could completely dismantle him with her presence.

"You only have a few months left of school," he said, trying to come up with a preamble that didn't sound stupid.

"Yes," she answered.

"I was talking to Zim, and he's moving back to Middletown. I might move down there to be... you know... closer."

She was silent. He could never tell if that was a good or bad thing with Sarah.

"You want to move down to Middletown to be closer? To me?"

"Yes," he replied.

The silence was torture. He knew he had to do better. He reached into his pocket and pulled out the gift—the gamble. He was ready to risk everything. This was his moment.

"Sarah," he said weakly.

"Sarah," he said again, with more conviction. "I don't want to be without you anymore. Ever again."

"Pax," she said, her voice a whisper.

He opened his hand.

"Sarah, will you marry me?"

She stared at it, resting on his palm. He took her hand and gently slipped the petite ring with the tiny diamond onto her finger. Now that she was wearing it, she stared even harder. He wrapped his hand around hers, waiting as his fingers nervously moved over hers.

He waited a lifetime, mulling over the possibilities. What would happen if she said no? What if she said, not now? What if she said—

She looked up at him.

ON THE DAY of the stress test, Pax went alone. He sat in the waiting room by himself. When they called him in, he joined four other people in the prep room, but since everyone was dealing with their own anxiety about the upcoming tests, he might as well have been alone there as well.

It began with an X-ray using tracing dye to establish a baseline before the stress test. Then more waiting in the prep room. When he was called in for the next stage, a med tech connected him to more wires than he could remember using for one of his shows and directed him to a treadmill.

He walked on a flat surface, then an incline, followed by a light jog, and finished with an uphill jog. Afterward, he had to wait again.

At the end of the test, he received another dose of dye and another X-ray. Then he was unceremoniously released, left to find something else to do for the rest of the day.

He returned to the fifth wheel to see if this experience had brought any words to the surface. It had not.

The test results from Dr. Engel arrived by email the next day.

Your stress test does not suggest any blockages or decreased blood flow to your heart. No changes are needed at this time.

He sent the email to Lara, who replied with an extra-large smiley face.

ON THE FOLLOWING FRIDAY, Pax sat across from Lara and Maliyah at the diner near the hospital. They met there regularly for breakfast when both doctors worked day shifts. He delivered the news: he was leaving.

"How soon?" Maliyah asked.

"Tomorrow."

"Tomorrow?" Lara nearly choked on her coffee. "That's some warning, Pax."

"I know," he said, feeling a bit guilty about the sudden shock. "I decided last night. I need to get back out there. I need to... find her."

Lara looked out the window, her face tensing and relaxing as she processed what she just heard.

"That sounds like a fine idea, Pax," Maliyah said when Lara's silence went on too long.

Lara turned back to the table, her face painted with disappointment. Dr. Allen took over.

"You received good news about your stress test, and we're all very happy about that. But you still have that concerning calcium scan, so you need to see a doctor regularly, Pax. You're okay now, but that won't last if you don't stay on top of it."

Pax nodded, feeling his emotions swell. He understood that Lara, in her professional way, was expressing her sadness about his departure.

"Was it Sara? Is she the reason?"

"Not entirely, but it felt like the end of something. Just as it had been with my Sarah."

He released a deep sigh.

"It was everything, though. Your perfume. When you kissed me—"

Maliyah laughed. "You kissed him?"

"Hush, I'll tell you later," Lara said.

Pax went on.

"It felt like the beginning all over again, and then, when little Sara..."

Lara stretched her arm across the table to rest her hand on his, just like he did for her when she shared the news about little Sara.

"It was the end, all over again. And now, I have a somewhat clean bill of health for the near term. I need to keep going. I already stayed here longer than planned, which was well worth it. But now it's time."

They sat in silence. The bomb had been dropped, and the three absorbed its impact.

After they parted outside the diner, Pax returned to the fifth wheel and packed up. At the end of the day, he waited in Lara's office while she completed her final rounds. He browsed through his phone, looking at pictures of Puck, Lainey, and Jazz, and thinking of little Sara. He texted Ally and Rob to let them know he would be on the road in the morning, heading to Austin.

Audra's contact record appeared on the screen. He studied it for a moment before tapping the text message icon.

Hi. I'm sure you've spoken with Ally and know about my trip. I just wanted to check in and let you know I'm doing okay. I am getting better every day, and every day, I think of you. I hope you're doing well.

He read the message, and it felt inadequate after such a long silence.

I have a lot of things to apologize for in my life. The way I treated you that day is at the top of the list. I hope you'll give me a chance when I return.

Lara walked into the room and saw him looking at his phone.

"You're turning into one of them, Pax." she chuckled.

"One of them?"

"A twenty-first-century American casualty of social media."

He laughed.

"No. I'm just sending some messages before I head out tomorrow."

"Maliyah's working late. Can I get a ride with you?"

"Sure," he said. "Let's grab something to eat and maybe a tequila or six."

"I know just the place," she responded.

The location was the Delta Harmony Lounge, and it was open mic night.

Pax and Lara sat at the same table where they met. He felt more calm than he had that first night. He had changed. He had grown. He knew it. He felt it. Lara stepped out of the restroom, and Pax immediately caught her perfume.

"You're just mean," he said with a smile. "But thank you."

She kissed his cheek, and they lifted their glasses in a toast to their friendship.

The acts were all typical—everyday folks trying to make themselves heard in different ways. Pax and Lara cheered each performer as they took the stage and again when they finished and stepped down. The night was moving along, and Pax felt the pull to head back to the trailer and get some rest before the long drive. Still, he enjoyed his time with Lara and didn't want to be "that guy."

"And finally," the club manager said, "we have an encore from our YouTube sensation, Pax Butler."

Pax glared at Lara who was laughing.

"I put you on the list!" she shouted over the applause.

He hesitantly stepped onto the stage.

"I don't have my guitar," he told the audience.

"Use mine," said a young woman near the stage, offering him her small Taylor acoustic.

The audience applauded again. Pax checked the tuning and paused for a moment.

"I don't have anything prepared," he said, glancing at the faces.

Then, as if struck by inspiration, "Maybe this."

He glanced at Lara, who was already recording his farewell performance on her phone. He fumbled with the chords but then found the right key and began.

Pax looked out at the crowd and started singing *Sara Smile* by Hall and Oates. Lara's hand went up to cover her mouth, her eyes blinking back tears. He knew he had made the right choice.

PART IV

THE FEEL OF YOU

"Some memories never fade because they are imprinted not in the mind but in the fingertips."

– Haruki **Murakami**

CHAPTER 5

Pax was determined to reach Dallas before stopping for the night. He estimated it would take a little over seven hours, planning to detour only once for fuel, food, and biological necessities. He hadn't, however, accounted for heavy traffic around Little Rock or a three-hour delay outside Texarkana, where authorities were working to clear at least one lane after a multi-vehicle crash involving two semis, several passenger vehicles, and a motorcycle.

After fifteen minutes of not even and inch of forward motion, Pax turned off the engine, got out of the truck, and walked to the median to gauge how far ahead the backup might stretch. Fellow travelers wandered around the parking lot that used to be the southbound lanes of I-30.

"Traffic report on the scanner says there's a bad accident just before Exit 7," said a man sitting on the guardrail.

Pax glanced at the next mile marker—11.2 staring back at him.

"Jesus," he said. "Four miles of this?"

"Yessir, and that's just what's in front of us."

The man pointed to the growing line of cars behind them.

Pax whistled and resigned himself to a long wait. Luckily, he had his "rolling hotel suite," as Sal would call it, complete with food, drinks, and, if needed, air conditioning—at least until the batteries gave out.

He returned to his unplanned parking spot, locked the truck, and climbed into the fifth wheel. He took a bottle of sparkling water from the cooler, sat on the bed, and used his phone to look for more information about the accident or an alternate route. Finding nothing helpful, he settled in for the wait.

He checked his text messages but saw nothing new since leaving Memphis that morning, including no replies from Audra. His emails were filled with the usual insurance offers, scams, ads, and digital junk mail. He decided to play one of the games Travis had loaded on his phone. Although he wasn't good at it, it helped his mind find a default mode which often sparked his creativity. It did not.

He then took out his guitar and played through the chords of *The Sound of You.* The few lyrics he had fit well with the simple structure he found on the guitar. He thought about adding some embellishments or changes between verses but ultimately decided to keep it simple, as he felt it was meant to be.

He was making a sandwich for lunch when his phone beeped. He hoped it was a message from Audra. Any reply from her would at least ease the uncertainty that was troubling him.

It was from Travis.

Dad, I finished decoding Erin's CDs. I didn't listen to all of them, but they are interesting. Don't try to download them on your phone until you're connected to a Wi-Fi network. There are about 5 hours of recordings, and downloading them over your mobile service will use up your data plan. I'm sending an email with links. Let me know when you see this.

Pax replied.

Message received. Will check tonight.

He arrived at Lakeshore RV Resort at 9:50 p.m. It was easy to find, just off the highway once he crossed Lake Ray Hubbard. After spending so much time parked and waiting in traffic, he was glad to be off I-30, even for a brief respite.

He connected the power but didn't bother with the water since he planned to be on the road to Austin early in the morning. He then sent a group text to the kids to let them know he was off the highway for the night. He followed that with a longer email describing his day and how the long wait made him realize how fortunate he had been to get that far as a novice towing a fifth-wheel trailer.

He read the email from Travis that included a list of links for downloading recordings from "the cloud," whatever that was. Travis also included instructions for connecting his phone to WiFi to avoid using his data plan. He managed to get successfully connected to the RV park's guest network on the first try and began downloading all the links without needing to ask Travis for tech support.

"Old dog, new tricks," he said as he watched his phone start downloading the large audio files.

While he waited, exhaustion from the drive, the long highway delay, and the stress of heavy traffic caught up with him. He decided to call it a night rather than deal with any more technology.

A light rain fell in the morning, making him uneasy about driving to Austin in wet weather. Pax sipped his coffee while standing in the RV's doorway, watching the drizzle. His phone pinged with a new text message. He checked it, again hoping it was from Audra, but it was from Sal.

Got offered the job. Shit ton $$$. Took it. Come visit me in Orlando.

He smiled, genuinely happy for his friend. He composed

several snarky replies but deleted them all before sending something more heartfelt.

Good for you. $$$ isn't everything, but it's nice to hear what someone thinks you're worth. Heading to Austin today. Lots to share. Call later?

As he sent this reply to Sal, a message arrived from Lara.

Hi you. I hope your drive was ok and you got some sleep last night. Can I post the Sara Smile video on YT? Miss you already.

He chuckled as he remembered the ambush from her first recording at the club and thought his reputation couldn't get any worse after that.

Sure. Miss you both. Safe outside Dallas. Austin later today.

He checked the downloads from the night before and saw that the audio files were safely on his phone. Travis had numbered and dated the file names so Pax knew the order to play them.

He started the first one, and the media player began. After half a minute of silence, accompanied by background noise that sounded like things being moved around, he suddenly heard... Zim? It sounded like he was several feet from the microphone.

"Yeah, right there. You want to be close so it will pick up your voice over any background noise. Ok. Ready? Just sit there and start talking. On 3-2-1, mark."

"Hi, Pax."

He stopped the playback, his heart pounding, eyes wide and brimming with tears. He couldn't swallow and hurried to the sink to spit out the mouthful of coffee he had just sipped before hearing those words. *Her* words. *Her* voice. *Her* sound.

It was Sarah. He glanced at the filename, which included the recording date: *(1) 2016-03-21.mp3*. The track had been created just over two weeks after they got the bad news about her cancer.

He looked in the folder where the audio files had downloaded. There were more than a dozen individual recordings. Were they all from Sarah? How had she managed to record them without him knowing? And Zim? He couldn't keep a secret. How had he not let this slip?

He forced himself to focus. Both nervous and eager to continue, he pressed play and heard Zim again.

"Slide forward just a little more, honey. Don't touch the mic screen, but get as close as you can without kissing it."

"Here?"

"Perfect. Go ahead."

"Hi, Pax. Um, I don't have anything planned for this. I just wanted to start something, but I promise I'll be more organized in future recordings.

"I guess if you're listening to this, Zim gave you these recordings, which means... well, we know what it means."

Pax could hear both the smile and the tears. Her voice was gravelly from the treatments and dehydration, but he could hear what he needed to: *Third fret—Second string.*

"Pax, I don't remember the day we met because I was a baby, but from my earliest memories, I was in love with you. You were the smile I longed to see. You were the voice I yearned to hear. Since we were just kids, you were my brother, my best friend, and ultimately my greatest love.

"I know I probably annoyed you when you were in high school and I was still in elementary school. I remember treating your house like it was my own, walking in whenever I felt like it. Your parents were so kind to accommodate my daily intrusions.

"I would walk into your bedroom without knocking while you were doing your homework or learning the guitar. I loved just being in the room with you, and I couldn't help but be nosy about what you were working on. I simply wanted to be close to you.

"Then, when you graduated, I thought I might lose you to a distant college, but you stayed. I convinced myself that you stayed for

me, that you were waiting for me. I was in junior high, so those fantasies were fueled by hormones and countless romance stories borrowed from the library. But you did. You stayed. I never asked why.

"And then, when you started dating that girl from Dryden, Caroline. Ugh, Caroline. I was so jealous. You seemed happy. I felt like you were heading down another path that would take you away from me. Whenever I saw her car in your driveway, I wanted to slash her tires or throw dog turds on the windshield. It was the only time I wanted to hurt someone, but I didn't want to hurt you in the process. Then, like a miracle, she was gone. I never asked what happened. I never brought up her name. I knew you needed a distraction. Even if I was the annoying kid next door, I could provide that for you. Hey Pax, play me a song. Hey Pax, do you want to see a movie at the State Theater? Hey Pax, can you help me with my math?

"I never needed help with math. I wonder if you ever figured that out.

"The boys I dated in high school were, what, practice, I guess? I never truly felt anything for any of them. It was an adolescent exploration. As Mr. Hainey said in health class, I was a teenager trying to figure out all these emotions and nerve endings. I know you don't want to hear that, but you must understand that the emotions were never there, not for any of them. They were all locked up in you. I'm sure that was part of why I never dated the same guy for more than a month or two. They just... weren't... you.

"And that makes me think about prom. That night. Oh my, that night.

"I still get tingles when I think about that first kiss. That night, the emotions and nerve endings connected perfectly. I remember your big brother attitude all night, giving my male classmates the famous Pax scowl when they asked me to dance, and dismissing the attention of my female friends. And God, that suit.

"Anyway, that kiss. I was risking everything with that kiss. Either *you would brush it off and stay that big brother and best friend, or you would change, and we would become something new. Together. And what we became—"*

Pax heard Sarah sniff, and the sniffing turned into a cough.

"Zim, can we take a break? I need some fresh air."

"Sure, honey. Take your time."

The track ended, and Pax wiped away his tears. Why hadn't Zim given him these recordings? He knew his friend could be a flake at times, but he couldn't imagine him forgetting about something like this. Maybe he was waiting for the right time, and Pax never showed any signs of what that might look like. And then, Zim was just... gone.

He saw that the next recording was over an hour long. He resisted the urge to play it, knowing he needed to get on the road. He would have to wait until he reached Austin to listen to it. Driving was too dangerous while feeling the emotions these tracks would surely stir up.

Before leaving the campsite, Pax replied to Travis's email and copied Ally and Rob.

I listened to the first track on Travis's playlist. I think we all should listen to them. I don't know if anything is coming up that I don't think you should hear, but at this point, I don't care. Listen, and we can talk about it later. Thank you, Travis.

Austin appeared without any further traffic issues. Pax navigated to the RV park south of the city, spending the rest of the morning and part of the afternoon setting up his reserved spot.

The manager told him that with the Austin City Limits Festival coming up, he could only stay a few days before the festival bookings arrived. He could return after the festival or he could be added to a wait list in case a slot opened up earlier. Pax opted for the wait list and hoped he wouldn't have to play musical fifth wheels over the coming weeks. He thought he might have to find a nearby hotel until the festival was over or until a spot became available, but he knew the hotels would likely be just as crowded.

Once settled, Pax went to a local convenience store for snacks and beer, expecting he would need several adult beverages to get through the first hour of Sarah's recordings. He wasn't sure what to expect, but knowing his late wife, she would deeply explore his emotions and make him "feel feels," as she used to say. The beer would help distract him from the overwhelming emotions he anticipated.

With two beers on the table and the other four in the fridge, Pax plugged in his phone and played the next track: *(2) 2016-04-08.mp3.*

"Okay, I think I'm ready, Zim. I won't know for sure until we start."

Sarah was giggling, as was Zim in the background. Pax had heard that giggle from Zim a thousand times.

They're high, he thought. *Zim got Sarah high?*

"Pax, hi Pax. Sorry about the abrupt end to that first track. I'm not going back to edit or re-record any of this. Time moves in one direction, and whatever they are, they are."

She took a deep breath and suddenly burst into laughter.

"Stop looking at me like that. I'm trying to be serious. Turn around!"

Zim mumbled something unintelligible in the background, and then Sarah started.

"For the record, I had one of Zim's edibles, Pax. Don't hate him for it. It helps. I haven't felt a buzz like this since college, but I couldn't smoke it, so this is the next best thing. Maybe even a better thing. I

imagine you're sitting there with a glass of tequila, so we're even. Anyway..."

Pax listened for an hour as Sarah recounted the evolution of their relationship, including, to his growing frustration, her brief college flings, despite having opened her heart to him on prom night. She insisted on transparency—no secrets, no lies. She wanted to show Pax that she always returned to him, despite her experimentation. No one else could replace him. She was always his.

Pax downed his first beer and opened another as he listened. His emotions shifted from joy to anger, frustration, and betrayal, then back to joy each time he heard her happy tones. Even though he hated the content of this recording, he listened closely, if for no other reason than to hear her voice.

When he finished the second beer, he paused the playback. He quietly processed what he had heard. He reminded himself that it all happened before he proposed, which eased his feelings about her infidelity. But another voice in his head told him she had pledged her love to him before sharing her bed with others, reigniting the sense of betrayal.

"Oh, fuck this."

He tossed his phone onto the bed. Grabbing two more beers —one in hand and the other tucked in his back pocket a la Leo Murphy—then stormed out of the trailer to walk off his anger.

Even with the ACL festival still a few days away and schools already in session, the RV park was nearly full. People moved around their sites, walked their dogs, talked on their phones— lived their lives. Pax saw none of it.

He sipped his beer as he walked along the roads and paths, between RVs and campers, trying to calm the cortisol-fueled rage coursing through him.

Why did she tell me all of that? he wondered. *I could have died ignorant and happy.*

He realized that sharing this was more about her conscience than about educating him. She was clearing the slate and explaining that during their youth, emotions and nerve endings often didn't connect. Initially, hormones, not emotions, drove desire—especially with newfound independence. Later, as desire intertwined with love and connection, a powerful chemistry developed between them, bonding them as a couple.

He remembered their times together during her holiday breaks and how, out of respect, he never tried to go beyond a kiss. With this new information, he wondered why she never made a move either. Was she waiting for him? Did she interpret his restraint as disinterest? Was she unsure of his attraction or not yet ready for a deeper connection? Or was she gaining experience with college flings in preparation for when they could no longer wait? His hurt faded as he considered these possibilities, and his anger diminished.

Then he heard it.

Third fret—Second string.

Literally.

Pax turned toward the sound and followed it until he found its source—a boy in his early teens tuning a guitar that was almost too big for him. The kid adjusted the tuning pegs and plucked the second string again.

F-sharp, Pax thought as he sipped and observed. The kid glanced up at the older man watching him.

"Open D?" Pax asked.

"Yeah," the kid replied. "Better to use the slide."

The kid held up a glass finger slide, touched it to the strings, and tore off a few delta blues riffs that surprised Pax.

"Wow," Pax said. "You've got some chops, man."

"Some what?" the kid asked.

"Chops," Pax replied. "Skills. Talent. An ear for what's good. What song are you tuning for?"

"Paris, Texas. Ry Cooder style."

"Ry Cooder?" Pax was in awe. "How old are you, man? How do you know about Ry Cooder?"

The kid didn't respond but kept tuning his instrument. A noise from the RV caught his attention, and he looked toward the door as it swung open. A woman leaned against the doorframe, looking out at Pax, adopting a posture like one he often used.

"Do you play?" she asked.

"Not like that," Pax replied.

The woman nodded. "Beto is something of a prodigy, like his father."

"Beto," Pax said, repeating the boy's name to help remember it.

"Time for lunch, Beto," the woman said. "Finish what you're doing and come on in."

As prompted, Beto started playing *Paris, Texas*, extracting every ounce of grim emotion as the slide moved gracefully up and down the neck. Pax watched silently for five minutes until the kid finished. He stood stunned for another minute as the kid packed up his guitar and took it inside the RV.

"Jesus," Pax said, almost to himself, but the woman smiled. "What just happened? I might have to quit playing now."

He laughed, and she joined in, her laughter like music.

"He's our pride and also our embarrassment," she said. "He just knows how to do it. It makes the rest of the family look like amateurs, except my husband. He's another maestro. The two of them together..."

She trailed off, glancing back into the RV as she followed the boy's path.

"I'm Pax."

"Marisol," the woman replied. "Are you staying in the park?"

"Yeah," Pax said. "Until they kick me out for the Austin City Limits thing."

"Are you going to the festival?"

"I planned on it, yeah. I'll need to find a place to park my rig unless they get a cancellation. Then I can stay."

A comfortable silence settled in as Pax finished his beer, tucked the empty bottle into his back pocket, leaving the other unopened bottle in his other pocket.

"You said you play?" Marisol asked.

"Yeah," Pax replied. "I've been doing this since I was a teenager, around his age. But I'm nowhere near as good as Beto. I'm more of a singer-songwriter type. I don't do much lead guitar work—at least not anymore."

"You should stop by in the evenings," she said. "We're usually out here playing and singing. Unless it's raining."

"I'll do that," Pax said. "Every night?"

"Most every night," she confirmed.

"Nice to meet you, Marisol. Tell Beto I said the same. I would love to hear him unload on that guitar."

"Nice to meet you, too, Pax. And I will."

Feeling lighter and calmer than when he left, Pax returned to his trailer. As he stepped inside the fifth wheel, he tossed his empty bottle in the trash and put the other in the fridge, then sat on the bed and hit play on his phone to pick up the session where he left off.

"I know you're probably angry after I told you all that, but I need you to hear me, really hear me. What happened in college shaped my life with you. Without that experimental phase and without making my own decisions—both good and bad—I wouldn't have been ready to say yes to you on that bench in Ithaca. From the moment you put the ring on my finger, you placed your heart in my hands and became my everything. You gave me your trust, and I held it like an egg,

protecting it, nurturing it, and helping it hatch and grow into the love we became.

"When you proposed that day, I felt something I had never understood before—certainty. My soul has belonged to you from that moment, and it always will. I have never strayed, not even for a second or with a single thought, because there is nothing and no one else I would want. You are my everything, Pax, and you always will be.

"Every moment we've shared since that proposal, every choice I've made, has been for us. You've shown me what love is supposed to be—patient, kind, forgiving. Because of that love, I can say with all my heart that you're the only man I've ever truly belonged to. No one else ever stood a chance. From the day I was born until..."

He could hear her words starting to choke with tears.

"We were meant to be. That was the certainty I felt that day, and I still feel it every day. Zim, I need to stop."

"Sure, honey."

Sarah giggled a little through her tears.

"You said these things would make me happy, you big liar."

IN THE EARLY EVENING, sitting on the steps of the fifth wheel with his guitar in hand, Pax tried to imitate what he had seen Beto do so effortlessly. He felt like a fraud. Despite nearly fifty years of playing guitar and over thirty as a professional musician, he couldn't match the talent the teenage boy displayed in just five minutes.

He realized that although he was a decent guitar player, a more than decent singer, and a passable songwriter, he was merely dabbling in music rather than excelling. He acknowledged that he should be better at this point in his career—if he could even call it that—but he wasn't. Then, he faced the grim realization that he never would be.

He played the riffs he knew well, feeling his injured hand move more nimbly than it had since the accident. He worked through his fingerpicking exercises, sensing about an eighty percent improvement. He practiced chord changes, key changes, and pentatonic riffs. He thought he could adequately demonstrate his skills and explain the stiffness as a result of age and injury.

He packed his guitar, grabbed his folding chair and the rest of the six-pack, and headed back to where he had met Beto and Marisol. When he reached the small RV, no one was outside. He set down his chair and put the six-pack on the seat. He checked his watch just as Beto opened the door.

"You're early," Beto said. "Mama said to invite you in for something to eat."

Pax realized he hadn't eaten since storming out of the trailer to clear his head of the images Sarah had painted with her words. He followed Beto into the cramped space of the old RV and found himself in the company of Beto's family. Marisol got up and prepared a plate for Pax while Beto introduced him to the rest of the clan.

"That's my papa, Roberto," Beto said. "That's my uncle Jose. We call him Pepe. And that's my brother, Nico."

Roberto and Jose stood up to shake Pax's hand and invited him to sit down. Pax quickly learned that the Cruz family had formed a band called Pleasure Cruz. They were scheduled to perform on one of the side stages at the Austin City Limits festival. Booked for both weekends, they planned to stay at the RV park for a few weeks before heading back to Florida for the winter.

Marisol was the manager, booking agent, accountant, and

cook. Roberto and Pepe took turns driving the RV and often earned extra money at the parks by doing odd jobs for other patrons. Roberto had a certificate in auto mechanics, while Pepe had been a math teacher before joining the band. Roberto helped people with vehicle issues, and Pepe provided tutoring and computer support.

Beto and Nico contributed by offering dog walking, babysitting, and trash pickup services. The Cruz family had a flyer posted on the office bulletin board and were regularly called on to help their nomadic neighbors.

Marisol also had a teaching degree, so she and Pepe homeschooled the two boys. To Pax, Beto, fourteen, and Nico, ten, seemed very mature for their ages. As he reflected on Ally and Rob at that age, he felt inadequate as a parent.

"My wife, Sarah, was a teacher," he said. "We had two kids as well, about the same ages apart. I mean, I still have them, but they have their own families now."

"Is your wife not traveling with you?" Marisol asked, handing Pax a plate of rice, meat, and vegetables.

Pax clenched his jaw and squinted, trying to find words that wouldn't bring on tears.

"Oh!" Marisol said, interpreting Pax's body language. "Oh, I'm so sorry."

Pax nodded but stayed quiet. Roberto and Pepe reached across the table and squeezed Pax's arm, a kind gesture of support for someone they had only just met. Nico asked what was happening, and Beto elbowed him, whispering. Nico's expression changed as Beto explained the situation, and, like his father and uncle, he reached over and squeezed Pax's arm. After the awkward beginning, dinner turned into a mix of storytelling, inside jokes, Tio Pepe's pop quizzes, and laughter.

Pax nearly inhaled the plate of ropa vieja, calling it one of the best things he had eaten on this journey. He jokingly told Marisol he'd love the recipe but then admitted he'd prefer she made it for him, knowing he could never duplicate it.

"Nico," Pepe said, "do you know what Señor Butler's name means in Latin?"

Nico put his fork down and let his hands rest in his lap, gazing at his plate, lost in thought. After a moment, he looked up.

"I think it means peace?"

"Muy bien," Pepe replied.

Nico looked at Pax and chuckled.

"So, are you the peace butler?"

Pax couldn't restrain himself. He burst out laughing, and the family joined in.

"Well," he replied. "Don't let the name fool you. I doubt anyone I know would call me that."

Pax started answering questions. He felt alive with these people. He knew that Sarah would have loved this moment, so he absorbed all of it to share with her through their strange entanglement.

He told the story of what had put him on the road. He talked about where he had been, where he was headed, and what he was searching for. Roberto nodded in understanding, knowing what Pax meant by *Her* sound.

"Mi Sol's happy note is A," he said. "When she laughs or talks to the boys, she's a D minor chord."

"I am not!" Marisol chirped. "That's a sad chord. I don't have a happy sound with a sad chord."

Pax chuckled and nodded.

"Yeah, you do," he said. "But the F note is dominant, and it sounds beautiful when you laugh."

Roberto smiled as he reached for his wife's hand.

"Your voice turns sadness into happiness, Mi Sol."

Marisol pulled her arm back in pretend annoyance.

"I think you gentlemen should find a different way to describe my sound," she said. "Otherwise, there won't be any tres leches for either of you."

After dessert, which was served despite Marisol's playful threat, the group moved outside to the fire pit, bringing out and tuning their instruments. Nico carried percussion instruments with Afro-Cuban origins. Pepe brought out drumsticks and a plastic bowl.

Roberto and Beto uncased guitars, tuning them before settling on the D minor chord—a tribute to their matriarch's voice—and launched into an acoustic version of *Sultans of Swing*. Pax was amazed at how smoothly Roberto and Beto traded riffs, and when it was time for the iconic guitar solo, Beto played it with an ease that would make Mark Knopfler proud.

As the evening went on, other park residents came by to listen to Pleasure Cruz, with special guest Pax Butler. The songs ranged from pop to classic rock, and Pax admired how the family added Cuban spice to many of the numbers, making them sound original.

Roberto and Marisol gave a heartfelt version of *Shallow*, with Beto adding Latin guitar flair and fingerpicking that felt natural to the song's flow. Cheers echoed throughout the park from everyone within earshot, not just those nearby.

Roberto adjusted his tuning and asked, "Do you write songs, Pax?"

"Yeah, I've written a few. I have a new one I'm working on, but I haven't finished the lyrics. My wife used to like one I wrote while I watched her sleep."

"Play it for us, Pax," Marisol urged.

He hesitated, feeling overwhelmed and out of his depth with his new friends' musical talent.

"Maybe not tonight," he said. "The last time I played it, I lost a friend."

Marisol nodded but didn't press the issue.

"What else do you like to play, Pax?" Beto asked. "If we know it, we can probably play it. Doesn't have to be Latin."

Pax played a few riffs on his guitar as he thought, then glanced at Marisol.

"Jump in on harmony if you know this one."

Pax started the familiar opening riff of *Two of Us*. Roberto laughed and joined in, while Beto quickly picked up the chords and rhythm. Nico contributed on the guiro, and Pepe shook a tambourine. Marisol sang beautifully with Pax as if they had performed together for years.

He was in heaven. This wonderful family had welcomed him without hesitation, and he felt as if he had found a temporary home in the wild. The music played until nearly ten o'clock, and then Marisol told the group to pack up and head in. She invited Pax to join them anytime, weather permitting. Pax expressed his wish to play with them every night, if possible, but he didn't want to be a bother. Marisol assured him he was always welcome and encouraged him to share his songs with the family.

At the fifth wheel, Pax flopped onto the bed, grabbed his phone, and called Sal.

"Sal Cornish, consultant extraordinaire," Sal answered, her thick New England accent emphasizing the "-*aire*."

They talked until after midnight, with Pax listening as Sal shared the story of negotiating her new position from the perspective of someone who didn't want the job and how that made the hiring manager offer more and more until she had to say "yes."

Pax recounted his drive to Memphis, mentioning the bikers, Lara, and the cardiac scan. He described the torturous trip down to Austin and talked about the Cruz family, knowing she would really like them.

"Do they need a busted mandolin in their band?" Sal asked. "I'll quit tomorrow and drive to Austin."

Pax laughed and told Sal they didn't need a mandolin, but he would love to explore the upcoming music festival with her. Sal admitted that taking time off from her new job for a cross-country music trip might be too soon for her boss.

After everything was said, Pax told Sal about the YouTube channel Rob created and how to find it. She promised to check it out and leave some playful comments about watching Pax perform in Nashville. The call ended with plans to talk again soon, and within minutes of putting down his phone, Pax was asleep.

SUNLIGHT FILTERING through the blinds woke Pax before his alarm. He turned away from the glare and, like every morning since turning 60, assessed his body—what hurt, what no longer hurt, what hurt more than previously, and what might begin to hurt. He reflected on his conversation with Sal and reminded himself to call Lara.

He thought about the evening with the Cruz family and smiled. He hadn't felt such a sense of belonging in a long time and wondered why he didn't feel that way with his own kids. Concluding that it was probably his fault, he congratulated himself on this moment of self-discovery and promised to find a way to change things when he got home.

He made himself some coffee and a light breakfast. He considered listening to the next track of the Sarah and Zim Show, but decided to wait.

Instead, he sat down with his guitar to see if he could still play the bluesy flow of *Dream of Me, Please*. His fingers responded, and the chords and fills flowed naturally, albeit at a different tempo, which he preferred over the original. He wasn't sure how the song would sound without Zim's gospel keyboard during the bridge, but he decided to play it for the Cruz family that evening, weather permitting.

A knock on the trailer door interrupted his practice. When he opened it, he saw Beto and Nico standing on the grass.

"Mama thought you might want to walk some dogs with us," Nico said.

Pax took a sip of his coffee and eyed the boys.

"How many dogs are we talking about?" he asked.

"Two," Beto said. "Maybe three, but not all at the same time."

Pax nodded, understanding that Marisol was inviting him into the family through this simple act of kindness.

"Three sounds like it might be a lot," he said with a scowl. "You guys might need some help."

Beto chuckled as Nico pumped his fist. Pax slipped on his sneakers, refilled his coffee, and followed the boys into the park to look for those helpless dogs.

"Was that one of the songs you wrote?" Beto asked as they headed to their first assignment.

"You heard that?" Pax replied.

"Yeah," Beto said. "I hear music everywhere. It's always in my head. So, when I hear someone singing or playing, I pay attention."

"I get that," Pax replied, feeling as if he were talking to a fourteen-year-old version of himself. "I hear music even when there isn't music. Like in the way people speak. Or the sound of a creaking door. Traffic sounds. I hear the tones, and my brain records them."

"Like Mama's happy sound?" Beto asked.

Pax chuckled and restrained himself from ruffling Beto's dark hair out of respect for his maturity.

"Yeah," he said. "Just like that."

The first assignment involved two mismatched dogs: a Shih Tzu named Lacey and a Rottweiler named Sophie. Impressively, the boys showed no fear of Sophie's size as they attached the leashes to both dogs and followed instructions from their owner, Lonnie.

Pax introduced himself to Lonnie, who asked if he was new to the park. They had a brief, superficial chat about Pax's arrival. Lonnie mentioned she was also caught in traffic outside Texarkana but was closer to the front of the backup than Pax. She had decided to drive through the night to reach Austin instead of stopping somewhere between.

"Interesting combination of breeds," Pax said, referring to the dogs sitting patiently, waiting for their walk.

"Yeah," Lonnie said. "I have my 90-pound lap dog and 10-pound watchdog."

Even the boys laughed at this as Nico confidently stroked Sophie's thick head.

"Are you watching over these two guys?" Lonnie asked, her body language relaxing as she grew comfortable in Pax's company.

"Oh no," Pax laughed. "I'm a trainee right now. They're showing me how this whole dog-walking thing works. It's very complicated stuff."

After a few more light comments and laughs, the boys led Pax away from Lonnie's small trailer onto the paths to give Lacey and Sophie a long stretch while they circled the park.

"She likes you," Beto said once they were out of range of Lonnie's trailer.

"What makes you think that?" Pax replied, realizing that Beto was right.

"The tone of her laugh."

"Yup," Pax said, and the three continued into the park.

As they passed various sites, the boys were often called over to help with odd jobs for older nomads. These tasks were usually quick and easy, but they added up as the boys made their loop with Lacey and Sophie.

Pax became their extra set of hands, jogging to the management office to pick up packages or mail, helping to raise or lower awnings, stacking firewood, and connecting or disconnecting utilities. He even assisted an elderly woman getting into the passenger seat of a pickup truck. She struggled to lift her leg onto the running board and eventually grabbed his hand, placing it on her wide bottom to help push her into the seat, then gave him a sly grin once she was settled.

Every time someone tried to tip Pax, he pointed to Beto and told them to "pay his manager." These small acts of service filled Pax with a sense of community and belonging.

When they returned the dogs, Lonnie said they must have walked the entire RV park, considering how thirsty the dogs were. Pax asked if she had an extra water dish because he felt just as parched as the dogs. Laughing, Lonnie brought out a bottle of water for each of them and paid Beto for their services.

Pax noticed that Lonnie had brushed her hair and put on makeup while they were gone. He smiled and was kind, but he didn't give Lonnie any reason to think he was interested in anything beyond helping with the dogs.

"Come on, Peace Butler," Nico laughed. "We have another dog waiting."

Pax shrugged and said goodbye to Lonnie, mentioning how his trainers were harsh taskmasters. As the three walked away, Beto chuckled.

"She really likes you, dude."

"Yeah," Pax replied, but let it go.

The second job involved a single dog—a massive black Great Dane named Apollo, who proved to be very gentle despite his size, standing as tall as Nico.

Beto took the lead with Apollo, while Nico walked alongside the big dog. Pax followed, listening to the boys' chatter about homework and Tio Pepe's upcoming state-mandated math exam.

He asked about their learning experiences with their mother and uncle, and both agreed that their brief time in Florida's public schools was easier than homeschooling. However, they enjoyed traveling with their family and meeting people at various RV parks and music festivals where they performed.

"Are you going to play that song for us tonight, Pax?" Beto brought him back to the morning practice session, where he worked through *Dream of Me, Please* for the first time since The Club.

"Yeah," Pax said. "Normally, there's a piano solo during the bridge, but my piano player is... well, he's..."

"Did he die?" Nico asked, showing the typical bluntness of a ten-year-old boy.

"He did," Pax replied, realizing he hadn't said this out loud since Erin's call. "He was in a bad car accident."

"I'm sorry to hear that," Beto added. "It's always sad to lose friends. Probably worse to lose friends who are bandmates."

"It is," Pax confirmed. "Much worse."

"I think I could figure out a blues solo for the bridge if you want me to, Pax," Beto said. "I heard you playing in A minor, right? Three-quarter time?"

Pax smiled at the oddness of having an in-depth musical discussion with a fourteen-year-old.

"That's right," he said.

"I could add a pentatonic break in there. Maybe add a little Phrygian flair."

"Phrygian flair?" Pax laughed. "Who are you, kid?"

The trio laughed and chatted, sometimes like musical collaborators and other times like kids with their older family friend. The walk with Apollo was faster than the previous outing since most random tasks for the residents had been handled earlier. Beto and Nico stopped by Pax's trailer on their way back to their own mobile apartment.

"You want to see a video of me performing?" Pax asked the pair, happy that they both agreed.

He sat on the steps of the trailer, his phone in hand, showing the boys the videos from Memphis. At the end of *Red Roses*, both boys expressed their feelings with a single word for the emotions Pax drew from the audience.

"Wow."

They felt a little more uplifted after watching the *Sara Smile* video.

"That was your wife's name?" Beto asked, demonstrating emotional maturity beyond his years.

"It was," Pax replied. "Sarah Bing Butler. I met her when I was six, and she wasn't even one."

"That's some love story, man."

"Yes, it is," Pax agreed.

"I like that you're singing to her even though she's gone," Nico said. "It's a tribute. You should sing a song for her with us when we play at the festival."

"Do you think so?"

"Yeah," Nico said. "Beto can ask Mama. She'll say yes."

"Maybe you should do the song you're afraid to play," Beto said. "I can help you."

Pax was in awe of the empathy and kindness shown by these two kids. Reflecting on Rob and Ally, he realized he had let them down as a father. He vowed not to disappoint Puck, Lainey, or

Jazz when he returned to his family. He aimed to be a better role model for them, drawing inspiration from Beto and Nico.

The boys stood up.

"Well, we need to get home for lunch and English class."

"I think your English is just fine," Pax replied, offering encouragement in return for their kindness.

"I'll talk to Mama," Beto said. "Bring your song over tonight. Let's figure it out."

Pax nodded, and the boys headed back to their family, playfully shoving and kicking dirt at each other as they walked down the road, the way brothers their ages do.

Pax retired to the trailer, made a quick lunch, and popped the cap off a beer. He plugged his phone into the charger and selected the next recording on Travis's playlist. Uncertain of what to expect, he composed himself and settled into the chair, prepared for anything.

HE SPENT each day that week working with the boys or with Roberto and Pepe, helping RV park residents in various ways. Every night, he played and sang with the Cruz family, collaborating on original songs and classic blues pieces that moved everyone when Marisol let loose with her full voice. Beto helped him turn *Dream of Me, Please* from a gentle gospel-blues tune into a powerful Chicago-style blues number with crisp bass lines and electric guitar riffs.

After practicing each night, Pax listened to another track from the Sarah and Zim tapes. Sometimes he laughed, sometimes he cried, but he always appreciated Sarah's shared philosophy and rules for living a good life. Although the later tracks were mainly meant for the kids, Pax found that the lessons resonated with him, realizing he needed the principles of being a better person just as much as anyone. Maybe more.

He reflected on the people he had met—Lara, Sal, and the Cruz family—and felt that Sarah was guiding him in learning these lessons. He recalled the miserable cuss he had been at the start of his journey and hoped that someone new would return to South Carolina when his journey was over.

He was learning that leading with kindness was essential and that offering an empathetic ear was medicine for the soul. He also understood his mother's message when she said, "You never have to remember the truth." Truth and trust share more than just four letters, and although the truth sometimes hurts, being lied to eventually hurts more.

He was becoming a better version of himself, and he liked what he saw in the mirror each morning.

His efforts with the residents didn't go unnoticed. One morning, the park manager left a note on his door, stating there was a cancellation for the upcoming weeks and that he was welcome to stay as long as he wished. The note also offered any tools he needed to continue his good work with the park patrons.

He was enjoying his morning coffee and emailing Sal, Lara, Rob, and Ally when he heard a knock at the door. He put on his sneakers and a light jacket, expecting to head out with the Cruz boys. Instead, he opened the door to find Marisol holding a paper plate stacked with pastelitos.

"I brought the pastry if you have the coffee," she said, her wide, enchanting smile brightening the world around her.

Pax invited her in, poured her a cup, and then took a moment to refill his own.

"I have milk in the fridge, but I don't usually put anything in my coffee, so it's nothing special."

"I like it black," she replied, unwrapping the plastic from the pastries as she sat at the small table.

"I knew there was a reason I liked you," he said with a laugh as he handed her the cup.

"Oh, is that why?"

They chatted casually while having their light breakfast. The younger boys were out on the dog and trash pickup route, while the older boys were working on a golf cart motor for one of their neighbors.

"I was ready to join either team," Pax said with a laugh as he bit into a pastelito and moaned in ecstasy. "But I think I like this job much better."

Marisol took a bite of her pastry, then followed it with a sip of coffee.

"You had some good news about staying in the park?" she asked, though it was more a statement than a question.

"Yeah," Pax replied between sips of coffee. "I get to stick around a little longer. At least I'll have a place to crash during the festival. Now, all I need is a ticket."

"No, you don't," Marisol replied coyly as she reached into her back pocket and pulled out a lanyard with a Performer credential and a 3-day armband. "You're our roadie and backup musician for the weekend, Pax."

He stared at the badge and armband, completely amazed.

"What did you do?"

Marisol laughed and said, "I didn't do anything for you that I didn't do for the rest of the band. You're one of us, Pax. At least for as long as we're both here in this part of the world, you're a member of Pleasure Cruz. You'll be on stage with us and enjoying the rest of the festival when we're not performing."

"Beto?" Pax asked, remembering that his young friend had said he would talk to his mother about letting him sing a song on stage.

"Partly," she replied. "But Roberto and I had already discussed including you somehow. The boys see you as another uncle or maybe their adopted abuelo. But the rest of us love having you around. It feels so comfortable. Don't you think?"

"It does," Pax replied with a nod. "It feels natural. I don't know if it's because of the music or because you all were exactly what I needed when I needed it. I know we'll head in different directions soon, but until then, I can't imagine not seeing all of you every day."

"I watched the videos of you in Memphis," Marisol said. "Beto showed me."

"And?"

"And what? I cried. Shut up."

Pax shared with Marisol what had happened that night: the perfume, the panic attack, and the change in his song choice. He also talked about the friendship he built with Lara, which led to stories about Nashville, Sal, and ultimately Claire.

"It's been a weird road so far," he said. "But now it's... a Pleasure Cruz."

"You're an amazing man, Pax Butler."

"You're easily impressed, Marisol Cruz."

Pax embraced Marisol as if she were a long-lost daughter and expressed his gratitude for including him in her family.

"We should do a duet at the festival, Pax. We sounded good that first night we sang together."

"We should. Do you have something in mind?"

Her smile indicated that she did. It also told him that he should be ready to practice all night if needed.

Pleasure Cruz was scheduled to perform on a secondary stage at 7 p.m. on Friday. It was an excellent slot for attracting the day-one crowd, leaving the rest of the weekend free to enjoy other bands, food, and festivities.

The family stayed in the RV park as long as they could to finalize their set list before heading to the festival. Their 90-minute performance featured several original songs, a few popular covers, a duet between Pax and Marisol, and a version of *Dream of Me, Please* with a new arrangement by Pax and Beto. Pax hadn't been this nervous about a show since Butler Service played at a summer festival in Connecticut in the late '80s.

When it was time to head to the festival, the group packed into Pax and Roberto's trucks and drove to the site.

The stage was near the performers' parking lot, and they set up their equipment quickly. Pax was reminded of the busy back-stage area at the Ryman in Nashville but never imagined he would be doing a load-in at his age. Still, he enjoyed the experience with the Cruz family, slinging and taping cables like a pro.

Beto tuned and sound-checked the guitars and bass, while Pepe managed the percussion and microphones. Nico went to the concession stand and returned with a small pallet of bottled water. Even with a fall chill, being a roadie was thirsty work.

After a quick sound check with Pax and Roberto standing about a hundred yards away, they determined that everything was ready and gathered backstage to change into their performance outfits.

An announcement over the main PA system informed the attendees that Pleasure Cruz would perform at the Samsung stage at 7 p.m. The area in front of the stage began to fill up. Pax and Pepe watched from a discreet spot as the crowd grew to a few hundred people.

"Shit," Pax said. "I thought maybe a hundred or so."

Pepe responded by lighting up half a joint, taking a hit, and then passing it to Pax. He stared at the smoldering spliff for a few seconds, trying to remember the last time he had enjoyed what Zim called *pakalolo*. He thought his age might have started with a four back then. Twenty years? He wondered.

"Fuck it," he said, taking a couple of good drags before handing it back and breaking into a coughing fit. Pepe laughed, stubbed out the joint in the palm of his hand, and offered Pax a bottle of water to help with the spasms.

"Not the same shit you remember from the old day, is it?" Pepe laughed.

Pax shook his head as he tried to catch his breath. Marisol approached the two men, saw Pax still coughing intermittently, and swatted Pepe on the arm.

"Damn it, Pepe. I need him to sing tonight."

"I'll be ok," Pax said, feeling the almost immediate impact of the weed on his perception of things.

Marisol gently held his face in her hands and looked into his eyes. In his THC-fogged mind, he thought she might be about to kiss him like Lara had in Memphis. Instead, she smiled and shook her head.

"I'm not sure which of you is a worse influence," she said. "Are you ready?"

"Ready," the two responded in unison.

The band was announced, took the stage, and the night began.

Pax slung an electric bass in preparation for the first few parts of the set. He was used to being the frontman, but this wasn't his band. His acoustic guitar was also tuned and resting on a stand behind him as he moved to stage right and stepped back to let the family take the spotlight. Beto approached him.

"I love this part, man," Beto said with a big smile. "These people have no idea what they're in for. Watch Mama. Or just listen."

Pax eased off the gain on his pedal to quiet the bass and waited as Marisol stepped onto the stage and headed toward the center mic. The crowd erupted as the stunning woman made her way to the front, waving to the now several hundred people in front of her. Pax knew the opening song but had to wait for

Roberto's signal before starting. He sensed he was about to see something special.

She started a cappella, slowly drawing out each note with her rich, bluesy tone. Pax felt chills as he watched Marisol sway to music that only played in her mind while she chanted her rendition of *Piece of My Heart*, her voice pleading with the audience and provoking cheers from many men in front of the stage.

She used her hands and voice, tapping out the syncopation of the lyrics in the air, with her finger raised like a conductor's baton. She turned to Pax, winked, then faced the audience again and shouted in a call-and-response style.

"I want you to... come on!" she pointed the mic toward the audience, who were more than happy to respond.

"COME ON!" they roared back.

Roberto signaled, and Pepe pounded the bass drum as all the guitars started softly, then grew louder.

"Come on!" Marisol called again.

"COME ON!" the audience thundered as one voice.

As the music began, Marisol effortlessly captivated the audience, restarting the lyrics and taking control of the stage. Pax was amazed. The band opened with such intensity that the audience had no choice but to stay and immerse themselves in the sound.

After the initial hook of *Piece of My Heart*, they moved into family originals. Pax took on the role of the quiet bassist, enriching the sound without seeking the spotlight. He was in heaven performing again.

Marisol and Roberto performed a duet, with Roberto serenading her with a love ballad in Spanish. Beto stayed in the background during the originals while Nico played percussion on a platform near Pepe.

The crowd continued to grow.

After playing several songs without a break, Marisol stepped up to the microphone to address the crowd. She introduced each family member and then waved Pax forward from the shadows. Roberto took the bass from him and handed him a wireless microphone.

"This is our friend, Pax Butler," she said to the audience as she placed her hand on his shoulder. "If you haven't seen Pax on YouTube, make sure you do sometime this weekend. And if you don't cry when you see him, your mama didn't raise you right."

The audience clapped and cheered.

"Now, Pepe is back there on the drums. Hi, Pepe! Besides being a drummer, Pepe is also a math teacher."

Pepe waved his sticks in the air, and the crowd cheered for his service as a teacher.

"Pax was married to another teacher, weren't you, Pax?"

He nodded and shrugged, letting Marisol own the moment.

"Now, with all that math knowledge, we thought we'd share some mathematical wisdom with y'all. Does anybody out there know how many it takes?"

The crowd cheered and whooped.

"I said," she continued with a laugh. "Does anybody out there know how many it takes?"

Beto started a rhythmic riff on his guitar. Pax recognized it as the cue, and he and Marisol launched into *It Takes Two* in the style of Marvin Gaye and Kim Weston.

The crowd erupted.

Pax had never had so much fun performing. The Cruz family were natural entertainers. Roberto and Beto seamlessly took turns with guitar solos during a cover of Santana's *Europa*, while Pax followed along with the bass. He watched the crowd pulse and sway as the father and son demonstrated what true mastery looked and sounded like. Meanwhile, Nico danced across the stage, playing his guiro as if it were the only instrument that mattered. Pepe was a master timekeeper and a skilled player of syncopated fills. And Marisol? She was the queen of the stage, and as such, she knew exactly when to step back and let the men in her life shine.

He wished Sarah could see this. He wished Zim could be there to play with them. He wished he had found the spark decades ago to be the musician he felt like that night. Pleasure Cruz had let him experience that moment—the spotlight, the rush of captivating the audience. It was a genuine performance vibe that he had never reached before.

As the set wound down, Marisol called him forward again and told the audience their last song would be a Pax Butler original. The crowd cheered, even though they didn't know what to expect. Beto handed him his acoustic guitar and stood beside him. Pax went through the routine of checking the tuning, even though he was sure Beto had already done it. To his credit, the kid didn't stop him but simply waited until Pax was ready to start.

He looked down in front of the stage and saw Roberto slip into the audience and start recording on his phone. He nodded to Roberto, who responded with a thumbs-up, and then he turned toward the audience, gazing out into the darkness. He was unaware of how many people were now in front of him, but he knew it was more than he had ever performed for in his life.

"The last time I tried to perform this song for an audience," he said, plucking at the strings absentmindedly. "I fell off the stage, cracked my elbow, and busted my picking hand."

Pax waved his hand above his head.

"I also killed one of my closest friends."

The sudden silence from the audience told him that he had them hooked on the story.

"His name was Tomas, and he was the best guitar I've ever had."

The new sound showed they were relieved he wasn't a killer

but sad about losing his favorite guitar. One voice shouted, "Oh no! Not Tomas!"

"I know," Pax replied as he continued. "So, my elbow is healed. My hand is mostly healed. But tonight, I have to do this without Tomas."

The crowd cheered.

"But I have this guy," he smiled, pointing at Beto. "This is the best guitarist I have ever performed with."

From the audience, Roberto called out, "Me too!"

"You ready, pal?"

Beto responded with a slow, soulful blues riff that transitioned into the song. With Pepe laying down the beat, *Dream of Me, Please*, in its new form, flowed smoothly from Beto's fingers and Pax's voice. When Beto's final sustained note faded into the night, the crowd erupted.

Pax hugged Beto tightly, expressing his gratitude for helping him regain his courage. Marisol returned to the stage, wiping her eyes, and headed to the microphone.

"Pax Butler!" she shouted to the crowd. Pax bowed and turned to applaud all the members of Pleasure Cruz.

"Thanks for stopping by!" Marisol shouted at the crowd. "We're Pleasure Cruz, and we'll be back next weekend to do it all again."

Roberto rejoined them on stage after finishing the recording of the performance, and the entire ensemble took a deep bow to the cheers of an unknown number of new fans. Backstage, Pax hugged Marisol as tightly as he had hugged Beto and thanked her for adopting him.

The ACL load-out crew descended on the stage to help disassemble the drums and remove all the cables and tape, preparing for the Saturday morning shows. Pepe, Roberto, and Pax moved the equipment to the trucks while Marisol, Beto, and Nico sold merch to their new fans. The trio took plenty of selfies, signed CD cases and T-shirts, and chatted with everyone.

"Pax!" Marisol shouted to him as he was climbing back onto the stage for another load of cables. "Get over here and talk to your fans."

Pax scowled and moved toward the merch tent, where fans asked for selfies and autographs, mostly middle-aged women who had been moved to tears by the beauty of *Dream of Me, Please*. He felt overwhelmed by the attention. The closest he had ever come to feeling this level of appreciation for his music was a round of tequila after a show.

As the crowd of merch buyers thinned and Pax and Beto grew a bit tired of selfies, he heard a voice he recognized.

"Pax!"

He looked toward the voice and saw someone he never expected to see again. He felt both intrigued and uneasy.

"Hi, Mike," he said, walking cautiously toward the big biker he met in Tennessee. "What are you doing here?"

Mike extended his meaty right hand and shook Pax's until Pax laughed and cried, "Uncle."

"Cassie and I were walking toward the beer tent when I heard your name called on the PA."

Mike nodded at Marisol, who had been watching the interaction with concern.

"Cassie?" Pax asked.

The tall, blonde, heavily tattooed woman who had dropped Mike's brother Joe to the ground with a well-placed knee stepped into the tent's light and offered her hand.

"We didn't get a chance to be properly introduced," she said. "It was kind of a stressful day."

He smiled and recalled her kindness in returning the box with Sarah's rings that Mike's brother had stolen from his trailer. He shook her hand and suddenly felt at ease.

"Where's Joe? What about the rest of the crew?" he asked, not caring but looking for something to talk about.

"I sent Joe home that day," Mike said. "Taking your rings was beyond the pale, and I needed him to learn a lesson. Cassie's been riding with me ever since."

Mike and Cassie shared a look that expressed feelings far stronger than their love for motorcycles.

"The rest of them went home after NOLA. They all have jobs to get to. I have my own shop, so I called back and said I was taking some time off. Cassie and I have been riding around and exploring."

Pax introduced Mike and Cassie to Marisol and the boys.

"Your voice blows me away," Cassie said to Marisol. "I think I can sing, but when I hear someone like you, I'm glad I never tried to make a career out of it."

Marisol beamed at the compliment and handed Cassie a complimentary copy of the Pleasure Cruz CD.

"Beers?" Mike asked.

"Not for us," Marisol said, wrapping her arms around the boys. Beto pretended to protest, and the adults chuckled.

"I like beer," Pepe said as he approached the group to help pack up the remaining merch.

Pax was glad to hear Pepe offer to join them. He wanted a few beers after the stage work but didn't want to abandon the Cruz family after their incredible kindness.

"We need to get the equipment back to the site—" he began to say.

"I'll drive your truck, Pax," Roberto interrupted as he joined the conversation and introduced himself to Mike and Cassie. "Pepe can drive mine, and he'll come back to hang out and bring you home."

The logistics were settled. Pax agreed to stay, have drinks

with Mike and Cassie, and wait for Pepe to join them. He hugged Marisol and Roberto and high-fived the boys.

"We'll come back tomorrow and watch some other guitar players, okay, Beto?"

Beto agreed, then Pax, Mike, and Cassie headed toward the beer tent.

As it turned out, Mike Dunn wasn't your typical biker boss. He owned a seven-million-dollar custom motorcycle business near Atlanta. His motorcycle club, "Pains in the Ace," focused more on marketing and showcasing some of the custom wheels his company produced.

Cassie Lange, unsurprisingly, was a tattoo artist who handled all the club members' ink. She had started dating Joe before the crew went on their recent trip and ended things as soon as the ring incident happened. That was when she got to know Mike better.

Pax explained why he stayed in Memphis instead of going to the NOLA music festival. Mike laughed and said he had a similar medical issue, but his outcome wasn't as good as Pax's, and now he had stents in two of his cardiac arteries.

Mike said, "This getting old shit is the worst."

"I know, it's a terrible design for an animal, isn't it?" Pax replied as the second beer settled in. "We get older. We have some money. We gain some wisdom. But then all our bodily functions start to fail. It's a terrible fucking design."

Mike agreed by tapping his red plastic cup against Pax's just as Pepe arrived. He got up, and then he and Pepe went to grab more beers. Cassie leaned in toward Pax.

"Do you still have the rings, Pax?"

"In my pocket. Since the Joe incident, they're always with me."

"Good," she said. "And the one on your finger that you keep

spinning with your thumb? Why isn't that one in the box in your pocket, too?"

Pax looked at his finger and noticed the red line underneath the ring, indicating where it had been rubbing against his skin.

"A reminder, I guess."

"Of what, pain?" Cassie said pointedly. "If she's gone, she's gone. If she's in your heart, it doesn't matter what that ring means."

Pax didn't argue with her. He didn't know her well enough to explain the pain. However, he also knew that, eventually, he needed to take stock of his totems of Sarah and decide what was necessary.

"I want to do something for you, Pax," Cassie said. She reached inside her T-shirt and pulled out a gold chain with three rings. She held the large one up for Pax to see.

"He was only thirty. We had been married for just two years when he decided he needed to drive home after midnight with a blood alcohol level of 0.28. He never made it home. A week later, I miscarried. So, I know what loss is. I know what pain feels like. I know what anger at being left behind looks like, Pax."

Cassie took Pax's hand and placed her left hand in his so he could see the tattoo of a ring where her wedding band used to be.

"I still have it here if I want to look at it. Or if I want to hold it, it's always around my neck. There's no box in my pocket to keep track of. Let me do the same for you, Pax. Let me give you a permanent token of your wife, and then you can wear all the rings together around your neck."

She held his gaze even as Mike and Pepe returned with cold beers.

"What did we miss?" Mike asked, sensing the mood of the moment.

Pax nodded at Cassie.

"I think I'm getting my first tattoo," he said.

PAX REMOVED the small bandage covering his left ring finger. He looked at the message inked where his wedding ring used to be.

3F-2S

The simple message bordered by the edge of a virtual ring represented his lasting connection to Sarah.

Cassie always carried her tattoo gun and a few small ink vials. It took her several attempts to draw the letters at the right size to fit on his finger, but once she transferred the design to his skin, Pax knew this would be better than wearing his plain gold wedding ring.

"Will it hurt?" he asked Cassie.

"The skin is thin and close to the bone, so yeah, it will hurt. But this pain is nothing compared to how much your heart hurts when you miss her."

Ultimately, it hadn't hurt as much as he expected. Cassie was gentle, and the message was simple. There were no fills, no shading—just bold, serif letters to symbolize Sarah's joyful sound. His hand felt lighter, yet he could still sense the weight of the three rings on the chain around his neck. They felt good there. They felt secure.

Beto thought the tattoo was cool, but Nico scowled as if Pax had grown a second head. Since Roberto and Pepe already had tattoos, Pax's small ink spot was nothing to them.

Marisol arrived for coffee while the Cruz men went about their good deeds in the RV park. She studied the message, gently caressing his hand and feeling a maternal urge to comfort him during this significant life change.

"What does it mean?" she asked.

"Remember when we talked about your sound? I mentioned that my wife's sound was a D note. Third fret—Second string."

Pax showed Marisol the lyrics he had started for *The Sound of You*. She sniffed and wiped her eyes while reading them. When she finished, she handed the notebook back.

"You know, Pax," she said, chuckling a little, "Sometimes you come across as a total hard case. But you're probably the most romantic person I've ever met... after Roberto."

"I'll take that as a compliment," he said.

"Are you staying through the week to perform again?"

"I haven't decided yet," he replied. "But for now, yes, if you'll have me."

"Good," Marisol said as she stood up to leave the trailer.

"Listen," Pax said, stopping her before she reached the door. "I imagine you and Roberto don't get much quality time together with all of you living in that RV. Why don't you let Pepe and me take the boys back to the festival, and you and Roberto..."

Marisol faced him directly. Her body language suggested she might shout or throw something. He raised his hands in surrender.

"I promise I won't let them get tattoos," he laughed. "And only one beer each. Okay, maybe two."

Marisol walked over and bent down to look at him where he sat, her face unreadable. She reached up and placed her hand on his cheek.

"No tattoos. No beer. Have them back in time for dinner."

Pepe and Pax enjoyed beers while the boys stuck to soft drinks as they strolled around the festival grounds. Pax and Beto paused occasionally to watch random musicians performing in open areas. He told Beto that he learned to play fills and riffs by observing how guitarists' hands moved along the neck. Beto shared that he could recreate sounds just by hearing them, which made Pax feel even more inadequate with his chosen instrument.

Periodically, attendees from the previous night's Pleasure Cruz performance approached to express how much they enjoyed the show. Several mentioned having watched Pax on YouTube and hoped for more videos. Each time, Beto remarked on the tone he detected in people's voices beyond their words. As the day went on, Pax realized that he and Beto were of the same species.

They wandered around the festival for three hours, snacking on junk food, enjoying great music, and reveling in their minor fandom. Beto started complaining about boredom before Nico did, but Nico soon joined in.

Pax and Pepe wanted to give Roberto and Marisol as much time as possible, so Pax asked a festival worker for suggestions on entertaining some bored kids in Austin. They decided on the Austin Zoo, a fun way to spend a few hours before heading back to the RV park, though Pax suspected Pepe might have enjoyed it more than the boys.

After returning the boys to their parents and with dinner still a couple of hours away, Pax took his guitar and notebook to the picnic table outside the trailer, trying to work through different chord progressions for *The Sound of You*. No new words emerged, and he was uncertain about the bridge, so he shifted his focus to writing out the tablature for the new version of *Dream of Me, Please*.

"I saw you last night."

Pax looked up and saw Lonnie slowly walking down the road past his site.

"Oh no," he laughed. "Was I doing anything illegal?"

Lonnie laughed and toyed with her hair.

"Well, if making middle-aged women cry is a crime, then yeah, you are guilty, sir."

Pax played a quick riff and sang, "Baby, I never meant to make you sad."

Lonnie laughed and clapped, and Pax invited her to sit with him. He wanted to talk. He felt better than he had in what... months? Years? He wanted some good old-fashioned, free-flowing conversation.

"I stopped by early to see if you wanted to grab some lunch," Lonnie said.

"Lunch, huh?" he laughed. "I was out with the boys and their uncle at the festival. Had a couple of beers for lunch. I probably should eat something. Sometimes I forget."

"I already had lunch," she said, leaning on her hand. "Too late."

"Another time," Pax said.

Lonnie looked at the tablature Pax had written in his notebook.

"What's that? Is that music?"

Pax flipped the notebook to show the lines and bars of the tab.

"Yeah, this is music for a guitar. See, each of these lines is a string, and the lines that cross them are frets. The numbers on the strings show which finger to use on that string, on that fret."

Pax counted the first five frets on his guitar neck.

"The o means you play it open, and the x means skip it. So here..."

Pax filled out a new grid with numbers.

"This is a D chord. Second fret on the first string, third fret on the second, second fret on the third, open on the fourth. Skip the top two strings, although there are some variations you can add for different extensions, inversions, and such."

Pax played the D chord, leaving Lonnie entranced.

"How do you know which fingers to use on each string?" she asked.

"That comes with practice, but generally, you're trying to find a pattern that doesn't require you to cross your fingers or stretch too far. Most of the patterns are already known, but sometimes you have to improvise."

He continued explaining tabs and guitar fingering to Lonnie. He thoroughly enjoyed sharing his skill and thought he could teach guitar lessons if that was the direction his life went.

Lonnie leaned back and looked at Pax.

"How about dinner instead of lunch?"

Pax paused before sending a text to Marisol.

Can I bring a +1 to dinner?

He smiled at the response.

"Do you like Cuban food, Lonnie?"

HE HADN'T FELT this good in ages. Maybe it was the food, the beer, or the tequila Pepe bought on the way back to the RV park. But more likely, it was the feeling of belonging, camaraderie, and family.

Although Lonnie was initially attracted to Pax, she felt a stronger connection with Pepe. They sat close, sipping tequila, enjoying Marisol's delicious food, and genuinely laughing. As the night went on, they moved even closer, sharing gentle touches on shoulders and knees and exchanging lingering glances. Pax watched them, appreciating their growing infatuation. With a simple gesture, he had brought them together and avoided yet another conversation about why he wasn't looking for a romantic relationship.

"I don't think she likes you that way anymore," Beto said as he sat next to Pax and opened his guitar case.

"You are correct, sir," Pax replied. "And that's a good thing."

"Pepe hasn't had a girlfriend for a while. Maybe it's time."

Pax felt a hand on his shoulder and looked up to see Marisol standing behind him.

"Thank you for today, Pax. For me. For Roberto. For Pepe. For all of us."

"You're welcome, Miss Lady," Pax said with a smile. "It's a small token of gratitude for everything you've given me this week."

Marisol leaned down and kissed Pax on the cheek.

"Kindness has no price," she said.

"That sounds like a good title for a song," Beto said. "I told you once. I told you twice. Kindness doesn't have a price. Something like that."

Pax thought Beto might be onto something. As the other Cruz family members brought out their instruments, he pulled out his guitar, and another night of music began.

PAX HUMMED a random tune as he packed his trailer for the trip north. The second show the night before had been as fun as the first, although a light drizzle had kept the crowd small. Still, even with a scheduled set list, he loved the spontaneity of the performance and believed Marisol could be a big star if she wanted to be. And as before, Beto had amazed him with his guitar skills and his natural ease and comfort on stage. Pax knew he would watch the kid's career grow for years.

Once everything was stowed, strapped, and secured, Pax walked down the path to the Cruz family's RV, where everyone sat outside without instruments.

"Everything packed away?" he asked.

"All set," Roberto replied. "Heading back to Miami in the morning."

Pax looked around at his adopted family and felt a bittersweet flutter in his chest. Roberto and Marisol reminded him of Sarah and himself. Beto and Nico made him long for more quality time with his grandchildren. Pepe was like Zim but without the craziness that often erupted from his best friend.

And there was Lonnie, sitting on Pepe's lap. Pax had watched their budding romance grow over the past week and knew it was more than a fleeting connection. There was real chemistry and a genuine bond. If the roots were true, Lonnie wouldn't end up like Erin, in love with someone who couldn't commit.

Pepe had decided to stay a little longer until Lonnie's vacation ended, and she had to return to Georgia. They would have several hundred miles to spend together, figuring out where their romance might lead. For now, they were infatuated and carefree, unconcerned with others' opinions.

"North, Pax?" Marisol asked, a hint of sadness in her voice.

"Yeah," he replied. "You know, I hadn't planned on getting on any stages when I started this journey. I was trying to find what was missing after Sarah passed, and I think I found some of it, although not where I expected it to be. I enjoy performing for people, no matter how many are in the crowd. It's a place of joy for me."

"Your YouTube channel is getting a lot of views," Beto offered, "so maybe you're giving as much as you're getting from performing."

Pax looked at Marisol and Roberto in disbelief.

"Where did you find this guy?" he laughed. "He's part philosopher, part musical prodigy. Man, I wish I had been that cool when I was your age, Beto."

"We all do," Pepe added.

The group spent the rest of the evening sharing stories, food, and laughter. There was singing, too, all a cappella, and Marisol proved to be the only one in the group who could hold a tune without any backing music. Hearing others sing off-key brought even more laughter, and Pax thought he hadn't laughed that much or that loudly in a very long time.

As he watched his adopted family savor each moment of his last night with them, he realized that perhaps the greatest gift was receiving joy by giving joy—Beto had been onto something with his profound comment.

Pax stood, and the eyes around him followed his movement. One by one, they all got to their feet.

"I'm heading out early tomorrow," he said. "I'd love to stay and sing and laugh with you all night, but the longer I stay, the harder it is to leave."

Nico was the first to hug him, the brave little man fighting his emotions as his adopted abuelo embraced him and told him what an amazing young man he was. Next were Pepe and Lonnie, and Pax wished them the best in their adventures together.

"Listen," he told them as he pointed to Roberto and Marisol. "That kind of love is rare, but it is not unattainable. You two have to find your own song and not try to live up to the standards set by others. Always communicate. Always share your soul. If you are meant to be together, well, do these things and you will be."

Pax sought redemption for failing to recognize Zim and Erin's unfulfilled love. He believed his advice to Lonnie and Pepe could be a good starting point. He knew it was rough and incomplete, but being new to this philosophy racket, he hoped his guidance would improve with practice.

Roberto shook his hand and hugged him, thanking him for being part of their family, even if only for a short while, and invited him to visit them in Miami if he ever passed through. Pax said that he now had two reasons to go to Florida—two more than he ever thought he would have. Roberto laughed and patted him on the back.

Marisol said nothing. She hugged him with a ferocity he had

only ever felt with Sarah. She sobbed quietly, then wiped her eyes, looked into his, and gave him a chaste kiss on his lips.

"Gracias, pájaro cantor," he said, his Central New York accent mangling the syllables.

Marisol laughed, her tone rising to an A note that showed her enjoyment of his attempt.

"Google?" she asked.

"Does it show?"

She replied by patting his chest.

"Sing, Pax. Wherever you are. Sing. Find her sound in your voice."

Pax kissed her hand, acknowledging the message she conveyed, and then Marisol turned and entered the RV.

Beto approached Pax and extended his hand. Pax reached into his pocket and pulled out a folded piece of paper. Instead of shaking Beto's hand, he handed the paper to him. Beto looked at it, and his eyes widened.

"You wrote that song?" he asked, surprised. "Kindness Has No Price?"

"No," Pax said. "I wrote the lyrics. You write the song. Do something with this."

Beto read the page, his jaw tightening and relaxing from the emotion of the lyrics and the moment.

"I see myself in you, Beto. Only, I didn't have your natural talent. You'll be a world-beater if you combine that talent with the drive I had at your age."

Beto looked at Pax and pursed his lips.

"Maybe you and I could write more songs together. I don't think there has ever been a writing partnership between a teenager and a..."

"Senior citizen?" Pax laughed. "I would like that, Beto, but even more, I would like to help you write for yourself. Find your voice. You have my email and phone number. If you have any thoughts or questions about songwriting, I'm just across the wires."

"That sounds like the title of another song," Beto said. "I'm Just Across the Wires."

"Write it."

Beto hesitated before embracing Pax tightly. No words were spoken; only the past blended with the future.

In the morning, Pax left the RV park and headed to the highway. With no urgency driving him, he took his time traveling the back roads to explore parts of the world he had never seen before. He listened to the recordings of Sarah and Zim, some of them multiple times—sometimes laughing, sometimes crying, and always feeling their love through their dedication to preserving Sarah's legacy for Pax and his family.

CHAPTER 6

ARRIVING IN GOLDEN, he parked the fifth wheel almost perfectly on the first try. The hookups for power, water, and even a connection to flush his chemical toilet were easily accessible, and he was set up and situated in record time, a personal best.

The RV park was pleasant and clean, situated near a park that bordered Clear Creek, offering a picturesque view as he walked along the paths that ran parallel to the stream, exploring his temporary neighborhood. He talked with a few other nomads in the park, getting a lay of the land—where to eat and shop, the cheapest gas, and the sights to see. He didn't plan on staying long in Golden, so he intended to keep to himself for the first few days while he strategized his goal to stand on the stage at the most incredible outdoor venue music has ever known: Red Rocks Amphitheatre.

With a full tank and some essentials from the grocery store, Pax parked his truck in downtown Golden and wandered the streets. The air was crisp and dry, with no sign of snow. The forecast predicted increasingly cold, dry weather for the next several weeks, making a "White Christmas" unlikely for residents of the greater Denver area.

As he walked down Ford Street, Pax saw a sign for Bob's Atomic Burgers, one of the eateries highly recommended by the residents of the RV park. The place didn't look like much from the outside, and that impression didn't change as he stepped through the door. Pax frowned, unimpressed with the ambiance, but trusting in the culinary aptitude of his fellow nomads, he approached the counter and filled out the order sleeve to customize a cheeseburger and fries. He figured it was hard to mess up such a staple of American cuisine, and even if it was mediocre, it would still satisfy his appetite.

As he waited, Pax took out his phone and sent updates to Rob and Ally, informing them of his location, how long he planned to stay, and his destination once he had his shot at Red Rocks. He scrolled through spam emails that appeared like weeds, blocking the senders as Travis had instructed.

"George of the Jungle?" a tattooed and pierced young lady called out.

He looked at the slip of laminated paper he had been given, recognizing the exact words the server had just spoken, and realized this was their way of calling his number. The waitress delivered his food and made small talk until his smile signaled he was ready to eat.

Pax took a bite of the burger and immediately felt his senses heighten as it hit his tongue. The flavor, texture, and rich blend of the cheese with the burger fat caught him off guard. He had to consciously control how quickly he ate, as his hunger only increased with each bite. This simple meal triggered all the right brain chemicals, making him want to devour the food and order more.

As he chewed, he glanced around and noticed a clever yet kitschy facade hiding the culinary mastery coming from the kitchen. His initial impression of the place changed, and he felt it was one of the best surprises he had encountered on his journey.

The young lady returned and asked how he liked his meal. Pax raised his hand as he swallowed before speaking.

"I'm going to need another one to go," he said, struggling not to chew and speak at the same time.

"We get that a lot," the waitress laughed as she turned to fetch Pax another order sleeve.

"Make that two," Pax said from behind her, hearing her laugh again.

Pax chuckled while continuing to eat, realizing how he must look to the woman. She returned with two sleeves.

She watched as the final bite of the burger vanished into Pax's mouth.

"Jeez, you ate that fast. Did you even taste it?"

Pax swallowed and took a sip of his drink.

"Oh, I tasted it alright. That's probably the best burger I've had since I was about your age. Maybe even younger, considering how my memory is these days."

"Cool. If you like it that much, give us a five-star on Yelp."

Pax nodded. He didn't know what Yelp was, but he assumed it was an online service and trusted his IT department contact, Travis, to know for sure.

That evening, Pax sat at the picnic table outside his fifth wheel, watching the light fade over the park as he ate his cold cheeseburger from Bob's. The air temperature had noticeably dropped since his arrival, falling another five degrees each time he thought about it.

He browsed through his emails again and saw something from Rob, but he noted to read it later. He was more interested in cleaning out the spam messages. Most came from bogus senders with bogus offers for equally bogus products and services. They were easy to spot and quickly flagged as junk.

One message caught his eye. It was from someone named Alicent Klein. Although the email came from a generic Hotmail address that somewhat matched the name, it was the message's subject line that truly grabbed his attention.

Call me when you get to Colorado.

He scowled. How could someone he didn't know have any idea about his visit to Colorado? Travis had warned him that some spammers were very clever with their messages and often found ways to grab your attention by mentioning something personal. He decided to play it safe and marked the message as junk.

With his inbox clean, he glanced at the other cold burger in the bag and debated treating himself, even if it meant a restless night with a stomach full of meat. He decided it would be just as tasty for breakfast, so he rolled up the bag, finished the rest of his beer, and went back into the fifth wheel to listen to some music while hoping to find inspiration to work on the song that had been brewing inside him since Nashville.

He tuned his guitar and played a little blues riff. The fingers of his picking hand were no longer as stiff as they had been at the beginning of his journey. He could fingerpick a few patterns that had once eluded him, which made him happy.

He turned on the music app that Travis had loaded on his phone and chose a country-folk playlist. He spent an hour playing along with the songs and even sang a bit with the tunes he knew. The experience was calming and cathartic, but no new words for his own song came to mind.

When he decided to take a break for the night, Pax looked at the fingertips of his left hand and saw the indentations from the strings. His calluses had come back. He then flexed his right hand and noticed the improved mobility of his fingers. Playing with the Cruz family had done more to heal his hand than anything else he had tried. From now on, he would play every day, never letting those calluses soften or his fingers stiffen again. But for the moment, he would use his rehabbed fingers to play a game on his phone until sleep took over.

A bright red text message indicator appeared when he looked at his phone. The notification ping had been muted because of the music. Opening the text app, he stared at the sender's name: Audra. He tapped her name to read the message. His other hand instinctively moved to the rings around his neck, clutching them through his shirt.

Hi. Ally told me about your trip. I'm glad you're well. Thanks for reaching out.

He read the message over and over, trying to figure out if it was a call to connect or a sign of closure. He felt a swirling feeling in his chest. Happiness? Fear? He couldn't tell which.

He set the phone down and looked out the window, weighing his options. In the end, he decided to reply, but later. He was too caught up in the Red Rocks project and wanted to ensure he had nothing else pulling his attention when he reached out to her again.

And then, words came, but not the words he had been waiting for.

Pax grabbed his pen and looked for his notebook, finally finding it under the table against the trailer's wall. He slammed it down on the table, flipped it open to a blank page, and started to write. Though the words flowed like water from his pen, it took over an hour to shape the lyrics into something he could set to music—an ode to Audra and his reckless treatment of what could have been.

LATE THE NEXT AFTERNOON, Pax parked his truck in the Upper North Lot of Red Rocks Park and Amphitheatre, slung his travel guitar case over his shoulder, and headed up the path to the Visitor Center.

He knew the Visitor Center would close in a couple of hours. Still, he didn't regret making another trip to Bob's for lunch, even though he had lost track of time reading about Red Rocks and the logistics of getting there. Once he realized how late it was, he hurried back to his truck, still chewing, and drove to the park before it closed.

He hadn't driven recklessly from Bob's, but he might not have always come to complete stops at intersections or when turning right on red. Nonetheless, he arrived safe and ready to try to charm his way onto the stage.

The walk to the Visitor Center was quick, and as Pax entered, he was amazed by the Hall of Fame. The walls were decorated with photos and memorabilia of the legends who had walked the same boards he hoped to stand on. He felt a little embarrassed even thinking he might deserve a shot at that sacred stage, but that didn't slow him down as he looked for someone to help turn that dream into reality. He silently wished Sal were with him to use her powers of persuasion as she had at the Ryman in Nashville.

Near the entrance of Ship Rock Grille, Pax saw a large man in a security uniform. He approached and asked to speak with the facility's manager.

"Why?" the big man asked, clearly annoyed that his time spent staring off into space was interrupted.

Pax had no plan, so he just laid it out.

"I want to stand on the stage and sing a song to my late wife."

The guard examined Pax carefully, and his face seemed to soften. Pax hoped he was a romantic and would help him realize this vision.

"No," the guard said, his attention drawn to a group of

middle school kids reaching out to touch some of the items in the Hall of Fame. "Do. Not. Touch. The artifacts."

The kids glanced at the guard and Pax before hurrying away. The guard's eyes tracked each boy as they left, mischief brewing in each step.

Pax felt confused.

"Were you talking to the kids when you said 'no,' or—"

"I was talking to you," the guard said. "No getting on the stage."

Pax hadn't expected to be shut down so directly. He tried a different tactic, reaching out his hand.

"I'm Pax," he said. "Pax Butler. You are?"

The guard glanced at Pax's hand before turning his attention to his face.

"Robert."

"Robert. That's my son's name. Robert, great. Listen, Robert, is there someone I can talk to about this? I'm talking about 5 minutes on the stage, then I'm gone."

"No," Robert interrupted him again and continued to survey the Visitor Center.

Pax sighed in resignation and then decided to search for the administrative offices. He channeled his inner Sal, trying to find a more subtle way to reach the manager.

"Well, thanks anyway, Robert. It was a long shot. Listen, where are the restrooms? I had a big lunch and—"

"That way," Robert said, sweeping his hand authoritatively to signal to Pax that he needed to move on.

Pax followed the big man's directions and found the restrooms, but he didn't need to use them, so he wandered around looking for a door that said "Authorized Personnel Only," or something to that effect. Soon, he found himself at the top of the famous bowl, gazing down at the stage a hundred feet below.

He thought about all the music that had poured off that stage over the years. He knew he was undeserving, but damn it, Sarah *was* deserving. The stage was right there. He could walk down and—

"Pax Butler?" The young woman who spoke his name advanced almost aggressively toward him. Robert followed closely behind her.

"Yes."

The woman extended her hand, and Pax shook it. While she talked, she adjusted her glasses several times.

"Um, yes, I am Alicent Klein. I manage the facility, at least today and on many other days, but there are others who... In any case. Did you get my email? Your son said you would call when you got into town, but I didn't hear from you, so I assumed you were either not here yet or not coming."

"My son? You talked to Rob?"

"Yes," she replied.

Pax thought about the unread email from Rob. He remembered the other email from a stranger saying, "Call me when you get to Colorado." Rob had been back-channeling on his behalf, and he hadn't even known.

"I'm sorry," Pax said, a little confused. "I remember your email, but didn't know who you were, so I marked it as junk."

Alicent straightened her glasses again with a tight smile.

"Well, you can't be too safe these days," she said. "I, myself, have been the victim of a catfishing incident... in any case. Welcome to Red Rocks, Mr. Butler. Would you like to perform today, or do you want to schedule something?"

Pax chuckled. Rob had arranged everything. Somehow he had persuaded this quirky young woman to let his aging father sing an ode to his late wife on the most scenic stage in the world.

"Wait," he said. "How did you know it was me?"

Alicent aimed her pen at the guitar slung over his back.

"Your son mentioned that you were coming and shared your plans, along with a link to some of your other recent performances."

She pointed her pen at the security guard and adjusted her glasses again.

"Robert told me a man was searching for someone in charge. I connected the dots."

Pax was filled with admiration for his son. He made a mental note to call Rob when he returned to the fifth wheel.

"Is today okay?" Pax asked, knowing that the facility would be closing soon.

"Absolutely," Alicent chirped, turning to Robert. "Robert, can you help Mr. Butler down to the stage?"

Turning back to Pax, she said, "If I had known you would be here today, I could have had a microphone ready for you."

Pax chuckled.

"No, no, this will be enough. Thank you, Alicent, for making this happen."

"It is my pleasure," she replied, then added, "Robert, can you use Mr. Butler's phone to record his performance?"

Robert rolled his eyes and nodded.

"Please send me a copy, Mr. Butler? I have watched your other performances on YouTube. We at Red Rocks are proud to be part of your musical journey."

He agreed and followed Robert who was clearly unhappy about helping him with something he had declined just minutes earlier. Robert led him to the stage and took his phone to record the impromptu performance.

Pax stepped reverently onto the stage, quickly removed his guitar from the case, and tuned it. His breath caught in his throat as he gazed up into the rows of bleacher seats that rose between the enormous red sandstone formations. The awe he felt at viewing the iconic venue from that vantage point was matched only by the feeling he experienced while looking into the face of his newborn daughter. He took several deep, cleansing breaths to prepare himself for the mission that brought him to this spot, then he kissed the small rings around his neck.

"Let me know when you're ready," Robert said, positioning himself in front and slightly to the side for a clearer view of Pax on the stage.

Pax emerged from his trance and looked out at the bleachers. A small tour group of about twenty adults and children had taken seats in the lower rows to his right. Among them were the boys he had seen in the Visitor Center. One of them called out, "Foo Fighters!"

Pax laughed and nodded at Robert, who nodded back to indicate that the phone was recording. Then he felt himself slip into performance mode.

"I know you probably didn't expect a performance on your tour today," he said, looking specifically at the adults in the group. "Frankly, I'm shocked they let me up here."

"Me too," Robert replied, and the small crowd tittered.

"Thanks, Robert." Pax drew a deep breath and slowly fingerpicked a D chord. "A few years ago, I lost my wife. She was my breath. My pulse. My soul. I've been on a kind of pilgrimage for several months, visiting places we always talked about and trying to find her again through the music of those places. I'm still searching and listening.

"The song I'm about to play is in the key of D, for those of you who are music students. The D note was the sound she made when she was happy. It was in her laugh, or even just in saying 'Hi' when I got home from a gig. This note here."

Pax pressed down the second string on the third fret and plucked it, then continued fingerpicking. He glanced at Robert, saw the big man's jaw clenched tight, and knew he was feeling something, too.

"Sarah was a high school teacher, but she also taught life lessons that, frankly, when I was younger, I thought were cute. The older I get and reflect on them, the more I realize how incredibly wise she was."

Pax played the chords in the key of D major as he spoke, smoothly shifting from the introduction to the performance. He asked the small audience if they could hear him, and they nodded or clapped to show they could. He kept playing while he spoke.

"'Know who you are and whose you are,' she would say. I guess she meant that you should always be aware of yourself and understand who sees you as essential in their lives. Living is not just about what we do and say, it's also about who we impact with what we do and say."

Pax changed the guitar chord and played a little finger roll as he continued.

"She also said, 'People matter more than things—every time.' I understand that one. It's harder to lose a friend or family member than a book, bicycle, or any other replaceable item. Even a guitar, and I know that personally. People can't be replaced. Everyone is unique, so you need to cherish that uniqueness."

Robert nodded. The small audience grew quiet, including the students. Pax looked up and saw Alicent sitting several rows above the tour group along the aisle. He started playing with intention, the voice of his guitar filling the cool air.

"She also said, 'Love big, forgive quickly, laugh, be present, and always be thankful.' Thank you, Alicent. Thank you, Robert. And thank you all for indulging me during your field trip."

And then he sang. Without a microphone or amplifier, Pax

sang, and his voice echoed through the acoustics of the bowl. For three minutes and fifty-seven seconds, he poured his heart out to this small group of strangers, using the words of Neil Diamond and the muse of Sarah Bing Butler. The small audience clapped as the final chorus and chords of *Play Me* faded against the rocks.

Some of the adults in the tour group wiped their eyes. The students cheered and shouted. Alicent stood and went back up the stairs to the Visitor Center, while Robert stopped the recording, handed Pax the phone, and gave him an unexpected bro-hug.

"Tight, man," Robert said. "My mama loved that song."

The tour group's students and chaperones approached Pax to thank him for his unexpected wisdom and music. Pax nodded and expressed his thanks, as Sarah had taught him, then made his way through the group with Robert until he could climb the long stairway along the bowl's perimeter back to the Visitor Center. Alicent met him at the top of the stairs and walked with him back to her small office.

"I'm happy we could provide you this opportunity, Mr. Butler," she said, adjusting her glasses nervously as they made their way to the small room.

"Pax."

Alicent beamed happily.

"My parents taught me to refer to—"

"Old people," Pax said, finishing her thought.

"*Older* people," Alicent corrected with a grin. "They taught me to respect my elders and refer to them as Mr., Mrs., and Miss."

Pax sat in the only chair that wasn't stacked high with books and papers.

"Well, I think that explanation was probably more of an insult than calling me Mr. Butler," he chuckled. "But please, just Pax. I grant you permission now and forever to call me Pax."

Alicent sat, pretending to tidy her desk while avoiding his gaze.

"Pax, then," she said.

He took out his phone and bypassed security, then handed it to Alicent.

"I don't know how to send you a video, so just do what you need to do to send yourself a copy."

Alicent skillfully handled the smartphone for a moment before passing it back.

"You can upload it yourself to that YouTube thing Rob set up. I don't know how to do that either."

Alicent said she would and leaned back in her chair.

"Where to next, Mr... Pax?"

He leaned back, copying the young lady's posture.

"Probably heading north to Portland. There are a few places in the Northwest I want to visit, then I'll head down the coast to see if I can perform on any other stages that were previously out of my reach."

"Anywhere in particular?" she asked, genuinely curious after being drawn into Pax's strange, meandering story.

"Well, in Los Angeles, I'd love to try getting on stage at the Troubadour. I know that's probably a long shot, but Red Rocks was too." Pax smiled at Alicent, silently appreciating her generosity.

"I hope you get that chance, Pax," she said.

"Thanks," he replied. "But I think next, I'd like to have a drink and some dinner. Do you eat or drink, Alicent?"

She looked at him oddly before realizing he was joking.

"I do," she replied.

"I'd like to buy you dinner if you're interested. Just dinner. Or a drink. Or both," he laughed. "Maybe Robert could come too."

Alicent picked up her radio and called Robert to ask if he wanted to join her for dinner with Pax. Robert declined. Alicent looked conflicted. Pax could sense her unease about going to dinner with someone she had just met.

"It's okay, Ally," he said, then corrected himself. "Sorry, my daughter's name is Allison, but we call her Ally. That just slipped out."

Alicent's face lit up at the mention of the nickname. Pax thought she might never have been called anything other than her full name.

"Well," Alicent said. "I have some work to finish, and we don't close until 4:00 p.m. So, I might not be—"

"It's okay, Alicent. I'll be at the Buffalo Rose in Golden around 6:00 p.m. if you want to join me. I'd like to buy you dinner as a way to thank you for today. But if you're uncomfortable, that's fine. I'll thank you now and be out of your hair."

Alicent stood and reached out her hand. Pax took it with both of his and gave it a gentle squeeze.

"Thanks for including Red Rocks in your journey, Pax. I think that video will be a big hit."

Pax thanked Alicent again as he moved toward the door, and once more when he left and headed back to the parking lot.

HE CALLED Rob when he got back to the fifth wheel in Golden. Rob was thrilled that Pax had played even one song on stage at Red Rocks and that someone had recorded it.

"Upload the video, Dad."

"I don't know how to do that, Rob. Alicent said she would upload it to YouTube when she had time."

"Hang on a second," Rob said, and Pax heard typing. "It's there."

Pax heard his voice on the phone while Rob played the video on his computer.

God, I sound so old, he thought.

"Who are you talking to in the video, Dad?"

"Oh, there was a tour group with some middle-school students there. They were an unexpected audience."

"Oh wow, Dad. This stuff about Mom. Jesus."

Pax could hear the notes of sorrow seeping through as Rob listened to and watched the video. At the end, Rob sniffled, and the conversation resumed.

"I'll let Ally know it's up there. You've built quite a collection on this little channel, Dad."

"That was all you, Robbie. I wouldn't have known how to do that if you hadn't set it up. And Jesus, thank you for reaching out to Alicent. I don't know what you promised her to get me on that stage, but she was excited. In her own way."

"She's kind of an odd duck, isn't she?" Rob laughed. "But in a good way. It took a few calls, but I finally pointed her to the YouTube site after those folks uploaded that show from Austin. I think the videos got to her."

A long, comfortable silence followed, with Pax feeling the love both for and from his son through the phone.

"Where to next, Dad?" Rob finally asked.

"North, I guess," Pax replied. "There are a few places in Portland I'd like to see. Then, down the coast to San Francisco, and then on to LA. I'd appreciate your help if you could get me on stage at the Troubadour in LA. You'd make a great booking manager if I still had the chops to be in a band."

"You still have plenty of chops, Dad. The Austin show is a perfect example of that. Butler Service may be on permanent hiatus, but Pax Butler's solo career could just be getting started."

Pax chuckled at that and briefly thought about touring solo or reaching out to the Cruz family to see if he could join the band.

Rob's tone changed. "Dad, have you heard from Mom?"

Pax felt a shiver run through him at the question. Rob understood why he was out in the wild and what he was searching for.

"Yeah, Robbie, I have," he said, thinking about the wind chimes in Memphis and the single note on Beto's guitar that drew him to the Cruz family. "In unexpected ways, though. She's following me. Or leading me. I can't tell which."

"I listened to the recordings she made with Zim," Rob said. "I don't think I have ever cried so hard. She was something else, wasn't she?"

"That she was, Rob," Pax replied, suddenly needing to end the call. "Yeah, she was something. All the best parts of you and Ally you got from her."

Another silence followed, and Pax realized it was time to hang up the phone before he lost his composure with his son listening in.

"Hey, Rob," he said softly. "I'm going to get something to eat and maybe see a local band tonight. Thanks for everything. Thanks for the video channel. Thanks for sweet-talking Alicent. Thanks for the pictures of Jazz. And thanks. Thanks for being my kid. I love you, Rob."

Rob's voice cracked, but Pax could hear the smile behind his words.

"Why, Pax Butler. Listen to you. Not such a hard ass after all."

Pax sighed.

"I guess my secret is out," he chuckled.

"Anyone who has seen these videos knows your secret, old man. I love you too, Dad." Rob disconnected before the sentiment made things more awkward for either of them.

BUFFALO ROSE WAS the closest Pax had ever come to going to church. An eclectic combination of restaurant, lounge, bar, and an adjoining event center that hosted live music several times a month, it offered everything he wanted in one place.

He sat at the bar to avoid occupying an entire table by himself. It also let him chat with the bartenders about the different acts performing that week to see if any caught his interest.

He swirled his tequila on ice while he looked over the menu, undecided whether to eat lightly after gorging himself on Bob's Atomic Burgers or to order a big meal to celebrate his epic performance at Red Rocks.

"What are you drinking?" a voice behind him asked. Pax turned and looked into Alicent Klein's charming yet quirky gaze.

"You made it," he replied, grinning widely.

Alicent sat beside Pax at the bar and took a sniff of his drink.

"You should try some dark chocolate with your tequila. That's how I like it."

She took off her glasses and Pax watched as she carefully cleaned them with a cloth, put them in a case, and then slid the case into her purse.

"I only need them for reading," she said. "But once I put them on, I keep them on so I don't have to keep cleaning them."

Alicent called over the bartender.

"Two glasses of Casamigos añejo, please, Carlos."

Pax chuckled. "Carlos?"

Alicent smiled. "I come here a lot. I live three blocks away."

Pax nodded and finished his first drink just as the replacement arrived. He clinked glasses with Alicent, and they took a sip.

Pax swallowed and said, "Mmmmm, that's nice. A little peppery but in a good way."

"It's my go-to," Alicent said. "It's even better with some dark chocolate. I drank it first because of its association with George Clooney. But I stayed with it because it's just so good."

"George Clooney?" Pax asked, realizing that Alicent had many layers beneath her unique surface.

She replied, "He was one of the founders of Casamigos, and he and I share a birthday."

Pax clinked his glass against Alicent's again and said, "Happy birthday. Whenever that is."

They ate at the bar, sharing appetizers instead of ordering large plates. At Alicent's suggestion, they drank glasses of club soda between tequila refills. Under the increasing influence of the Jalisco truth serum, however, Alicent opened up to Pax about her childhood in Denver, attending CU Boulder for environmental science, her fruitless job search using her degree, and ultimately taking a job at Red Rocks, where she could at least be near an environmental landmark, even if her role was just to prevent tourists from damaging it.

"And, letting fascinating gentlemen sing love ballads to their wives," she concluded with another clink of the glass.

"I can't thank you enough for that, Alicent," Pax said, his sentimental side brought out of the shadows by glasses of his favorite medicine.

"It was my pleasure," Alicent said, her words slurring slightly as she patted Pax's hand on the bar. "I was extremely reluctant when your son called me the first two or three times. But when he sent me a link to the YouTube channel and I watched you... Oh my god... pouring your soul into the universe on those stages. I knew that you had to sing here. It was destiny."

Pax raised his glass, filled with gratitude for this young woman's generosity.

"To destiny," he said, and Alicent touched her glass to his in agreement.

They finished their current round, and Alicent turned to ask if he wanted another, but his attention was drawn elsewhere. There was a deep vibration in his chest. Initially, he worried it was a medical issue related to the cardiac scan he had in Memphis, but then he heard harmonics, and he realized this wasn't a coronary event. It was music.

"Hey," he said to Alicent. "Do you want to go see who the band is tonight?"

She wasted no time searching for the answer on her phone.

"It's a band called The Turbines. They are a cover band of an '80s band called Power Station. Oh, that's clever. Turbines and power stations."

Pax smiled with his whole face.

"Do you like it hot, Alicent?"

"What?" she replied, confused by the non-sequitur.

"You'll find out. We're going in! Come on!"

He quickly paid for dinner and drinks, took Alicent's hand, and followed her through the doors to the event center. The music throbbed, and the dance floor was packed with people moving to the beat. Pax didn't recognize the song, but that didn't matter. Within a minute of arriving, he and Alicent were dancing and jumping with the crowd as The Turbines energized the audience.

When the band played *Some Like It Hot*, Alicent turned to Pax, and her face lit up.

"I get it now!" she shouted over the pounding drums. "I like it hot! Wooo!"

They danced, and Pax sang along with the band. Alicent jumped and swayed, waving her hands in the air—the shy day manager transformed into a wild club girl immersed in sound and light.

As the tequila mixed with the music, fueled by dancing and singing along with the band, Pax was transported to Jones Beach on Long Island, where he and Sarah saw Power Station alongside other bands during a long weekend in the city. He glanced at the young woman dancing and shouting next to him and smiled, feeling the same vibe he had felt all those decades ago. The sensation was so familiar that he suddenly felt overwhelmed with emotion and feared that a panic attack might consume him like the one he experienced in Memphis.

Pax tapped Alicent on the shoulder and signaled that he needed to step outside for some air. Alicent nodded and followed, concern on her face.

Outside the venue, Pax sat on the curb, looking up at the iconic sign welcoming visitors to Golden. Alicent sat next to him and asked if he was okay. He nodded.

"Yeah, I had an overwhelming sense of déjà vu in there. It made me a little dizzy. I'm sure the tequila didn't help."

Alicent shivered and zipped her coat up.

"Better out here, Pax?" she asked.

He stood and extended his hand to help her up.

"Yeah, better. Sorry, it's cold. I didn't mean to drag you out here with me, Alicent."

She shrugged and said, "Will you call me Ally? When you called me that before, it felt right."

Pax smiled. "With a 'y' or an 'ie' at the end?"

Alicent's eyes moved back and forth as if she were looking at the two choices in the air in front of her.

"A-l-l-i-e," she said. "I think the 'ie' makes it stand out. And the extra 'l' makes it feel…fuller. More full? Fullier?"

They both laughed.

"Allie, it is," he said. "Can I walk you home, Allie?"

They strolled slowly for three blocks to Alicent's apartment.

"Do you want to come up?" she asked, shivering on the sidewalk. "My roommate is there, but so is a bottle of Casamigos. I might even have some chocolate."

Pax looked up at the building and sighed.

"If I was twenty years younger, maybe. But I'm not."

Alicent smiled and patted his arm.

"It's okay, I understand. But Pax, age is just a number. At least that's what they say."

He laughed, "Well, the people that say that still have cartilage in their knees and probably don't have grandchildren."

Alicent joined in his laughter.

Second fret—first string. F-Sharp: the major third above the root of D. Harmonic with Sarah's note of happiness.

"Well," Alicent said as the silence grew in the cold air. "You have my email, and my phone number is in the signature, in case you are back in the area. I also sent a text from your phone to mine earlier, so we have each other's numbers that way, too."

Pax smiled and nodded, gazing into the face of this stranger who radiated generosity and embodied what Sarah had preached.

"Can I at least hug you, Pax?" Alicent asked. "I had so much fun tonight, and I admit I'm a little tipsy, so I apologize if I seem a bit over-friendly."

Pax opened his arms, inviting Alicent to step into them.

"I think you're a little more than a little tipsy, Allie," Pax said. "But that's okay. You've earned it in my book. You made me a very happy man today."

He hugged her, and she hugged back. That sense of déjà vu returned, his pickled brain thinking he was holding a young Sarah again. As the hug ended, Pax cupped Alicent's face and kissed her forehead.

"Look at you, with a new name and a fresh start. I hope you find a job that makes you happy, Allie."

She was beaming.

"I hope you find what you're looking for, Pax."

She walked into her building and gave a small wave before disappearing behind the door.

Pax walked back to where he parked his truck and stared at it for a long moment, questioning whether it was wise to drive the mile back to Clear Creek RV Park with so much agave juice in him. He decided to walk to the trailer instead. He could pick up his truck the next day. The cold air would do him good, and the walk would give him time to reflect on the day's events and absorb everything that had happened.

He couldn't remember a better day in a very long time. Singing at Red Rocks, the call with Rob, drinking and dancing with Alicent, and flashbacks of Sarah—he wanted to relive it all with every step he took back to his bed.

He was still smiling as he finally lay back in bed, his fingertips numb and his nose running from the cold night air. It wasn't a forced smile like most of his were; it was a genuine smile of pure joy at how perfectly that day had gone. Even the slight panic attack from the familiarity of everything at the restaurant wasn't enough to wipe that smile from his face. He reached for the chain around his neck and kissed Sarah's two rings, holding them to his chest as sleep took him away.

In the morning, the demon of Jalisco did not wake Pax as he had expected. The alternating club sodas from the night before prevented any aftereffects, and he lounged in bed, reliving the day and night once again before getting up, dressing, and walking back to where his truck was parked.

The air was just as cold as it had been the night before, maybe a little colder. A few snowflakes drifted through the air, defiantly ignoring the weather report.

Once at the truck, Pax realized he had not brought the keys. Despite having no hangover, his tequila-addled brain was still misfiring, and he walked back the way he came to retrieve his keys from the trailer.

On the return trip to the truck, keys in his pocket, the snow started to fall with purpose. Pax checked the weather report on his phone as he walked along Clear Creek. The patch of pink and blue moving in from the west urged him to pick up his pace. He wanted to get as far north of the area as possible before the worst of that squall trapped him in Golden for an extended stay.

The snow kept falling, dusting the ground as he disconnected the trailer, attached it to the truck, checked out at the office, and pulled out of the RV lot heading to I-25 North. He slipped a Supertramp CD into the player and drove as fast as he felt comfortable, the ironic refrains of *Take the Long Way Home* filling the air.

CHAPTER 7

Pax grew up in the Finger Lakes region of Central New York, where he learned to drive in winter conditions as a teenager. Driving on snowy roads was a rite of passage for Pax and his friends. Ithaca and the surrounding areas were notorious for their lake-effect storms, which could deposit several feet overnight. However, he had never learned to drive in snow and wind while towing a forty-foot trailer.

The weather worsened just outside Fort Collins. It became severe as he crossed into Cheyenne. The weather advisory on the radio told everyone to stay inside for the day and into the evening, but "inside" didn't mean the inside of a truck speeding down the highway.

Each crosswind on northbound I-25 caused a mini whiteout and violently shook the trailer. Pax realized that nature might force him off the road if he didn't exit voluntarily. He slowed down to fight snow blindness and the battering wind of the dimming afternoon until he reached the town of Wheatland, Wyoming.

At the end of the off-ramp, Pax saw a sign for Motel 6. More than needing a room, he wanted a place to park his trailer until the snow and wind let up. The motel's desk manager agreed to let him use as much space as he needed since the few hotel guests this time of year meant the parking lot was mostly empty. He asked if there was a nearby place to get food or groceries, and the young man suggested some local options that might still be open.

He parked the trailer on the leeward side of the motel and lowered the front stabilizers. After living in the Carolinas for a few years, he had forgotten what true cold felt like, and his coat was insufficient for this part of the country. He needed something warmer, and once again, the desk manager helped by pointing him toward the Wheatland Country Store, conveniently situated just a few blocks away.

"Get some gloves while you're there if you ain't got any," the manager said. "Days like this will bite right into your bones."

Pax's brief time setting up his trailer showcased his unpreparedness for the harsh weather. He felt the sharp pins and needles of the bitter cold in his fingertips. Although he had spent much of his life in the snow belt of Central New York, he had not adequately prepared himself for multiple seasons in different climates before setting out on his journey.

Deciding it was smarter to drive to the store instead of walking, Pax made the quick two-minute trip. As he entered, a few patrons inside laughed at the sight of a middle-aged man in sneakers and what was essentially a padded windbreaker. Pax blew into his cold hands and glanced at the rugged-looking man at the checkout.

"Coats?"

The man pointed back toward the clothing section.

"Got gloves, too," the man said. Pax waved without turning around.

He rummaged through the coat rack, which had been picked over before winter arrived. He tried on a large, his usual size, only to find it snug. It seemed he had gained a few pounds over the past few years, probably due to Audra's delicious southern cooking, Marisol's Cuban dishes, or a combination of both. It couldn't possibly be due to all the beer and fast food he had consumed on his quest. Reluctantly, he tried an extra-large and was happy to find it too big.

"You're in-between," a voice said from behind him.

Pax turned and saw a woman roughly his age pushing a shopping cart full of bags of dog food.

"Story of my life," he laughed in response.

"If you had come last week, you probably could have found a better fit."

Pax returned the XL and browsed the rack, looking for another L without the X that could at least get him through the drive north.

"You look like a 44-regular, between large and extra-large," the woman said, and Pax's trained ear detected the trace of a European accent.

"44? Shit."

The woman chuckled at his response.

"Sorry," he replied, trying on another tight large. "I grew up in New York, where we're all fluent in Vulgarian."

"It's not an issue," she laughed. "My husband spoke a similar dialect."

Pax smirked at that response and offered her a faint smile.

"And he wore a similar coat size, 44-regular."

Pax noticed the past tense in her word choice and realized she used it twice. He looked at her a little longer and recognized the same distance in her eyes that he had seen reflected in the mirror every morning since Sarah passed.

"He doesn't need it anymore," she said.

"I'm sorry," Pax said, hating the finality of those two words while struggling to find a better response for a stranger.

"Thank you, but it's fine," she replied. "It's been two years. We must continue, yes?"

"I guess so," Pax responded, hoping his tone wouldn't reveal his own emptiness.

He reached for another coat on the rack, but the woman stopped him by placing her hand on his arm.

"Hold on, Mr. New York. If you can't find one that fits, you might as well head south for the winter. I have one of my husband's coats in my truck. Let's try that."

Pax reluctantly agreed and offered to help her with her shopping cart.

"You're still needing gloves and boots, Mr. New York. I'll meet you by the door when you're ready."

He blushed slightly and fumbled over his words while searching for the boots and gloves.

Fortunately, feet don't grow like waistlines, so he found insulated work boots that fit perfectly, along with thick socks and gloves. He wore the new boots and socks to the checkout, paid, then put on his gloves and met the helpful woman near the door.

"No hat?" she said with a grin as he approached.

"Shit," he replied. "Sorry."

"I have a hat for you, too. Come along!"

Pax followed her and helped load her bags of dog food into the bed of her pickup truck.

"I'm Pax," he said, removing his glove to shake her hand, but immediately regretting it as the cold quickly pierced his skin.

"Katja," she replied, noticing his discomfort. "Put your glove on, Pax."

Katja reached into the space behind the passenger seat of her pickup truck and pulled out a slightly dirty, well-worn Carhartt coat. She found a wool hat in the pocket and handed it to Pax, who promptly put it on to keep his ears warm.

She was right about the fit. The coat was snug where it needed to be, yet allowed room to move. The thick canvas and lining effectively blocked the wind's bite.

"This is great," he said, already feeling the difference. "How much—"

"Stop, Pax. Just take it. It's my pleasure."

"Are you sure?" he begged. "Can I at least buy you dinner? You literally just saved my life."

"Don't be silly. It's fine. Enjoy the coat. Carsen did for many years."

He watched as Katja drove away, feeling as if he had no control over his life. Some cosmic force had guided this generous woman into his path just when he needed help, and then, like a drive-by angel, she was gone.

He hopped into his truck and followed the route the motel manager had given him to the grocery store. He stocked up on his favorite snacks, planning to hit the road again in the morning, and then returned to Motel 6 to wait out the weather.

He decided it would be wiser to wait inside the motel rather than in the trailer. So, he rented a room for the night, grabbed some essentials from the fifth wheel, including his guitar, and sat down with a six-pack of beer and a bag of chips to watch TV. Halfway through the chips and his second beer, Pax realized he would no longer be a 44 regular if he kept up this current pace.

The snacks were put away and he spent time on his phone trying to figure out his route through the mountains to Portland.

THE MORNING WAS SUNNY, and the wind had settled when Pax stepped outside to check his trailer. The cold air hit him like a wall of ice. Even with a warmer coat, hat, and gloves, he could feel the risk of frostbite as the cold, dry air drained heat from his face. He knew he had to limit his time outdoors.

The lock on the trailer door was frozen. No amount of shaking or hitting would loosen it. Pax went back to the lobby to warm up and consider his next move.

"Frozen lock?"

Pax turned to the skinny twenty-something day manager behind the desk.

"Yeah," he replied, his gloved hands stuffed in his coat pocket, trying to find warmth within the layers. "Is there an auto supply store nearby?"

The young man grabbed a can of deicer from the office and handed it to him. Grateful, Pax thanked him and went back to the trailer, eventually unlocking and opening the door.

Once inside, he immediately realized that sleeping in the trailer, which had been exposed to increasingly colder air since leaving Austin, wasn't feasible at the moment. He needed to winterize it and find somewhere to park it. A more troubling thought quickly followed—he was stranded in Wheatland.

"How long does this kind of cold weather last out here?" Pax asked as he returned the deicer to the desk manager.

"Depends," the young man replied. "The mornings and nights are the worst, but we can reach the forties, sometimes fifties, during the day. The dry air is a bigger problem because it makes the air feel colder than it is. This cold, though? This is something special. I heard something about La Niña making it colder this year."

Pax considered the situation. He decided he could stay in the area for a few days, maybe even a week, hoping the weather would warm up enough for him to head south again. He would have to delay his trip to Portland until he could safely use the trailer for overnight stays, though he had no idea when that would be.

He took the rest of his clothes into the motel, emptied the refrigerator and pantry, and put everything in the motel bathtub until he could decide his next step. Not knowing how to winterize his trailer, he realized he needed help. He also wasn't keen on staying in the motel for a long time, so he would have to find temporary housing elsewhere in town.

He spent the rest of the morning researching how to winterize his trailer, but he grew increasingly discouraged by the complexity of the steps. Growing confident that he would mess it up if he tried alone, he accepted his limitations and called the local storage facilities to see if they had space and could help with winterizing. The public storage facilities offered only storage, but none could assist with winterizing.

While searching online for nearby fifth-wheel dealers, Pax discovered that his best option was to take the trailer to Cheyenne for winter storage. Dreading the drive back down the highway while towing the trailer, he thought about hiring someone to retrieve it or at least come to Wheatland to help winterize it. After making several calls, he found an enterprising young man named Harley who was willing to drive to Wheatland to assist him.

"I got family nearby where I can stay while I lend you a hand," Harley told him.

"You're a lifesaver, Harley," Pax said, relieved that his current crisis was coming to an end. "How much do you want for the effort?"

"Well, material costs obviously for the antifreeze, but I'd take $200 to do the work for you."

Pax didn't flinch. He sat quietly on the phone, weighing the value of the service against the alternatives.

"Harley," he said in a soft, serious tone. "You wouldn't be trying to take advantage of an out-of-towner, would you?"

Harley responded confidently after a long pause.

"No, sir."

Pax smiled.

"Well, I guess you should probably charge $300 for the work," he said.

Pax could hear the smile in Harley's reply.

"Yes, sir. I'll be there tomorrow."

THEY AGREED to meet at a diner a few miles from the hotel to handle their business before tackling the cold task of winterizing the trailer. Harley suggested that Pax work with him to learn the process in case he faced a similar situation down the line.

While sipping coffee and waiting for Harley, Pax heard a new tune in his head. He realized that the lyrics for the new song he was gradually composing fit perfectly with the chord progression and melody he was hearing. He asked the server for a pen and quickly jotted down the chords and shorthand for the song's structure in this fresh pattern.

"Mr. Pax?" A tall, bearded man in his twenties stood next to the table.

"Just Pax," he said as he stood and offered his hand. "Harley?"

"Yes, sir," Harley said with a smile as he slid into the booth across from him.

Pax looked around at the roughly twenty people in the diner.

"How did you know I was the guy you were looking for?" Pax asked.

Harley looked around the room once more with a chuckle, nodding in greeting to some of the patrons.

"Well, sir, I reckon I know just about everyone else in here. I spent summers at my uncle's ranch, and we often ate at this diner. The faces have aged a bit, but I recognize a lot of them."

"Those must have been some fun summers. What kind of ranch?"

"Horses. I loved riding in the open spaces. But after he passed away, my aunt couldn't manage the workload, so she sold the horses. Now she takes in injured wild ones, nurses them back to health, and then finds them homes."

Pax felt a sense of admiration. "That sounds like a very altruistic calling."

"Yeah, she's something else. Here she comes. Hope you don't mind. I'll be staying with her, so I told her to meet me here."

Pax turned and saw a familiar face. Katja, who had given him the coat and hat on his first day in town, was walking into the diner.

"Hi, Aunt Kat," Harley said, walking into her open arms.

Harley turned to introduce her to Pax.

"Aunt Kat, this is—"

"Mr. New York, Pax, yes?" Katja smiled, her eyes showing her genuine pleasure.

Harley looked at them. "So, you've met?"

Katja laughed, pointing out, "It's your uncle's coat crumpled on the seat next to him."

Pax felt self-conscious and carefully reached out to fold the jacket.

"Oh, stop it, Mr. New York. Carsen would have done the same."

"It's very nice to see you again, Katja," Pax managed, feeling a bit overwhelmed by the peculiar nature of this meeting.

"Pax," Harley started, then corrected himself in front of his aunt. "Mr... New York?"

"Butler," Pax chuckled and corrected.

"Mr. Butler hired me to winterize his fifth-wheel trailer for storage."

Katja sat in the booth, glancing over at Pax.

"So, you're staying in our small town for a while?"

"It appears that way," Pax replied. "At least until this weather breaks. I'll probably head back south for the rest of the winter."

Katja smiled as Harley watched the interaction with interest.

"I grew up in New York, Central New York, Finger Lakes area, not the City," Pax said, waving his hand at an invisible map as if it would mean something to the others. "We had rough winters, but it rarely got this cold. Mostly just mountains of snow. I've lived in South Carolina with my daughter... and others... for the past few years. So, my winter brain was hibernating when I went on the road and neglected to pack for this kind of weather."

Katja laughed while sharing her introduction to Pax with Harley, saying, "This poor man walked into the Country Store in something slightly warmer than a spring jacket."

"Your aunt was kind enough to give me one of your uncle's old Carhartt coats and a wool hat," Pax added to the story, squinting his eyes as he looked at Katja. "And then she drove off without letting me properly show my appreciation."

"The look on your face was reward enough," she laughed as the server approached the table. Harley and Katja recognized the woman and made small talk while they placed their orders. Pax ordered his usual breakfast of coffee, an english muffin, and more coffee.

"And they don't get to pay," he told the server as she took their order to the kitchen. "This is on me."

"Yeah, right," the woman replied oddly.

Pax discussed the winterizing process with Harley and asked for suggestions on where to store the trailer. Harley didn't have many positive comments about the commercial storage facilities in Wheatland and recommended that Pax drive it back to Cheyenne to store it at his workplace. He considered the challenge of retrieving it when he was ready, especially if it was parked an hour away.

"I have a barn," Katja said, sipping her coffee.

The two men looked at her as if they were expecting her to elaborate.

"If you're going to leave it outside, you might as well keep it covered. There's plenty of space in the barn."

Harley looked at Pax and shrugged.

"It's not a bad idea," he said.

Pax was somewhat surprised by the offer.

"Katja, you barely know me. Where I come from, we don't make offers to strangers like that."

"I don't come from where you do," Katja replied. "Where I come from, we care about people in need."

Pax frowned, but it was a good kind of frown. It was the frown of a man who didn't know how to respond to an unexpected act of kindness.

"Besides," Katja added, "I have seen your soul, Pax Butler."

"My soul?"

Katja pulled out her phone and, after a few swipes and taps, placed it on the table. The volume was low, and Pax watched the video of himself singing at the club in Memphis. It was the *Red Roses* performance from the night he met Lara.

"One of the women in my book club saw this and shared it with us. And then the other song, Sara, something?"

"Sara Smile," Pax replied. "There are a few new ones in that group, channel, whatever it is."

"You revealed your soul to the world in those videos, Mr. Tough Guy from New York. And then, the other day, you needed help buying socks. Not so tough after all."

Pax thought, *"Rob and Ally are never going to believe this."*

"So, then," Harley said, breaking the silence. "You'll be parking the trailer in the barn, I suppose?"

Pax kept his eyes on Katja, who looked back at him. They both quietly sipped their coffee, as if engaged in a silent negotiation.

"Yeah," Pax said as their food arrived. "I guess I am. But to be clear, I didn't need help buying socks. And Katja, I'm going to pay you for this. It's a rental, not a handout."

Katja smiled and nodded in agreement.

The three of them engaged in small talk over breakfast. Pax shared stories about New York and South Carolina, mentioning the kids and grandkids, but he never brought up Sarah. He learned that Katja was from Aarhus, Denmark, and had met Carsen Browne one summer while she was in Copenhagen with friends. Carsen had been on a European beer tour with college buddies. She described their connection as instant, as if they had known each other in a past life.

"Entangled," Pax said, deeply familiar with that feeling.

"Just so," Katja replied with a smile. "Entangled."

They kept the conversation light and cheerful, steering clear of contentious topics entirely. After finishing breakfast and finalizing the day's plans, Pax called the server over for the check.

"It's already taken care of, sir," the woman said.

Pax glanced at Harley, who averted his eyes with a grin. Katja looked at Pax over the rim of her coffee cup, saying nothing. Neither of them had left the table since they sat down, yet somehow the check had been paid. Pax felt a little annoyed and was confident that Katja was behind it, but he was also impressed by her stealth. He accepted the situation with a shake of his head.

The two men spent the day winterizing the trailer. It took longer than expected because some water lines had already frozen. Still, the job was finished with patience and perseverance, along with several warm-up coffee breaks in the motel lobby. Pax reconnected the trailer to his truck and followed Harley to Katja's ranch.

The Brun-Dahl ranch got its name from Carsten's last name, "Browne," and Katja's maiden name, "Dahl." It covered fourteen hundred acres of fields, forests, and fens. The main house was set far enough from the highway to be almost completely hidden unless someone accidentally took the wrong side road.

That road was, in fact, the driveway, changing from pavement to gravel to hardened dirt, running beside a fence that seemed endless to Pax. As they neared the house, the driveway reverted to gravel, and Pax saw Katja standing on the front porch in a thick wool sweater, flanked by two large dogs.

Harley was greeted by the giant, furry beasts that nudged him with their massive heads and licked his face as he knelt. Pax, who was also a dog lover, knew to wait for the mountains of fur to approach him. Once they sniffed his hand, he reached out to pet them.

"What kind of dogs are these?" he asked, having never seen a shaggy dog quite as big.

"Bernese mountain dogs," Harley replied. "This is Ike, and that's Tina."

Pax chuckled in appreciation of the music reference, giving them some attention.

"It took longer than you expected, yes?" Katya said as the two men climbed the porch steps.

"Yeah," Harley said as he hugged his aunt. "The cold got to the water before us, so we had to de-ice it before we could clear the lines. Fortunately, the black tank was emptied, so that didn't require as much attention."

"I don't think I want to know what a black tank is," Katja replied, hinting she already had an idea of its purpose. "Mr. New York, you could use something hot."

"Yes, I could," Pax replied. "But if you keep calling me Mr. New York, we can't be friends."

Katja laughed, and the men followed her inside.

"Pax it is, then," she said as she poured the coffee. "It means peace. Did you know that?"

Pax smiled, indicating that, yes, he did know that.

"I had a friend who told me that whenever he saw me getting angry, especially when he was the one getting on my nerves. I guess it was an ironic name when I was younger. I was a bit of a hot head."

While Pax and Katja sipped warm drinks, Harley drove the trailer to the barn behind the house, slightly higher on the hill. After parking and disconnecting the trailer, he returned Pax's truck to the front and went inside, where Katja was giving Pax a quick tour of the house's history.

Pax noticed the framed photos of Carsen on the walls and nearly every surface. The number and theme of the pictures made it clear that Carsen had been central to Katja's life. He understood that deeply, as well as the emptiness left when someone so important is gone.

As they stepped into the side room, Pax saw an antique upright piano against the wall. He pressed a few keys and played a simple C chord.

"Do you play?" he asked Katja.

"No," she replied. "Carsen was the musician. He played piano and guitar."

Pax watched as Katja experienced a moment of nostalgia, a sad smile creeping over her face. Then, just as quickly, she snapped back to the present and looked at Pax.

"He was a terrible singer, though," she laughed. "Do you play, Pax?"

He shrugged.

"I can, a little. It's more like fumbling than playing, but my friend was the keyboardist in our band. I play guitar, though."

"I know, I watched you," Katja said, referring to the videos.

Pax nodded in appreciation. Having never felt comfortable with compliments, Sarah advised him to nod, smile, and say "thank you" instead of trying to come up with some pithy retort.

"Trailer is all set for as long as it needs to be," Harley said as he took off his coat.

Pax showed his appreciation and turned to Katja.

"Please tell me how much you want to rent the space, Katja." He hoped his seriousness would come through. He didn't want her to dismiss the idea of him paying her for her kindness.

Katja smirked slightly, clearly thinking of something sarcastic to say, but she brushed off the comment and changed the subject.

"How about a late lunch, gentlemen?" she asked as she turned and walked into the kitchen.

Pax looked at Harley, who shrugged and followed his aunt.

As Katja arranged dishes of beans in olive oil, pickles, and homemade bread, Harley reminisced about summers spent at the ranch.

"I remember getting up early and riding out to check on the horses every morning, rain or shine. Foaling in late spring and early summer. It was hard work sometimes, but it didn't feel like work, you know?"

Pax nodded, feeling the same way about playing gigs with the band.

"When Uncle Carsen passed—" Harley continued, then stopped and looked at Katja.

Pax saw the struggle on Harley's face and took the chance to change the subject, giving Harley a break from the pressure of continuing the conversation.

"Harley told me you rehabilitate wild horses, Katja. How

does that work? I wasn't aware there were still wild horses out there."

"The BLM estimates that tens of thousands still roam free. However, the numbers decline each year."

Pax thought about Audra and her fierce support for the Black Lives Matter movement, but he couldn't connect it to what Katja had told him.

"BLM?"

"Bureau of Land Management," Harley added. "The government organization that oversees federal lands."

"Oh, I thought BLM was—"

"Yes," Katja interrupted. "An unfortunate coincidental acronym with another important cause."

Pax could hear her passionate dedication to her mission in her voice—sorrow, anger, and frustration all competing for dominance behind her drive to make a change.

"Why are there so few? If they're wild, wouldn't there be new little horses each year to grow the herd?"

"Well," Katja continued, "are you a political man, Pax?"

"Not really. I feel like truly intelligent people would never run for office, so it's unlikely we'll ever see the right people making decisions for us."

"Exactly," she replied with a smile. "Well, the same government that talks about conservation also passes laws that reduce land for wildlife and let landowners kill wild horses, burros, and even wolves to make room for more livestock. Americans love their meat, and when you see it in a grocery store, it doesn't look like the animal it came from, so it's easy to pretend it's something else."

Pax thought about his last steak and realized her statement was true. He then noticed there was no meat on the table for lunch. This made him think of Bob's Atomic Burgers and wish he had brought a sack of them with him.

Katja continued, "The horses I take in are often injured, making them easy targets for what these same men call 'compassionate death,' but I still call it slaughter. They are brought here by kind, caring people, and I work with some veterinarian friends to help them become healthy again. Returning them to the herd is often not an option, so we find homes for them with people who will love and care for them. Their wildness is sacrificed to save their lives."

"How many horses are you taking care of right now?" Pax asked.

"Only four. I've heard through my network that two more might be on their way soon."

"How many people do you have helping with the ranch?" Pax asked, fascinated by this world he had never known existed.

Katja smiled and looked at Harley.

"Counting me?" she said. "One. And sometimes Harley, when he has some free time. But he needs a life and eventually a family of his own."

"I'm working on it, Aunt Kat," Harley responded to her less-than-subtle taunt.

"How do you care for that many sick and injured animals alone?" Pax asked.

"I manage," Katja shrugged. "We manage. When you're doing something meaningful to you, it's not work. It's... life."

Pax knew Sarah would adore Katja. They would have become great friends, sharing traits like compassion, kindness, empathy, and honesty, all wrapped in a layer of sarcasm. Sarah loved horses, too. He remembered the summer job her father arranged for her at Cornell Equine Park, and how she always smelled like a barn when she came home. But most vividly, he remembered how her eyes lit up when she talked about the horses she worked with.

The silence lingered as Pax reflected on how his familiar

world back east was not so far removed from this unfamiliar one. He wondered what else he might have missed over the years by keeping his emotional focus so narrow. Eventually, Katja broke the silence by steering the conversation in a different direction.

"What will you do now, Pax?" Katja asked. "Your moving metal house will be safely in the barn for a while. Do you want to fly back to South Carolina for the winter and then return when the thaw allows you to continue your journey?"

Pax frowned, not having even thought about going back yet.

"No. I guess I'll stick around here for a while. I'll look for a long-term rate on a hotel room or see if someone is renting a place for a reasonable price. I'm not ready to go back yet."

Katja sipped her tea until the silence in the room became overwhelming.

"Let me show you something, Pax."

She stood, walked out of the kitchen, and ascended the long, straight staircase to the second floor. Pax felt a bit uneasy walking up to the sleeping level of the house but followed her. She stood by an open door, sipping her tea as he reached the top of the stairs and proceeded down the hallway. When he reached the door, Pax looked inside a small, unremarkable bedroom.

"You can stay here if you like," Katja said. "At least until you feel you must continue your journey. A few days. A few weeks."

Pax scowled. He felt overwhelmed by the woman's generosity and felt like he was taking advantage of it, even though he hadn't asked for it.

"Katja, I can't—"

"Shut up." She stopped him. "Of course you can. If you can stay in a hotel or at some other stranger's bed and breakfast, you can just as easily stay here."

Then, quoting his own snarky remarks, she said, "And you'd

better start calling me Kat, like everyone else, or we can't be friends."

"I don't know what to say," Pax said softly. "Why would you take a risk with someone you barely know?"

Katja laughed.

"I took a risk with a young, lively man who convinced me to move from Denmark to Wyoming. I'm still here, even if he's gone. I take risks by speaking out to the BLM about their treatment of wild horses. And yet, I'm still here. Life is about risks, Pax, whether physical, emotional, or spiritual. If we don't take risks, we don't grow."

He considered the offer against his other options. He saw no reason to turn it down.

"How much is the rent?" he asked, thinking he already knew the answer.

"Oh, how much? How much? So much talk about how much," she said with a laugh as she walked toward the stairs. "It's twice as much as renting the barn. That's a ridiculously expensive woolen hat you wear these days, Mr. New York."

THE NEXT DAY, Pax woke up before dawn. Not wanting to make too much noise with a shower and his morning routine, he dressed, pulled a chair up to the window of his temporary bedroom, and gazed out over the vista that unfolded before the ranch house. He was in awe, not just of the view but of how this happy accident had placed him in that chair.

In the corner of the small room were his clothes, guitar, and other belongings he had brought from the hotel. Katja, now Kat, drove with him to clear out the room and then dropped off all his unopened groceries at the local food pantry. Sarah would have done the same to prevent him from eating all the junk food. Knowing Sarah as he did, he could almost predict Kat's actions. They were so alike that it was comical.

He craved a cup of coffee but didn't trust the floorboards in this old house not to creak as he made his way to the kitchen, so he sat and browsed through his phone. The cell signal at the ranch was weak, and he tried to send text messages to the kids, but they didn't seem to go through. He would need to get closer to town to let them know where he was, why he was there, and for how long. With nothing else to do, he gazed out the window, rolling Sarah's rings between his fingers.

A board creaked outside his open door, and he saw Harley standing in the hallway. He hadn't been the first person up and moving that morning, as he had thought.

"Ready for some fun?" Harley asked, a knowing smile on his face.

"I'm always up for fun, but somehow, I think what you see as fun is going to be hard work for me," Pax said with a chuckle.

He asked Harley if there was Wi-Fi in the house for him to connect to, and Harley responded with a laugh.

"No. Aunt Kat is as off-the-grid as you can get. She has a landline if she needs to call someone. And there's satellite service for TV and Internet, but that's about it. She usually keeps them unplugged to save energy, but I turn them on when I visit."

"Is electricity expensive out here?" Pax asked, wondering what he meant by saving energy in the current device-driven economy. In response, Harley pointed to the lights in the hallway.

"Solar," he said. "All of it is solar-powered with batteries for backup. Wood stoves are used when the electric heat pump isn't enough to keep the pipes from freezing. She keeps the house cool because you can always put on more clothes, but there's a limit to how many you can take off. Summers can get pretty warm in here, but there's no A/C. She'd sooner walk around naked than install even a window unit. She's a twenty-first-century hippie."

Pax marveled at the idea of living without mainline power as the two men went down the stairs and found Kat in the kitchen, coffee brewing, toast on the table, and jam on the counter.

No bacon and eggs? Pax thought, then remembered this was a vegan kitchen.

"Have you ever been on a horse, Pax?" Kat asked as she poured each man a cup.

"A few times," Pax replied. "Sarah, my wife, used to work at the Cornell Equine Park in the summers when we were younger. She tried to teach me to ride. I never quite got the hang of it."

"Well, we'll act like it never happened."

"Good plan," Pax chuckled.

"There is a lot of work to do, and I could use some extra hands," Kat said bluntly, as if the two men in the room had a choice. "Feeding, mucking, brushing. Six hands for four horses. Should be quick work."

Pax realized that he was now paying rent. She didn't want his money; she wanted his help. Despite the uncertainty of the work ahead, Pax vowed to do his best and try, through physical labor, to make a dent in the debt he owed this generous woman.

After breakfast, Kat gave Pax and Harley each a thermos of coffee and took one for herself, along with a piece of toast with marmalade.

"August," Kat said to Harley. Pax frowned, confused about what she meant, given it was the middle of winter.

He followed the two to the barn where Harley had parked the fifth wheel the day before. He wondered why they had thermoses of coffee when the barn was so close to the house. His unspoken questions were soon answered when he followed Harley and Kat through a side door into a small set of stalls, each holding a large, well-muscled horse.

"These don't look like babies," he remarked.

Harley laughed. "No, these are for riding. The barn with the wild horses is a two-mile ride from here."

Pax realized his horsemanship class was happening right now.

"There's a dirt road leading to the barn from the other side of the ranch. That's how we bring in and send off the horses. Aunt Kat doesn't like using gas when a more eco-friendly method is available. So, we ride."

While Harley showed him how to saddle and prepare a horse for riding, Kat groomed and talked to the other horses in the stalls. Pax did his best to keep track of the various aspects of saddling, but he knew he would need another lesson. And another. And probably another. Harley had to remind him more than once to watch his step.

"The horses move as we do this, and they can't see where their hooves land. You don't want one landing on your foot," Harley instructed.

"Not even with steel-toed boots?" Pax asked.

Harley laughed and shook his head. "No."

When the horse Pax was to ride was properly saddled, Harley showed him how to mount the animal. It took several attempts for Pax to find his balance and swing his leg over to the other side of the beast, who remained calm despite the erratic motion of the human trying to climb onto his back. When he finally got himself in the saddle, Pax smiled like a kid who had just conquered an obstacle course.

"August is named after my father," Kat said as she led her horse to the stall where Pax had been training and patted his horse's neck. "He's older. Calm but stubborn."

Pax appreciated Kat's choice of mounts for him. The two seemed to have similar demeanors.

They rode slowly to the barn to allow Pax to find his balance on August. The sun breaking over the horizon lit the open areas of the ranch with a warm yellow light, making the prairie grass poking through the snow appear to glow. The air was cold, but not biting, unlike the previous few days. The breath of the horses and riders alike formed rapidly dissolving clouds as they approached a building in the distance.

At the barn, Pax dismounted—slowly. Although the two-mile ride hadn't been strenuous, the novelty of the experience and fear of falling had caused him to tense up, leaving his thigh muscles aching.

The barn resembled the one behind the main house, but it featured a large, fenced paddock on one side. A sign over the side door read, "Vild Lade," which Harley explained meant "Wild Barn." Pax noticed the solar panels on the barn's roof and admired this woman's commitment to her cause. She was that rare activist who truly "walked the talk."

"Carsen had all that installed before it was fashionable," Kat said as she walked over to Pax. "I fear that some of them may not work as well as they should, and I will have to replace them all soon. Expensive, yes. Worth it? Also, yes."

Kat slipped her arm through Pax's and led him to the barn.

"This will be a lesson in handling wild animals, so I ask you to stand aside and watch. Even though these horses are smaller than the one you rode here, they are still wild and can be dangerous if you ignore their body language."

As they entered the barn, Pax once again thought about how different this world was from the one he had left. A motion detector turned on a few interior lights, and Pax noticed the four young horses scattered across various stalls.

"Why are they separated?"

"Three males and one female," Kat replied. "Not too different from humans in some ways. It's best to keep adolescent boys separate, yes? Otherwise they will get into mischief."

Harley entered the barn and quickly headed to the back to prepare the grain mix they used to feed the young ones. Kat took Pax to the stall with the filly.

"She was found wandering on a large ranch up north. We don't know if she was lost, abandoned, or if her band was somehow wiped out. We only know that she was very thin when she arrived and is now filling out nicely. We want to keep her for another week or two, then we will find someone to adopt her."

"Who adopts wild horses?" Pax asked.

"Different people. We can't release them back into the wild, so they are tamed to save their lives. Often, they end up as work-horses on ranches. It's quite ironic, don't you think, that big ranches often make these young ones into orphans, but sometimes those same ranches become their new homes."

Pax looked at the beautiful young horse in the stall, and the horse returned his gaze.

"How can I help?" he asked.

"Stop buying beef," Kat replied absently as she looked at the filly.

Pax smiled and rephrased his question.

"I mean, how can I help today?"

IT WAS mid-afternoon when Pax sank into the chair by the front door. He removed his boots and checked them for bits of manure. His legs ached. His back ached. He felt as if he'd never really worked a day in his life before this. Everything else seemed like busy work compared to the simple tasks involved in caring for those four young horses.

Harley walked into the kitchen and returned with a bag of frozen peas, tossing it to Pax.

"You'll need these," he said.

Pax looked curiously at Harley, who pointed to the spot where the peas should go. Pax placed the pack on his groin and moaned in relief as the cold helped reduce swelling in his nether regions.

"Now you know why old cowboys are bowlegged," Harley chuckled.

Kat exited the kitchen and spoke to him as if nothing was unusual about seeing a man getting friendly with frozen produce.

"Show me your elbow," she said.

Pax stretched his arm. The spot where he slammed into the stall post after one of the yearlings backed into him still ached, but he doubted anything was broken.

"It wasn't a direct hit," he replied. "Hurts like hell and will leave a mother of a bruise, but it's solid. The bone is intact."

Olecranon Process, Pax thought, recalling the damage to his other elbow when he fell off the stage and destroyed his hand, and more importantly, Tomas.

"When you're ready," Kat said, "we'll take your shirt off and have a look. Do you need anything for the pain?"

"Tequila would be nice," he chuckled.

Kat looked at Harley wordlessly, who left the hallway to fetch the Jalisco Painkiller. She helped Pax out of the hardback wooden chair by the front door and moved him to the softer couch in the next room. She sat beside him and tried to examine the damage by lifting his sleeve.

"So, now you know that the rent is very high, yes?" Kat laughed, but her laughter carried hints of concern and guilt.

"Worth every sore muscle, Kat," Pax replied. "Any day I can learn something new is a good day."

"Exactly," she replied. "Tomorrow, we will recite what we learned today and learn something new."

Harley entered the room carrying a bottle of tequila and

three glasses. They shared a silent toast to the day's work and the lives of their wards in the Vild Lade.

"Now, let's see that arm," Kat said, helping to lift Pax's sweatshirt over his head.

After several minutes of examining the injury from every possible angle, Kat left the room, then quickly returned with a salve that she rubbed into the bruised area and over his elbow. Pax watched her as she treated his injury with no sense of embarrassment at him sitting shirtless next to her with a bag of frozen peas on his crotch.

"CBD," she said. "I use it on my joints. It's wonderful."

Pax thought of Audra, who also used CBD to help with his soreness after his grueling physical therapy sessions. He had laughed when Audra told him where CBD came from and asked her if his hand was going to get the munchies later.

Kat looked up at Pax's face as he watched her tend to his injury. Her smile was faint, but her eyes sparkled. He felt a connection. She was unlike any woman he had ever met, yet in many ways, she was like Sarah.

"I'd help you put on your shirt, Pax," she said as she stood. "But you might want to shower and put on something clean. Did your mother ever tell you that you smell like a barn?"

"Often," he chuckled.

"Well, today, she would not be exaggerating."

Freshly showered and dressed in clean casual clothes, Pax went downstairs and saw Kat and Harley. They were laughing when Pax entered the kitchen, and the conversation stopped, making him think they had been talking about him.

"How did you two get cleaned up so fast?" he asked, noticing they were in different clothes than earlier.

"We shower quickly," Harley said. "Solar electricity is nice, but the quicker we shower, the less reheating the water heaters take. You think about energy consumption differently when you don't have a constant supply from the grid."

"True, true," Kat said. "So now that you've had your luxurious New York shower out of the way, maybe we can make them shorter in the future?"

Pax agreed and took a seat at the table.

"Black bean burgers and potato salad for dinner. How does that sound?"

"Can I help?" Pax asked.

Kat looked at him, lifted his injured arm, and then let it fall to his side, watching him jump from the pain as gravity pulled the arm into his hip bone.

"Fffffuuu—!" Pax bit back the profanity, but half of some words is enough to know the rest.

"With that damaged wing?" Kat snickered. "Do you think you can play your guitar?"

"I think so," he replied. "As long as you don't do that again."

"Then sing to us while we make dinner," she said. "Carsen would play the piano and sing to me while I cooked sometimes. I didn't complain about his awful voice because I loved that he wanted to do it."

"I can do that," Pax said, grateful for the opportunity to use his talents.

He retrieved his guitar from the bedroom after stiffly climbing the stairs, then even more stiffly descending again. He found a seat in the kitchen, out of the way of the two cooks.

"What would you like me to sing?" he inquired.

"That one you sang in Austin," she said. "The one with that young man on the electric guitar."

"Oh, you saw that?"

She smiled and nodded, saying, "Yes, I got caught up last night before I slept. Red Rocks was also stunning."

Pax played slowly, evaluating the damage to his left arm. He realized he could comfortably perform the song by sticking to the chords, which created a new arrangement for *Dream of Me, Please*. The unplugged, coffee-shop style without any solos brought a smile to Kat's face that stayed long after the song finished.

While the black bean burgers cooked in a pan, Kat assembled a bacon-free German potato salad, and Pax played some soft rock acoustic tunes to keep the mood light and fill the room with music. When the food was ready, Harley went to the barn where the trailer was parked and returned with a six-pack of beer.

Pax looked at the green can. "Carlsberg?" he said.

"Danish," Harley said.

"I have a friend bring it to me when he visits from Laramie. I can't get it here," Kat added. "A little taste of home, although pasteurization laws in the US remove some of the more memorable flavors."

From vegan fare to Danish beer, Pax enjoyed his first meal as a guest worker at Brun-Dahl Ranch. He knew he was going to feel like death in the morning, but he was determined to push as hard as they needed him to.

Harley was heading back to Cheyenne after they took care of the horses in the morning, which meant that Kat would be alone. Pax understood that a few days of learning how to help care for the *unge heste*, as Kat called them, would not be enough to make him masterful, but he would work beside her to lessen her burden. It would be worth the aches and pains.

He mounted August on his first attempt the following day as they prepared to ride out. He swung into the saddle without losing his balance or overloading his injured limb, relying more on his leg muscles to push than on his arm muscles to pull. He was still sore in his thighs and undercarriage, but Harley and

Kat took turns reminding him to relax, making the ride less strenuous.

After finishing the day's chores, Harley told Pax he could call him when he felt it was time to hit the road again, and he would come back to help make the fifth-wheel road-ready. Pax thanked him for everything. Kat hugged Harley and made him promise to visit the ranch more often. Then, Harley drove down the long driveway as Pax and Kat watched and waved from the porch. Pax felt a strange sense of separation, even though he barely knew the young man.

"This feels like one of those scenes in a movie where the older couple waves as their child drives away to their future."

Kat looked at him with curiosity.

"A couple, are we?" she laughed as they entered the house. "No, Mr. Butler. Not yet."

THE LATE-MARCH SUN rose over the horizon, illuminating the ranch. With the deep snow gone, prairie grass waved in the light as the ground warmed beneath it. The sky was dotted with fluffy cumulus clouds, and the breeze was crisp but not bitterly cold. The absence of vapor trails from high-flying aircraft made the world feel as if it had slipped two hundred years into the past. Nothing else in the sky or air hinted at the crisis gripping the world beyond this small Wyoming ranch.

In more populated areas, panic and pandemic became the new normal. Cable news channels constantly broadcast fear-mongering conspiracy theories. The world was bracing for the worst, which many referred to as the biblical "End Days." Yet, on the prairie of the Brun-Dahl Ranch, the sun continued to rise and winter receded.

Pax sat atop August, gazing across the prairie, warmed by the early spring sunshine despite patches of snow still speckling the ground. After his first week of daily contact, August had become his friend, and now, a few months into their relationship, they communicated silently through touch. This new form of communication felt both strange and comforting for someone who had relied on sound all his life.

The jacket Kat had given him on that long-ago frigid day was also more comfortable. A vegan diet and daily hard work on the ranch had trimmed the excess weight he had gained since Sarah passed. He felt good and strong, with muscles again.

He let his beard grow, embracing a more rugged cowboy look. He liked what he saw in the mirror, except for the silver mop of hair on his head—the color, not the length. Kat had offered to trim his hair as she did weekly with his beard, but he declined, wanting to awaken that old, long-haired rock-and-roller inside him.

With a simple motion, August turned and brought him back to the path where Kat met him on Freyja. The two rode quietly down the path to the Vild Lade.

"You're leaving soon?" Kat asked as they rode along, her words just as likely to be a statement as a question.

"No," Pax replied simply.

"No?" she laughed. "The snow is melting. Aren't you planning to be on the road again to continue your quest?"

Pax looked at her and shook his head.

"No," he said. "This pandemic is going to last a while. Some states are talking about lockdowns, which means... I don't know what it means, but my pilgrimage is on hold."

"You don't want to go home to see your family?"

"I do," he sighed. "But I think they're all going to be locked down too. One more body in the house will only add to their stress."

She rode silently, listening.

"And if I left, who will sing to the new horses when they arrive?" he asked.

Kat smiled and nudged Freyja into a trot as they approached the barn. Pax silently urged August to keep pace.

As he got used to working with the wild foals and yearlings under Kat's care, he found that singing while filling their feed and water or mucking out stalls helped keep them passive. After being knocked around on his first day at the ranch, he started singing to himself to stay calm around the horses and realized that when he was relaxed, so were they. So, he made singing a daily routine. The males enjoyed his version of *Me and Bobby McGee*, while the filly loved *Banana Pancakes* by Jack Johnson.

"Know your audience," he had told Kat when she saw how the horses reacted to his voice.

He sang for Kat as well. She enjoyed classic '70s ballads, and he did his best, even though he sometimes struggled to remember all the lyrics. Thirty years earlier, he would have known every word of every song on the radio. Now, he remembered most of them and made up the rest. Kat never called him out for his creative license.

He also sat at the piano, reliving his childhood lessons. Although many keys beyond the second octave above middle C were out of tune, he let his fingers play some of his original songs to hear how they sounded.

Even their living arrangement had evolved.

One night in early February, he woke to the sound of a board creaking outside his bedroom door. He turned to see the door open, revealing Kat standing there, backlit by the full moon shining through the windows behind her. He knew why she was there. The tension between them had been growing, accompanied by subtle displays of affection—a gentle touch of her hand on his chest, her arm linked with his, and a lock of hair brushed from his face to behind his ear.

"Kat, I," he tried not to sound harsh, "I can't."

She leaned against the doorframe. He could see the outline of her fit body in silhouette, but her face remained shrouded in shadow.

"You can't? Or you won't?"

He thought about it. Could he? Yes, he was quite sure he was capable. Was he ready to? That was another question.

"I can," he said, meaning he was able. "But I won't. So, I can't."

She sniffed slightly, and he recognized that it wasn't the sniff associated with a cold or dust in the air. It was the sound of disappointment.

"I'm sorry," she said, stepping away from the door and heading back to her room.

He lay for a full minute, nervously fingering the rings, before getting out of bed and walking to her partially open door.

"Kat?" he whispered.

"It's okay, Pax. I'm okay."

"Can I come in?"

She shifted in bed and glanced at the door. He entered the room.

"I'm sorry I was so blunt," he said. "I don't want you to think it's you. It's absolutely not you."

He laughed softly, signaling to her that he was attracted to her and that any obstacles to their being together were his responsibility, not hers.

She moved over, letting him lie on the bed next to her. He felt comfortable doing this. They had grown close and shared deeply personal stories, including their experiences of loss. They often listened to music and lay together on the sofa in the living room. They felt at ease like this.

"I'm not ready, Kat. That's all. It's not you. It's all me. I'm not ready, but wow, if you feel that way about me, I'm... wow."

She crept closer as he slid his arm under her head, allowing her to rest in the crook of his shoulder. Her hand rested on his chest. They remained that way in silence for a long time. He accepted that he would stay there through the night, and as he drifted closer to sleep, he heard a whisper.

"You feel like him."

The next morning, he woke before dawn. The remnants of his dream state fogged his perceptions, and he felt... *Her...* against his chest, spooning as they had so many times before, his arm wrapped around her, and her hands wrapped around his arm. She didn't smell the same, but she felt perfect in his arms.

"Sarah," he whispered.

"I'm sorry, no," came the response.

His eyes flew open. The woman he was holding wasn't his wife, who had left his life years earlier. This woman felt like her, but she wasn't her.

"Kat?"

"Yes," she sighed. "Just Kat."

His response surprised them both. Rather than pulling away in shock, he hugged her tighter and resisted the urge to cry.

"I'm sorry, Kat, I thought you were—"

"I know," she said. "All night, I thought you were Carsen, and then I would remember that he's gone and it was you."

They lay quietly entangled for a few long moments.

"I'm sorry I'm not him," Pax said.

"And I'm sorry I'm not her," Kat replied.

They lay spooning, holding each other, feeling something strangely familiar. He wanted to kiss her, to give her what she desired, to love her. But he knew he couldn't—not in the way she wanted. Kat meant too much to him, and he wouldn't give in to these basic desires, fearing he would break her heart when he eventually left.

From that moment forward, their days were filled with trips

to the out barn to care for the wild ones, rides back to tend to the tame ones, and then music, laughter, and stories. They occasionally went into town for groceries and to give Pax a chance to send messages to his contacts before returning to the ranch, where there was almost no mobile signal or wired internet.

Every night, they slept together, holding each other and finding a peaceful sleep neither had experienced in years.

Happy birthday, Dad. Please call.

It was early May, and Pax stood on the corner outside the Wheatland Country Store, where he and Kat were picking up some supplies and dog food. Their masks were in place, and they maintained their distance from others, especially those protesting the safety mandates and, in many cases, the existence of the virus itself.

He looked at Ally's text message, and the last two words made his stomach churn. He dialed.

"Dad? Wow, that was quick."

"Hi Kiddo, got your text, what's up?"

"I didn't think you had a signal at Katja's."

"We're in town to get dog food and some other provisions," he said.

"Provisions? That's a funny word coming out of your mouth. How's cowboy life treating you?" she asked, her voice laced with sarcasm.

"I don't think you would recognize me, Kiddo," he chuckled. "So, what's up?"

"I thought I would give you a birthday present," Ally said, her voice a confusing mix of tones.

"Over the phone?"

"I'm pregnant, Dad."

The words took a moment to register with Pax. Pregnant. Ally is pregnant.

"You're pregnant?" he laughed.

"Yup!" she replied, her voice wavering between laughter and tears.

"How did that happen?"

Ally laughed. "You know how it happens, Dad."

He couldn't tell from her tone if she was excited or upset or some blend of both.

"Wow, that's great, Kiddo! I mean, it's great, right?"

"Yeah, yeah, it's great. It's scary as hell with a goddamn pandemic around, but yeah, it's great!"

Kat approached him on the street while he was talking to Ally.

"Ally is pregnant," he told her.

Kat brazenly took the phone from Pax's hand and started talking to Ally while he stood by, stupefied that his conversation had been usurped. She laughed and spoke loudly, and he watched as this woman conveyed love and compassion over the phone to someone she had only spoken to a handful of times, but never met in person. He realized that his feelings for Kat were growing, and he was entering a phase of their relationship where he would have to choose between staying and being content with what his life would become with her, or leaving and continuing to search for Sarah. He knew he wasn't ready to make that decision.

Kat graciously handed the phone back to Pax and playfully slapped his shoulder.

"Why didn't you tell me it was your birthday? You're a ridiculous old man."

Kat walked away, presumably to find a suitable birthday gift, while Pax continued his chat with Ally.

She told him that when they found out about the baby, low-key Travis beamed like a man who had won the lottery. She talked about Lainey and her tendency to sing everything instead of just saying it. She mentioned Puck, who had, so far, dodged COVID, although most of his school friends had been exposed. She said he was still feeling run down and sad, presumably because he couldn't see his friends.

"We bought him a starter guitar," she said, "and he liked playing it at first, pretending to be like you, Dad. But he hasn't touched it in a while. Maybe when you get back, you can work with him."

"Yeah," Pax replied. "Something recently made me think that I would enjoy teaching guitar lessons. He can be my first student."

"That's great, Dad. I think you would be a phenomenal teacher, especially for kids. You're much more patient with them than with adults."

One of their typical awkward pauses filled the ether between them.

"Dad," Ally said, needing to break the silence. "Have you heard from Audra?"

"Yes, Kiddo," he replied after a long pause. "She responded several months ago. It was short and... not sweet, I guess... but not really flavored at all. I've meant to reach out to her again and see how she's coping with the pandemic."

"She's fine, Dad. She told me she replied to your text, but I wanted to see if you would tell me the truth."

That stung, and he bit his tongue to suppress his knee-jerk reaction.

"Let it go, Dad. For now, anyway."

"Why?"

"She is really busy right now. When you come back, you can sit down with her and apologize for being such an asshole."

He chuckled. Ally was remarkably similar to him in many

ways, but she was still more like Sarah when it came to compassion and empathy. He still felt guilty about leaving things with Audra as he had, but it seemed she had moved on. Ally was telling him he didn't need to pick at that scab.

"When are you coming for a visit, Dad?"

A visit? Did she know more about his dilemma than he did? Did she assume he was staying?

He didn't answer right away because he didn't have an answer. He was comfortable, perhaps too comfortable, living with Kat. The purpose of his trip had faded into the background, a soft but steady rhythm. But as he searched for a response to his daughter's question, he heard that rhythm a bit louder, and it felt foreign.

"Soon, Kiddo."

IN THE WIDER WORLD, the pandemic continued. However, in the U.S., as most of the population practiced social distancing and wore masks, states lifted lockdowns, allowing society to inch closer to the "old normal." There were still pockets of deniers and conspiracy theorists, and some learned the reality of the virus the hard way.

Still, people needed to socialize, and Pax and Kat were no exception. Months spent isolated together had bonded them, but the desire to see others and experience live entertainment began to grow. When the last wild foal was adopted in early June, they decided to head into Cheyenne to socialize before the next group of four arrived in late July.

Pax and Kat drove to Cheyenne, enjoying the light traffic—a pandemic side effect—which allowed them to take in the beautiful highway views of southern Wyoming. They checked into a hotel for their one-night stay and called Harley to see if he wanted to join them for dinner. Harley suggested a restaurant he liked that had karaoke, and they agreed to meet there for dinner and some entertainment.

True to its name, T-Joe's Steakhouse & Saloon was a saloon-style steakhouse with a lively karaoke atmosphere. During the early days of the pandemic, while business shutdowns were recommended and sometimes mandated, T-Joe's stayed open. Despite the challenges other restaurants faced, it continued operations by following health guidelines, taking precautions to ensure the safety of its staff and patrons, and offering takeout services for those who preferred to eat at home. As the country slowly reopened, T-Joe's was ready to welcome back patrons from the broader Cheyenne area for in-person dining, providing a much-needed change for residents tired of seeing the same faces at the dinner table every night.

The room buzzed with the energy of people who hadn't socialized in a very long time. It wasn't crowded, but it felt full—full of hope, laughter, and old routines picked up as if they'd never been dropped. Kat leaned into Pax's shoulder as they moved through the bar, scanning for Harley.

"There he is," Kat said, pointing to a table near the front where Harley was waving them over.

They enjoyed a heartwarming reunion after their long spring separation. Harley lived alone in an apartment, and the isolation had weighed on him when the pandemic began. He kept his sanity by playing online video games with friends across the city and organizing socially distant meetups at Lions Park, where his friends would bring their favorite bottle of whatever, sit comfortably apart, and share stories they'd heard from relatives in other parts of the country. It wasn't perfect, but it was something, and it kept the depression of isolation at bay.

Pax sat quietly as Kat and Harley caught up, neither slowed by the N95 masks they wore. He listened to the sounds of the room, with different groups chatting about what they had heard from other parts of the country, which businesses were open again, and which were still "believing the bullshit from the government."

As his attention wandered among the widely spaced tables, he noticed an older man approaching them. He had a white goatee, wore a vintage denim jacket, and had his mask pulled down below his chin, revealing a curious grin that didn't quite reach his eyes. As he neared the table, he pulled the mask up to cover his mouth and nose. Behind him was another man about Harley's age, who waved to the karaoke DJ. Harley greeted the two men and introduced them to Pax and Kat.

"JD," the man said to Pax. "Friend of Harley's from work. He said I'd like you. Must be ageism."

"He oversells," Pax replied. "Good to meet someone who remembers life before hashtags, though."

Donnie, Harley's other work friend, sat across from Kat and began chatting with them while Pax connected with JD. The older man's laugh was easy and familiar. Within minutes, the two were engrossed in a conversation about '70s music, TV shows that were never meant to be binge-watched, and how rotary phones taught people patience.

"Back then, you had to want to talk to someone," JD said. "If you forgot which number you just dialed, or dialed all seven digits and messed up the last one—"

"You started over," Pax finished with a chuckle. "And the cords! You had to have a 25-foot cord to get away from your parents while you talked to a girl on the other end. People today just don't get that there were times when you were unreachable, like driving home from work or just going to the store. I think all this constant availability has ruined us. Although I missed the birth of my daughter because I was a few counties away with no way to reach me."

Kat and Harley exchanged glances, smiling at the sight of the men bonding over nostalgia. They saw a different Pax than the one who had been working on the ranch for the past several months. There was something comforting in how the two men fell into a rhythm so quickly, like strangers realizing they had both been at the same concert decades ago.

Pax's ear was attuned to JD's accent, and he thought they might have walked the same streets long ago.

"Where are you from, originally, JD? You sound... eastern?"

JD nodded and laughed. "Yeah," he responded. "Born in Albany, New York, grew up in Colonie—northwest of there, if you're not familiar."

"Oh, I'm familiar," Pax laughed. "What got you out here?"

JD quieted. "My father-in-law drove a big rig for about thirty years until arthritis in his knees ended that unchosen career. He decided to move out this way when he retired. My wife and I moved here about five years ago when Bobby got sick, before he retired for good."

Pax understood the indirect reference in JD's message. He also suspected there was a reason why JD's wife wasn't sitting next to him, but he didn't want to pry. Finally, JD broke the drawn-out silence.

"Harley mentioned you're from the Finger Lakes area. That's not too far from my old stomping grounds."

Pax nodded. "I was born in Ithaca, but my wife and I moved to Middletown when we got married, so I know the Hudson Valley from one end to the other. My band played in Albany more than once. Schenectady, too, so we would stop in Colonie now and then for food or beer. Man, it felt like you could play up and down Central Ave for miles and never play the same club twice."

JD shook his head and chuckled as Pax listed off half a dozen venues in the capital city area where Butler Service had once enjoyed a loyal following.

"Wow, my buddies and I killed a lot of brain cells in some of those places," JD laughed.

Pax clinked his tequila glass against JD's bottle. "Right there with you, pal."

Eventually, JD excused himself and walked toward the stage. "I promised our waitress I'd sing at least once," he called over his shoulder.

Kat turned to Pax, raising her eyebrow. "And you?"

"I'm good right here," he said, his hand on the back of her chair, his thumb gliding over the space between her shoulders. "This is the first night in a long time I've wanted to just be in the room. That's enough."

JD's voice filled the space as he sang a warm, slightly raspy rendition of *Try a Little Tenderness*. People sang along, adding to the sound of laughter and conversation mingling like the first signs of spring after an unreasonably oppressive winter.

"It's strange," Kat said, leaning in close. "Everyone's still a little careful. Like we're afraid to enjoy it too much."

"Yeah," Pax said, eyes on the crowd. "But you can feel it. People want to return to their lives before all this. Even if they're not sure how yet. I'm glad we're doing this."

"Me too," she said. "Even if it's just this. Just a good night."

When JD returned to the table, slightly winded from singing through a surgical mask, Pax raised his glass. "To good nights."

JD clinked his bottle against Pax's glass. "And to more of them."

The group expressed their agreement. "And more of these," Pax added, waving to the server to bring another round.

They ordered dinner. Although T-Joe's wasn't inherently vegan-friendly, Kat only needed to know what ingredients they used and worked with the server to create a unique meal for herself and Pax.

When their dinners had been partially eaten and another round was ordered for each of them, excluding Kat, who opted for water, JD sang again, followed by Donnie. Other patrons took turns at the microphone, some delivering good performances, some not so good, and some truly great ones. Pax listened quietly, his musician's respect giving each their due. Between the songs, the group continued chatting.

Under the table, Kat reached over to touch Pax's hand. He opened it and held hers gently, stirring memories of holding Sarah's hand on a park bench many years ago. So much about this woman reminded him of her.

The night was exactly what they all needed after a long stretch of isolation. Pax and JD reminisced about the 70s and 80s, discussing the various music venues they had both visited. Some were places where Butler Service performed, while others were where Pax and Zim drank through the money they earned from the previous night's gig. They suspected they had probably been in the same bar at the same time on more than one occasion. Meanwhile, Donnie and Harley's conversation shifted from college football to NASCAR racing to the expanding swinger community in the greater Cheyenne area.

Kat remained silent as he held her hand, savoring the evening and enjoying the unexpected connection between JD and Pax. She watched them chatting, laughing, and exchanging stories about life before the Internet—the quality of marijuana grown on a farm instead of in a lab, skinny dipping and streaking, sitting around the TV on Thursday night so you didn't miss out on the latest episode of one show or another. He spoke excitedly about his family and grandchildren, and for the first time since she met him, he mentioned Sarah.

Kat noticed the change in him. He was no longer the broken

man she had seen in the YouTube video months earlier. He was stronger, not just physically from the ranch work, but emotionally as well. He was open and accessible. This change pleased her, but it also planted a seed of anxiety.

JD got up and sang another song, and despite Kat nudging and encouraging him, Pax refused to take the mic. Singing would mean letting go of her hand, and he preferred to quietly hold it under the table, even if it meant eating and drinking with his non-dominant hand.

When karaoke finished at 10:00 p.m., the group broke up, exchanging numbers and promises to meet again. Harley drove to his apartment while Pax and Kat headed back to their hotel.

As he closed the hotel door, Pax noticed Kat standing by the bed, an anxious expression deepening the shadows on her face. Without hesitation, and emboldened by the Jalisco Love Potion, he walked over, wrapped an arm around her waist, and kissed her deeply. She melted into the kiss, and they remained in that embrace for several long moments. When it ended, Kat touched his cheek and smiled.

"Thank you, Pax," she said quietly. "That was—lovely."

He smiled and leaned in to kiss her again, but she stopped him by placing a hand on his chest.

"I can't," she said softly.

He waited. She tucked some of his long hair behind his ear.

"You can't, or you won't?"

Kat laughed, reminded of the exchange they had months ago, although this time it was the other way around.

"Pax," she said. "You're leaving soon. So, I can't."

Her words struck him much like Audra's had when she said she was "done with him" on the last day of his physical therapy. This time, though, the pain felt real, not just because this woman who had taken root in him was rejecting him, but because of the reason she was rejecting him. She believed he was ready to leave. After months together, she thought he would simply pack up and go.

Pax stepped back and looked at Kat, whose thin smile revealed her happiness that he was healed, but also the sorrow of their imminent parting.

"I could tell when you spoke with Allison on your birthday. There was a longing in your voice. And now you have a new grandchild on the way. Your old life is calling you, Pax."

"No," he said emphatically. "No."

Kat rested her head against his chest and listened to his heartbeat.

"It's fine," she said quietly. "No, not fine, but it's okay. You made no promises."

"Kat, I—"

"Don't, please," she said, looking up at him, her eyes wet. "I don't want false hope. I don't want promises."

"Come with me, Kat. Come to South Carolina. We'll visit and then we'll come back."

He knew he was reaching. He couldn't imagine life without her. Could he possibly have both her and home? But wasn't she now part of what he considered home? Kat patted his chest and kissed his cheek.

"You know I can't, Pax," she said. "You know my work is here with the horses."

He understood the reality. Her life was at the Brun-Dahl Ranch and always would be. His life was... where? In South Carolina, where his family was? That felt both right and completely wrong at the same time.

He felt like one of the young horses Kat cared for—physically broken, then healed, before their wildness was tamed to save their lives. He had been emotionally broken and healed by this remarkable woman. Now, he was more focused, more peaceful, and more himself than he had been in a long time, maybe ever. His wildness was tamed. But unlike the horses, he knew that leaving her could break him again.

Pax sat on the bed, trying to find the words to convince Kat that she was wrong. He was good with lyrics, so why couldn't he stitch together the words to make her believe him? Sarah had always been a persuasive speaker. He wished she would whisper the right words into his heart.

Kat sat next to him, her hand resting on his knee. They stayed silent for several minutes until Pax turned to meet her gaze, feeling like he had the beginning of something.

"If I told you that I love you, would you believe me?" he asked, nodding as if the truth of it were immutable.

"I would," Kat replied, leaning into him with her head on his shoulder. "And if I told you I love you, would that change anything?"

"You have already changed everything, Kat."

He scowled, wishing for a better follow-up comment, but her response to his declaration had disarmed him.

"I love you, Kat." Even those powerful words felt flat in his mouth.

"Ah, now you say it," Kat laughed and sniffed.

"I wonder why we never said it before."

Kat sighed.

"Because I believe we both knew this day was inevitable."

"No," he said again. "No. I'm staying. Yes, something is tugging at me to go back there. But it's not to return. It's to visit."

"If you go, Pax, when will you come back here? Do you come back at all once you've held your grandchildren again?"

They held each other in the dim light of the hotel room, enveloped in a silence that seemed to last forever. Pax intertwined his fingers with hers and thought again of the bench in Stewart Park. He raised her hand to his lips and kissed her fingers. For some reason, he listened for a sign from Sarah, a signal, a tone. *Third fret—Second string*. It didn't come. He wondered if that was because he no longer needed it or because she approved of where his heart and mind were.

"I can," he said, breaking the silence, the unspoken part of his statement lingering in the air. "And I will, if you want to."

She stayed silent.

"I want to," he added quietly, making sure she understood that things had changed.

Kat gazed at him, her eyes filled with tears that defied gravity.

"I'm afraid to," she said, sounding uncharacteristically vulnerable.

He kissed her fingers again and then stood, uncertain of his destination. His instinct was to leave, not to storm out as he had with Audra, but to walk around the hotel to let Kat clear her head or to clear his own. He hesitated briefly, then slowly moved toward the hotel room door. As he opened it, she suddenly stood.

"Pax."

He turned and saw the anxiety in her expression and heard the desperation in her voice. She took several deep breaths, and then, to his surprise, she nodded.

"I want to," she whispered.

Pax shut the door.

PART V

THE SIGHT OF YOU

"I didn't realize how much I had missed you until I saw you again."

– Unknown

CHAPTER 8

PAX LOOKED DOWN AT THE WORDS that had just spilled out of his pen. They came to him while he was showering, prompting him to jump onto the floor and slip frantically down the hall with a towel around his waist, hoping to capture the words before they vanished from his aging mind.

Another night, another place
She has your smile but not your face
And holding her completes the space
Like I once felt with you.
And though I love you, this I know
I have to stay, not let her go
For in her arms I found my soul,
And learned to love anew.

It's time this pilgrim found a home
To build a life, not walk alone
To share my song with those I've known
And hold to what is true.

The children thrive, their songs their own.
New voices heard, new verses flow.
Her hands now holding theirs, although
They still remember you.

This song, *their* song, included Katja. He ached for Sarah, but Kat's presence softened that pain. Their sounds were different—inharmonic, in fact—but together they made his song feel more complete. Sarah was still the notes of joy in his heart, but Kat was the sound of peace in his soul. The children and grandchildren would remain his echo of *Her*.

He pushed away thoughts of how to make this long-distance familial arrangement work. He would figure it out with Ally and Rob. He wouldn't rush into something unprepared as he had many times before.

He reflected on Ally's comment about his poor decisions and acknowledged how dead-on she had been. He had always been impulsive and single-minded. Even during his time with Kat, his narrow focus remained fixed on Sarah, rather than genuinely listening to his own heart. He thought about the silence and peace he experienced with Kat, not only in her embrace each night but also in the daily moments when he was within range of her smile.

He remembered the night in Cheyenne when their bodies moved together as if strings connected their hands, hips, and legs. She was the one Sarah wanted him to find. Not just a body to replace the one he could no longer hold, but a soul in tune with his own. Entanglement in a different key.

This is home now, he thought. *I don't need to go back.*

Finally, he had the words to back up his decision to stay. He would tell Kat when she got back from her morning grocery run.

He finished his shower, dried off, and got dressed. As he was brushing his long hair, his phone pinged, and he realized that the notification tone was a B note, like the heart monitor in the hospital room the night Sarah died—not as high-pitched, but still. He picked up the phone and put it on vibrate to avoid hearing that tone again, then he read the message.

Please call.

Rob's simple words stared back at him. The exact two words that had caused him anxiety from Ally's birthday text stirred up the same unease. He picked up the upstairs house phone and dialed.

"Dad," Rob said. Pax could sense his distress.

"What's going on, Rob? Is it something with Jazz or Naomi?"

He could feel his tension rising as if it were pumped through the wires from Rob's call.

"No, Dad," Rob replied. "They're fine. Ally wanted me to call. She has her hands full, but—"

He was losing patience. The tones in Rob's voice were fueling his fear.

"Rob. Please."

"It's Puck, Dad."

PAXTON LEEDS—PUCK to his friends, and he had friends now—looked into the camera from the hospital bed, his mask pulled down so Papa could see his smile.

Her eyes. *Her* mouth. Pax thought as he scrolled through the series of pictures that Ally sent him. He blinked back tears repeatedly, though some still found their way down his cheek.

Ally had remained calm and professional with Pax, explaining everything they had discovered over the preceding few weeks. She had mentioned Puck's lack of energy when she

called on his birthday, but it was common for kids to feel disconnected and uninspired during lockdown, so they hadn't linked
his lethargy to anything physical.

Then, spontaneous nosebleeds, headaches, and dizziness
began to appear. His pediatrician diagnosed anemia and recommended a dietary change, including more iron-rich foods. Next
came fevers, with no indication of COVID or other infections.
Ally ultimately consulted specialists she knew through her role
in patient advocacy, and they suggested additional testing,
hinting at something more serious. She called in some favors to
quickly secure an appointment with Pineville's top pediatric
specialist, and Puck underwent testing.

Initially, he cried when pricked with a needle, but after
several instances requiring blood draws, he became accustomed
to the process, and the "little pinch" he was warned about
became no big deal.

Based on those results, additional tests were ordered,
including X-rays, MRI scans, bone marrow samples, and, most
frightening of all, a spinal tap. Throughout it all, Ally and Travis
were by his side, speaking calmly, keeping him still, and helping
him understand what was happening to his eight-year-old body.

Pax looked at the words in the text Ally sent.

Acute Myeloid Leukemia (AML)

He couldn't understand what she was saying on the phone,
hearing only the word "leukemia" and feeling the panic it
caused, so she texted him the full name. After giving her an
earful for not telling him sooner, he let her finish.

"He's low to intermediate risk, Dad," Ally said as she smoothly
switched between mother, daughter, and patient advocate. "It's
manageable, and we will ensure he gets the best treatment."

"What are the odds of him getting better?" he asked, his
voice uncharacteristically quiet.

"The odds are very good with most kids his age, Dad, but we won't talk about the odds of other kids. Puck's odds are one hundred percent that he will get better, got it? That's what you get into that stubborn brain of yours. He is going to be okay. There is nothing else to know about it."

She hadn't mentioned a number, which indicated she didn't like it.

"How can I help, Kiddo?"

"I don't know, Dad. I really wish you were here, though."

Downstairs, he heard Kat come back from her trip to the store.

"Kom ned og spis, gamle mand!" Kat shouted to Pax to join her for breakfast.

He chuckled softly and wiped away his tears.

"Kat's going to say, 'I told you so,'" he said softly.

Ally was sniffing. The patient advocate had been replaced by the mother in crisis. "What?"

"A couple of weeks ago, she told me I was ready to go home, and I told her I was staying. I've been trying to convince her ever since."

"Oh, god, Dad," Ally cried. "Oh, god, don't lose her. She's been so good for you."

Pax stared at the floor, his mind bouncing between Puck, Kat, Ally, and...

"I'm on my way, Kiddo."

After ending the call, Pax took several deep breaths and blinked away his tears. He needed to hold it together, get things done, and get rid of the fifth wheel so it wouldn't slow him down. He picked up the phone and called Harley.

"Hey, Aunt Kat," Harley answered on the first ring.

"No, it's me, Harley. Listen, does your outfit buy used trailers?"

"We do," Harley replied quizzically. "You looking to sell yours?"

"Yeah. I'm heading back to South Carolina. I don't need it to slow me down. Can I meet you in Cheyenne and make a deal with your people?"

"I'm on my way to the office now," Harley said. "I'll let them know you're coming and tell them not to screw you over. Friends and family treatment."

"Thanks, Harley. I can be there in a little over an hour."

"Pax?" Harley's tone was flavored with concern. "Does Aunt Kat know?"

"She will, in about two minutes."

"Ok, good luck. See you in an hour."

He disconnected the call, took a deep breath, and walked down the stairs to the kitchen, where Kat was making vegan blueberry pancakes. She heard him enter the kitchen, but when she turned to make a snarky comment about how long he had taken in the shower, she noticed the expression on his face.

"Pax, what is it?"

He unloaded everything Ally had told him. He told her that he was selling the fifth wheel and that somehow, in that hotel room, she had been right, but for the wrong reasons.

Kat looked into the eyes of the man she had lost her heart to, and she felt his ache. She sensed the tug between his family and his place by her side. Just as he had done for her when her anxiety peaked in that room in Cheyenne, Kat lifted his fingers to her lips and kissed them.

"Well," she said quietly. "It has been a very long time since I took a vacation."

∼

EVEN THOUGH HARLEY'S colleagues offered him a fair deal, Pax had to absorb $15,000 in depreciation and wear and tear. He reflected on the places he had visited, the people he had met, and the experiences he had gained from the rolling apartment and decided he had received more value from the trailer than that.

After finishing his dealings with the RV dealers, he said an emotional goodbye to Harley, explaining the situation with Puck. Then, he drove north, where Kat had been making her own arrangements.

She met him on the porch and wrapped her arms around him, burying her face in his neck.

"We will get through this," she whispered against his skin. "He will be fine."

Pax heard the "we" in her words, and his breath caught. She was in this with him. He wasn't alone.

Kat pulled back and placed her hand on his chest. This was something she did, something that was theirs without any echoes of Sarah.

"Now listen," she said thoughtfully. "This is a trip, not a move. I must return here in July."

"I know," he said. "Maybe at that point, I'll have my emotional shit together enough to come back with you."

"Make no promises, Pax."

"I know," he said, grabbing her bags and putting them in the truck. "Do you have someone to keep tabs on the place while you're gone?"

"Yes," Kat replied. "Even though I'm a hippie and a nuisance to my cattle ranch neighbors, we look out for each other. The oldest son of the largest ranch is coming to stay for the few weeks I'm with you."

Kat packed vegan snacks for the drive and filled two thermoses with coffee. She locked up the house and slid into the passenger seat.

"I can drive when you need a rest," she said.

"I know," he replied. "It's about 25 hours of driving, so we'll take at least one overnight break, maybe two. Most of today is gone, and I want to reach Lincoln before we stop for the night."

"So, let's not waste any more time," Kat stated.

They drove to the ranch where her neighbor's son lived, and she handed him the keys along with a list of items to care for the dogs and ranch horses. She also provided him with directions on how to reach the Vild Lade on horseback to check on it a few times each week, even though there were no wild horses currently in their care. Pax watched as the tall man in his mid-twenties nodded and showed Kat the respect she had earned in the area. Despite her strong opposition to their business pursuits, the local ranchers respected Carsen and Katja.

Once back in the truck, she buckled her seatbelt and patted Pax's leg. Then they were on their way, heading toward Puck.

Since starting his pilgrimage, Pax had driven alone for many months, so silence was easy. Kat respected the quiet but kept an eye on him for the anxiety she knew would come in waves as he thought about his grandson. Each time she saw him scowl or clench his jaw, she would reach over to caress his neck, stroke his hair, or sing to him in Danish.

Once they were on I-80, Pax took the truck up to a speed that matched the highway number and kept his eye open for speed traps. Kat shared the snacks with him, sometimes feeding him directly, and making sure he drank some of the water she picked up when they stopped for gas.

After a few hours of quiet, disrupted only by reminders to eat and drink, Kat finally broke the silence.

"I only have one regret," she stated.

Pax glanced at her, as if he had just realized he wasn't alone in the truck. He laughed.

"Only one?" he asked.

"Yes," she replied. "Only one. I regret not making you sing karaoke with JD so I could record it and upload it to your YouTube channel."

The YouTube channel felt so distant from his active memory that he couldn't recall the last time he had looked at it. His nomadic life was behind him. He didn't think he'd ever perform on a stage again, but he reflected on the stages he had stepped on, the people he met, and the words rolled out of his mouth.

He talked, and she listened. He told her about Nashville and Sal, Leo, and Claire. He spoke about the clubs he and Sal visited, as well as the families in the RV park. He even shared the story of the Claire incident, which made Kat laugh.

"Oh my," she said. "I guess she had no idea who she was trying to seduce?"

Pax laughed. "Neither did you, but here we are."

He described the incident involving the bikers between Nashville and Memphis, as well as how he met the club's leader again in Austin. He spoke about the Cruz family, especially young Beto, the guitar prodigy. He recounted how Cassie convinced him it was time to take off the wedding ring and how she gave him his first and only tattoo. He reminisced about Red Rocks and Alicent and how it was likely the peak of his musical life to stand on that stage, even though the crowd was much smaller than at Austin's performance.

"And what about that first performance?" Kat asked. "The Red Roses performance. How did it come about?"

He began talking about the night he met Lara, but as he did, a thought stirred, and he sensed something in the back of his mind.

"Lara," the voice said. *Third fret—Second string.*

The silence stretched for a few minutes as he sorted through his thoughts. Was it possible? Could she help?

"Pax?" Kat prompted, concerned at his silence.

"What does the GPS say is our ETA in Lincoln?" he asked.

Kat glanced at his phone.

"A little before 10:00 p.m.," she said. "Why?"

He looked at her. His expression had shifted. A thin smile curved beneath his clear blue eyes.

"Have you ever been to Memphis?"

THEY STOPPED near Kearney to refuel and grab a bite to eat. Even after months on horseback, strengthening his legs, stepping out of the truck, and stretching felt like a welcome relief for Pax's hips.

While Kat ordered a custom vegan meal at Cunningham's Journal Tap and Kitchen, Pax called Lara to update her on the situation. Lara explained the typical referral process and promised to contact the head of Pediatric Oncology to check the backlog for inbound referrals. In the meantime, she advised Pax to have Ally gather as many referrals as possible from Puck's doctors and send her all the diagnostic reports, test results, laboratory reports, and surgical information.

"I can't make any promises," she said. "But we'll do our best to get him into the program. At the very least, we'll get him into outpatient services so he can be treated while we wait for a bed."

"So, if I'm hearing you right, Lara," Pax asked. "Get him to Memphis, and we'll figure it out when we get there?"

She chuckled.

"Get him to Memphis, and when he gets here, we'll be ready for him as an outpatient. Do you have a place to stay?"

"Not yet," he said.

"Well, you do now."

Pax struggled to find the words to express his gratitude.

"Thank you, Lara," he said softly.

"We'll take care of your guy, Pax. When can I expect you?"

"Tomorrow."

"Wow, so soon. And Puck?"

"I'll call Ally as soon as I get off the phone with you. I'll text you when I know."

"Ok, my friend. It's going to be so wonderful to see you again." She sounded genuinely excited to be reunited, even in the dire circumstances.

"Oh, and Lara?"

"Yeah?" Lara's tone was hesitant.

"Okay if I bring a plus one?"

Ally couldn't believe what he was telling her. Somehow, her father managed to pull off a miracle while she struggled to determine their next steps. When she discovered he was serious about temporarily moving Puck to Memphis, she broke down and cried.

"Dad, I can't afford not to work," she said. "I can't move Puck to Memphis."

"Yes, you can. I will stay with him. He'll live with me at Lara's place until we can get him into the hospital."

"Dad, this could take months or years. How are you going to do that?"

"That's on me, Kiddo. You get Puck's referrals and documentation over to Lara. She's texting you her office address. Then you and Puck get on a plane to Memphis—ASAFP. No delay."

Ally could hardly speak through her sobs.

"I don't know what happened to you out there in the world, Dad, but oh my god, thank you."

"I found your mother, Kiddo. I'll tell you more about it when you get to Memphis. I love you. I'll see you in a couple of days."

"Yes, Dad. A couple of days."

Pax got off the phone and listened. He heard *Her* in the back of his mind. *Third fret—Second string.* She was happy.

Back in the restaurant, Pax sat next to Kat, leaving the other seat in the booth empty. Kat glanced at him while eating some hummus.

"Mind if I sit here, Miss?" he joked as he moved closer to her.

"I'd be devastated if you didn't, sir," she replied, kissing his cheek. "Well?"

"Memphis tomorrow. Ally and Puck will meet us there this week."

"And your friend, Lara?" Kat asked. "Will she get jealous if I'm there with you?"

Pax laughed, recalling something Lara had mentioned at the start of their friendship.

"No," he said. "Her wife won't let her be."

They ate quickly and returned to the road, still two hours from Lincoln. They held hands as they drove down the interstate, Pax feeling lighter now that there was a semblance of a plan.

"If I tell you I love you," she said with a smirk, "will you sleep with me tonight?"

"If I tell you I love you," he replied, "will there be any sleep?"

(5) 2016-04-26.mp3

"YOU'RE ON, HONEY," Zim said from the background. "Whenever you're ready."

Sarah inhaled deeply a few times, then coughed and groaned.

"All night," she said to Zim. "All night with the goddamn cough."

"Drink some water, honey."

Another deep breath, and she began. She sounded exhausted.

"Hi, Pax. Hi Rob and Ally. And my sweet grandbabies, even if you're too little to understand this right now. If you're hearing this, well... I guess I've moved on. But I wanted to leave something behind for you. A way for me to be here, even when I can't. Well, that didn't make any sense."

Zim spoke from a distance, "It's okay honey, still rolling."

"So, let's talk about life. Let's talk about what matters. And let's talk about the things I want you to remember, always."

Another pause followed as she drank more water.

"Ok listen—show up. I mean it. The birthdays, the weddings, the little league games, the recitals, the graduations. Be there. Be in the audience. Be on the sidelines. Be in the pictures. People don't always remember the words you said, but they will always remember that you showed up.

"And it's not just the big events. Show up when someone's hurting. Show up when they need a ride to the doctor, a hand to hold, or someone to sit in silence with them. Show up when life gets heavy.

"Because at the end of it all, it won't be the things you bought or the jobs you worked that people remember. It'll be that you were there. When they needed someone to be there, you were there. So be there.

"If I could make you understand one thing, it's this: People matter.

"Not the job, not the house, not the bank account. Just people.

"Every time you have a choice between a thing and a person, choose the person. Choose the time spent with them. Choose the conversation. Choose the moment.

"Because all things must pass and all things must fade. But love? Love endures."

THEY WERE BACK on the road early the next day. Pax gripped the steering wheel as the first light of dawn painted the sky in soft hues of amber and rose. The road to Memphis unfolded before him with more promise and hope than when they left the ranch. It was a passage back to his life before he embarked on his journey, closing the loop, in a way, from his past life to the future that lay ahead. Beside him, Kat's stoic presence was his anchor, her eyes reflecting both sadness and fierce determination. But she was there. She was there for him.

They grabbed breakfast in Kansas City and ate it on the road as she drove the next leg to Springfield. They picked up a drive-through lunch in Springfield, and he took over the wheel again for the final stretch to Memphis.

She talked about growing up in Aarhus. He shared stories about Central New York. She spoke of all the horses she had known on the ranch, while he recounted the gigs he and Zim played all over the Eastern Seaboard. Between long stretches of conversation, there was a comfortable silence.

"Do you ever think about how we ended up here?" Pax asked softly, his gaze drifting between the horizon and her profile beside him.

Kat gazed out the window as the highway signs passed by. "East on Interstate 80, then south on 29, and now... I don't know what freeway this is. Or do you mean how we ended up together?"

He chuckled. "Now, I don't know what I meant. I was thinking about Sarah and how she was always there for people. I was usually in a studio pretending to be something more than I was or on a stage somewhere. But she was where she needed to be for those who needed her. It was as if she had a sixth sense, knowing who needed her most at any given time. Most times, they didn't even have to ask. She would show up with food, a bottle of wine, a cake, or something to show them that she was there no matter what they were going through, good or bad."

"What made you think of that?" she asked.

His eyes scanned the empty lanes ahead. His conscious mind puzzled over the circumstances that had landed them in a pickup truck on the road to Memphis, while his subconscious navigated the highway, absorbing the sounds of the engine and the hum of the wheels.

"You," he said. "You're here. You're not just here with me. You're here *for* me. She would have done the same. People matter more than things, she would say."

"Every time," Kat added.

He looked at her and smiled. "Exactly what she would have said."

"She sounds like she was a remarkable woman. You were lucky to have her. It may not have worked both ways."

She giggled as the slight left her lips, with a little more Danish flavor than usual.

Pax laughed and nodded. "You got that right. I always thought my job was to take care of her, but looking back, I don't think I was qualified to do that. She took care of us. She took care of others. And she took care of herself... until she couldn't."

"You miss her greatly."

His silence spoke volumes.

She gave a gentle smile, her voice thick with memory.

"Every day, especially on drives like this one, when there's nothing to do but think for miles, I think about Carsen and how his laughter once filled every corner of my heart and how his absence left an emptiness that still seizes me."

Pax nodded, the afternoon light shimmering in his eyes.

"I know that feeling, too. I remember our relationship started with flirtatious gestures and private secrets. It evolved naturally until every word and touch seemed to bring us closer. Losing her left an emptiness that only she could fill because she created the space. But when I'm with you, Kat, that emptiness is... well, it's bearable. You fill it differently. Not the same, but enough that I almost feel complete again."

The miles slipped beneath the tires, each one carrying fragments of their past into their presence through their words and stories. The road, with its endless curves, reflected the unpredictable paths of relationships over time.

Kat's gaze drifted over the changing scenery.

"Carsen taught me that every love leaves its mark, no matter how tender or painful it is. He said I got too emotionally involved with our animals, and when we had to sell them or if they died, I took it personally. It's no different when I think of him. I still catch myself smiling at the memory of his silly grin, even as I feel the pain of its absence. And yet, as I sit here with you, I feel something else. A calm. Peace. Healing, yes?"

Pax's voice softened even more, as if confessing to a childish secret.

"I think Sarah led me to you. I know that sounds silly, but—"

"It's not silly," she said abruptly, her breath betraying her emotions. "It's not silly."

He looked at her to ensure he was okay. She leaned her head against the headrest and took his hand in hers. Pax felt uncertain about how to break the growing silence as she regained her composure.

She turned to him. "You were nobody to me. A man in a video sings to his dead wife. Beautiful yes. Sad, also yes. But no one. Just a man. And then... there you were. Inches from me, needing help. Watching you struggle with those coats... I felt how lost you were, and with it, how lost I was. She would have helped you find a coat that suited you. It was like you didn't know how to act for yourself. I had to take her place. Not because you needed it, but because I did. I needed to help you."

He squeezed her hand, sensing their escalating emotions with every word.

"Why didn't you stay?" he asked, recalling how quickly she had left after he offered to buy her dinner.

"I couldn't," she replied. "It was too much. You fitting perfectly into his coat? I cried all the way home. I felt him, Carsen, in you. It was too much."

He loosened his grip and gently rubbed the back of her hand with his thumb, a trick that had once worked with Sarah. She responded in kind, her breath calming.

"And when I saw you in the diner with Harley..."

"Joy," he said. "Comfort."

"Yes, just so."

Pax's heart swelled with newfound resolve during this intimate communion between them. Their memories of Sarah and Carsen, each a bittersweet melody of love and loss, became more bearable for both of them when they were together. He truly believed that Sarah, Carsen, or both had guided them to each other and ultimately to the answer to his initial question.

How had they gotten there?

Zim would have said they were entangled through layers of dimensions, and arriving at the same place was inevitable. Pax smiled, thinking of his friend and realizing there was a fine line between crazy and brilliant.

"The pain of our old loves may still linger," she said, "but our connection numbs it, yes? Our journey isn't just about moving forward. It's about healing and finding beauty in every broken piece that brought us here."

Pax reflected on his broken pieces and how they had reassembled into something stronger, more resilient, and more capable of growth.

With those words echoing softly in the early evening light, they entered the outskirts of Memphis—two souls bound by memories and implied promises of a future where every moment together brought healing and every memory brought hope, not hurt.

MEMPHIS GREETED him like an old friend. As Pax and Kat pulled into the driveway of a modest, welcoming home, the glow of early evening embraced them. From the doorway stepped Lara, her arms open in welcome, and beside her, Maliyah, whose ever-present smile and kind eyes immediately put the weary travelers at ease.

"Pax, Katja—welcome," Lara said, her voice a mix of relief and joy as she wrapped Pax in a tight hug. "We've missed you."

Maliyah reached out to Kat, adding, "Come in and relax. You both deserve it after that long drive. It's so nice to meet the woman who tamed the mighty Pax Butler."

Kat giggled. "It is much easier to break a wild horse than tame a man like this one."

Inside, the living room was softly lit, its walls adorned with memories and mementos of the Allens' lives. Despite the lingering fatigue from the journey, the four gathered around a low table, letting the hours dissolve in shared conversation. The aroma of herbal tea mingled with the sound of a blues playing on the streaming service, set the tone for a night of reconnection.

"That was a long road. Every mile stirred up memories of Sarah and Zim—but it wasn't as painful as it once was," he admitted, his eyes finding Kat's.

Kat leaned forward, her hand resting on Pax's arm.

"We all carry our past loves with us, don't we? But here, at this moment, with all of us together for the common purpose of helping Puck, it feels like those old pains are nothing compared to what that little boy needs."

Lara studied Kat's eyes as they lingered on Pax.

"I like this one, Pax," Lara said. "You have chosen wisely."

Pax, usually embarrassed by such comments, nodded and said, "Yes, I have. But I think she might argue that she did the choosing, despite early misgivings."

Lara turned to him and smirked. "So, no panic attacks this time?"

"Not yet," he replied, "but the night is still young."

Their conversation flowed through laughter and memories, each story drawing Kat deeper into Maliyah's and Lara's trust and affection. And although fatigue tugged at the edges of his awareness, Pax was eager to stay in the warmth of the love he felt from these women.

When he could hardly keep his eyes open for another minute, Pax stood and said goodnight, leading Kat to the guest room, where they surrendered to the darkness. The morning would bring new challenges, joys, and sorrows, but it could wait, at least for a little while.

A GENTLE KNOCK at the door signaled another turning point as the Memphis afternoon ripened. Ally arrived at the doorstep with Puck in tow. She had driven through the night. The little boy, filled with wonder and anxious about all this sudden change, clutched his mother's hand tightly.

Pax stepped forward and enveloped Ally in his arms for a long, nearly silent hug, interrupted only by occasional sobs as the magnitude of the moment overwhelmed both father and daughter. Her swollen belly, carrying the next in the Butler line

—though the last name would be James—pressed against his taut abdomen. Pax looked at the baby bump and smiled.

"Ally, I want you to meet somebody," he said, grinning widely. Then Kat's arms were filled with Ally, no longer a stranger, and much more than just a voice on the phone.

He lowered himself to Puck's level and smiled, his eyes shining with joy at seeing his grandson, despite his current health challenges. Puck didn't recognize Papa at first, but when he did, he smiled back. *Her eyes. Her mouth. My nose.*

"Papa? Is that you?" Puck asked, reaching over to tug on his beard and long hair.

"Yeah, buddy. It's me. Did you bring your guitar?"

Puck's smile disappeared as he turned to Ally.

"No, baby, we didn't bring it, but I bet Papa has his, and we can get you a new one here if you'd like."

Puck nodded and wrapped his arms around Papa's neck. Pax lifted him into his arms and hugged him as tightly as he dared.

Lara and Maliyah, both emotional as they watched the reunion, exchanged a brief, resolute glance—each medical professional silently affirming their commitment. With everyone gathered and introductions complete, the work to help Puck began.

Ally and Puck slept for a while. Lara and Maliyah, both doctors at St. Jude's, called everyone they knew to discuss the referrals and test results that Ally had brought with her.

Pax and Kat went out to get takeout for dinner. While they waited for their pizzas to cook, they walked across the street to a music store, where Pax spotted a used beginner's guitar in the window.

"Buy it," Kat said. "He will be so happy when he sees it."

"No," Pax replied. "I need him to see it here. It's kind of like that movie about the kid wizards where they say that the wand chooses the wizard. Well, the guitar chooses the player."

As the entire crew ate that night, they shared stories about how they all came to be together. Pax was the unwilling focal point of it all.

"I truly thought he was having a heart attack," Lara said, describing the night they met at the Delta Harmony Lounge. "I was there with some colleagues after a fundraiser, and here's this handsome man suddenly having a panic attack because of the scent of my perfume. It's good that I was there with some of my team to help stabilize him. You scared the bejeezes out of us, Pax."

Kat perked up. "Was that the Red Roses night?"

"Yes!" Lara replied. "God, the place was a puddle after he sang that night. I'm just glad I got it on video, although I thought he might strangle me when he found out I posted it on YouTube."

Kat laughed. "Well, I must thank you, Lara. That video got me to see him for who he is, not who he pretends to be."

Pax smiled and enjoyed his slice of vegan pizza under the curious gaze of his daughter, who had never seen him without meat or cheese on his plate.

"There are few times in my life when I felt completely out of control," he said. "That was one of them." Waving his slice of pizza in the direction of Kat, he said. "That was another."

"Which time?" Kat asked, laughing.

"The coat," he replied, and she nodded.

"I think we were both a little out of sorts that day," she said, then recounted the story of meeting Pax at the Wheatland Country Store. "Like you, Lara, I felt compelled to help him. It wasn't a panic attack, but he was very confused just trying to find a warm coat."

"Why were you out of sorts, Kat?" Maliyah asked.

Kat set down her slice of pizza and licked her fingers, wiping them on a napkin before cleaning a dollop of sauce off Pax's lips.

"Because he reminded me so much of my Carsen. And when he fit perfectly into his coat, it was too much for me. I had to leave him there with a confused look on his face."

She smiled at Puck, who was biting into his slice of cheese pizza, recognizing a hint of Pax in his small face.

"And then, two days later, he was there again. But I wasn't upset to see him this time. I was glad to see him. It was—" Kat paused to look into Pax's eyes. "It was destiny."

The table fell silent, everyone absorbing the sentiment of the story.

"Who's destiny?" Puck asked, and the group laughed.

CHAPTER 9

THE NEXT DAY, in the hum of the hospital corridor, Puck's journey began. Every word and action was infused with the strength of a family united. Despite the unknown challenges ahead, hope bloomed anew as each member of his support network pledged to do everything possible to help Puck heal.

With Lara's knowledge and guidance, coupled with Ally's expertise in patient advocacy, enrolling Puck in an interim outpatient program unfolded like a well-rehearsed dance. In a side office at St. Jude's, surrounded by the choreographed chaos of hospital life, doctors were assigned, schedules created, and the treatment plan for Paxton Leeds, age 8, of Rock Hill, South Carolina, was put into motion. Concurrently, young Mr. Leeds was added to the waiting list for the Hematology-Oncology Department to receive more comprehensive treatment when a bed became available.

Despite being "outside the normal age range for family donors," Pax insisted on being tested as a bone marrow donor for Puck. Ally also submitted to the Human Leukocyte Antigen test, and unlike Pax, her sample showed promise.

Disappointed with his HLA results, Pax offered to donate as

much of his O-negative blood as the hospital could safely take from him, both for Puck's treatment and for any other patient who needed it.

Once the plan was in place, Puck was introduced to Dr. Jain, the pediatric hematologist-oncologist assigned to his case, who would lead the team in keeping Puck stable until a bed became available.

Dr. Jain was small, only slightly taller than Puck himself, which, she said, made the children she worked with feel more comfortable than having a tall man in a mask looming over them. Puck's response to her proved that thesis.

"Is Jane your first name?" Puck asked, familiar with pediatricians he had met who used their first names to create a sense of familiarity, such as Dr. Steve and Dr. Doug.

"No," Dr. Jain replied. "My first name is Pooja."

"Pooja?" Puck laughed at the sound of the name, and Ally told him to stop.

Dr. Jain remained unfazed, having heard children laugh at her name before.

"It's a silly-sounding name, isn't it?" she said, smiling along with Puck.

Puck nodded but no longer laughed.

"I'll make a deal with you, Mr. Leeds, Puck," Dr. Jain offered. "I won't laugh at your name if you don't laugh at mine. Deal?"

Puck nodded once more and said, "Deal."

At the end of the introductory meeting, Dr. Jain provided Pax and Ally with a schedule of tests and guidelines to maintain Puck's stability while awaiting inpatient care. This included daily blood tests until a baseline was established, followed by tests every 2 to 3 days, and transfusions if necessary to address severe anemia or low platelets. It also included potential prophylactic antibiotics to prevent infections, as well as strict hygiene measures such as wearing masks, washing hands, and avoiding crowds. The family's experience with COVID had already prepared them for this.

"If he needs a transfusion," Pax said. "Take it from me. Tap right into an artery if you need to. I'm O-Neg, and he can have it all."

Dr. Jain looked up into Pax's eyes, the only recognizable features amid the "mountain man" beard and hair.

"I think a very big heart is pumping all of that blood," she said. "He's a lucky boy."

After a long day at the hospital, they felt drained both physically and emotionally, but hope still lingered. Dr. Jain confirmed that they had identified Puck's condition early and was cautiously optimistic that a positive outcome was not only possible but likely.

Lara drove them back to the house where Kat had prepared dinner. Pax and Ally filled Kat in on their day and the plan. She nodded quietly and absorbed it all, acknowledging the seriousness of the situation with her stoic attention.

Maliyah was working the second shift at the hospital, which Lara and Pax were accustomed to, so dinner that night was short one person.

"Pooja is a rock star," Lara offered as they ate. "She's a no BS kind of doctor, but she has a way of explaining things, even bad news, in the most digestible way."

Ally said, "I felt very comfortable with her. Did you like Dr. Jain, Puck?"

Puck nodded while he picked at his food, eating almost none of the strange meal that had neither meat nor cheese. Kat noticed.

"Do you like peanut butter and jelly, Puck?" Kat asked.

"I love it," Puck said as he sat up.

"Good. When my nephew, Harley, was your age, I made him a mountain of peanut butter and jelly sandwiches over the years. Come with me then, and we'll make you one," she said. "Or maybe two."

With Kat distracting Puck by preparing him a vegan meal that didn't appear too strange, the adults conversed.

"Pax," Lara said. "The beard and long hair need to go to make the hygiene plan easier."

"Really?" Ally said. "Aw, Dad, I like this rock star look on you."

Pax laughed, saying, "Kat will be sad, but we make sacrifices, yes?"

Everyone laughed at his failed attempt at Kat's accent.

"Her name means *worship*," Lara said after a pause in the conversation. "Pooja, that is. Be prepared to do so, team. That woman is a goddess."

"Sounds like you have a little crush?" Pax smirked.

"A professional one, yes," Lara replied. "She's a decade younger than me and a decade more talented. She's one of the best in the building."

Kat and Puck came back from the kitchen. Puck carried two PBJs on a plate, which he immediately sank his teeth into as soon as he returned to his seat.

"Did I hear you making fun of my accent, Mr. New York?" Kat said with a grin.

Pax looked up from his plate with a "hand in the cookie jar" grin.

"Hmmm," Kat replied. "I suppose while cutting your hair and shaving your beard, I'll have to be sure not to slip the razor." She stroked his beard and then ran her finger across his throat.

The group laughed as Pax leaned over to kiss Kat on the cheek.

That night, as Puck lay in bed, Pax read one of the books Ally had packed for him. He remembered how Audra always read to the kids whenever they asked, and he promised himself to make this a regular part of their routine.

"Papa?" Puck asked, interrupting the latest adventures of *The Clockwork Boy*.

"Yeah, buddy?"

"Is Kat my new grandma?"

Pax was surprised by his grandson's question. Although he didn't have an answer, he realized this would occupy his thoughts going forward.

"Would you like that, buddy?"

Puck nodded and then said, "But maybe you or Mom should cook dinner instead of her."

Pax chuckled and set the book aside.

"Deal," he said, kissing Puck on the forehead. "Goodnight, buddy."

"Goodnight, Papa."

PAX STARED at the old man in the mirror. His long hair had been clipped down to its pre-COVID length, and the beard that had made him look more cowboy than New Yorker was gone. He examined the crow's feet around his eyes and scowled.

"When did I get so old, Kat?"

"You were old when I met you," Kat laughed. "And every day you get older. But I wouldn't have it any other way."

He and Ally were taking Puck to the hospital for the first of many blood draws. When Puck was told, he responded with the exasperated "again?" typical of an eight-year-old. Given how annoyed he sounded, Pax thought it could have been something as mundane as time for a bath or time to finish his homework. His grandson's lack of fear impressed him, reflecting Ally and

Travis's efforts to keep him calm and help him get used to the "little pinch" fib.

Pax would get jabbed in solidarity, allowing the hospital's blood bank to have his first deposit. He also wanted Puck to see that his family supported him in every way, even if it meant sharing his pain with him.

As they sat in the hospital lab's reception area, waiting for their turn, Puck remained quiet, his book open on his lap, his gaze focused on Papa's shaved face.

After a few minutes, he said, "Mommy, I don't want to be called Puck anymore."

Ally looked up from her magazine. "What? Why not?"

"It's a little kid nickname, and I'm a big kid now."

"Yeah, you are," Pax agreed. "You're a big kid, and you're fighting a big fight. Big kids like you deserve to be called what they want."

"Yeah, Papa," Puck replied, glancing around the hospital reception area. "This is some big kid shit right here."

Ally's eyes widened, and Pax resisted the urge to laugh so that his daughter could correct her son in her way.

"Paxton Leeds," she stammered. "You might be a big kid, but you're not big enough to start using the 'S' word. That's a four-teen-plus word."

"Sorry, Mommy."

"Fourteen-plus?" Pax inquired.

"The rating systems they put on everything now—movies, books, video games. Puck... I mean, Paxton has been checking all those ratings to see if he's old enough for whatever the thing is. So now I tell him what something is rated if it isn't obvious."

Pax confirmed, "So, s-h-i-t is ok after he's fourteen?"

"Yes, Dad, and he can spell so..."

Puck, now Paxton, returned to his book, while Ally mouthed

the words 'Fucking Russell' when he wasn't looking, implying the source of her son's colorful language. Pax laughed.

"Is this the famous Puck?"

The question came from a tall, well-dressed woman holding a clipboard. At first glance, Pax thought she could have been Audra's sister. Jess Brynne was a Child Life Specialist assigned to assist Puck and his family in coping with the stresses of his journey toward healing. She had a big smile and kind eyes, and Puck liked her immediately.

"I'm not Puck anymore," he said with an air of maturity. "I'm Pax now."

Jess crouched next to his chair and pulled her mask over her mouth and nose.

"I see," she said. "And when did that transformation happen?"

"Just now," Ally replied as she introduced herself to Jess.

"And this is..." Jess said as she extended her hand for a fist bump with Pax.

"Pax the Elder, I guess," he laughed. "But if you call me that, we can't be friends."

Jess laughed, and her laugh made Pax smile.

"He's Papa," said Pax the Younger.

"Papa, it is, then," responded Jess.

After the introductions, Jess explained her role at the hospital and that once little Pax was checked in, she would see him daily during his treatments.

"We're going to be great friends," she told Pax. "We'll read books, play games, talk about how to care for yourself when you leave the hospital, and all kinds of other things. How does that sound?"

The little guy said it sounded pretty good, trying to emulate Papa's direct approach to things. Jess handed the adults her business card, informing them they could call anytime, but she might not answer right away.

"My kids come first," she said, "but I will always call back as soon as possible."

They made small talk until the lab receptionist called their names. Jess left while the others were taken back to the lab. Puck, now Pax, would be the first to provide his small samples, followed by Papa, who chose to donate whole blood despite the guidelines that prevented him from donating again for eight weeks.

"Whole blood this time," said the phlebotomist. "We can start weekly platelet draws when your red blood cells recover."

With their matching Cookie Monster band-aids in place, the "little pinch" victims left the hospital and returned to the Allen house, equipped with more knowledge than they had when they departed that morning.

Little Paxton would need to return every day that week to ensure his blood wasn't showing any signs of advanced anemia or other conditions related to his disease. Pax wished he could donate blood every time he accompanied his grandson, but he decided to trust the doctors and open his vein again in two months.

His most pressing concern was Ally. She spent much of her time that week on the phone with Travis and Lainey, who cried every time Mommy had to hang up. Pax knew she was struggling with being away from her daughter, but he understood a mother's need to stay with her child in distress. He decided to help her resolve her dilemma. He was going to send Ally home.

Later that afternoon, Pax and Ally walked together in a sunlit corner of the backyard.

"Ally, listen," he began, his gaze fixed on the pattern of light and shadow on the wooden fence bordering the yard, reminding him of the branches waving in the sunlight on Audra's wall. "I'm going to be here every day of Puck's treatment, no matter how long it takes. I promise I'll be by his side until he's healed and we can bring him home."

His tone softened as he continued, "But I know Lainey needs you. Little girls need their mothers. You needed yours, and she was there for you. And that's why you are who you are."

Ally's eyes sparkled with a blend of gratitude and uncertainty.

"I know, Dad," she whispered, tears starting to flow. "My heart feels pulled in two directions. It kills me to hear her cry every night, but I can't bring myself to leave my boy when he needs me."

He took her hand and kissed her fingers just as he had kissed Sarah's the night she passed.

"I've got this, Kiddo. Go home. Hold your girl. Tell her Papa loves her and will see her as soon as we fix her brother."

Ally nodded, wiping away her tears. She rested her hand on her swollen belly, where the next descendant of Pax Butler was doing cartwheels inside her.

"Oof," she said and belched. "Then there's this kid."

Pax touched her belly and felt the motion beneath the surface.

"Wow, a dancer."

"Oh, God," Ally sighed, returning to the previous topic. "It's such a long drive."

"Fly."

"What about my car, Dad? I need it at home."

Pax thought about how easy it was to let the fifth wheel go when he knew he had to be elsewhere.

"Sell me your car," he said. "Sell me your car for a dollar, and fly home. Buy another car when you get there. I'll sell your car here and send you the money."

Ally stared at him, astonished. This wasn't her father. This was her mother in a Paxton Butler suit, solving problems in an instant.

"What happened to you out in the wild, Dad? You're... you're not you anymore."

Pax sighed deeply and smiled as a sense of calm washed over him.

"I found her, Kiddo. I found her. She wasn't out there. She was here and here." He pointed to his head and his heart. "She never left me. Yeah, her body did, but she is still here."

Ally was weeping.

"That's beautiful, Dad. Can you hear her?"

"I can. It's not her voice, but it's like a note playing in my head when I do something that would have made her happy. Her note. And the funny thing is, the whole time I was with Kat on the ranch, working every day, just the two of us during lockdown, I didn't hear her once. She was letting me find someone else. Like she approves of Kat."

Ally wrapped her arms around her father, and the two stood in the sunshine, embracing, shedding tears, and experiencing emotions they hadn't felt since Ally was a teenager.

"I can hear her now," he said, and Ally tightened her grip on him.

"Tell her I miss her," she whispered.

As they pulled away, Ally felt resigned to return home, confident that Pax Butler 2.0 could help her son through this crisis.

"I need to call Travis," she said. "And I need a plane ticket for tomorrow morning."

"I'll let you handle the details," he laughed. "I'm still fumbling with my smartphone. Trying to do anything on a computer would be torture."

Ally laughed while wiping her tears, and the two went back to the house.

"Get Rob tested as a transplant candidate when you get home," Pax said. "And Russell."

Ally laughed at the idea of Puck's deadbeat father donating anything to anyone, much less something from his body.

"I'll talk to Rob," she said. "He'll do it. And I'll catch Russell up on all this, but that's it. Who knows how many flavors of hepatitis that asshole has in his system since the divorce? Probably the entire alphabet."

The next day, Ally said her goodbyes, expressing gratitude to Lara and Maliyah for their generosity and to Kat for helping her father become more human. She urged her son to behave for Papa and the others and to listen to his doctors.

"You're a big kid now, Pax. Big kids are brave and strong. I know you'll do great, and I will talk to you every day so you can let me know how hard you're fighting. I will come and visit you as often as I can. Whenever you need me."

Little Pax hugged her tightly, squeezing tears from her eyes.

"Don't cry, Mommy," he said. "You're going to be okay."

For the next week, Papa Pax's days were filled with managing treatment schedules and keeping "Mighty Pax," as his team of doctors called him, distracted from the discomforts of outpatient life.

Then, on a cool morning when the light seemed brighter than usual, Kat found Pax alone on the front porch, sipping coffee in the sunshine. In her most gentle and direct way, she spoke the words he had dreaded but knew would eventually come.

"Pax, I'm going back to Wyoming." She paused, her eyes searching his for understanding.

He managed a bittersweet smile, his heart weighed down by the conflict of responsibility and impending separation.

"Do you have to?" he asked, his voice barely above a whisper.

She nodded. "Young horses will be arriving soon, and I think you need to put all your energy into your boy. You need to focus on young Pax."

He didn't argue because he knew she was right. He was already so distracted by Pax's treatment schedule and other needs that he often didn't realize he had barely spoken to Kat all day until they were in bed at night.

She patted his chest and kissed him softly, her lips lingering on his as she whispered.

"If I tell you that I love you, will you call me every day so I can hear your voice and know you're okay?"

"If I tell you that I love you, will you get an answering machine so I can leave messages when you don't pick up the house phone?"

Kat laughed. "I suppose that's a fair request."

She kissed him once more.

"I love you," she said.

"I'll call," he replied. "I love you."

"I'll answer."

The next day, she was gone.

"WE HAVE A BED," Dr. Jain said one day while the Mighty Pax gave another blood sample in the hospital lab. The elder Pax stood and towered over Dr. Jain, fighting the urge to crush her in a bear hug.

Eight weeks of waiting. Eight weeks of walking a tightrope regarding his grandson's health. The patient's patience slowly eroded as it often does with eight-year-olds when they have only adults to interact with.

"When?"

Dr. Jain looked up at his eager face, and Pax could tell that beneath her mask, she was smiling.

"Three days," she said. "We are releasing one of our little fighters back into the world tomorrow, and we'll have the room cleaned and prepared for the Mighty Pax to move in by Saturday."

Pax stopped fighting his emotions and lifted Dr. Jain into his arms, hugging her tightly as her feet dangled above the floor. She laughed and swatted his arm, telling him to put her down, as he was contaminating her jacket and it was completely unprofessional.

Behind his mask, Pax couldn't stop smiling. This was the moment when the real fight began, and he felt more confident than ever that they would overcome this challenge. He heard *Her* sound in his head, her happiness harmonizing with his own.

Lara and Maliyah were equally as excited when he shared the news. Lara sat down with him to discuss the guidelines for the few things Pax could have in his room. Under his grandson's supervision, he packed familiar items: books, pajamas, photographs, a handful of plastic dinosaurs, and his Nintendo Switch.

"I'll bring you some new books and games when you get bored of these," he told young Pax.

"How long will I be in the hospital, Papa?"

Pax didn't have an answer and didn't want to make something up. He sat on the bed beside his grandson.

"I don't know, buddy. It's probably going to be a while. There will be good days and bad days—maybe some really bad days, but also some really good days. It's all so we can make you better and take you home. But you're a fighter like your Papa, aren't you? You can be tough, right? Show me how tough you are."

The little guy raised his arms and flexed his tiny muscles. "I'm the Mighty Pax!"

"Yes, you are!" Together, they flexed and howled their toughness into the universe until the Mighty Pax felt tired and needed to lie down.

Pax called Ally the next morning before dawn. He knew she would be awake and getting ready for work, and he wanted to share the news before she became immersed in the needs of the patients she assisted in Rock Hill.

"We got a bed," he said, then paused.

Ally let out a breath that sounded like it had been knotted up in her chest for months. "I'm coming."

While Pax took his grandson to the hospital for admission, Ally caught the first flight available from Charlotte to Memphis. Maliyah met her at the airport, and they drove to the hospital.

Pax smiled as he greeted her in the waiting area. "Hey, Kiddo."

She embraced him tightly. "How is he?"

"Asleep for now. He's been very brave."

With guidance from an intake nurse, the two scrubbed and got dressed, their faces, hair, and clothes layered with sterile coverings and hands protected by surgical gloves. Then, she took them to the room where little Pax would spend the next several months.

He was not there when they arrived, having been taken away to get fitted for his various catheters to assist with blood draws, IV transfusions, and chemotherapy. His new best friend Jess was by his side to explain everything they were doing and to distract him from the worst parts.

The room was small, yet it offered a nice view out the window, a glimpse of something beyond the sterile walls. When they rolled in the Mighty One, his sleepy eyes spotted a woman clad in sterile garb, but he recognized her immediately.

"Mommy," he whispered, then drifted back to sleep, floating on a raft of sedatives. The orderlies settled him into the room before leaving their new charge with his family to adjust to this unfamiliar world.

Ally wrapped the thin hospital blanket around his small frame. She ran a gentle hand over his head, brushing away the damp curls.

"You're a warrior, buddy," she whispered.

Little Pax stirred but didn't wake. His tiny fingers twitched, instinctively reaching for comfort. Pax held one hand, while Ally held the other. For a moment, there was only the rhythm of their breath, the beeping of the monitors, and the hum of the hospital beyond the door.

The following week was a blur of consultations, tests, and whispered conversations in hospital hallways. Ally took charge where she could, her background in patient advocacy taking on a new level of intensity as she worked with Jess to ensure her father had everything he needed to be the Mighty One's legal and family voice. When she wasn't in her professional mindset, she sat with her son, told him stories, and brought him small surprises from the gift shop—anything to make the hospital feel a little less like a battlefield.

In the evenings, Ally consulted with Lara about hospital protocols, the expected level of communication, and, once again, the importance of having Dr. Jain lead her son's team. Pax sat quietly through most of this. It wasn't his world. It wasn't his language. He was a surrogate parent who needed to be his daughter's eyes and ears while caring for his grandson.

Each day, Pax improved in his hygiene routine, which allowed him to be on the floor. Each day, Jess would stop by to chat with little Pax, asking him how he was handling the transition and checking if he needed anything. Pax listened to her speak in words and tones that put children at ease during stressful circumstances, then marveled at how quickly she could adjust her dialect to converse with Ally, ensuring they were both on the same page.

Eventually, reality intruded for Ally. Work, Lainey, and responsibilities in South Carolina that needed her attention couldn't wait forever.

"I don't want to leave," she confessed to Pax on the day of her flight home.

He nodded, understanding. "I know. But you've done everything you can. He knows you love him and that I will be with him daily. We'll call you every day. Come back as often as you can."

They stood together in the dim light of the hospital room, watching little Pax sleep. She had told her son that she needed to go home for a while, but would be back. He cried a little, but he understood, as much as an eight-year-old can, that Mommy had other people to take care of. Still, he had Papa there to make sure everything would be alright.

Ally pressed a kiss to his forehead, lingering for a moment before pulling away.

"When he's better, we'll bring him home," she said, her voice firm with conviction.

Pax squeezed her hand. "Yeah. We will."

With that, they exited the room.

As the weeks dragged on, the hospital corridors echoed with solitude and the weight of the unknown. Pax called Ally daily, updating her on the progress and the next steps. He often had the little guy say hello when he felt up to it. He talked to Kat whenever she was available, and with her promise to get an answering machine fulfilled, he left long messages when she wasn't home, often singing to her, with many calls ending in tears. When they did speak, he felt whole again.

Pax's focus sharpened as he sat beside his grandson each day in that quiet room, the steady beep of monitors underscoring the reason for his vigil. Every treatment represented a step in the long, arduous battle against the disease that had shadowed the little boy's life. Those once haunting beeps and pings had taken on a new meaning. They were no longer the sounds of loss— they were the sounds of healing.

Another sound they occasionally heard was the Victory Bell, rung enthusiastically by each child in the ward when they completed their treatment and were sent home, victorious over their disease.

Pax would wheel his grandson into the hallway for each new ceremony, and they would cheer for the victor. Each child who rang the bell would say, "You've got this, Mighty Pax! You're going to ring this bell, too!" Ally had been present for a few of these events and encouraged little Pax to get better every day so that he would ring that bell one day.

After each ceremony, howls of strength and determination could be heard from the room where the Mighty One was flexing with his grandfather and sometimes his mother.

In the moments between celebrations, chemotherapy and radiation treatments, blood draws, and transfusions, Pax sang to the Mighty One while the little guy slept or lay peacefully, exhausted from his treatments. Songs of strength and hope: *I Won't Back Down*, *Eye of the Tiger*, *Stand by Me*, and *Here Comes the Sun*, among others. However, the most requested song on the Mighty Pax playlist was *Lean on Me*. Pax sang that song so many times that within a few weeks, they were singing it together. Little Pax sang it as much for Papa as Papa sang it for him, and with their voices united on those amazing Bill Withers lyrics, the two shared strength and support.

One evening, several weeks into his treatments, Pax watched his grandson sleep and gently smoothed back his namesake's sweaty, disheveled hair, a consequence of his latest chemo treatment. He frowned as some hair came out in his hand, with more scattered across the pillow. While this was expected, he had hoped they might be fortunate enough to avoid it. He understood that this fight was more than a medical battle; it was also an assault on little Pax's sense of self. It was a struggle against pain and the loss of control over his bodily functions, which was a lot to ask of an adult, let alone an eight-year-old. Losing his hair would be a challenge.

That night, as he and Lara shared a drink on the porch, he told her about the hair loss and asked how other people helped their sick children cope with something so beyond their control. Lara responded by walking into the house and returning to the porch with scissors, shaving gel, and a razor.

Pax sent Ally and Rob a photo of his cleanly shaven head along with an explanation of what was happening to the little guy. Within an hour, Rob sent back a picture of his own shaved head. Then came Travis. Pax smiled at the photos and shared them with Lara. She remarked that this often happens in families—solidarity in the fight. Pax believed that if Sarah were still alive, she would have shaved her head without hesitation.

When the Mighty One saw Papa the next day, he laughed as much as his frail body could handle.

"You look like Caillou," he said. Pax had no idea who that was, but if his new clean head triggered some recognition in the boy, he knew it would be easier for him to accept it.

Little Pax didn't understand why Papa would do such a silly thing until he saw the hair on his pillow, realizing that what Dr. Jain had warned him might happen was indeed happening. He felt sad and a little scared to see the strands of his hair in his hand instead of on his head.

"Things like this are going to happen," Pax said. "Dr. Jain told us, right? Just like the upset tummy and diarrhea. But you know, even though we can't do anything about those things, we can do something about this."

With Jess's help and Dr. Jain's approval, a stylist from St. Jude's Great Clips Salon came to the room and assisted the Mighty Pax in beating chemotherapy at its own game. Within minutes, his little head was as clean as Papa's, and they flexed their muscles and howled as loudly as they were allowed to in the ward. Pax texted pictures of the two of them to Ally and Rob, and the responding emojis expressed their love and support.

With his hair gone, Pax looked into his grandson's eyes, *Her* eyes, *Her* mouth. He could see Sarah more clearly than before, and he heard *Her* approval in his mind.

PAX SAT AT THE TABLE, his english muffin half eaten and his second cup of coffee half empty. He was writing. It had been months since new words had appeared, and these didn't make sense. They felt right as part of the libretto, but didn't carry the weight of personal experience like the other verses.

A woman walks into a bar,
Her graceful motion from afar,
I see her and think, "There you are."
I want it to be true.
She moves about the crowded space,
Between the patrons of this place,
And in the light, I see her face,
That woman isn't you.

Second string, third fret.
The note of joy I can't forget.
In my mind, I hear it, yet
My ears can't find the tune.
That single note remains unblurred,

But missing in the voice heard.
I long to hear a single word.
In the perfect sound of you.

"What's that?" Lara asked as she poured herself a cup of coffee.

"A song I've been writing for what seems like forever. Since the night I met you, in fact."

"Can I see it? Or hear it?"

Pax slid his notebook filled with disordered verses across the table. Lara sat down and read each stanza as she sipped her coffee. Suddenly, she stopped.

"This one is me. That night we met when you had the panic attack because of my perfume."

Pax smiled and replied, "Yes."

"This one is... Kat? 'Holding her completes the space'?"

"Yes."

"So, who is the new one?"

"I don't know. It just came to me while I was shaving."

Lara snapped her fingers to get Pax to hand her the pen. She wrote down numbers next to each verse and chorus, then slid the notebook back to him. He read them in sequence.

"Yeah, that works," he said. "That's good."

"Maybe we're the next Ashford and Simpson," she said.

"You're aging yourself."

"Shut up."

As Pax read the words in the order Lara had arranged them, the dam broke, and he started writing again. Lara left him to his creative moment while she finished getting ready for work.

When she returned to hug him before leaving, she glanced over his shoulder and read his hurried script. Some words were crossed out, but the main idea was emphasized by being underlined.

I know someday I'll hear you clear,
When time for me is over here.
I'll hear your voice. I'll feel you near,
And love will start anew.
Third fret, second string
Will be the perfect way to bring,
You back to me, so we can sing
In harmony, we two.

Together, we will always stay
Entangled in the strangest way
And perfect, when I hear you say (Hi)
In the blissful sound of you.

"Is there more to the last chorus?" she asked, noticing that it was only half the length of the others.

"No," he replied. "I left it there because that's what I've been searching for. Just that."

"Just hi?"

"Just hi."

She smiled and wrapped her arms around his neck.

"She'll love it," she said, kissing his bald head before she headed out the door.

CHAPTER 10

PAX'S ONCE IMPULSIVE LIFE had become a self-imposed twelve-step routine to ensure he fulfilled his promises to his family and himself.

1. Begin the day with a cleansing shower and shave (face and head) at dawn.
2. Have breakfast with Lara, and sometimes with Maliyah if she wasn't sleeping in after her late hospital shifts.
3. Drive to the hospital, either alone or with Lara.
4. Undergo a ritualistic sanitation process: hand scrubbing, switching from outdoor shoes to indoor shoes, and wearing a mask, gown, and shoe coverings.
5. Get updates from the doctors on how little Pax did during the night.
6. Spend five to eight hours with the Mighty One reading, playing games, or sharing stories about Ally and Rob when they were eight. Have lunch with Lara, Maliyah, or both.

7. Meet with the doctors again for updates before departing for the night.

8. Drive back to the Allen house and have dinner with Lara and occasionally Maliyah.

9. Contact Ally and Rob with email updates or a phone call.

10. Call Kat.

11. Unwind with his guitar, take a walk through the neighborhood, or sip bourbon on the porch with Lara. Sometimes all three.

12. Sleep.

Rinse and repeat.

Once a spontaneous and erratic musician, Pax Butler had transformed into Papa Pax, the steady and reliable guardian of his namesake.

He reflected on the changes in his life over the past few years. The carefree musician who booked as many gigs as possible, often spending more on gas and hotels than he earned, was gone. Now, every day followed the same routine. In Las Vegas, they might call this a "residency," but this routine wasn't career-driven—it was about family.

Also missing were the late-night jam sessions that stretched into the early morning, the occasional mind-expanding drugs to spark creativity, and the persistent hope of being discovered as a future star. Now, he was in bed by 9:00 p.m. and up by 6:00 a.m., the only drugs being medications for little Pax, and his only hope centered on his grandson's future.

Every week, he updated Sal and Marisol. In return, they shared news about their lives and offered words of hope, love, and support to keep him focused. When he couldn't reach Kat by phone, he left her a message and then called Sal. The two joked and laughed, temporarily easing the burden of his responsibilities until the next day, when the alarm clock signaled the start of the twelve steps again.

When he felt confident about the lyrics for *The Sound of You*, he shared them with Marisol and Beto. Within a day, Beto returned a chord progression for the verses and chorus, along with tablature for fingerpicking the intro and transitions between stanzas. Pax played through the composition and was amazed at how well Beto had captured the flow of the lyrics and selected the right chords to convey the song's emotional core. Naturally, it began and ended on the D chord.

One evening, Lara heard Pax playing his guitar on the front porch. She poured each of them a drink and joined him.

"That sounds nice, Pax," she said as she handed him the glass. "Is that the new one?"

"Yeah," he clinked glasses with Lara and sipped his drink. "I sent the lyrics to Beto, the kid from the Austin video. He wrote out this excellent intro riff. I was trying to see if my hand would work properly. It's not too bad when I slow it down and play higher on the neck."

Lara listened and watched. Pax hummed the verses, and Lara caught the melody. To his surprise, she sang without the lyrics in front of her.

"In crowded rooms, alive with sound, the stink of beer and sweat abound. I catch your scent and turn around in hopes of seeing you. But disappointment falls again, like bitter tears in summer rain. The passing memories in vain, it's someone else I view."

Pax paused his play and smiled.

"That's the only part I know," Lara said, sipping her drink. "The part about me."

He continued fingerpicking softly.

"That was the first part I wrote," he said. "You think the

panic attack in the bar was bad? You should have seen me in the truck when the rain came down that night."

"What happened?" Lara asked as she leaned forward.

Pax recounted his meltdown and memories of the prom and that first kiss with Sarah, which closely resembled the kiss Lara had given him.

"How did the lyrics come to you?"

"I heard her, Lara. She came to me as a wind chime in the same tone as her happy sound."

"Third fret, second string," Lara said.

Pax nodded, pleased that Lara could understand his unusual, music-powered memory.

"What's my happy sound?"

"Third fret, fifth string. C. Same as mine—only it's my usual tone, but with you, your register drops when you're happy—more sultry. Like an old FM radio DJ."

"It does not."

Pax laughed.

"Ok," he said. "Imagine Maliyah coming home to you after a long night shift. You see her and want to hold her. You've missed her all day and are happy she's back in your arms again. When you've got that image, say 'Hi.'"

Pax watched her, and as the word escaped her lips, he plucked the C note on the fifth string. It matched.

Lara blushed when she realized he was right. Her voice softened when she felt happy.

"It's normal for many people," he said. "When you're comfortable, you make lower, softer sounds. Higher-pitched tones take more effort and more air. When you're happy and relaxed, boom, third fret, fifth string."

She sat quietly for several minutes, sipping tequila and listening to Pax play Beto's arrangement on the guitar.

"Pax," she said, her tone higher than before, now that of Dr.

Allen, not Lara, his friend. "For months, you have spent all day, every day, with little Pax. I'm concerned about the toll this is taking on your mental health. You have almost nothing going on outside of this daily routine. Would you talk to someone for me? Someone at the hospital? A friend?"

"A psychiatrist friend?" he smirked, his hands still practicing the riff while his attention stayed on Lara.

"Psychologist, but yes. Someone to talk to about all this and find out if the stress is building up and if you're handling it properly."

"I'm okay, Lara," Pax replied, knowing he would lose this argument no matter how hard he tried to convince her. He thought about how right she was to suggest the calcium scan so long ago and relented. "But I love you for wanting to be sure, so I'll do it."

Lara smiled and tilted her head to the side. His friend had returned from the shadow of the stern doctor.

"You love me, Pax?"

He played the riff a little faster.

"You know I do. Shut up."

She leaned back and took a sip of her drink.

"I love you too," she said, deliberately adopting a low sultry tone.

They laughed.

(7) 2016-05-11.mp3

"AND 3-2-1, GO ON, HONEY."

"Kids," she croaked, then paused to cough.

"Maybe we wait for a day or two, Sarah." Zim's voice was filled with concern.

"No," she croaked again, followed by the sound of gargling and then spitting.

"Sorry, Zim. I got some on your floor."

Zim laughed, saying, "That's not the worst thing that's been on that floor, honey."

"Ew."

"Ready?"

"3-2-1," she said, taking a deep breath and letting out a slight chuckle.

"Alright, let's talk about something important. If you don't know who you are, the world will try to tell you. And let me tell you right now—most of the world doesn't know a damn thing about you."

A pause for another drink of water.

"So, let's start with this: You are not defined by what other people think of you. You are not just what you do for a living. You are not just a collection of your past mistakes. You are not merely a set of traits that people assign to you. These are facts about you, but they are not you.

"You are—listen to me now—you belong to yourself. You come first. Nobody can own you. People can claim you as something—a friend, a lover, a spouse, whatever. But nobody can possess you. You belong to yourself.

"But there's more to it than that. Because as much as you belong to yourself, you also belong to something bigger. You're part of a story that started long before you got here and will continue long after you're gone. You're tied to people who came before—your parents, grandparents, their parents. And you're tied to the people around you now—the ones who see you, the ones who show up for you, the ones who love you even when you make it hard."

Another short pause and a deep sigh.

"And you're also tied to your family. And when I say family, I don't just mean the one you were born into. No, sometimes that's just the starting point. Family isn't only about blood. It's about the people who stand by you when things get hard. It's about the ones who tell you the truth when you need to hear it, who hold you up when you don't have the strength to stand on your own, and who never let you forget where you come from, even when you want to."

"You need to know 'whose' you are. That means knowing who loves you, who includes you as part of their life, who stands with you. It means honoring those connections and understanding that you don't go through this life alone. No one does. You can try—Lord knows some people do—but you won't get very far before you start running on empty."

Soft laughter and a pause.

"Now, I hear that Jackson Browne song in my head, Running on Empty. *Pax will be happy about that.*

"I had to learn that the hard way. You all know I can be stubborn. I wanted to prove I could stand on my own, and I did for a while. But then I realized something—it's not weakness to need people. It's not weakness to lean on the ones who love you. It's a gift. It's the thing that keeps you from falling apart."

Another pause accompanied by the sound of her shifting in her seat.

"And let me say this: Just because someone is supposed to be your family, that doesn't mean they deserve to have a place in your heart. Some people don't earn that right. You don't owe anyone your peace just because they share your DNA. Family is about love, not obligation. You have the right to build a family that lifts you up, not one that tears you down. Blood makes you related, but love makes you family.

"You are worth being loved. You are worth being chosen. If someone in your life makes you feel like you have to prove that to them over and over again, let me tell you right now—they aren't your family. They're a lesson. Learn it and move on."

A deep, near-gasping breath.

"So, my loves, know who you are. Be proud of it. And know whose you are. Stand with the people who stand with you. Love the people *who love you. And for God's sake, don't waste your time on anyone who makes you feel like you have to earn what should be given freely."*

A gentle laugh. Voice heavy with emotion.

"I love you. That's a fact. You are mine. And I am yours. Always."

DR. JAIN PULLED up a chair across from Pax in the hospital cafeteria. He thought she seemed taller while sitting and resisted the urge to glance beneath the table to see if her feet were dangling.

"Have you talked to the team today, Papa Pax?" she asked, using the informal title the other doctors on the team used to distinguish him from the Mighty Pax.

"No," he replied. "I was surprised that none of them met me at the elevator."

Dr. Jain powered on her tablet and entered some commands. She also placed a thick folder of papers on the table, marked with a sticker that read, "Leeds, Paxton (8-AML)."

"I'm sure you don't remember, since it was a long time ago and quite overwhelming at first. But several months ago, I showed you a small visual tool I use to track my patients' progress. I would like to discuss it with you and update you on where little Pax stands on my radar."

Dr. Jain pulled out a piece of paper that had a drawing resembling a radar screen in the center, surrounded by acronyms and abbreviations above each of the six spokes radiating outward. Ten circles extended from the middle to the edge. She marked dots along the lines while reporting Little Pax's condition. Pax couldn't help but smile upon noticing that Dr. Jain's analytic device looked like a guitar tablature with a different shape and four additional strings.

"The first indicator is CR—Complete Remission. Undetermined, as yet. We need another bone marrow biopsy to be sure, but he hasn't needed a transfusion in ten days." She drew a question mark on the fifth line from the center, along the spoke labeled "CR."

"Blood count stabilization. ANC, hemoglobin, and platelets are all within standard tolerance." She marked a dot on the first line from the center. "One."

"Infections or uncontrolled complications. There were no persistent complications from his last chemo treatment, but we will continue to monitor him. Two." She marked a dot on the second line on the spoke.

"IV medications or transfusions. No IV antibiotics in a month. All other medications have been delivered orally. No transfusions in ten days, as I mentioned." She drew a dot. "One."

"Post-treatment follow-up plans. I spoke with Dr. Llewellyn, the doctor who conducted his tests in North Carolina. He will be ready for Pax in an outpatient capacity once we release him."

"Wait." Pax nearly shouted as he sat back, wide-eyed. "Release? You said, *release*?"

"Shhh," Dr. Jain admonished him with a smile, patting his hand on the table. "Listen."

Pax leaned in, his heart racing, hands trembling, and eyes fixed on the paper.

"Post-treatment follow-up plans." She drew a dot. "One."

"And finally, a safe living environment and caregiver readiness. This means clean and infection-controlled. Family members, all of them, trained on infection prevention, medication management, and nutrition and hydration plans." She drew a question mark on the first line of that segment. "I suspect this is a one, but I want to ensure his parents are ready. They can meet with Dr. Llewellyn or someone on his staff to get all the details."

After covering all the segments, Dr. Jain connected the dots and question marks to show Papa Pax where she believed the Mighty One was on her readiness diagram. She then traced the circle representing the third line, making it thick and bold.

"This dark line indicates where we want everything before considering release. Ideally, all should be within that line, especially the first four segments."

Pax looked at the solitary spike outside the dark line, the question mark that represented little Pax's bone marrow biopsy. Dr. Jain circled it.

"That's the only remaining unknown," she said. "He's scheduled for Friday. I assume you will be there?"

Pax nodded, taking a deep breath. Then... he wept.

Lara cried silently that evening as Pax shared the copy of the radar chart—a map of hope drawn with clinical precision by Dr. Jain. Each dot and question mark represented a milestone in little Pax's battle. As Lara's tears fell, they released a sense of resolve that everyone had given their all to keep the Mighty One fighting: Pax, Ally, and the doctors directly supporting little Pax, along with Lara, Maliyah, and Kat supporting Pax the Elder.

After a hurried dinner, he called Ally with the news that "there was light at the end of the tunnel." The entire family had gathered at the James house to hear the news, and as it was delivered, the immense pressure valve of uncertainty opened, releasing their worst fears into the ether. Rob and Travis, always the stoics who typically masked their feelings behind jokes and practicality, cried openly.

When Pax called Kat after finishing the emotional flood with Ally and others, Kat's voice trembled as she shared her happiness with him. He promised to see her again soon, though he couldn't give an exact date. Every heartbeat in that moment was a testament to the fragile, precious nature of hope, and Pax felt lighter and more loved than ever before. Sarah's presence inside him filled him with the hope that they might all find peace soon.

He and Dr. Jain decided to wait until they had clear results from the bone marrow scan before telling young Pax. Of all the tests his young body had gone through over the past months, the bone marrow biopsy was his least favorite. Waking up from sedation always made him feel nauseous, and the area around his hip bone, where the needle was inserted, stayed sore for several days.

The Mighty One was not thrilled about another biopsy. He groaned, and tears fell that Friday, knowing it would bring a few days of agony and a few more of discomfort. Pax, however, had been looking forward to that day with as much hope as he had felt since before receiving Sarah's terminal diagnosis. He wanted the test done, the results confirmed, and the Victory Bell Ceremony scheduled as soon as possible.

"Look at it this way, buddy," he said, trying to comfort his namesake without revealing the source of his hope. "This could be the last time you have to go through this. What if they find good news in that scan and say you're healed?"

Mighty Pax wiped his tears. "Do you think that will happen?"

Pax thought about how to explain hope to his grandson. He wanted him to understand that it wasn't a guarantee, but also not a fantasy that he might be going home soon.

"Pax," he began. "Do you know the difference between something being possible and something being probable?"

"I think so," little Pax responded. "Like, it might be possible that my hair grows back purple. But it probably won't. Like that?"

"Exactly," Pax agreed. "But that would be pretty cool, right?"

Young Pax smiled and nodded.

"So," he continued. "Even though we hope for something possible, we are better off hoping for something probable."

Little Pax sat up in bed. Pax watched him move without help. Disease, drugs, and chemotherapy had worn down his little body, but here he was, showing the strength to adjust while talking with his grandfather. Pax seized the moment as an example.

"You see, only a few weeks ago, we would have wanted it to be *possible* for you to pull yourself up in bed. But you were too weak, so it wasn't *probable*. Now, you can do it. You just did. So, if it's probable that you're getting stronger, then it's probable that you're healing. Therefore, it is also probable that this bone scan will be the last one. Get it?"

Little Pax nodded and brightened.

"So, a little more ouch. But maybe that's the last time?"

Pax extended his knuckles for his grandson to fist bump.

The Mighty One faced his final bone marrow biopsy with a bravery that belied his small frame. As he emerged from sedation in the recovery room, his eyes met Pax's, and for a brief moment, the pain and nausea were replaced by a smile and a weak thumbs-up.

"Last time?" Pax whispered, softly bumping his knuckles against the boy's tiny hand. The words were simple, yet they carried the weight of every promise made and every tear shed during those long months.

Three weeks later, on the Friday before Christmas around 11:30 a.m., Pax entered his grandson's room at St. Jude's, pushing a wheelchair. Little Pax sat in bed, playing a new game on his Nintendo Switch.

"Hey, buddy," Pax said. "Would you like to have lunch with me today?"

Little Pax looked up. "You mean in the cafeteria?"

Pax stifled a smile and nodded.

"Yeah!" the Mighty One said. "Do they have macaroni in cheese?"

Pax laughed at the use of the word "in" instead of "and," something Ally had done her whole life. She believed the macaroni was in cheese sauce, not just served with it.

"Maybe," Pax replied. "What kind of cafeteria in a kid's hospital wouldn't have it?"

He helped his grandson get comfortable in the wheelchair, then rolled him out of the room and down the hallway. After several twists, turns, and a brief elevator ride, Pax positioned the Mighty One in front of a large gathering of people. In the group were a very pregnant Ally, Travis, Lainey, Dr. Lara, Dr. Maliyah, and the entire team of doctors who had worked with him over the long months to fight his disease and prepare him to go home.

Little Pax cried as soon as he saw his mother, stepfather, and sister, all of whom were hugging him with tears streaming down their faces.

Lara and Maliyah wiped their eyes. Although they loved every child they worked with, Pax Leeds was special because of the personal bond they formed with his family.

The entire crowd of doctors, nurses, orderlies, other patients, and their family members cheered for the Mighty One as he rang the Victory Bell, symbolizing his triumph over his illness.

"You've got this, Mighty Pax!" a nurse cheered as the bell rang out.

Pax knelt beside his grandson's chair as the families thanked the doctors and shared tears, hugs, and fist bumps. Little Pax was still struggling to stop crying, overwhelmed by the entire ceremony.

"Pretty good surprise, huh?" Pax asked.

Little Pax nodded and hugged his grandfather around the neck. "Can I go home now?" he asked.

"Yeah, buddy. You're going home. You still have a lot of fighting ahead, but you'll be seeing doctors in North Carolina, and Mommy, Travis, and the whole family will be supporting you every step of the way."

"Will you be there, Papa?"

"Eventually, yes. I'm going back to Wyoming to spend some time with Kat, but then I'll be back in South Carolina for a visit, and maybe I'll bring her with me. Would you like that?"

Little Pax nodded.

As with such emotional events, the family felt torn between expressing gratitude and taking their reunited child home as quickly as possible. They left the hospital as the doctors and other staff gradually returned to their routines. Lara and Maliyah promised to see everyone for dinner.

Later, as the sun set behind the Memphis skyline, Pax sat on a wooden porch step outside the Allen house. The murmur of voices from inside, the clinking of plates and silverware, and the breeze rustling through the trees, created a pocket of comfort as he decompressed.

He listened, his heart rate steady and slow. The stress that had lingered beneath the surface for months was finally lifted. He took a deep breath, picked up his phone, and sent a message to Sal and Marisol.

"Today, we celebrated life," he typed slowly, each word heavy with emotion. "Little Pax's Victory Bell was more than a sound. It was our testament that love will always guide us home. The support you provided me during these months was essential. There were days when defeat lurked in the back of my mind, but your words of encouragement and support got me through, and because of that, we got little Pax through. I'll never forget that. You are family forever, not family by DNA, but family, nonetheless. Sarah used to say you have the family you're born to and the family you find. I'm so glad I found you."

Lara came out to the porch to join him.

"New song?" she inquired.

"No," he laughed. "Just updating some important friends on the day's events."

She handed him a beer, which he surprisingly set down without taking a sip.

"How are you doing, Papa Pax?"

He turned to Lara and leaned back on the step.

"It's strange to think it's over, at least this stage. But I feel good. I feel... light."

Lara rested her head on his shoulder and sighed. "You were a warrior, Pax. Day to day, nothing else mattered but that little boy. I kept looking for signs that you might be melting down like you did the night we met, but you were solid."

"I've changed a lot since then," he said. "Met some interesting people, present company included. Found out who I am and what family means to me. It made a difference in how I handled this. Each day in the hospital wasn't a test of endurance. It was just another day, and my only job was getting little Pax through it."

They sat quietly for a few minutes, listening to the laughter coming from inside the house. Lara sat up.

"I have an idea," she said. "Get your guitar."

"Why?"

"It's Friday. You need to sing."

LARA AND MALIYAH entered the Delta Harmony Lounge, followed by Pax. The manager greeted them at the door and led them to a VIP box—a table for four, roped off with holiday streamers to make it look special. As they took their seats, a young woman with a guitar performed an original folk-rock song.

Knowing that Lara would record the performance and upload it to YouTube, Pax considered the song he was going to perform and how Kat might interpret it. He knew she would watch the video as soon as it was uploaded.

After a few other acts, the manager took the stage and recounted the first night that Pax Butler performed at The Lounge. The audience chuckled during the funny moments and "aww-ed" during the sweet ones. He discussed the other performances on the YouTube channel and concluded by reminding the audience that it was right there on that stage that this pilgrimage began.

"So, now," the manager said, looking at Pax. "After thousands of miles, other performances, and a new hairstyle, ladies and gentlemen, Pax Butler."

The applause took Pax by surprise as he stood. Lara began recording right away. Before stepping onto the stage, Pax looked into Lara's camera, his question directed at his lover over a thousand miles away.

"If I tell you I love you, will you still love me after I sing this song?"

Then, to loud applause, he walked onto the stage and tuned his guitar. As the crowd quieted, he slipped into performance mode, much like putting on his favorite pair of jeans.

"Right here," he said, fingering a few notes in the D chord. "This isn't where my pilgrimage began, but it's where it became something special. Who could have thought I would be back here over a year later?"

The audience cheered and clapped. Pax ran his hand over his head.

"Today, my grandson rang the Victory Bell at St. Jude's.

That's what this whole Kojak thing is about. He's a mighty warrior, and he's going to be okay."

The audience clapped and cheered even louder than before.

"Sorry if you're too young to know who Kojak was, but you can always look it up."

Someone in the audience yelled, "Telly Savalas!"

Pax laughed, and the audience joined him.

"It's important to fight for family," he said, looking back at the table where two women who shared no lineage with him sat. "That's some of my extended family back there. Others will see this online, I'm sure. They know who they are. This song is for all of them."

He began *The Sound of You*, playing through the riffs Beto had composed. The arrangement was a winner, and the song flowed from his fingers and lips. He sang the first verse to the audience, then turned to Lara for the second. Finally, he looked directly into Lara's camera as if searching for Kat while singing the third. His heart ached as he sang about the woman who felt like her, marking the end of his search. He wished she were there.

As the song ended, the crowd erupted. Pax thanked the audience and packed his guitar before returning to his seat. He took a big gulp of tequila and then looked at Lara, waiting for her verdict.

Her silent nod was everything he needed to know.

THE MORNING LIGHT filtered through the lace curtains of the Allen house, bathing the modest dining room in golden hues. The aroma of freshly brewed coffee gradually drew every adult in the home to the kitchen.

Pax sat at the table, tracing the rim of his mug with his

fingers, his mind replaying the previous night—the applause, the unexpected emotions as he sang *The Sound of You*, and the way Lara had grinned at him afterward, telling him he needed that performance more than anyone in the audience.

Ally sat down at the table, her hair still a mess from sleep, her hands curled around her steaming cup. She regarded him for a long moment before speaking.

"Have you made a decision, Dad? Are you coming home for Christmas?"

Pax exhaled slowly, gazing into the dark liquid before taking a sip.

"Maybe after winter for a visit," he admitted. "I know where I belong. She's been my anchor, even from a thousand miles away."

Ally nodded as though she had anticipated that answer.

"You deserve that," she said. "And I know you'll visit when you're ready."

Pax met her gaze. "You and the kids need me. I mean, I need all of you."

She smiled, a hint of sadness yet a deep understanding.

"We always need you, Dad. But I think you need this. You need her. And I think she needs you. Mom would want you to be with someone who loves you, Dad. There's no doubt where Kat's heart is."

Pax reached across the table and took her hand, squeezing it. "You're an amazing woman, Ally. Your mother would be so proud. She is."

She squeezed back and chuckled softly.

"You're going to make me cry before I finish my coffee," she teased. "Ugh...I'm so tired of crying. We all need some emotional downtime."

Pax raised his coffee mug in agreement.

"Can you hear her, Dad?"

He nodded.

They sat in silence, allowing the morning to unfold before them, neither feeling the need to rush the moment. But the moment came, as all moments must, to say goodbye.

Outside, the cars were packed, and the last bags were loaded. The cold Tennessee air carried the murmur of casual comments that masked the heavy, aching silence of farewells about to be spoken.

Little Pax clung to his grandfather's hand, his eyes wide and uncertain. He had spent months tethered to Papa Pax, sharing every fight, every tough day, and every tense moment in the hospital. Now, for the first time in a very long while, they would be apart.

"You sure you don't want to sneak into my suitcase?" Pax asked, his voice light, though he felt a weight in his chest.

Little Pax giggled, yet his lips pressed into a firm line, his tiny hands gripping Pax's tightly. "You won't be gone forever, right?"

Pax knelt so they were eye to eye.

"No, Mighty One. We'll see each other soon. But you've got a big job ahead—getting stronger, playing with Lainey, driving your mother crazy. That's a full schedule for an old person like me, let alone a man of eight."

Little Pax sniffed and nodded. "And you'll call me?"

"I will," Pax promised, ruffling his grandson's hair. "And when I come to visit, we'll do something special. Maybe go fishing?"

Little Pax's face lit up. "Like at the lake?"

"Exactly like at the lake." Pax wrapped him in a tight hug, kissing the top of his hairless head. "I love you, Kiddo."

"Love you too, Papa."

Ally witnessed this tender moment. She had to catch her breath, overwhelmed with emotion, as the nickname her father had given her was passed down to her son.

Lara and Maliyah stood in the driveway, their arms around each other's waists, their faces showing a blend of joy and sorrow.

Maliyah knelt next to little Pax, gently rubbing his small bald head.

"Remember something for me, Mighty One," she said softly. "Home is who you're with, not where you are. Family isn't just the people in your house—it's love, and you'll always have that here. You'll always have us, Lara, and me, okay?"

Little Pax nodded solemnly, as if absorbing a truth he might not fully understand yet but would carry with him. His hug around Maliyah's neck reflected precisely the emotion that she had planted with her words.

Lara hugged Pax tightly. "You were a rock through all of this," she whispered. "And I hope you know you'll always have a home here, too."

Pax swallowed hard against the lump in his throat. "I do," he said. "And I won't be a stranger."

She pulled back, her eyes shining. "I won't let you be."

Lara cupped his cheeks, gazing deeply into his eyes. "Tell her I said 'thank you' for whatever she did to turn you into the man you are now. I don't think you could have handled this so capably last year. She found something in you and pulled it into the light."

One final round of hugs, one last wave goodbye, and then the cars drove off.

After the two vehicles fueled up near the interstate, Pax watched Ally, Travis, Lainey, and little Pax disappear down the road, heading toward South Carolina. His heart ached, but it was a good ache, reminding him that love stretched across every mile.

His hand moved instinctively to the rings around his neck, sensing their weight.

"Ready?" he asked the universe, then climbed into his truck and headed north, toward Wyoming, toward whatever came next.

HE DIDN'T CALL when he got near. He simply arrived.

She met him on the porch, wrapped in a large, crocheted shawl to ward off the cold, holding a steaming cup of coffee. He walked slowly through the crunching snow and up the steps. She offered him the cup, but he set it aside and kissed her. To him, it marked the first kiss of the rest of their lives.

She beamed, patted his chest, and they went inside. She settled beside him on the couch, warming herself by the fireplace, legs tucked up on the seat, her fingers drumming absentmindedly against her knee.

"Did it feel weird?" she asked. "Being alone on the road again, after all that time."

Pax nodded, keeping his eyes on the fire.

"Yeah. It felt... unnatural, almost. Like, I should still be there."

She studied him, searching his face.

"You were there for so long, Pax. For him. For them. You fought beside him every step of the way."

"Yeah," he said, his voice heavy with emotion. "And now I'm not."

She sighed and shook her head.

"It doesn't work like that, darling. You don't stop being with him just because you're somewhere else. You're with them right now, even though you're here with me. Every time he thinks of you, you're there. Just as you were here with me while sitting with him in Memphis. We were together every time we thought of each other."

He said nothing. He knew she was right, but it didn't make things any easier. Little Pax had been a part of him, day and night, for months. Now, there was an emptiness where that constant worry and care had been. But being back in that house, he knew how to fill it.

After a long moment, she spoke again, this time more softly.

"I missed you," she admitted. "I know I told you to stay, and I meant it, but I still missed you every day."

He placed his hand on her knee, intertwining his fingers with hers.

"I missed you, too, Kat, but I couldn't leave him."

"I know," she said. "And I wouldn't have wanted you to."

They fell silent once more, the weight of their words lingering, the tension of their reunion straining for relief.

She shifted. "So, what now, Pax?"

He exhaled and smiled. "I'm here," he said contentedly. "Where I am meant to be."

She looked into his eyes, doubt in her own. "You're not already planning when you will go back?"

He hesitated. "No. I'm here. I'm home."

She moved toward him, her eyes curious about his use of the word "home."

"You found her, Pax?" she asked softly. "Sarah. You found her? Your quest is over?"

He swallowed hard, his gaze fixed on the crackling fire.

"I was never looking for Sarah. I thought I was, but—"

The silence lingered, words left unspoken, and the tension grew.

"I don't regret anything, Pax. And I don't resent it. You needed me. We needed each other. And for a while, we still do. But I think we both know how this ends."

Pax tightened his hold on her hand.

"No, no, no. Stop. Please understand me. I found what I was

looking for. But it wasn't Sarah. It was a feeling. I realized in Memphis that what I was missing wasn't her. It was the fullness of her. It was the love that filled me when I was with her. I found it, Kat. It's here with you."

Despite her Nordic stoicism, she turned away to conceal the tears that gathered in her eyes.

"Don't tease, Pax. It's not kind."

He pulled her onto his lap and gently wiped tears from her eyes.

"If I tell you that I love you," he said, then paused. "Oh, screw it, I love you, Kat."

She melted into him, their arms entwined and their lips engaged. The universe contracted into the space between them.

When the kiss faded, they kept their lips touching, sharing breath.

"And the song?" she said, referring to the YouTube video of *The Sound of You*, still uncertain of his commitment to stay. "The ending? You're not still looking for her?"

"It's just a song, Kat," he said. "This pilgrim has left the road."

WINTER SPREAD over Brun-Dahl Ranch like a woolen blanket, muffling the world in layers of soft, powdery snow. The wind carried the scent of pine and distant smoke from the chimney, curling in the crisp air as Pax and Kat rode side by side through the sugar-coated fields. The horses' breaths came in thick, visible plumes, their hooves crunching into the snow with each step, forming a steady rhythm against the silence.

Pax had nearly forgotten what this peace felt like, the raw beauty of Wyoming in winter, the slow and deliberate pace of life. He had first experienced it a year ago, in that same place, under that same sky, with Kat's voice guiding him. And now, after months spent in hospital rooms, surrounded by antiseptic smells, and the relentless struggle to keep his grandson alive, he was back.

Each day followed a common rhythm—mornings spent on horseback, afternoons caring for the animals, and evenings wrapped in the warmth of Kat's small but sturdy home. They prepared dinner together, sometimes with music playing softly in the background, and at other times in the comfortable silence that only exists between two people who understand each other without needing to fill every moment with words.

At night, they lay entwined beneath thick quilts—skin on skin—with the cold never quite reaching them in the cocoon of each other's arms. There was no urgency or restless need to prove anything. Their love had settled into something tangible, something known, something undeniable.

They drove down to Cheyenne every few weeks to meet JD and Harley for karaoke at T-Joe's. Pax, never one to refuse a stage —even one as humble as this—found comfort in being in the audience rather than at the microphone. He would sit and listen to bluesy ballads, classic rock tunes, and the occasional folk song, all sung in various voices—some in key, and others not quite so much. Kat and JD often tried to persuade him to take the mic, but he would smile, sip his drink, and let their requests dissolve into the bar's atmosphere.

"I only sing for Kat, now," he said on one occasion, to put an end to their badgering. "And only at home."

Late one early spring night, as they drove back to the ranch, Kat watched him from the passenger seat. He felt her gaze, but it wasn't unsettling. It was comforting.

"You're feeling it again, aren't you?" she asked. "The pull."

He exhaled deeply, watching the headlights carve through the dark, endless road ahead. His initial response was going to be one of frustration, but as he let that dissolve, he realized she was right.

"I am," he admitted. He had been thinking about Ally and Rob, along with the growing brood of grandchildren. They held periodic video calls with the South Carolina contingent, always making time for the little ones. Sometimes it was enough. Sometimes it wasn't.

Kat didn't push him. She simply waited for the words he was struggling to find. Her fingers traced slow patterns on the back of his hand. She concealed her anxiety with her patience, waiting for the words that would eventually come—the words she dreaded.

"I was thinking we should get another dog."

The silence of her surprise made him chuckle. "What? You like dogs."

She started to laugh. Her fear of his departure faded, replaced by a joy that filled her to the brim.

He couldn't help but laugh with her; her happiness fueled his own.

"Pull over now, Mr. Butler," she ordered, pointing to the shoulder of the side road. Pax complied.

Had another car passed by that night, or a nighthawk, or a lone coyote, they would have seen two people in the throes of passion in the front seat of a pickup truck, windows steamed, sounds of rapture emanating from within—the intensity of their lovemaking would have been the envy of lovers a third their age. As it was, they were left undisturbed, and although they arrived at the house later than usual, when they walked up the steps hand in hand, they were no longer just a woman and her itinerant lover. They had become a couple, married in every sense of the word except the paper.

That night, skin-to-skin, Kat rested her head on his shoulder, her hand brushing against the three rings that hung on the chain around his neck.

"Does she approve?" she asked.

He chuckled. "If she were here, then yes. But then, if she were here, would I be?"

"I don't know what kind of woman you think I am, sir," Kat joked. "But if she were here, I would hope it would be as my friend."

"She would have loved you, Kat. You're so alike. You two would have spent every day teasing me in some secret language."

She cuddled closer and stopped playing with the rings.

"But yes, Kat. She told me to find someone to love and to love that person with all my heart."

Kat smiled into his chest.

"A wise woman," she said. "I like her very much."

THEY GOT ANOTHER DOG.

The two big mounds of fur, Ike and Tina, weren't much for running along the trails between the barns, but Gracie, the Australian Shepherd, couldn't get enough of it. They adopted her from a shelter in Cheyenne, and on the first day, she was down the trail, running alongside August and Freyja as they rode to the Vild Lade.

Kat wasn't sure about having such a hyper dog in the same house as the others, but after a few days, it became clear that Gracie was *her* dog while Pax was just the human who threw tennis balls and gave treats under the table.

Ike and Tina became Pax's foot-warmers every night as they lay beside his chair in the living room. Gracie found a spot on the couch where she could lie with her head on Kat's lap while

Kat read or cross-stitched. They had to close the door at night to keep Gracie out of the bed, especially when they desired something more than a comfortable sleep. Gracie would lie at the door, whining to come in until either Kat relented or Gracie fell asleep.

Kat and Dog, Pax would think. *There might be a song in there somewhere.*

As spring warmed the landscape, Kat and Gracie would go for walks together, sometimes with Pax and other times without him. He didn't mind. He loved seeing Kat happy, even if it was from a distance.

With Harley's help, he also persuaded Kat to install Wi-Fi in the house. They set up satellite internet service at Vild Lade, allowing them to communicate with family and friends and share live feeds of their wild charges with the vets and other members of their activist circle. Harley and a friend came over and installed all the technology that required more capability than either Pax or Kat possessed.

Once Kat realized she could post videos and photos to people who shared her passion for the cause, she was convinced. She soon started actively uploading videos on social media to raise awareness about the endangered animals in a country that preached conservation. Pax laughed as his lover became and influencer, using terms like "vlog," "likes," and "views."

"I can be very loud now with the BLM," she would say, and the increasing number of followers on her social media account confirmed that.

Two days after Pax's birthday, Kat and Gracie rode and ran along the green path toward Vild Lade. She was heading to the wild barn to capture some footage of a new male yearling.

The young horse had suffered severe injuries from barbed wire, as well as cracked hooves from kicking down the fence posts while trying to escape. A veterinarian sedated him and treated his injuries, and a full recovery was expected, but the psychological effects were more difficult to solve. Kat planned to play soothing music while she filmed the young horse and made her heartfelt plea to raise awareness against fencing wild areas.

Pax stayed behind, writing his weekly emails to Ally and Rob and sending pictures of the horses for his grandchildren to see. Ally had sent photos of baby Robbie, her brother's namesake, and included her fervent pleas for Pax to visit South Carolina to meet his new grandson before he was old enough for college.

After lunch, Pax checked his watch and wondered how long Kat would be filming. He wasn't sure if he liked her newfound passion for social media, but he wasn't there to tell her how to serve her cause. He was there to love her while she was doing it.

He checked his account and found no notifications for new videos on her feed.

"The hell is she doing down there?" he said to the room, but the room didn't answer.

Gracie's enthusiastic bark in the distance caught his attention, and he relaxed as he walked to the door to greet their return. She came running up the path from the direction of Vild Lade, but there was no Kat, no Freyja. Pax felt his stomach drop.

Gracie barked at him and dashed back down the trail. He briefly thought she was just being unusually hyper, but he realized something was wrong when she returned to him and barked again.

He ran to the barn behind the house and saddled August as quickly as he could. Gracie kept barking at him, and once he mounted and rode the old horse out onto the trail, the barking stopped and she ran toward the Vild Lade. Pax rode as fast as he dared, not wanting to risk falling off or causing August to stumble. The trip took too long—too damn long.

Freyja was tied up outside the Vild Lade barn, munching on hay. Kat was nowhere in sight.

Pax jumped off August and secured him to the same rail as Freyja.

"Kat!"

Silence. He moved quickly to the barn, his heart racing.

"Kat!"

Silence. He went to the stable where the young male was stalled. It was empty, and the gate had been kicked off its hinges.

"KAT!"

He ran to the door that led out to the fenced paddock. As he approached, he slowed. Something—no, someone—was lying on the ground outside the door.

He ran.

IT RAINED on the day of her funeral. Her cremation had taken place the day before, and the weather had been sunny. But the sky wept when they all gathered at the cemetery where her ashes would be interred with Carsen's, reunited once more after so long.

Pax breathed. That's all he could do as the words were spoken, as the memories were shared, and as what remained of the second woman he had loved with his entire being was placed behind a stone panel, laser-etched with her smiling likeness. He breathed and listened to both the words spoken aloud to the group and those murmured quietly behind him.

"One of them wild yearlings busted right through the stable wall. Happened quicker than a wink," someone who hadn't been there whispered. "Kat got caught up in the ruckus when it bolted out of the barn."

"It wasn't much—just a nasty knock to the head on a fence

post—but she was out at the wild barn. Nobody could reach her in time."

"Pax found her. She was already gone by then."

"She was an incredible woman. He loved her somethin' fierce."

"What's Harley gonna do with the ranch? Is he gonna to move here?"

"He's good with horses, but that's a tough charge for him. He'll have to sell it."

Pax swallowed hard, contemplating the sale of Brun-Dahl Ranch. Any buyer would likely be an adjacent ranch, and Kat's sanctuary of peace and protection would be consumed by a business aimed at satisfying the greed of humans.

When the will was read, as the sole survivor of Carsen and Kat's estate, there was enough money to keep Harley comfortable for the rest of his life, thanks to Carsen's wise investments and Kat's prudent management of the funds. However, the fact remained that while Harley could work the ranch, he lacked the knowledge and skills to run it as a business. Leases, fractional assessments, land valuation, property taxes, and arrangements with various sources for the care of the wild horses were beyond his expertise. He reluctantly decided he had to sell the property.

Pax helped Harley find a lawyer to handle the sale. Although they could have received a higher price for the acreage by selling to a cattle rancher, a few calls to Kat's contacts uncovered a non-profit organization dedicated to the exact cause that motivated Kat. The land was sold to the non-profit for pennies on the dollar, but at least it was protected and could continue to be used for rehabilitating wild animals in need.

The Brun-Dahl Ranch would remain a safe harbor for wild horses, and the Carsen and Katja Browne Trust would evolve into a southeastern Wyoming charity supported by conservation groups, school fundraisers, and even cattle ranchers who had known the couple during their lifetime. The ranch would also welcome tourists seeking their *City Slickers* experience, allowing the organization to educate others about the disappearing wild horses and burros across the "wild" West. Vild Lade would continue to function as a working barn but would also transform into a classroom. A small plaque painted with a Marguerite daisy, the national flower of Denmark, was mounted on the wall near the spot where Kat fell.

After the papers were signed and a closing date was set, Pax and Harley returned to the ranch and pulled every bottle from the liquor cabinet. They sat on the porch under a full moon, each with a bottle in hand, glasses unnecessary, and got drunk.

The old place felt empty without Kat's presence, her laughter, her steady hand. He let the memories wash over him—the nights spent in each other's arms, the intimate moments, the spoken and unspoken acts of love.

They exchanged stories, with Harley's encompassing multiple lifetimes, including his father and Carsen's adventures as young men, along with his first encounter with Kat as a child. Pax's stories were fewer and more recent, but they still reflected Kat's love for the world and the two most important men in her life.

"She loved you fiercely, Pax. Honest truth."

"It was very true, Harley. For both of us."

After midnight, Harley went upstairs to sleep off his grief and the liquor. Pax stayed on the porch, reflecting on the women he had embraced and loved. There were just three of them, and Katja Browne was the first woman to fill his emptiness since Sarah.

The wind flowed through the fields, and Pax raised his bottle in a silent toast to the woman who had healed him, loved him, and made him more than he was when she had met him not so long ago by a coat rack. Then he took a long drink and let the memories carry him away.

PAX RETURNED to South Carolina with a sense of finality. The drive had been long, the miles passing like flickering sunlight through a picket fence. His time with Kat had been warm, filled with joy and comfort, and ended all too soon. She had always anticipated that he would leave her to return to South Carolina, but his home had become where she was, and without her, he felt lost once more, compelled to return to where familial love awaited him. Gracie rode alongside him. Ike and Tina had moved in with Harley.

As he pulled into the driveway of Ally and Travis's home, he exhaled, bracing himself for the welcome he knew would be both joyful and bittersweet. Ally and Travis greeted him on the porch, their expressions full of understanding. They had witnessed the cost of his return—what he had lost in Wyoming. It was their turn to heal and protect him, just as he had done for their son.

Ally wrapped her arms around him tightly, whispering, "Welcome home, Dad."

Little Pax was thriving, full of energy and resilience. He was a living testament to months of struggle and sacrifice. His hair had grown back, and the doctors were optimistic. The battle had been long, but the prognosis was good. There would be years of checkups and a lifetime of vigilance, but the worst was behind them.

As Pax sat with him on the couch that first night back, watching his grandson play a video game, he felt a sense of release in his chest. The weight, the constant ache, lifted.

A few weeks later, Pax discovered a small house on the

outskirts of Rock Hill—a modest home with a fenced backyard and a front porch where he and Gracie could sit and listen to the wind in the trees and the neighbor children playing in the cul-de-sac. He embraced his new role as a grandfather and patriarch, finding his purpose in the rhythms of family life, something he couldn't remember feeling in his six-plus decades.

He stayed connected with those he had left behind in the world. He occasionally spoke with Sal and Marisol on the phone, but more often, they exchanged emails and texts about their travels, music, and life in general. Marisol sent him videos of Beto playing guitar—his talent growing by the day.

"We miss you, Pax," she wrote. "The music will always be better when we're together."

He also kept in touch with Harley and Erin, even an occasional message to Alicent, now Allie, when he saw something online that reminded him of her. He tried to keep those messages lighthearted, leaving the more difficult moments to share with Sal or his daughter.

And he started doing things he never imagined he would—things that Sarah or even Kat would have had to force him to do.

He found a straightforward doctor he liked, who convinced him to get a colonoscopy—all clear, see you in ten years.

He volunteered at his grandkids' school to help with traffic control during parent pick-up at the end of the school day. This allowed him to see Lainey and Little Pax, still called Puck by his friends, every school day. He also got to know many of the other children and some of their parents. They all called him Papa Pax, and he was okay with that.

His experience working with Harley to resolve inheritance challenges prompted Pax to find an estate attorney and organize his financial affairs. He considered this the most adult thing he had ever done and toasted himself with some tequila on ice, saying, "Who's a big boy now? I am. I'm a big boy now."

Then, on an unremarkable day in June, Pax stopped by the pharmacy to pick up a prescription refill. As he rounded the corner of an aisle, he halted abruptly, looking into Audra's wide eyes and anxious face.

Her smile was a mixture of surprise and something else—relief, perhaps? Or anxiety? In her shopping cart sat a young child, no more than two years old, sucking absentmindedly on a sippy cup. His stomach tightened, and he tried to do math in his head. *How long was I gone?*

"Hey," she said tentatively.

"Hey," he replied, his voice strangely quiet. His eyes were on the child, searching for features he might recognize in himself.

They stood there, the silence stretching between them, before Audra glanced at the little girl and then back at him.

As if reading his thoughts, she smiled and said, "She's not yours."

A strange combination of emotions flooded him—relief, guilt, regret, disappointment.

"I—," he started, but stopped, unsure what he had meant to say.

Audra offered a faint smile, lightening the weight of whatever lay between them.

"How's your hand?"

He chuckled and showed off his dexterity and range of motion with the exercises she had taught him.

"I had a lot of help getting it back," he said, feeling less disoriented by her sudden appearance.

"It's good to see you, Pax. It's been a long time."

They spoke for a few minutes, catching up the way people do when too much has happened, and the moment wasn't quite right for sharing.

"I've been playing guitar again," he said, searching for shallow topics to discuss.

"I know," she replied. "I saw the videos."

He didn't know why, but he was suddenly embarrassed at being so visible to the world.

"You look good," she said. "You look fit."

He quietly nodded in appreciation. "That's a long story."

"Maybe we can grab a coffee sometime," she suggested. "Just to... tell stories."

Pax nodded in agreement and glanced at the child once more.

"Her name is Zuri," she said. "After my mother."

"Beautiful name. Beautiful child."

"She is," Audra agreed, stroking Zuri's wavy black hair.

"You look happy," he said, trying to keep the sound moving between them.

"I am," she said. "And you?"

He contemplated the question. "I think I'm getting there."

The silence returned, broken only by the chirps and sounds from Zuri.

"Your hair is different," he remarked.

She laughed. His heart fluttered slightly at the sound of her laughter after so long, and it brought a smile to his face.

"Yes, it is," she replied.

"I like it."

The silence returned, waiting for the next random effort at continuity.

"I'll call you, Pax."

"Please do," he replied. "You have my number?"

"I do."

His paralysis finally lifted when she turned at the end of the aisle and disappeared.

That night, he sat on his porch with his guitar, tuning it slowly. The music flowed quickly, and the melody felt familiar. He began to shape the chords into something new, something full of promise. The song he started for Audra in Colorado was coming back to him.

As he played, he felt a settling inside him. Not closure, not quite—but a step forward. A new sensation filled his empty spaces. He couldn't name it, but if he had to, he would say he felt hopeful and content.

He settled into his life in Rock Hill, finding comfort in the rhythm of routine—walking with Gracie, playing with the kids, spending weekends with families, and still making time to enjoy live music in the area.

He started teaching guitar lessons, welcoming students from the local community and sharing the knowledge that had shaped so much of his life. It wasn't the stage, but it was fulfilling in a different way—watching young minds learn the language of music and seeing their eyes light up when a chord progression finally made sense.

His reunion with Audra over coffee started awkwardly, but the more they shared, the more they wanted to share. They avoided reliving *that* day and instead focused on their love and care for each other, albeit in a different form.

He met her husband, Leroy, an instructor in Computer Technology at York Tech. He and Leroy also shared stories, and Pax knew after the first meeting that this man was a better fit for Audra than he ever would have been.

Audra and Pax formed a silent alliance—Leroy would never learn about their past, allowing their friendship to flourish in this new shape. Over time, Papa Pax became Zuri's surrogate grandfather, spending many afternoons entertaining her with simple melodies or reading children's stories, just as Audra had once done for Ally's kids.

The connection between Audra's family and those of Ally and Rob deepened, creating a tangled yet loving network of relationships. Pax found himself enveloped in unexpected love, watching children grow and life move forward. He heard Sarah's tones every time he watched the children playing together, convinced she was seeing through his eyes and listening with his ears. He privately heard Kat's matter-of-fact tone when he needed to make a decision about something or view something differently than before.

Though the stage still called to him, he never stepped onto it again. His guitar remained a personal refuge, a companion rather than just a tool.

Sitting on his porch, strumming a D chord with Gracie by his side, he reflected on his journey. With all the miles behind him, along with all the love, laughter, and loss, Pax Butler had discovered himself, and in doing so, found something resembling peace.

~

(11) 2016-05-23.mp3

"READY, ZIM?"

"Go ahead, honey. No countdown— just talk."

"Hey, my loves. I hope you can still feel me in your bones because I promise you, I haven't gone too far. I know this is hard. I know there'll be days when the hurt feels bigger than the love, but let me remind you: the love is bigger. It always is.

"I want to talk to you about gratitude. Not the polite kind, where you say thank you because it's the right thing to do, but the kind that fills you up from the inside. The kind that makes you stop in the middle of the day and know—really know—how lucky you are, even when things aren't perfect.

"Be thankful for the people around you, even when they make you want to pull your hair out. Every eye-roll, every squabble, and every time you have to count to ten before saying something you can't take back—that's a privilege. Not everyone gets to have that for as long as they should. Love each other fiercely, even when you're mad.

"Be thankful for the everyday stuff. The dishes in the sink mean you had food to eat. The mess in the living room means there was laughter. The laundry pile that never shrinks? Well, it means you're still living every day. And isn't that something? Isn't that what we all hope for— to still be here, still making a mess of things?

"Be thankful for time. We never get enough of it, and Lord knows it moves too fast. But what a gift it is to have at all. Use it wisely. Don't put off the good stuff for "someday," because someday isn't a guarantee. What you have is today, and that's more than enough.

"And more than anything, be thankful for love. It's the strongest thing there is. It'll hold you up when your legs give out. It'll keep you warm when the world turns cold. It'll remind you that you aren't ever really alone, even when the house is quiet.

"So today, if you're missing me—if that ache feels like too much— take a deep breath, look around, and find something, anything, to be thankful for. Do that for me. Do that for you.

"I love you always. And I am always thankful for you."

PART VI

CODA

"Endings are not always bad. Most times, they're just beginnings in disguise."

–Kim **Harrison**

JUST, LISTEN.

THE FIRST SIGN OF THE HEART ATTACK felt more like an annoyance than anything else. His back ached, his shoulder was sore, and he mumbled something to Ally about feeling old. He claimed it was indigestion, but she kept an eye on him. Her career in patient advocacy had taught her that even at sixty-five years old, anything sudden was worth monitoring.

Pax spent the afternoon with Travis watching Gamecocks football. He barely touched the beer beside him and didn't want to dig into the chips that Ally had put out. Heartburn, he thought. Maybe. He wasn't sure. He just felt shitty.

The second wave hit him harder. His breathing became difficult. His ears were ringing. His teeth hurt. *Why do my teeth hurt?*

"Ally," he said, getting up to tell her he needed a Rolaid and collapsed to the floor.

He didn't remember Ally screaming. He didn't remember Travis shouting into his phone. He didn't remember whether or by how much Clemson beat those goddamn Gamecocks. However, he did remember the sirens, the stretcher, and the ambulance to the hospital. He remembered the frenetic actions of the ER team, the machines, and the injections, and he remembered everything going silent.

The next thing he remembered was that bent fucking B note on the machine with its fucking nineteenth fret on the fucking first string. He didn't know where he was. He didn't know when he was.

Does that mean that she's coming back? He thought. *Is she going to make it?* He opened his eyes. She was there. But it wasn't her. *Her* eyes, but not *Her* face.

"Sarah?" he said, but something was stuck in his mouth. He tried to dislodge it with his tongue, but it wouldn't move, and he started gagging, struggling against the urge to vomit.

"Dad. Dad. Stop!"

Rob.

Rob held Pax's arms away from his face.

"Hey, Rob," he attempted to say, but the sedatives and the tube in his throat made him sound drunk.

"Dad, they have you intubated," Rob explained, releasing Pax's hands when he felt them relax. "You left us for a bit, but they got you back."

He shook his head, or at least he thought he did. Everything hurt. He reached for Rob, and Rob took his hand.

"What do you need, Dad?"

He pointed to the tube and mimed pulling it out. Rob nodded and quickly left the room.

And then *She* was there. He blinked several times. How was she there? She had been gone for years. He felt something in his chest, and at sixty-five, he finally understood what people meant by feeling butterflies in their stomach.

He reached for her, and she took his hand. He felt it. How can this be possible?

"Dad?"

He blinked. His dry eyes cleared slightly, and he saw Ally.

Disappointment washed over him as he cried, the breathing tube stifling his sobs and causing him to choke.

"It's okay, Dad. Rob is checking with the doctor to see if they can remove that tube."

He turned toward the window and gazed outside, tears streaming down his face.

"Where?" he gurgled around the tube.

"Rock Hill, Dad."

He turned back to Ally just as Rob returned with a doctor.

"Mr. Butler," the doctor said. "I'm very surprised to see you awake, sir. You have a superhuman constitution to push through the sedatives we gave you. We're going to get this tube out for you. I can't lie; it won't be pleasant."

He nodded and gave the doctor a thumbs-up.

Pulling the tube felt like extracting a burning alien from his chest, and when it was out and he could feel his tongue again, he wept from the sheer pleasure of it.

The doctor explained the situation. Angioplasty was performed to insert stents into three cardiac arteries to keep them open. That was the quick fix. Bypass surgery was the longer-term solution, and it was scheduled. However, the damage to his heart muscle was extensive, requiring significant testing to determine if he could live with the damage or if a transplant was necessary.

Despite their protests, Pax sent his kids out of the room while he spoke with the doctor privately.

"No bypass," he said calmly. "No transplant."

"But Mr. Butler, it is highly unlikely—"

"No," he repeated.

The doctor tried again to steer Pax toward reason, but he wasn't having it.

"I'm old," he said. "If you find a heart, it should go to

someone younger who needs it. Don't waste someone else's sacrifice on me."

The doctor nodded, not in agreement but in understanding.

"And no more stents or bypasses. Don't make things worse just to make them better for a bit longer. Let me have time with my family, and eventually I'll be out of your hair. I'll sign whatever you need me to sign."

"We can speak again about this, Mr. Butler," the doctor said.

Pax smiled. *No, doc, we cannot.*

ROB AND ALLY took turns staying with him. With a job that allowed him to work from anywhere, Travis was always present when Ally was there. Naomi joined Rob occasionally, depending on the demands of her job. Travis brought him the chain with the three rings that had been removed before surgery, and placed it around his neck.

He's a good man, Pax thought. *He'll take care of everyone.*

He slept a lot. Dreamless sleep. Uncomfortable, joyless sleep. He wanted to tear all the electrodes off his chest and pull out all the tubes, but he knew they were keeping him alive. If he wanted more time in this world, he needed to stop being his typical ornery self for a while and let this happen.

He woke up, and Ally glanced up from her book and smiled at him.

Travis stepped forward.

"Do you need anything, Dad?"

He opened his mouth, but no words came out, so he shut it and gently shook his head. He closed his eyes, but sleep wouldn't return, so he listened. He heard Ally breathing as she read. He heard Travis humming something. He heard sounds in the hallway outside his room and traffic from the street below.

He heard *Third fret—Second string.*

He fought against the urge to let that tone pull him away. He knew what it was: a siren song. It was Sarah. His time was near.

"Ally," he said quietly, and she looked up from her book. "Get Rob."

HE HADN'T FELT this calm in years. His kids and Travis sat close by, each holding a hand. Travis held Ally's free hand, connecting the group by one degree of separation.

He lay smiling with his eyes closed. The medications they had given him to prevent agitation and help him sleep felt nice. It wasn't quite what he had experienced in his younger days, but it was a pleasant, floaty feeling when he allowed it to happen.

He suddenly turned his head and looked at Rob.

"Rob, sell that truck. Or keep it. I don't care. It's yours."

Rob glanced at Ally nervously.

"Don't worry about her," he said. "I have her covered."

He closed his eyes and drifted off for a moment, mentally thumbing through the checklist in his head. He had things that needed sorting, and he had little time to do it.

Several minutes passed, and he suddenly leaned up again, startling all three of them.

"Ally, what's left of the money from selling the fifth wheel and the house in Middletown is in an account. Split it with Rob. It's in the will that way."

"Dad, I—"

"Stop it," he snapped. "This is happening. None of that happy horseshit. I've got places to be."

Ally began to sob quietly as he settled back into the bed, drifting on the edge of sleep.

Damn, these drugs are good, he thought, and it reminded him of the days when he and Zim would smoke a little, snort a little, and eat some mushrooms.

"People like me because I'm a fungi," he whispered, echoing Zim's stupid joke from days gone by. He smiled nostalgically, then opened his eyes and saw Ally's tears.

"I'm sorry, Kiddo. I've been an asshole most of your life, and I wish I could take it all back."

"Dad, it's ok," Ally started.

"It's not. Don't ever let it be. Your old man was an asshole. It doesn't make excuses for your behavior, but it also doesn't mean you shouldn't just own it."

Ally tightened her grip on his hand.

"I know you were an asshole, Dad," Rob chimed in. "But you grew up on the road."

He looked at Rob and smiled, then turned back to Ally. He closed his eyes, feeling... wow, what was this? Better? He heard something through the haze of drugs.

Third fret—Second string.

Not yet, baby.

He opened his eyes and sat up, startling the group once more.

"Now, I don't know if any of you were ever arrested or jailed while I was being selfish and not paying attention. And I don't want to know. But even if you were, I love you anyway."

They all exchanged glances, silently confused.

"I spent a night in jail," he laughed. "In Hartford. A long time ago."

"What, Dad?" Rob asked, dumbfounded. "You were arrested? For what?"

He laughed again, feeling a bit euphoric from the medication.

"I hit a man. Knocked him out."

"Why did you hit him, Dad?" Ally asked.

"I thought he was Zim."

He drifted once more.

Goooood drugs, he thought, but maybe he said it out loud.

"What, Dad?" Rob asked.

He tried to keep his eyes open, but they wouldn't obey. Other sounds filled the room, and he forced them open. Audra and Naomi had brought the grandkids.

He smiled, tears welling as he looked at the five of them. Lainey had Jazz and Zuri in hand. Pax was carrying Robbie. All of them seemed terrified of what was happening in the room. He needed to make them feel less afraid. He smiled when he saw *Her* eyes, four pairs of them looking at him.

"Hi, you guys," he said, smiling and thanking Audra and Naomi for bringing them. Audra looked alarmed and pulled Ally into the hallway to talk.

"Listen," he said, feeling his words turn into taffy in his mouth. *Damn, what kind of drugs are these?*

"You didn't know your grandmother, but she was... she was..."

He shook his head, trying to clear his mind.

"Your grandmother was the best person I have ever known, and she would want you to know some things about the world. So here it is."

He took a deep breath, resisting the euphoria.

"Kindness. You must always be kind to people, even if you don't like them. Especially if you don't like them. Kindness will help keep you out of fights. It will help you deal with difficult people. Your grandmother was the kindest person to ever walk the planet. I was not good at that. But she was. Be like her. Be... like... her."

Third fret—Second string.

When he came back from the haze, he jumped a bit and

once more surprised everyone in the room. Zuri began to cry, and Robbie joined her.

Travis took the young ones out of the room, leaving Pax, Lainey, and Jazz to listen to Papa's philosophy. Rob and Naomi stayed behind to comfort the older kids.

"Trust. Trust is not something you do. Trust is something you give. It is a powerful and humble gift. However, it is also fragile. When you give your trust, you share your vulnerability —things that scare you. When someone gives you their trust, you accept the responsibility that comes with it. It's like a delicate egg. If you break it, you may be able to hold onto it, but it will never be the same as when they gave it to you. If you accept another person's trust, respect it, protect it, and honor it."

He settled back, filled with a desire to say more—something more tangible, a lesson to hold onto. His voice would echo in their minds for the rest of their lives. As he tried to organize his thoughts, Ally, Audra, and Travis stepped back into the room. The two little ones calmed with their sippy cups.

Pax looked at the little ones, content with their drinks, and wondered if he could have one last tequila in a cup like that. He chuckled.

"Pax," he said to his namesake, not so little any longer as pre-puberty bubbled in his system. "Keep playing guitar. Keep practicing. Reach out to Beto when you have some ideas for songs."

"Yes, Papa," his namesake replied.

"Lainey, girl, just keep singing. You are a songbird. A pájaro cantor... or something like that." Pax chuckled, thinking of Marisol as the words rolled off his limp tongue.

"I will, Papa," Lainey replied, her voice cracking as she fought back tears.

Pax searched for Jazz, but she was hiding at the foot of the bed.

"Jazzy? Jasmine? Where are you, sweetie?"

Jazz looked up over the bar at the foot of the bed, *Her* eyes in Naomi's face.

"Hi, sweet girl."

"Hi Papa," Jazz whispered.

"Jazzy, you're going to be a strong and beautiful woman like your mommy, Aunt Ally, and Aunt Audra. I'm so proud of you and I'll be watching, okay?"

Jazz nodded but then slid back behind the footboard. Pax smiled and relaxed as he looked at the faces of his family. They would all be fine. They had each other. He drifted a little and then opened his eyes again, this time not causing everyone to jump.

"And this goes for all of you, older kids and younger. Look up from your damn phones and see the world. Look into the eyes of people who need you. People who care about you. See them. You can't do that in a text or on the socials."

Rob snickered slightly at his use of "the socials."

"Look and *listen*. People make sounds. They make music with those sounds. Listen and learn. You can hear when they're happy, or angry, or in distress. Listen to that music. Listen. Just, listen."

He looked at Rob.

"Rob, let them hear her voice. The recordings. When they're old enough, let them know her."

He looked at Travis.

"Travis, you're a good man. Good for Ally. Good for my family."

Travis expressed his gratitude. "Thank you, Dad."

"Travis, my phone. Everyone is in there. Call them and tell them... tell them..."

He drifted and then blinked, his eyes opening again.

"Tell them I love them all. Tell them they... tell them they will always be a part of me."

He sank into the bed, ready now. *That's all I got*, he thought. *That was good, though. Good job. I'm finally a big boy.*

He slowly settled back into the pillow. He felt hands—hands in his hands, hands on his shoulders, hands on his legs—this was his family. He smiled. He heard sniffling, weeping, and deep sighs of resignation. He listened to their music.

He opened his eyes and looked at Ally. He saw *Her* eyes but not *Her* face, *Her* mouth moved, but it wasn't *Her* voice. But then, he *could* hear *something*.

"I hear her voice," he said.

Ally glanced at him. "Dad?"

He smiled as he clutched the rings around his neck.

"There you are."

"Dad?"

His ears were ringing, like wet cotton muffling the sounds around him. He saw a shroud of haze creeping over the faces of his family and, behind them, a chaotic blur of motion.

He heard Travis say, "Baby, let them work."

"Dad!" Ally's voice trailed off into the distance as the room was filled with white light.

"I HEARD YOUR VOICE," he said.

"Hi."

Third fret—Second string.

—END—

ACKNOWLEDGEMENTS

This story is stitched from real memory—the passing scent, the missing voice, the touch of a hand we thought we'd never hold again. It isn't a sweet road-mance or a tidy tale of healing. It grew from grief, from love, from the spaces where we face the parts of ourselves we spent years letting someone else fill.

Pax's journey is a reflection of real stories I've collected: the old man who kept his wife's photos on the table so he wouldn't have to eat alone; the neighbor who lost his wife and was himself lost in the world without her; the beautiful soul who lived into her nineties by following a handful of simple rules that kept her heart open; and the unexpected discovery of a cousin we never knew existed. These lives became the framework for this book.

At its core, this story is about what happens when we are forced into the open. Who we become when the person we leaned on—loved, trusted, listened to—can no longer hold us up. Pax had to learn how to survive in the emotional wilderness, in the silence that settles in when the music stops. He, like all of us eventually, had to find the sound of himself.

To the people who lived the real versions of these moments, thank you for giving this story its heartbeat. And thank you, the reader, for listening to the sound of a lived, loved, and remembered life.

Lake Wylie, December 2025

ABOUT THE AUTHOR

DAVID TELFORD is a writer whose work lives at the intersection of speculative fiction, literary realism, and human-centered storytelling. His stories often explore themes of connection, belief, memory, and choice, set against backdrops that range from the personally intimate to the expansively cosmic.

Blending elements of science, philosophy, and emotional truth, his writing is driven by people: how they love, how they fail, how they search for meaning in uncertain worlds. No matter the nature of the story, his focus remains on empathy, consequence, and the fragility of being human.

He lives near Lake Wylie, SC, with too many outlines, never enough coffee, and an endless playlist of songs that remind him of the people he loves.

ALSO BY DAVID TELFORD

Novels

Minstrel of a Modern Time

Genesis Rift: Tales From a Future War

COLLECTION I: INIZIO

 A Gentle Leap

COLLECTION II: GUERRA

 The Dove

COLLECTION III: DA CAPO

 The Lohj

www.ingramcontent.com/pod-product-compliance
Lightning Source LLC
Chambersburg PA
CBHW030234120726
47903CB00005B/1488